DERT

KYLE K WOLFSON

Also by Kyle K Wolfson

The Haunting of Abraham Lincoln.

———————————

To my dear sister Lexie.
I miss you.

CHAPTER ONE

STORM

The light breeze ruffled my hair. Ignoring it, I continued with my gardening. I've never had much of a green thumb. Once on a trip to Wrigley Field I managed to snag a handful of the ivy, but it never had a chance at living. My approach to plants has always been sorta superficial—dig the hole, put the plant in, and wait for it to grow. That theory, though, tends to only work on plants considered invasive species. Normally my gardening ends up with crispy leaves of death and a bare spot in the yard. My newest foray into gardening hasn't been successful, but it hasn't been a failure yet either. Necessity has made me a more attentive warden of their lives.

The breeze hit me again. There was a sharpness to it that broke my focus on the plants. The wind brought a smell with it. The smell of rain. We all know the feeling of a storm approaching; even before you can see it, your senses tell you it's there, just over the horizon creeping towards you. Sitting up and scanning the sky, I saw it was still sunny, a few clouds in the sky, but not the rainy type. Still, the signs were everywhere. The senses don't lie. "Sami!" I yelled in the general direction of the house. "Sami!!"

The soft thump in the house told me my wife had heard my shouts and was coming to the window. "What?" she asked, her voice mildly annoyed but in a good way, like she kinda enjoyed being annoyed by me.

"There's a storm coming."

"What?"

"A thunderstorm's coming!" I responded somewhat urgently.

Looking away from me, she scanned the sky. Her second-floor vantage point gave her a better view. "I don't see anything." She paused and sniffed the air. "But it does feel like it's about to."

"Better start buttoning up."

"Okay." Disappearing from the window frame as she bent down, she returned a minute later, shoving the plywood contraption I had built through the opening.

"I can do that, babe," I called out. The improvised window shutter wasn't that heavy, but it was an awkward shape.

"It's fine, I got this one," she huffed, pushing the whole arrangement through and spinning it. Once it was right-side-up, she pulled tight against the exterior wall and slid it down, so that it rested in the brackets I had installed around the window. It clicked into place and I heard the window shut behind it. Only about twenty more of them to hang.

Looking down in front of me, I saw a single weed, the one I had been in the process of grabbing at when the wind arrived. It would get a stay of execution for now. It would even get some rain before too long, hopefully a bright spot in its life before I plucked it out of the ground reserved for my tomato plants. Stepping around the plants, I headed for the gate. By the time I had decided to put a wall up around the plants, there wasn't any chance of finding lumber in a store, much less having a good way of getting it back to the house. So the walls were a hodgepodge of tree branches and whatever scrap wood I could scavenge from around the house. I even had an old closet door nailed up in one area. It wasn't pretty, but it protected the plants from most trespassers.

After locking the gate I went for the rain buckets. I kept them in the garage when it wasn't looking like rain. When we first moved in, we had tried parking our cars in the garage, but it never really worked out. Our first idea was that my car would stay in the driveway, generously suggested by Sami. But even with just her car inside, the space never seemed big enough to access the car comfortably, so after a while Sami joined me in the driveway, and the garage became a workshop and storage space. Now most of the space was filled with the sandbag bunker I had built. That would have to go in a hurry.

The door from the garage to the house opened up. Sami was coiling up one of the extension cords. "You want to work on this, and I'll put out the rain buckets?" she asked, gesturing to the bunker.

"Sure." She set the coil down where it ran out of the sandbag wall, and I started in on the bunker. It was about three feet tall and five by five feet in area. Two sheets of plywood covered the top, with various insulating components thrown on top. There were also two pipes sticking out of it. The one that came out of the back went to the window; that was the exhaust. The other had a fan on the other side, to suck air in and provide some circulation inside the bunker. Throwing all the stuff off the top and into the corner, I pulled off the plywood and leaned them against the wall. There was my generator, dug in like a Nazi at Normandy. The worst part of the deconstruction was obviously the sandbags. They weren't all full of sand—there isn't much sand that can be found in Joliet, Illinois—but plenty of dirt.

I was about halfway through moving the bags in front of the large garage door when Sami came back in. "It's starting to get dark out there," she said.

"Damnit. Work on the windows you can reach. I'll get this out to the shed." I nodded at the generator. I had envisioned keeping all of our electronics running throughout the house with my cleverly hidden generator; however, its thirst for gasoline exceeded expectations, so it sat silently in its fortified home most of the time.

"Okay."

"Have you seen anyone out there? Anyone who might see me?"

"No, it seems pretty quiet."

"Alright."

I manhandled the generator over the remaining sandbags and got it to the door. Sami was right, it was getting dark, and the wind was picking up. None of the neighbors could be seen. Most of the surrounding houses' windows had been permanently boarded up with nails over the past couple months. Their owners apparently didn't want to put the extra effort into making them removable like I did.

I left the generator at the edge of the yard, crossing at a brisk pace to the tool shed on the other side. It was a good-sized building, big enough to fit a car in; never thought I would need to do that, but it turned out to come in handy. Unlocking the padlock, I pushed the door open, taking another look around the neighborhood. Still no one in sight; probably everyone was already huddled down for the storm. Jogging back to the garage, I dragged the generator across the yard as fast as possible, although they aren't really made to be moved swiftly. Back at the shed, I pushed it in and stepped inside. In the shed was my pride and joy, my Range Rover. Even with the tarp covering it completely up, it looked like it was ready for a drive. Giving The Duke a pat, I closed the door of the shed and put the padlock back on.

Sami had started putting the covers on the rest of the upstairs windows now, so I started on the ground floor. We did these from the outside; just pick up the board, slide it in, and put the lock on it. The upstairs didn't have locks on them, since they can't be easily reached. However, the ground-floor ones would be useless at keeping people out if they didn't stay in place somehow. So I added a chain to the bracket that we lock back on itself. It was pretty simple and secure, even if it didn't look it.

The last cover was going on when I felt the first raindrops on my neck. We had made it. Hurrying back to the garage door, I locked it behind me and put the bar in place. Sami was in the kitchen, frantically moving the perishables out of the fridge and into the freezer. I checked the front and back doors. They were locked and had their own bars in place. The noise of the rain on the roof was noticeable now, with the occasional rumble of thunder.

I dropped onto the couch in the living room, Sami joining me. The room was dark, no lights on inside, and only dim light making it around the corners of the shutters and in through the window. Sami leaned into me, putting her head against my chest the way I liked it. "Think it'll be a bad one?" she asked.

"I don't think it matters how bad the storms are anymore."

"That wasn't what I was asking about," she replied, her voice carrying a hint of fear.

"Maybe they've finally worn themselves out."

"Maybe."

"I don't understand all the fuss," she continued as I dug my fingers through her hair. She always liked it when I massaged her scalp. "It was raining when we met."

"I know. You kept telling me how soaked you were."

"I was!"

"And still prettier than all the other girls."

"Hmm."

"It was raining during my proposal."

"At least it didn't rain at the wedding."

"True. Wet wedding dresses are probably pretty heavy."

"I don't think my makeup would've looked good in the rain."

"Or mine," I answered.

Lightning cracked somewhere nearby and stopped our thoughts for a moment. "Maybe we should listen to the radio?" Sami asked, looking up at me.

"Okay." I struggled out from underneath her and retrieved the radio from the kitchen. Prior to last week, I hadn't owned an actual radio in years, probably not since I was a little kid, listening to Braves games late at night when they were playing out on the west coast. But here it was, an old '90s-style radio, now our only source of information to the larger world.

Static welcomed us when I first clicked it on, but I found the right channel pretty quickly. There were only a few stations still broadcasting anymore, all government-run. One for the news, one for the weather, and two for music. An oldies channel that played the least objectionable music from our parents' era, and one that played even older music, a mix of classical and big band. The songs even sounded scratchy, like they were playing them straight from a vinyl record player. Setting the radio on the coffee table, I slipped back in to the couch. The current song ended and a man's voice cut in.

"If you are listening from the Eastern Seaboard or Midwest, be advised that there are major storm systems moving very quickly into your areas today and overnight. Experts say to expect destructive winds, several inches of rain, and severe tornadoes over the next twelve hours."

A concerned woman's voice interjected, "I'm just so worried. Each time I keep hoping that the worst has passed, but then here comes another stormfront."

The first voice responded, "I know the feeling. However, it took us a long time even to get to this point, so it's going to take a lot more sacrifice before we make it to a cleaner, safer world."

The woman spoke again. "When things get dark, I actually like to listen to President Rodriguez's speech from last month. It really gives me hope that we're moving forward."

"That's a good idea," the man's voice answered. "Perhaps our listeners would like to hear it themselves right now."

"I think that would give a lot of people hope," she responded.

"Alright. Well, you asked for it, so here it is, President Rodriguez's address during last month's special session of Congress."

Sami reached out and spun the dial, resulting in static. "Jesus, they play that speech every day. To give us hope when it rains and to inspire us when it's sunny." She worked her hand down my arm to my wrist, where my Bracelet was located. "Why are you still wearing that?"

Most people just called them "'Lets," but "Bracelet" is the name it's marketed under. When we were kids, smart phones first appeared, then soon after smart watches, but they never really appealed to me. It seemed like tech that was trying to be relevant before its time. Eventually the smart phones and watches had merged into a bracelet. There were varying sizes; mine was about three inches long, spanning from my wrist up my forearm. It could do everything my old smart phone could, now with a hologram display. Of course, it needed to be charged to do that. But with power drying up and internet connections sinking back into the dial-up era, there wasn't much use in keeping it charged.

"I guess I'm just used to it," I answered.

"You should take it off so you don't get funny tan lines."

"Too late for that." I twisted it so the whiter flesh beneath the device showed.

"Ewwww."

"Besides, haven't you heard how dangerous the sun is? Extreme heat, burning the skin right off your body."

"Well, at least it'd look good before it started to burn off."

Leaning forward, I adjusted the radio knob. The static was bothering me. A few twists and we had some music coming through, songs that reminded me of my grandparents. Sami committed fully and stretched out on the couch, her head in my lap, looking up at me.

"I remember this one." The words finally started coming back to me.

"Don't."

"Like it was…"

Sami's hand shot up, covering my mouth before I could hit the full high-pitched note. "Shush."

"Fine, no singing."

"Nappy time," she whispered.

"Okay."

* * *

I'd fallen asleep quickly, even though I wasn't particularly tired. There just wasn't any other things to do, so why not sleep? As the modern world around us had started shutting down, we had begun to connect more with nature, both a goal and side effect of the current crisis. Through my experience in this forced reuniting with nature, I had found my spirit animal, a house cat. Why does a cat sleep all day? Because there's nothing else to do. No TV, no job, no reading in the dimness of the house. Might as well take an afternoon nap. We've been laughing at cats' laziness for years, but now I'm becoming the cat. I probably could be entertained by a ball of string if one showed up.

"It's too hot," Sami moaned. Her voice reached out from

beyond and pulled me out of my sleep. I could feel the slow-motion awakening happening deep in my mind. I was awake, drifting towards opening my eyes. I didn't want to—I wanted to stay asleep—but the river to consciousness had me, and a moment later I opened my eyes. My shirt was damp from sweat, and my pants were even worse from the combined heat of our two bodies together. The rain had brought the humidity, and the house felt like a swamp now with all the windows covered.

Climbing out from under Sami, I went for the front door, pulled the bar out of the way, and let the door swing open. The cold air of the outside hit me. It was still raining, not a storm but a steady drizzle. Sami joined me and slumped down the doorframe until she was sitting on the floor. "I hate waking up sweaty."

"Air conditioning should be a human right," I said, taking a seat across from her in the doorway.

"We should open the back door to get some airflow through here." She climbed to her feet.

"I need to eat something."

"Well, come on. Let's see what we have," she answered, heading for the kitchen.

Once the back door was open, the house started to unstuff itself, bringing us to a non-tropical level of humidity. "We can do some crackers and peanut butter, honey," Sami said, pulling them out of the cabinet.

"Alright. Some cheese would really be nice."

"Well, maybe you could grow some out there in your garden."

"Imagine if we had a queso plant. We could sell it by the ounce. We'd be like Pablo Escobar rich. That's the dream."

"*That's* the dream? Being a queso dealer on par with Pablo Escobar?"

"Babe, a plant that grows queso? You're telling me you wouldn't leave all this behind in a second for a chance at that life?"

She gave me her usual eye roll. "Just eat your crackers and peanut butter."

"Yes, ma'am."

Silence joined us in the kitchen, the only sound just the crunching of the crackers. Even the rain had seemed to stop. "Kyle…what are we gonna do?" she asked, still staring at the crackers on her plate.

"I don't know. I don't know what to do."

"Have you talked to Eric? Is there any chance of you being able to work again?"

"I can't get a hold of anyone. My 'Let is dead and I'm sure his is as well."

"Weren't you supposed to get a new shipment in this week? All EVs?"

"We were expecting them, but who knows where they are. Or if they even got shipped. Or if they even made it on the boat, for that matter. You know how things are going right now."

"How long can we go with no money coming in?"

"Well," I tried to lighten the mood, "at least our utility bills are down to nothing."

"That still leaves the mortgage."

"I know, I know." She finally turned and looked at me, tears dotting the corners of her eyes, and I continued, "I'll try walking to the dealership tomorrow. Maybe I can find out what's going on."

"Okay. I'm just worried we might have to join the Dirts. I know it doesn't pay much, but they get extra food vouchers and all their debts are being paused during the crisis."

"It's an option," I agreed, eating my last cracker. "Not a good one, but there aren't many left." We were about out of food.

"Inflation is starting to get worse. Maybe we can work that to our advantage on the mortgage payments."

"There are benefits to living in a banana republic." I smiled at her.

"We live in Illinois. I think corn is as close to bananas as we're getting."

"I think the rain stopped." I leaned back to get a look out of the back door. We both walked towards it. The back yard was soaked, water still dripping from the roof and trees, but the rain itself had stopped.

"Hope we got a good bit of water. We were running a bit low."

"Let's leave the buckets out for a bit. Maybe there'll be another shower," I said, turning back inside.

* * *

This time I sensed the disturbance on the first indication, noises coming from the front side of the house. Hurrying to the front door, I leaned around it to get a look down the street. There, in front of Jeff Mason's house, a crowd was gathering. Jeff was the neighborhood leader of the Dirts. That wasn't the proper name, of course; the organization started as the Gaia Party, led by up and comer state politician Alyssa Rodriguez. I guess some hippies back in the '70s stole the name from the Greek goddess of the earth and then Alyssa stole it from them. Back when the party was first created, there had been plenty of derisive nicknames for them, but "Dirts" was what stuck. Probably because their followers simply looked dirty. Part of the process of joining was abandoning wasteful goods and embracing a carbon neutral lifestyle, which included forgoing contemporary fashions and wearing the Dirts' signature brown uniforms. They looked like UPS drivers in need of a shower. Once Rodriguez won the election and became President, she formed the Department of Environment Reclamation and Trust, or "DERT". With her party faithful filling the ranks, they still looked dirty, but now with federal badges, the authority to confiscate property, and a mandate from Gaia to punish Polluters with a capital "P."

Our most direct contact with the new bureaucracy was our neighborhood DERT administrator, known as an "Arborist." A name stolen from the profession of pruning trees, their purpose was to prune local communities of any metaphorical dead wood. She had appointed Jeff as the hyperlocal commissioner of this neighborhood. Of course, as the existing head of our homeowner association, Jeff had already been generally disliked even before he donned the brown tunic he wore with the pride of Napoleon's Imperial Guard, so it wasn't a big stretch.

"Sami," I called across the rooms. "Close the door up."

She didn't hesitate this time. I heard the door slam shut and the bar going in immediately. I closed the door slowly, trying my best not to attract any notice, and slipped the bar into place.

"They're gathering up?" Sami asked, joining me in the living room.

"Yeah, looks like a bigger group than before."

"Should we go out there with them?"

"I don't know. We haven't joined them before. It might be weird for us to show up now."

"The rain buckets!" Sami squealed, running for the back door. I joined her. The buckets were technically against the current regulations. Of course, that could be said about nearly everything. The never-ending list of edicts coming out of Washington were impossible to keep track of. Collecting rainwater was considered interfering with plants' ability to feed, and therefore was "harmful to the earth," so that was illegal. But that line of thinking could also be applied to raking leaves or getting mud on your shoe, which hadn't been criminalized yet, as far as I knew. Though with water delivery being unreliable, almost everyone in the neighborhood had been collecting water for months. Even Jeff, the local face of the new regime, had built himself a collection system. I had stuck with a simple bucket scheme; it was effective and easy to keep out of sight when needed.

Emptying all the buckets into one, I took it into the kitchen and Sami threw the rest into the garage. "Hopefully they'll just march off somewhere, go trash a gas station or something," Sami said once we were back in the living room.

"Let's go upstairs. We'll be able to see better."

Upstairs in the bedroom, we could see around the improvised shutters pretty decently, because I had trimmed them down so we could peek out. There about fifty of them gathered out front of Jeff's, five houses down from ours, though there were more and more people showing up each minute, like buzzards gathering over a corpse. Our home was farther into the neighborhood than Jeff's, so if things broke our way they'd head in the other direction, out into the rest of the world to let off some steam. If they came this way, it was going to be trouble.

"I think they're drinking," Sami whispered. "You see Mark and Jackie over there, by the tree? Doesn't it look like they're handing out shots?"

"I don't know what environmental good would come from getting wasted beforehand."

Retreating from the window, Sami laid down on the bed. "If we had some liquor, we might be able to go out there and butter them up," she said with a sigh.

"If we had that queso plant, I'm sure we could keep them happy and away from us."

"No more jokes."

About thirty more minutes passed before the crowd began to move around a bit, growing restless. My hope was that they would finally get bored and drift back home without incident, but there wasn't really anything to do at home anyway, so the crowd remained, impatient for some action. Jeff finally summoned them around and started preaching at them. I couldn't make out the words from this far away, just the pitch of them and the growing murmurs of agreement. After what looked like a resounding climax, he motioned his followers forward, into the neighborhood and towards our house.

Stepping back, I joined Sami on the bed. "Which way are they going?" she asked. Her voice betrayed the fact that she already knew.

"Coming this way like, Sherman through Georgia."

The mob was getting louder, not just because they were creeping their way towards us, but they were generating more energy with every second. Suddenly there was a loud *smack*. We both jumped as an object struck our house. Even though the ambient noise outside was considerable, the sound rang through like a gunshot. Another one followed a moment later, until there was a steady rain of them against the side of the house. Rocks, bottles, pieces of wood, whatever the marchers could find, were being hurled towards our house.

Sami found my hand and squeezed. "It'll be okay," I whispered to her...to the both of us. "Just let them get their energy out."

"I love you," she said.

Squeezing her hand back, I replied, "I love you too, my dear."

"HAAARRRIIIISSSOOONNN!" The voice boomed through the air as if magnified, even though we knew it wasn't.

"Don't say anything," Sami said firmly.

Seconds slipped by. The crowd outside had grown quiet, waiting to see what happens. "KYLE HARRISON, WE KNOW YOU'RE IN THERE! COME OUTSIDE!!!"

"Don't do anything," Sami pleaded.

"What can I do? They aren't going to get bored and leave."

"ANSWER ME BEFORE WE BREAK THE DOOR DOWN!" The promise of destruction drew a cheer from the crowd.

I stood up. Pulling on my hand, Sami tried to stop me. "Babe!" she begged.

"I have to say something, otherwise they're coming in." I stepped over to the window. "I'm here!" I yelled out. "What do you want, Jeff?"

"Kyle! How nice of you to answer us!" His voice dropped to a more reasonable tone. "Why don't you come out here with us?"

"Uhh, no thanks, I'm fine in here!" I called back.

"Kyle, you're coming out here one way or another. You can either walk or be dragged."

"What do you want from me? We haven't done anything."

"Then why are you avoiding us?" This got another taunting jeer from the crowd.

"Because there's a mob of people throwing shit at my house!" I yelled this time.

The crowd hooted and hollered, followed by several sharp cracks against the downstairs door. After the third one, Jeff yelled, "Kyle, you come out here now, or we're chopping that door down and pulling you out."

Sami joined me at the window. "You can't go out there. They might kill you."

"They won't kill me if I come out peacefully. They might, though, if they come in all enraged." Walking towards the door, I paused. "Do you have any ideas?"

"Check the back. Maybe we can run."

I nodded and slipped into the guest bedroom. Its window faced the back yard. Four of my neighbors stood leaning against my garden fence, all holding baseball bats. I shook my head in a negative towards her, and she received it stoically. "Alright, I'll come with you." She began following me down the stairs.

"No, you can't come out there."

"You aren't going out alone!"

Crack. The front door shook as another blow was delivered. "Calm down, I'm coming!" I shouted at the door. "Sami, go hide in a closet or something."

"No, I'm coming with you. It might calm them a bit if I'm there too."

There was no arguing with her, and short of knocking her out myself, I wasn't going to be able to stop her. To be honest, having her next to me made me feel a little braver. Grabbing the 2x4 from its hooks, I pulled it out and yanked the door open. Tony, a neighbor from behind Jeff's house, stood there grinning at me, sledgehammer in hand. He had always been a prick. The scarcity of food had hollowed out his face to the point that he looked like a maniac. "Tony," I said politely, stepping past him into the open.

Another round of jeers welcomed us out front. They were formed up in a big semicircle in my yard, Jeff standing in the center like Caesar. "I'm here!" I yelled. My mood had shifted from nervous to annoyed. Banging on my door and throwing crap at my house was starting to piss me off. I looked Jeff in the eyes. "What do you want?"

"What do I *want?*" His voice was steeped in false modesty. "It's not what I *want*, it's what your neighbors want, what your friends want, what the people want!" The people—my neighbors, but not my friends—cheered.

"Fine. What do the people *want?*"

"They want to know what you're hiding."

"I'm not hiding anything."

"Really?"

"Really!"

Jeff turned, facing the crowd around him. "He worked at a car dealership. He laughed at us when we got our Turtles because they weren't cool enough for him. He doesn't care about Gaia. He's only ever cared about money."

"That's what this is about? That I made fun of the Turtles?" I snapped back. "Turtles" were the nickname given to the new breed of environmentally conscious vehicles that had been developed since Rodriguez's election. Rushed through the production cycle, they were mostly plastic, not much more than a bicycle with extra parts and a putt-putt electric engine originally designed for scooters.

Jeff was about to respond venomously before he caught himself and bit his words. Turning this into a battle over personal slights wasn't going to make him look very good in front of Rachel, the regional Aborist representing the bigger regime, lurking in the crowd behind him.

"You worked at a car dealership," Charlene Mossberg screamed, pushing her way to the front of the crowd to confront me. "You profited off all our lives. You're a *Polluter!*"

"None of you had a problem with me selling cars when you were asking for a deal on them!" I shouted back. But it was no use; the chant of "Polluter" had broken out. Charlene's use of the new ultimate slur had inspired the crowd. They screamed it at me, over and over, until it just became a high-pitched roar.

After a minute or two of the chanting, Jeff stepped farther forward and motioned the crowd into silence. "Crimes have been committed at this house, against the people, against the government, and against the Earth."

"We've all seen you collecting water and bribing the food deliverers!" Sami yelled at him. "Don't stand here preaching to us about something you don't even believe in!"

Heather from across the street jumped into the fray. "No! NO! Do *not* project your crimes on us! You don't get to keep living like a Polluter and expect us to put up with it!" This from the woman who used a Stalin-like hard sell for her daughters' Girl Scout cookies every season like clockwork.

"You were driving a goddamned Escalade until three

months ago!" Sami yelled back, coming all the way into the yard.

"Fuck you, Sami!" Heather responded. The two woman stared daggers at each other, almost resulting a girl fight right there.

There was a pause as Jeff looked back to Rachel, standing out in her stark brown uniform as she now decided the fate of the entire neighborhood. She gave a slight nod and Jeff spun around. "SEARCH THE HOUSE!" he screeched into the air. His command sent the people into a frenzy as they tore past us into our home. Grabbing my hand, Sami pulled me out of the way. For a moment I thought we might just make a run for it. But Tony grabbed my other side and a second man grabbed Sami, pulling us into the yard, facing the house. "On your knees, Polluter," he growled.

"What?"

The sharp poke from the handle of the sledgehammer hit me in the gut, doubling me over. From there his hands forced me to my knees. Sami went down without a fight.

"What do you think they'll find in there?" Jeff asked, smirking at me.

"Same stuff in every house on this street."

"You know what, Kyle? You'd have a much easier time if you weren't so sure you were right about everything." He laughed. "You had to talk shit about the Turtles. You had to make fun of the uniforms. And you're surprised we came to your house?"

I didn't answer, but glanced over to Sami, who was just glaring angrily at the two brown-shirted women who were exiting the house. One was Jeff's wife Naomi, the other Tony's wife Crystal. They had been officially deputized by Rachel a couple of weeks ago. They had followed the rush of people inside but were coming out quickly, carrying two plastic totes. They had been sent in on a mission to clear out any food they could find. They avoided eye contact with us as they slipped out onto the street and back towards their homes.

The rest of the people were streaming through our house. The shutters were being ripped out of their places over the upstairs windows. They were trying to get the bottom ones off too, but they were locked in. The upstairs ones began to rain down, followed by everything they could find up there. First it was just electronics—laptops, alarm clocks, hair dryers and the like—then it was everything they could get their hands on. Clothes, sheets, books.

Tony grabbed me and dragged us out of range once the shower started. "Some nice stuff in there," another guy I didn't recognize said. "All that luxury brand money, huh? Selling cars too expensive for normal people. It treated you pretty nice."

"Normal people have a way of biting back," Jeff said with a laugh.

Even in the haze of noise and destruction, there was a noticed increase from the back yard. They had finally broken into the shed. When the gas shortages had first hit, we had used Sami's car only. It got better mileage and attracted less attention than The Duke. A month ago, gas disappeared completely. The Green Swap Program was initiated shortly after. Just turn your car in to the local DERT office and they would issue you a voucher for a new Turtle. Of course, there was no timetable on when they'd be available. I had wanted a Range Rover ever since I was a kid, and when I fell into a sales job at a dealership, it seemed providential. Not long later and before I met Sami, I had enough money coming in that I was in a position to take advantage of one of the special deals that popped up at the dealership. So I finally had mine. I was proud of it; it's a nice car, not the greatest by any measure, but it was mine and I loved it. That's why it ended up in my shed instead of at the DERT lot. Maybe gas would start pumping again in the future; maybe things would go back to how it was, and I could dust The Duke off and roll him back out. It wasn't illegal (yet) to still own a gasoline car, just frowned upon, and since there wasn't any available gas anyways, it didn't really seem to matter.

"Commissioner!" One of the ransackers came running back around the house, calling for Jeff. "You should come look at this!"

"Well, well, well, what do you think they found, Mr. Harrison?" Jeff asked, motioning for this goon to guide us around the back. Yanking us up, we were marched around our yard. The crowd had regathered in the back, lining our path to the shed. The vibe had turned exceptionally angrier.

"Whoa," Jeff let out when The Duke was fully visible. It had already been rolled backwards out of the shed and was sitting in the middle of the yard. "That's quite the gas guzzler."

"How do you explain this!"

"Polluter!"

"OIL WHORE!"

"We're onto you!"

The crowd was pressing in on us around the car. Sami's hand slipped into mine as they inched closer.

Jeff continued his theatrical interrogation. "So Kyle, how do you explain this?"

"Explain what? Why there's a car in my garage?" I spit back. I was sick of being reprimanded like a child.

"It's not just a car, it's a symbol. How can you say you care about the planet while you keep one of these on your property?"

"It's just sitting there. I'm not driving it. It either sits there or it sits somewhere else! It doesn't matter!"

"It does matter! This is a symbol of destruction, a false idol of consumption capitalism, and it's sitting here in your backyard drawing the fury of nature onto our homes as punishment."

Looking around I saw only angry faces, hateful faces, compassionless faces. No hope or understanding was left in them. "Take it if you want!" I shouted, looking around at them. "Burn it if you think it's somehow magically causing it to rain. But it's sat here through plenty of sunny days too. Take it and push it into the lake. But the rain will come again, and then the mob will be at one of *your* houses."

"Let's see what we got here," Jeff said, ignoring me and stepping forward to the back of the car, where the gas tank was located. Pulling the cover open, he signaled to the man who had been holding Sami. He looked familiar, but I didn't know his name. The man released her and produced a contraption out of his backpack, mostly rubber hoses with a bicycle tire pump attached to the end of it. He took the other end and jammed it down the gas tank opening. It took just a minute of maneuvering it down into the tank until he started working the handle of the pump. A moment later, gasoline started flowing out of the hose into a bucket that Tony had placed on the ground. "Still got plenty of gas in it," Jeff yelled out to the anxious onlookers. "Looks ready to drive. Let's help him absolve himself of that crime. Destroy it!"

With a whoop the people descended onto The Duke. Glass flew and the metal dented from the blows. Those who were unarmed tried kicking and punching, ripping at the interior. Pulling me closer, Sami whispered, "It'll be okay, just let them get it out." Several minutes of orgy rage passed until the car was nothing but a shell, its guts spilled out all over the yard.

The gas siphoning hadn't stopped during the destruction; they had started pumping it into a trashcan once the first bucket filled up. Finally it ran dry and The Duke was now fully beaten and bled. Jeff produced a cup and dipped it into the yellowish liquid. He held up the cup for everyone to see. "As long as there are people like this in the neighborhood, we will continue to suffer!" he roared. In a smooth motion he stepped forward and tipped the cup over Sami's head. The stench of gasoline was overpowering as she gasped for air.

"What the fuck!" I shouted, jumping forward at him and catching another blow from Tony's sledgehammer. On the ground, it was my turn to gasp for air as Sami stood trembling in front of Jeff, who casually flicked his lighter in the air. Everyone's eyes were locked on the flame he displayed. "Wait! WAIT!" I screamed. "We're sorry! I'm sorry! We'll do whatever you want!" I pleaded, the words tumbling out of my mouth.

"Gaia is challenging us to be better people!" Jeff shouted. "Are you committed to a new world, a clean world?"

The people screamed their agreement. "CLEAN WORLD!"

"Oil Whores need to die!" he continued.

"Death to Oil Whores!" the crowd chanted, though with a little less conviction.

"We don't deserve this planet. We've wasted it. We've abused it. Yet she's giving us another chance. She's showing us mercy if we'll change our ways!" Jeff looked around at the neighborhood gathered around him. He was greeted with a vocal wave of agreement. "But there must be sacrifice!" he screamed, holding the lighter above his head. The entire community held its breath as they awaited his next command. I struggled to get up but the men behind me held me down. Sami remained still, glaring into his eyes. He paused, then yelled at the top of his lungs, "BURN THE HOUSE!"

The crowd erupted in screams of glee as they swarmed over the house, throwing everything they could find that was flammable through the open doors and along the edges of the walls. My garden fence was ripped out and The Duke was pushed against the wall, as the gas siphoner splashed the noxious liquid across the siding. Pulling free of the distracted imprisoners, I got to Sami. She was still standing exactly where she had been when Jeff poured the gas over her head, shaking uncontrollably but still on her feet. "Are you okay?" I asked, squeezing her still wet body against mine.

"Bring them out front!" Jeff roared over the commotion. Hands grabbed us and dragged us along. Holding Sami's hand as hard as I could wasn't enough; we were ripped apart in the tide of the crowd. "SAMI!" I screamed as I tried to get back to her, but the crowd held me, pushing us back to the front of the house. The crowd's energy was reaching fever pitch as we resettled in front, nearly in the same positions we had been in before the searching began, except this time being forcibly held. Sami was about ten feet to my left, looking as calm as could be. Jeff was in front of us again. This time Rachel was next to him and handed him a glass bottle with a rag hanging out of it. "Let this be a warning to us all —Gaia will no longer tolerate pollution, and we won't either!"

Holding the makeshift bomb and lighter as close as he could to Sami's face, he taunted her. "Would you like to do the honors, missy?" She just remained silent, so he flicked his lighter and the cloth caught the flame. Smiling at me through the blaze, Jeff lobbed it through the open door as the crowd erupted

CHAPTER TWO

SHELTER

The sun returned through the retreating storm clouds just long enough to wish us goodbye for the evening. The ashes of our possessions were still swirling around the two of us, alone in the trampled grass. The neighbors had melted away, though they could still be heard in some of the houses, the afterparty continuing, enjoying the high of wanton destruction.

"Let's go," I croaked out. The blood, smoke and shock had nearly taken my voice.

Sami was curled up, her head laying in my lap. The small shudders coming from her body told me she had been crying for a while. There was nothing to do about it; letting it out was the only thing that could be done. Nodding her agreement, we helped each other to our feet. "Should we say something?" she muttered. It was the only place we had lived together; it felt like a part of our marriage after all these years.

Taking her hand in mine, I simply said, "I'll miss her."

"Me too."

* * *

I hadn't been outside of the neighborhood after dark since

the curfew had started being enforced, about the same time the gas dried up. The area was oddly quiet. You got used to the lack of mechanical sounds back at home; but being on a public street, with commercial buildings all around, it was unsettling for it to be black and silent. Sami kept close to me as we picked our way through the shadows. The only light to guide our way was the moon barely visible through the still shifting clouds, and the glow of the fires still raging in the surrounding neighborhoods.

"Do you think they burned someone's house in every subdivision?" Sami asked.

"Looks that way." Though with the fires still going, it seemed like they'd gotten a later start than ours had. "They have to make sure their message is received by everyone. Without cars or phones, no one is going to know what happened over here and learn from it. Everyone has to experience the lesson with their own eyes, in their own neighborhoods."

"I guess that makes sense," Sami agreed. "At first it was just on TV, them protesting at refineries or whatever, and it didn't seem like something affecting me. But when they destroyed that Shell over on Briggs, it actually felt real for me."

"Let's stay in the middle," I said, pulling Sami away from the sidewalk. It had always been my theory that when walking through seemingly unsafe streets, it was the best decision to walk in the middle of the road. It guaranteed some distance between you and anyone who might be in the shadows. They'd have to come out after you if they really wanted to get you. My guess was that they'd rather hide in dark corners, waiting for someone to come within grabbing distance.

In the middle of the street, we had to dodge the occasional burned-out car. Most of the time they were tipped over. Like a ship run aground, they rested silently in the road. The first intersection we crossed had signs of life, though. The gas station on the corner had been burned down in the first weeks of the emergency orders. The CVS on the opposite corner still stood, but it had been gutted even before that. The rest of the buildings stood unburned, but in varying states of destruction. People milled around in the shadows, some peering through broken windows. Displaced people had moved into these spaces once the chaos had begun, an old laundromat or check-cashing place being preferable to wherever they'd been previously. Others were just out prowling, looking for more to scavenge or shady transactions to facilitate. Keeping our eyes forward, we slipped through their gazes, everyone content to remain unbothered.

The next neighborhood was on our left, simply called "The Estates." We had looked at several houses in there during our home buying search, but everything was over our price range, so we settled in the glorious "Meadows Acres" a few neighborhoods over. "I can't tell if it smells like smoke everywhere or if it's just our clothes," Sami said, the first words she had uttered in the past half an hour.

"Probably both."

The house that had been sacrificed in this evening's round of atonement was very close to the front entrance. We could see the flames leaping out of the house as we approached, and hear shouting. Apparently these Dirts were sticking around to watch the full demise. Reaching the entrance, we peered around the tasteful stone wall with the development's logo carefully. We were far enough away to not really need to worry about being seen, but we didn't want to push it.

"Oh my God," Sami exclaimed. My eyes took a moment longer to make sense of what we were seeing. The eyecatcher was the two-story house bathed in flames, but then next to it there was a crowd of onlookers, hooting and hollering in the road. They seemed to be watching the large tree in the front yard of the house. The flames from the roof were licking outwards towards the branches, threatening to engulf the entire tree. Through the gap in the people, there was something else that didn't look right.

"Are those bodies hanging there?" I asked, even though I already knew the answer.

"We need to go." Sami stepped out to run across the entrance.

Grabbing her arm, I yanked her back and said, "Go to the other side," nodding to the other side of the street. She hurried off, me just behind, once I checked to see that no one had noticed us watching. On the other side we snuck past the opening of the neighborhood as if we were sneaking past the gates of hell. The party continued to rage in front of the fire, dancing in the streets and drunken singing like it was the Fourth of July.

* * *

Four miles later, we stumbled through the gates at the Land Rover dealership where I used to work and maybe still did. All of the cars had long since disappeared from the lot, forcibly seized by DERT agents during the crackdown on gassers. Luckily for the dealership, it was rather off the main road; unlike most car dealerships, this had kept it from going under the torch in the first waves of burnings that caught a lot of the car dealerships in the area. The extra mile of walking to burn a building without any cars around apparently wasn't appealing enough to the mob. Even the floor-to-ceiling glass windows hadn't been broken yet. Everything looked completely normal, except for the missing merchandise.

Heading for the back side of the building, we found the employee entrance and the old-fashioned combo look on it. 456123 went into the keys and the door clicked open. "Leave it open," I said before Sami could close the door behind us. It was pitch-black inside. The light from outside didn't do much, but it was something.

Inching our way forward, we passed several doors before we found the break room. "In here," I said, pushing inside. The room had two big windows that were uncovered, letting in enough light for me to take a look around. Everything looked normal; the couches were right where I remembered them being, coffee table in between them. Slipping past me, Sami fell down into the first available one. "Wait here," I told her. "I'll be back in a minute."

"Uh-huuuh," she groaned.

From the break room I crept forward to the showroom. The exterior wall of the large empty room was entirely glass, so it was easier to traverse than the rest of the building. My destination was on the opposite side of the room, the large door into the repair shop. Opening easily under my weight, it revealed nothing but blackness. I know what the space looked like, a typical repair and service shop. Propping the door open, I ventured in. There was always a supply of flashlights and headlamps located on the back wall for the mechanics. Stepping into the abyss, I quickly realized how dark it actually was. Once, in Iceland, I took a tour of a cave that was basically a bubble that had formed underground during some ancient volcanic explosion. That was the darkest experience I had ever had. This was a close second.

Thunk. My shinbone immediately collided with something that was very metal in front of me, bringing the expedition to a cursing halt. Stumbling forward a few more feet, I bumped and banged into just about everything in a five-foot radius. "Fuck!" I shouted out at the darkness. It practically laughed back at me. Dropping down to my knees, I oriented myself in the direction I believed to be the back of the shop. Crawling forward like this was the slowest way to move, but the amount of things I felt ahead of me before I crashed into them made it worth it.

It felt like an eternity in the darkness before I felt the concrete wall ahead of me. I kept moving, to the right this time, looking for something that would let me know where I was in the garage. Five feet more and I bumped into something. A quick feel revealed it to be one of the posts that stand near garage doors to keep you from driving the car into the wall. I was at the back of the shop. Moving a little more confidently now, I was looking for the space between doors three and four. Finding the shelf, my hands shifted through the invisible objects; tubes of grease, old bottles...flashlight. The cold textured metal in my hand felt familiar.

Click. The beam shot out, nearly blinding me in the process. "Woo!" I exclaimed, feeling proud of myself. There were a few more flashlights on the shelf, even some battery-operated lamps. Scooping them up, I headed back, on my feet this time.

"I'm back," I announced as I walked back into the breakroom, setting the rest of the treasured lights on the counter.

"Did you find any food?" Sami asked. She wasn't as impressed with my crusade against the darkness as I thought she should be, but I was starving too, and the flashlight was just a means to an end, that end being finding something to eat.

Spinning to the right, the snack machine in the corner of the room was revealed in the glow of my flashlight. "Ah-hah," I said. Stepping over to the machine, I saw that it was still stocked fully—chips, gum, breath mints, cookies, pretzels, even some small sticks of beef jerky.

"I want it all," Sami whispered from next to me, reaching out and feeling the glass between us and it. "Did you find any quarters on your search?"

"I'll be right back."

This time the journey into the repair shop was a quick one. I found a two-foot-long socket wrench on the first bench I came to. That would work. Back in the break room, Sami had put one of the lamps on the coffee table, lighting the room up with a nice glow. Whipping the socket wrench into the glass made it break away easily. A few extra pokes and it was all on the floor around us. "What do you want?"

"Anything."

Tossing a few bags of chips at her, I grabbed a fist of beef jerky and some of the cookies. I wanted to eat everything in this machine, but we'd probably need it to last longer than just this evening.

"Is there any water in that?" Sami asked, pointing at the water cooler.

"Yeah, looks like it," I responded, giving it a shake. Normally these things came with paper cups supplied from a dispenser, but all paper products were ruled harmful to the earth in one of the first directives, so no cups. However, there were some coffee mugs in the cupboard above it. Filling one up for each of us, we could finally start in on our feast of vending machine snacks.

"Babe!" Sami yelled alarmingly.

I spun around. "What?"

She was staring hard at me. "You're all bloody."

"Am I?" I hadn't been in front of a mirror since before the storm. "I did get roughed up there for a minute."

Putting the food down, Sami was in front of me now, inspecting the cuts on my face. "Is there a first aid kit around here?"

"I think there's one in the garage. I can go get it."

"No." She pushed me down towards the couch. "You wait here, I'll go get it."

"It's alright, I know where it is." But, grabbing a flashlight, she headed off before anything else could be said, returning a minute later with an armful of supplies. "I don't think we need all that," I commented.

"Hush." Working me from head to toe, she washed the cuts with alcohol, slathered everything in Neosporin, then applied a few Band-Aids to the large cut across my forearm. "Do you feel okay?" she asked while giving me a final once-over.

"Yeah, just sore and bruised."

"Okay. Let's eat."

You can't have high expectations when dining on vending machine items, but we did the best we could. It was actually a better meal than we had been able to eat in a while. "I've never liked beef jerky," I said, taking another bite of my stick of dried meat. "Now I wish I'd learned to."

"It's not my favorite either. At least it's protein, though."

Finishing our meal was a letdown. After the day we had just experienced, we deserved to eat our fill, a small solace on this dark day. However, what was left in the vending machine might have to last us longer than we cared to admit, so neither of us went back for seconds.

"Bedtime," Sami said, kicking her shoes off. I gave her the couch we were sitting on, pulling the other one over so that they were butted up against each other. Laying out, she held her hand out to me. The arms of the couches didn't quite line up, so we couldn't cuddle without falling through the gap between them, so hand-holding was the most we could manage.

"Good night, dear," I said.

"Goodnight. Love you."

"Love you too."

* * *

As an adult, you don't often forget where you are or what's going on, at least while you're still in your thirties and not yet senile. Waking up is always a dose of confusion for me, the world hazy and distant as you slip out of your dreams and into reality. Today was even more jarring, though; my face ached, my feet ached, my stomach ached, my mouth was dry, and the morning light was shining in my eyes. I tried to roll over but I couldn't; the back of the couch was there, limiting my bedspace. Shaking myself fully conscious, I sat up. It suddenly occurred to me that I wasn't at home, that I wasn't in my bed, that those things didn't exist anymore. The noise that had woken me up continued from down the hallway, just thumping it seemed like, but my ears weren't completely awake yet. "Helllooo?" a voice echoed down the hallway.

"Wake up!" I hissed, shaking Sami awake. She woke up angrily, her brows already furrowed before her eyes had even opened. "Someone's here." That brought her into the moment in a hurry.

"Is someone in here!" the voice called again.

Scrambling off the couch, I grabbed the socket wrench from the counter I had used to open the vending machine. Edging towards the door, I peeked around the corner. At the end of the hallway, the exterior door was still open from when we had come in last night. Just outside the door was my boss, the manager of this car dealership, Eric Riley. I let out a breath of nervous air. "It's just Eric." I said to Sami. She was sitting up on the couch, first looking terrified, then confused.

"What's he doing here?"

"I don't know."

I stepped into the hallway and held my hand up in a stiff wave. "Eric, it's just me, Kyle. Sami's here too."

"Kyle? What are you doing here?" Eric asked, stepping into the building.

"It's a long story, man. We just didn't know where to go for the night."

"This is very irregular," he said, joining me at the doorway and then spotting the broken glass of the vending machine. "What happened here!?"

"Yeah, sorry about that. We needed to eat something last night."

"Hello, Samantha. How are you?" He held his hand out to her.

"Very well, Eric," she replied, taking it and shaking. "It's nice to see a friendly face."

"Of course, of course. Always a pleasure to see you." Nobody spoke as Eric looked around what amounted to our bedroom, an awkward moment to be sure. "So how did you end up here?"

"Well, there was that big storm yesterday," I started.

"Oh yes, oh yes, we've been having some very bad weather these days," Eric cut in.

"Yeah, well, the Dirts got all worked up and they, uh, burned our house down."

Silence followed again, Eric blinking furiously, looking between Sami and I. "They did what?" he finally managed to ask.

"They burned our house down. They blamed us for bringing the storm around."

"They can't do that. They're just a conservation group, doing recycling and stuff like that. They can't burn someone's house down. That's against the law. Did you contact the police?"

"Uh, no, we didn't," I answered.

"You need to! They need to catch the people responsible! Did you get a good look at who did it?"

"I mean, yeah, we know who did it."

"Then call the police! They need to be arrested! Storm or no storm, you can't burn someone's house down."

"The police haven't done anything about all the other fires," Sami interjected. "The fire department doesn't even show up to them anymore."

"Nonsense," Eric replied firmly. "The police won't let that happen. It's against the law."

"I guess it can't hurt to try and call them," I said. "Maybe we can sort something out."

"Yes, the landline in the office is working just fine," Eric said, striding to the door. "Kyle, you work on calling them and getting it sorted out. Sami, if you could clean the glass up, so it's not so dangerous while we get it repaired. I need to get a move on if I want to get this place ready to open for the day." He headed down the hall.

"Did he say he's opening the showroom?" Sami asked.

"That's what it seemed like."

"There aren't any cars left here, even if you were allowed to buy them or get gas or..." Her voice trailed off, the thought unfinished, but I imagined it had something to do with burning houses down.

* * *

"Yes, what's the nature of your call?" the dull voice of the operator said.

"I guess I need to report a crime."

"Current or concluded?"

"What's that?"

"Is the crime currently happening or has it already happened?"

"It, uh, happened last night."

"Please hold."

I was sitting in the sales office, at the sinister desk where we sold the extended warranties, upgraded tires, and floor pads that padded our bottom line. The office looked about the same as it had when I had stopped coming into work a few weeks ago, but it was clean. Eric had seemingly taken on the duties of caretaker of the dealership while he was here alone. Cellphone activity had dried up early since it became so difficult to charge them. However, it appeared that landlines remained active, even though the world had previously passed them by.

The minutes ticked by slowly as I toiled on hold. I had seen Sami find a broom and dustpan to get the glass cleaned up. Eric was hurrying around straightening things up for the anticipated opening of the store at 9 a.m., a time quickly approaching. But I didn't have a watch, so I wasn't sure how quickly.

"Hello?" A voice replaced the hold music.

"Yes, hello."

"What is the nature of your report?"

"Yeah, my house got burned down yesterday."

"Was it an act of nature or deliberate?"

"It was a person. Actually, several people."

"What was the cause of the event?"

"It was the Dirts in the neighborhood. They got all worked up and burned my house down because of the storms yesterday."

"What is the address of the event?"

"1200 Harvest Valley."

"Please hold."

The pointless music returned. Who composed such an aimless song? Did they kill themselves afterwards? Surely they hadn't grown up aspiring to create sounds like these. Hold music had to be the last stop for a musician before they accepted the reality of their failures and finished it off for good, like a stripper ending up in a brothel in Pahrump, Nevada, or a baseball player on the bench in the Croatian league.

Sami poked her head into the office. "Any luck?"

"On hold with the police."

"I pulled the rest of the glass out of the machine. Figured I might as well finish the job."

"Good idea. Don't want to get my arms cut up at lunch."

"Where's Eric?" Her voice dropped a level.

"In his office, I think."

"Does he seem alright to you?" Shaking my head was enough of an answer. "He's kinda creeping me out."

"Yeah, I know. But we'll just have to ride it out, I guess."

She left me alone again with the joyless music coming from the phone. Eventually the music stopped and the monotone voice returned. "Is this the owner of the residence I'm speaking to? A Mr. Kyle Harrison?"

"Yes, yes, that's me," I said, jerking back awake.

"Okay sir, I found your file and reviewed it. It shows that your property was found to be in violation of several sections of the Fair Weather Act, specifically Title 4. Would you like to hear them?"

"Yes, I guess?"

"First is storing and maintaining a fossil fuel motor vehicle with the intent to drive. That seems to be the big one. Second, the illegal collection of precipitation. Let's see, illegal cultivation of the earth, failure to submit to an inspection, failure to provide a sustainability plan. Disregard of the natural cycles of the earth. Intentional disregard of the climate safety of the area. Neighborhood endangerment. Those are the main issues, though there's a lot of minor violations noted as well."

"Okay, so what does that all mean? Do I pay a fine or something?"

"It looks like the Arborist on site made a ruling that there were too many infractions in one space to permit an appeal process. In order to protect the safety of the neighborhood, the penalty was issued on site as directed by Arborist Rachel MacMillan acting under the authority of the Fair Weather Act. Do you understand, sir?"

"No, not really."

"Because of the violations, the offending property was burned as the penalty."

"So they legally burned my house down?"

"Yes, sir."

"So…" I paused, sighing. "So I guess that's that."

"Is there anything else I can do to assist you today, Mr. Harrison?"

"No, thank you."

"Have a good day." The line clicked dead and I set the receiver down.

* * *

It was about noon when I finally pulled myself together and headed into Eric's office. He had been bustling around the empty showroom and offices all morning, but he had been in the office for a while now. "Knock, knock," I said as I mimed rapping in the open doorway.

"Oh, Kyle, come on in," Eric answered, setting the papers down on the desk.

"How's it going?" It'd been the standard greeting for so long, I couldn't stop saying it even when the world had been turned upside-down.

"It's been a long day. Papers have been piling up and I'm just playing catch-up all the time, it seems." He motioned to the pile on the desk. The papers were well-worn and stained.

"Right. I guess the important thing is staying busy."

"Oh, don't I know it. It keeps me young, keeping this place running." He gave a laugh.

"How's Debby handling everything?" I inquired.

"Debby's doing just fine. She keeps busy with all her little groups and her little projects."

"That's good. Sami and I were getting cabin fever the past few weeks back at the house."

"Did you get things sorted out with the police and insurance company?" Eric asked.

"I talked to the police. They said the house was legally burned down as a penalty for still having my car."

"That doesn't make any sense. Since when has owning a car been a crime?" Eric looked genuinely perplexed. "That's going to be bad for business."

"Yeah, owning an operable gasoline car has been illegal since the President's emergency decrees in July."

"Well what did the insurance company say?"

"They didn't answer the phone. Honestly, I wouldn't answer the phone either."

"Very difficult times these days."

"Yes they are."

"So what are you going to do?"

Shaking my head, I stood back up and looked around the room. "I guess I'm stuck here for the moment."

"You mean in the office?" Eric looked taken aback.

"Yeah, I guess so. We don't have anywhere else to go, and no money to try and get a hotel room, if there are even any hotels still open."

"Oh, that's not good. This is a place of business, Kyle. How would it look if one of our customers found out you were living here?"

"I think *having* a customer would be more surprising," I responded dryly.

"Oh, don't worry about that. Things are bound to pick up again soon."

"Do you have any ideas about another place we could stay for a few days while we try to figure something out?"

"Well, I do have a guest room that's available…" Eric said slowly. This was the outcome I had been hoping for. The break room had worked for the night, but a couple nights in an actual house would give Sami and I a chance to recover from the ordeal.

"That's very generous of you, Eric. Would Debby be okay with that? We'd hate to impose."

"I think Debby'll go along with it. Mind you, just for a couple of days."

"That would be very nice of you. We could use a bed to sleep in for a few nights."

"Very well. I've been a little naughty this week and locking up here an hour early, so we can leave for my house around four o'clock."

I went to the break room and found Sami spread out on the couch, flipping through old magazines. " What do you think happened to all the celebrities?" she idly asked. "You think they're sitting in their dark mansions, waiting for the lights to come back on like the rest of us?"

"If they were smart, they would've skipped out of the country before it got out of hand." I sat down on the other couch. I got her caught up on what the police had said about the house, and she simply sighed and said, "Yeah, that seems par for the course these days. So what's next?"

"Eric said we could stay with him and Debby for a few nights while we figure things out."

Shooting me a questioning look, she set the magazine back down. "Eric seems kinda out of it."

"Yeah, I know." My voice dropped a couple of levels. "But I don't want to keep staying here. Let's go to his place and buy us a couple of days to decide what we want to do. But while he's still busy, let's find every single thing here that can be useful and pack it up. There are a bunch of Range Rover backpacks in the store room we can use.

We worked quietly. Eric was still in his office, rustling weeks-old papers around. At this point, taking supplies from the dealership didn't feel like stealing, but Eric might view it differently, so we were keeping him uninvolved as long as possible. Plenty of flashlights were up for grabs now that I could see the room. They all made it into the bags. Spare batteries were collected and a bunch of knives of various sizes. Unfortunately, even though there were plenty of cool tools up for grabs, I couldn't envision much need for sockets, Allen wrenches and screwdrivers. Picking through anything that might be useful, I grabbed a tire iron and crowbar as well, the only weapon-like tools I could find.

Back in the office, Sami sorted out all the food and drinks she could find. She even scoured all the other offices for anything that might have been hidden away. That search produced a couple bags of chips, a bottle of peach schnapps, and a bunch more candy bars.

Spilling everything out on the floor, we realized we didn't need ten flashlights, so we picked out the two best and a couple of backups. Same thing for the knives and assorted tools I had brought back. After a bit of haggling, we had outfitted ourselves in the best manner that the Land Rover dealership could offer.

"Anything else you think we need?" I asked as I zipped my bag closed.

"A gun would be nice."

"We don't sell those here, dear."

"Then I guess this'll have to do," she said matter-of-factly, putting the last of the first aid supplies into her bag and zipping it closed with a sudden jerk.

CHAPTER THREE

KAREN

Karen Roberts didn't really worry about why she was where she was, or what had gone wrong in her life that had led to her living in the manager's office in a Bed Bath and Beyond off I-80. It had always been that way for Karen—she went with the flow, not worrying about where the current was taking her, just happy to be in the group. Her life followed a predictable course if you looked at it like a recipe.

The first step was back in high school when she was a cheerleader, though not the queen bitch cheerleader like Skyler Briggs, the head cheerleader. Everything was a test of fidelity to Skyler; if you didn't compliment her hair or if you spoke out of turn, you made the list. Karen had a knack for staying out of Skyler's way—she gave way, smiled when she was supposed to, and stayed quiet when she needed to. But Karen wasn't like Rose Tomlin either. Rose was desperate for attention and acceptance. Painfully so. Rose carried Skyler's bags, and she stayed sober so she could drive the other girls home when they were shitfaced. Rose even took the fall when Skyler and Jess trashed the locker room one night when they were messed up on some pills. Rose did it all with a smile. It reminded Karen of the Joker's smile, painted on in the best-case scenario, scarred into place in the worst.

Karen was comfortable in the middle. That's how she ended up with Jackson, a wide receiver on the football team. Steven, the quarterback, was obviously with Skyler; and Vickie, Skyler's enforcer, got dibs on Jerome the running back. The fate of the hierarchy put Karen and Jackson together. Jackson was tall for his age, good-looking and trim, like a wide receiver should be; but if he wasn't good at sports, people probably would've never even noticed him. He didn't have much to say, and when he did, it wasn't much to hear. Still, Karen and Jackson got along alright, Karen sitting on his lap when they squeezed into the back of Steven's truck, or sharing a popcorn at the movies whenever a new "Pirates of the Caribbean" came out. The first time they had sex, Karen was smart enough to be careful, making Jackson pull out early. The first time was good, in the sense that it wasn't horrible. It got better as they went along, but sex never really caught Karen's attention. Maybe it was the lack of orgasms, or the awkwardness of Jackson's efforts.

Skyler slept with Steven because she had to; he was the only one who could knock her from the top of the ladder she was desperately holding onto. A break with Steven would have resulted in scorched earth warfare for control of the school's social high ground. So, Skyler used what she had and kept Steven on his leash. She gave him whatever he wanted and he didn't fight her for the throne. Rose had sex because that was her job; she was dependable and expendable. Steven had a rotating cast of bit players from the fringes of the team; maybe a safety that made a big interception that week or a lineman that protected Steven's flank flawlessly for a change. They got invited to wherever the party was, and Rose accepted her mission to make them feel welcomed. Karen had sex because she got bored listening to Jackson ramble on about World of Warcraft or whatever stupid Japanese cartoon he was watching that week. Pull out some titties and shut the man up.

High school ended and the group started to break up. Skyler and Steven were going to different colleges, so she didn't need him anymore. The same for Jackson; he had gotten a Division 1 scholarship, not to a good school, but a decent one. Karen considered sticking with him—a few years in college and maybe he could get drafted. Life as a player's wife would've suited her fine, but she couldn't pull the trigger on living in Idaho for four years, and the smart money said Jackson wasn't going to get much better at football anyway. So she sent Jackson on his way, but not before a quality goodbye in the bedroom, one last practice session before he graduated to college girls.

Karen had set her sights on a teaching degree at a school in Florida. Warm weather and the beach sounded good to her. Three weeks after Jackson had left and one week before she was set to leave, though, she broke down and went to CVS to get a pregnancy test. For the past week, she had been ignoring the signs (or symptoms, you might call it), but she couldn't do it any longer. She had to know. She didn't cry when the test came back positive; it was the path she was on now, and she had no choice but to follow it.

College went the way of her periods, and she stayed home with her parents. They weren't thrilled about the diagnosis, but they were go-with-the-flow types as well, so the family just buckled down. Baby Amber came into the world in 2009. Karen was almost 19. The first few years weren't so terrible. She had her parents, who carried a lot of the burden. She floated forward through life, waitressing, bartending and enjoying her life the best she could. By the time the recession hit, her parents were out of patience and nearly out of money. Karen was finally going out on her own. She debated leaving Amber with her own parents, but decided against it.

Karen's biggest accomplishment in life had been getting through nursing school while being a single parent. No small feat and something that could've altered her life, but didn't. She didn't really like being a nurse and, within a week on the job, she knew she would never be a good one. Other nurses felt a genuine concern about their patients. Karen was punching the clock. She could handle the work, but it was just work; it paid the bills and left her with money to spare. The years flipped by and Amber moved out in 2027. Karen recognized Amber—she was a Skyler, bossy, bitchy and a climber. She didn't have time for her boring mother who had never really been interested in her in the first place.

With Amber gone, Karen's life took a turn up. More freed-up money, more freed-up time, and a sudden lack of any responsibilities outside herself. Karen decided to reinvent herself as a soccer mom. During her professional career and parenting time, she had always been a bit too drained to commit to anything social. Sure, she went drinking after shifts, fucking a cute intern or a fellow Chili's customer every so often. Blind dates and bachelorette parties; Karen had a good time, but nothing concrete. Now that she was basically childless, though, she finally embraced the mothering class. She didn't actually go to soccer games, but she found her group of mothers who all did themselves, looking to flock together. Most of them she knew from spin class, a couple from yoga. Girl trips to Nashville, beach weekends, scary movies, and flirting with the guys at the juice bar in the gym. Karen had found her new pack, and she didn't have to fuck any wide receivers.

It was spring of 2028 when Karen first noticed things were changing. It was little things at first—suggestions that the girls should carpool to spin class, or the planned trip to Vegas getting canceled because Tiffany and Michele didn't want to fly anymore. Then the activities starting shifting focus too, especially with the coming of summer and the hot weather. It was easy to understand the park clean-ups or helping out with the gardens each of the moms had suddenly started in their backyards. Ever since Alyssa started a garden and livestreamed it every day, it had become all the rage.

As summer turned to fall, however, it got more serious. Tiffany announced she wouldn't get inside an automobile anymore, so she was trading in her Lexus for one of the weird little Turtle things that Karen had started seeing around. They looked like a child's soapbox derby car, and were always holding up traffic as they sputtered and crawled down the road, hence the name. Karen thought they were the dumbest thing she had ever seen. She hadn't worked her way up to an Audi just so she could end up in something that leaked when it rained. However, the rest of the girls were so excited for Tiffany. They swore they were going to do the same thing. Driving real cars was just too selfish of a thing to do now, and the girls weren't anything if not socially conscious. Karen started keeping the Audi in the garage. It seemed oddly dangerous to leave it in the open now, but she was keeping it. For the rest of the fall she hitched rides in the Turtles or walked to the group gatherings.

In October the first really cold rainstorm hit the town. It was too warm to snow, but it was the first time all year that the weather reminded you of the impending doom of winter. You could go all spring and summer enjoying the warmth and clear days, naively forgetting about the oppressive cold that would return in the dark months. October was when it began knocking on the door.

Snuggling up in bed was Karen's plan for the day. So far she had managed to make it to the kitchen for some cookies and wine, but that was the extent of her ambitions. The vibrations of her phone were calling her attention away from the TV. The screen read "Tiff." Groaning as she muted the TV, Karen picked up. "Hey, girl," she answered with a false cheeriness.

"Are you okay?" Tiff's voice was borderline panicky.

"Yes?"

"Oh my God, I'm so glad. It's just so scary. I'm worried something's going to happen to us."

"What are you talking about?" She paused the TV, now that she could see that Tiff wasn't going to be quick about this.

"The storm! The weather! It's just so scary. We don't deserve this to be happening to us!"

Looking over to the window, Karen saw that it was still raining pretty badly outside, but it didn't seem any worse than the storms they had been experiencing over the last couple of years. "It doesn't seem too bad over here," she responded in the only way that seemed reasonable, even though Tiffany only lived about two miles away.

"That's just because you've gotten used to how bad things have gotten, just like Alyssa is always talking about. The wind hasn't stopped blowing all day, and the rain is insane. I'm worried the house can't take it. What am I supposed to do if the roof comes off or something like that? Remember when that happened to the Walmart last summer? It's not my fault this is going on. Those fucking polluters are the cause of this. It's not fair that we have to suffer too."

"Yeah." To tell the truth, as long as the internet didn't go out, Karen wasn't too worried.

"I mean, I'm doing my best to reverse their destruction, but there's only so much I can do. I don't know how we're gonna get through this if the storms get worse. It's like Alyssa says, Gaia is a delicate goddess, and we need to stop treating her like some cheap hooker."

"Okay…"

"You should come over. We shouldn't be alone during this kinda of storm. But oh my God, there's no way you could get here! You'd get swept away as soon as you got outside! Please don't go outside, please! Promise me you won't go outside!"

"Okay, I won't go outside."

"No, say you promise."

"I promise. I'll stay here."

"I'm just so worried. I can't stand it. This has to change. I can't live like this."

"Yeah, it's pretty rough." Rolling out of bed finally, Karen made her way over to the window overlooking the front yard. It faced in the general direction of Tiff's home. The high winds had knocked several tree branches off, and they were now littering the yard in random patterns, like that Pick-Up Sticks game her family used to own when she was a kid. Maybe Tiffany was right, and the storms were getting worse than they had been, Karen thought. They all sounded the same from the safety of her bed.

"I gotta call the other girls and make sure they're okay," Tiffany said. "I already have the kids hiding in the bathtubs. That's what all the warnings say to do."

"What was that about the bathtub?" Karen had started zoning out while climbing back into bed.

"The bathtub. It's the safest place to hide during a storm like this. If it gets much worse I'm going to drag the mattress in there and put it over them. Alyssa said that's the best thing to do for children in her last video. I just don't know where to hide myself."

"Do you think that's necessary? It might be a little scary

for them."

"It's necessary. I couldn't live with myself if they got hurt. I'm not letting them suffer because some fucking billionaire wanted another yacht." Her voice had taken on a tone of frenzied panic.

"Alright," Karen answered, unpausing the TV.

"I'm seriously terrified right now. I need to call the other girls and make sure they're safe. I don't think Courtney has watched any of the shelter in place videos I've been sending her."

"Sure, go ahead and check on them. I'm fine here." She was already pulling the phone away from her ear. "Bye."

"Goodbye. Call if you get scared!"

Dropping the phone on the pillow, Karen grabbed for the wine. If the world was ending, might as well enjoy it.

Two days later, the weather finally broke and the sun reappeared, bringing a fairly warm fall day with it. Normally Karen would prefer a day like that to be spent on a patio with a mimosa within reach, or really any activity that involved drinking. Not so with this day. It was already scheduled to be a park day. Generally Karen wasn't a fan of parks, today even more so since the group activity was going to be focused on cleaning out the creek, which was sure to be colder, muddier and nastier than normal after all the rain. The park was a few miles away from Karen's house, too far to walk; and not wanting to deal with the hassle of getting a ride in one of the Turtles, she hopped in her car without much thought and headed over.

The parking lot was devoid of cars, just the Turtles and her friends gathered up around them. Jumping out of her car, Karen greeted them. "Hey, everyone!" Silence was returned, blank faces staring at her. "What's wrong? Did something happen?" She looked between all the faces, a few of them pained, a couple seemingly as confused as she was.

"Karen, what are you doing?" Michele asked.

"What do you mean? I'm here for the clean-up." She pointed to her rubber boots, bought specifically for the ever-increasing amount of time she was spending in the muck these days.

"How can you drive that car here?"

"Oh, well, I was running late and didn't have time to ask anyone to come get me, and it was too far to walk." Her voice was uncertain.

At this point, Tiffany collapsed to the ground, sobbing uncontrollably. "Oh my God!" she wailed. The girls clustered around her, trying to comfort her.

"Look what you did," hissed Kayla.

"I...I...I...I.... *I can't fucking believe you're one of them*," Tiffany choked out, tears streaming down her face.

"What are you talking about?" Karen asked, kneeling down in front of Tiffany.

"How can you drive that car?" Michele screamed from her knees, still on the ground consoling Tiff. "It's killing the world. It's literally killing Tiffany right here in front of you, and you're still driving that piece of shit!"

"I'm sorry, I'm sorry!" she pleaded. "I don't drive it much. I just wasn't thinking."

"That's not enough," Michele continued. "These storms aren't accidents. They're a warning, a punishment, the planet pleading with us to do something before it's too late. We've mercifully survived and have come here today to honor and listen to Gaia, and you show up in this monstrosity."

Karen remained silent. Her life had been a trail of fitting in and staying under the radar of whatever social group she was attached to, climbing the ladder of the rankings, saying the right things, partaking in the right activities, and fitting seamlessly into the group. She had followed the rules for this group carefully, taking her time as she joined, not rocking the boat or stepping on toes. Now, all of a sudden the rules had shifted. The nice car, stylish clothes, and full embrace of the frantic rush to avoid the stigma of old age that usually possessed these upper-middle-class housewives didn't matter anymore. For the second time in her life, she was left standing alone, a victim of changed circumstances.

Sinking to the pavement, Karen joined Tiffany in tears. "I'm so sorry. I don't know what I'm doing. I don't know what's going on. I'm scared too."

The tension of the group broke down as all the women joined in, trying to comfort the two on their knees.

"Everything is okay!"

"It's going to be alright!"

They cooed and hugged until Tiffany and Karen calmed down, finally raising back to their feet in an embrace.

"I'm sorry, everyone. I'll do better," Karen said. It was the truth. Up until then, she hadn't really taken seriously the women's growing concern about the environment. It had just seemed like yet another silly fad to put up with, like that summer they had all gotten into intermittent fasting, or the Christmas they had all gifted each other chunks of jade in the shape of an egg, because they had heard a celebrity on a talk show claim that keeping it in your vagina would naturally balance your hormones and increase your feminine energy. But now this climate-change stuff appeared to be the central concern of the group.

"It's not your fault, Karen," Kayla announced. "You just didn't know any better. You've been fooled by the polluters. They're the true enemies." The rest of the girls murmured their assent. "They're the ones we need to be mad at. They're the ones we need to confront." The agreement was louder this time.

"I know what we can do!" Michele shouted. "Follow me!" She led the group back towards the street and away from the park. Karen was up front this time, her car left in the parking lot unlocked.

It was quite a walk and the sky had darkened a bit during the march, but the last mile wasn't bad. The noise of the crowd was drifting out that far, their debris marking their trail as the girls neared. Rounding the last corner brought the mass of people into view. They were clustered around a building, blocking the streets and generally causing a scene.

"What's that building?" Karen whispered to Michele.

"It's the local party headquarters for those pollution profiteers," Michele hissed back.

At the rear of the pack of people were a few organizers handing out picket signs. All the girls grabbed for them. Karen got one thrust into her hand. It read, "Gas The Oil Polluters."

"Let's try to find a good spot!" Kayla shouted over the noise, pointing to the far side of the protesters. The girls followed after her. On the far side of the building, they settled into a more open spot. The crowd alternated between group chants and random screaming punctuated with air horns and other noise-making devices. Then came the praying, which seemed more like some kind of native raindance where everyone just did their own thing, while people banged on drums in no particular pattern or rhythm. Karen did her best to keep pace with them, but even the other girls in her group weren't clued in on how to behave. It was the first time any of them had been at an actual protest.

After two hours of this, Karen was getting tired. Her mud boots weren't comfortable, and the long hike to get here didn't help the situation. But after the fiasco in the park, she couldn't look weak on the cause. The first thought that went through her head when she felt the raindrop hit her on the cheek was, "Good thing I still have my boots on." While Karen had now avowed herself to the cause of the Gaia Party in order to stay in the good graces of her friends, she hadn't actually given in completely to the belief system yet. So her reaction to the rain was more in line with how she had always responded to rain during her life, avoiding it but being prepared to deal with it. Since her bed and wine glass were far way, the boots were the next best thing.

The rest of the crowd, however, had already fully invested in the movement, so their response was different. At first there was an uneasy shifting that rippled through the people. "Is it really rain?" "Was that thunder?" The questions seemed to pop into everyone's head in unison. Then came the rage. The system that had brought us the five stages of grief now gave us the five stages of environmental panic: surprise, terror, rage, blame and revenge. The surprise was quick, the terror and rage bundled into one quick wave, and the blame was easy; after all, they were already standing outside of the source of their perceived plight. Revenge followed swiftly.

The crowd surged forward with a roar. The flimsy barricades around the perimeter of the property gave way as the leaders pushed forward. "Let's get these Polluters!!" the first person up the steps screamed while heaving a rock through the glass door. Lunging forward with the rest of the people, Karen and the girls were engulfed with the group bloodlust that had taken hold of the crowd. Pushing and shoving their way forward, they climbed into the building through a broken window and found themselves in someone's office. The door to the rest of the building was blocked with people trying to get deeper in, but this one was good enough for Tiffany. Most of the big items had already been smashed by the first wave, , although there was plenty of smaller stuff looking to be destroyed. Grabbing books from the shelf, Tiffany started ripping pages out. Michele grabbed a chair that had already been knocked over and started banging it against the wall. The rest of the squad spread out to lay waste. Still holding her protest sign, Karen put it to work against the wall. It took a few tries, but she got a good hole going through the drywall, although after a few swings it felt more like work than fun.

Just as the inspiration to destroy had appeared so quickly, it also disappeared. It wasn't a nice office space to begin with. The building looked like it had been an old bank that had vanished a dozen years before, during the big bailout, designed in a '70s Brutalist style, all tinted windows and brown brick slanting at strange angles. Occupied by some local officials and interns, it was mostly just a meeting point for like-minded individuals, as well as local storage for the party's promotional material. It lacked any luster when you actually saw it for what it was.

The rest of the raiding force started to trickle out through the doors once all the cool things had been smashed, which wasn't much. No one tried to leave through the windows that they had so eagerly entered. Once tempers cooled, civility returned, and civilized people use doors.

The girls regrouped on the sidewalk, sweaty from the siege. The rain had already stopped. "I guess we should head back to the park to get the Turtles," Tiffany said. Silently the girls turned back down the street and headed home.

* * *

The last few weeks before the election moved quickly, as the intensity ramped up for everyone. For Karen, it was memorable, not only because it was the first time she had ever actually followed politics, but because there was a large sense of community between everyone involved, not limited to her relatively small social group. One of the first things she did after the protest was register to vote. She had skated by this far in life without ever really feeling the need to get involved, and had always steered clear of the people with their clipboards whenever she saw them around election times. But that wasn't something she wanted her friends to know; they had already been disappointed enough in her lack of political involvement. Now that the girls had thrown themselves fully into the Rodriguez campaign, it would have been an awkward conversation if her name showed up on one of the lists of unregistered voters they kept using to chase down and pester people to join the Gaia Party.

The election was like a tailgate party for the whole country. Even the mainstream people were going nuts, because it was looking likely that Alyssa Rodriguez would become the first President since Millard freaking Fillmore in 1850 to not be either a Democrat or a Republican. Karen had never heard of President Fillmore before, but it was a fun bit of trivia the Gaia Party kept reminding everyone about, that electing Alyssa was a chance to make history. The night before the election, the girls marched in the Parade in the Dark, a silent march during the night to symbolize their commitment to abolishing the destructive waste of modern power grids. It wasn't as much fun as it sounded, but the next night lived up to the hype. The girls worked until the polls closed. After the results came in that declared Rodriguez the new President, the entire town seemed to turn out to celebrate. Fireworks, horn honking and binge drinking took over until daylight. It was like a frat party, the Fourth of July and the Super Bowl combined. It was the best night of Karen's life. Winning always felt good, and tonight everyone was a winner.

Though after the election, the luster faded. The march to Washington was being planned and people started heading that way, but all of the girls bowed out. The kids or some other pressing engagement came up that kept them comfortably at home. Karen didn't really want to go, but had mentally prepared to participate if it was demanded. The urgency of autumn had faded from daily life in winter, and things fell back into their normal routine. That was, until around April that next spring, when the weather took a turn for the worse.

The girls reunited to watch the reports and comfort each other as they watched the destruction that Super Storm Albert was unleashing on the east coast. It had seemed like their votes had been enough to affect the necessary change, yet the weather continued happening, and Gaia still wasn't happy. By June their little group had disbanded. Things had gotten too dangerous to make the treks to meet up. The Turtles that had been all the rage the previous summer hadn't held up well during the winter, and most of them were immobile by this point. As the world closed in, the effort of walking for hours was getting to be too much for them all to bother meeting up. With the sudden scarcity of food, you also had to start factoring in what you were physically capable of doing before you made plans. Three hours of walking to just sit somewhere and gossip wasn't a good use of your finite strength. Michele lived closest to Karen, only the next neighborhood over, they were each other's last connection to their old life, so they found the time to meet and talk every couple days. Not like they didn't have plenty of free time. The morning of June 23rd, they ended up sitting in the shade of trees that lined the edge of the former grocery store parking lot.

"All my neighbors are heading down to Centennial Plaza today," Michele said once they got seated. "We're sick of those corporations trying to charge an insane amount for those things they ruined the planet making in the first place."

"What things?"

"Everything. Food, shoes. I need a new pillow, but they cost like a hundred bucks now."

"A hundred dollars for a pillow?" Karen asked. She had been happy to stay near her home for the past few weeks as things deteriorated. She had heard people on her 'Let talking about "wheelbarrows of cash," but she didn't realize it had become so literal.

"Yes, it's insane. They're trying to punish us for electing Alyssa. Scare us into not supporting her and ignoring their crimes."

"So what are you doing down at the Plaza about it?"

"Taking what we need. I need a new pillow and I'm going to get one."

"I'd be happy with a cheeseburger," Karen mused. It had been awhile since she had seen a cheeseburger, or any kind of fast food for that matter.

"You aren't taking this seriously."

"I'm very serious about cheeseburgers."

"Fuck off," Michele shot back.

"Hey!"

"It's just frustrating. You've treated this whole thing like a joke. It's people like you who got us in this mess."

"What are you talking about? This is my fault?" Karen gestured around at the parking lot that could have passed for a scene from the third world. As the arteries of modern life shut down, more and more people had let go of their previous lives and now lived untethered in the urban wild that surrounded them. The looted-out grocery store served as the local bazaar for the region. Just about everything you could want could be found in the village of tents, huts and hulks of old cars that filled the parking lot now.

"Bitches like you are the problem. You don't care about anything! The whole world can suffer because you want another cheeseburger, as if you haven't had enough," she screeched.

"Yeah, you're so much better, wanting your precious pillow. You were a bitch when I met you, and no amount of praying to the damn trees is going to change that." Karen snapped off, climbing to her feet.

"You disgust me!" Michele screamed after her. She could get the last word in, it didn't matter anymore, the group was dead and she didn't have to play nice with the other girls anymore. It was time to move on.

Michele had been right, her neighborhood was riled up and ready to do something about it. All day long, the noise from across the street had been growing, and by late afternoon it was on the move. Karen's own neighbors were a little less restless, but there wasn't much left to occupy their time with at home, so following along seemed like the most interesting choice.

The trek to Centennial Plaza was only a couple miles, and with such a big crowd working that way, it seemed like some kind of slow-motion marathon. "How's it going, Roger?" Karen asked once she caught up to him when they turned out of the neighborhood. Roger was the neighborhood gay; that might sound harsh, but that's how he was viewed, and it didn't actually seem to bother him a whole lot.

"Just going shopping."

"Ha, yeah, it's just one big shopping trip."

"Well honey, I don't think those guys up front are just out for fresh air."

"No, I guess not. What do you think will happen up there?" The orgy of destruction at the party building had been her only experience with mobs, and wasn't really high on her agenda to recreate.

"Normally it's just a bunch of yelling and kicking trash around, but I think today it's going to be full-on."

"What are you going to do when it happens?"

Roger gave her a look. "I honestly don't know. I'm sick of how things are going...but burning down a Target isn't really going to change much."

"No, not really." She paused. "I hope they don't burn down Target. Maybe the bookstore or something."

"That's what I need, books!" Roger said. "These days are getting longer and more boring as we go along. They'll be a bitch to carry all the way back, though."

The last big turn put them looking straight at the Centennial Plaza shopping district, even if it was still a mile ahead of them. That's when the columns of smoke became visible on the horizon. The murmur of the crowd swelled quickly and the pace quickened. The mass fear that all the good stuff would be taken before they got there took over.

Most everyone ran the last mile or at least jogged it. Breaking through the last little line of trees, the group burst into the first of the large parking lots that surrounded the stores. Most of the stores were unburned; the majority of the smoke was coming from a few cars sporadically parked around the otherwise empty lot, plus the IHOP. Several other small hordes were milling around all the stores within sight. However, things still seemed rather calm. Most of the people were unsure of what to do next, now that they had gotten this far.

The leaders of Karen's group were still the loudmouths from Michele's neighborhood, and there was no holding them back. They lowered their heads, rushing forward to the first store in their path, Karen's favorite, Target. In the front of the store were three men who seemed to be guarding the place. They had cars parked in front of the doors like a barricade, and carried baseball bats. They stood firm at first, until the leaders of the mob got about a hundred feet from them and showed no intentions of slowing down. The defenders then scattered, their bats laying on the ground. They would've made the perfect tool to break the glass doors down without any injuries, but that thought didn't occur to the attackers. The first wave hit the glass at full force and burst through with a rebel yell.

Having worn herself out from the first sprint in, Karen lagged behind during the final rush, surveying the area. The rest of the people who were already there reacted to the new wave with glee and immediately picked out their own prey. Now that the looting had begun, no one was holding back. All the stores were being raided at the same time, up and down the mile-long stretch of middle-class shopping.

Peering through the smashed glass frames of the Target entrance, the situation inside was insane. The lights were out, obviously. Even though vision was limited, it yielded a mob scene. Several people laid in pools of blood inside the doors and even farther inside. The people closest to the doors were the ones who had jumped through, taking the brunt of the impact, then sliced up by the glass and trampled by the rest of the group before they could get back up. The last unmoving body Karen could make out, at the edge of the light, was sprawled towards the door, his arm still clinging desperately to a box whose contents Karen couldn't figure out. The fact that he had been injured after having made it inside and found something to loot meant he had been attacked by someone on the way out, not trampled on the way in. The roar of sound coming from within was frightful, individual screams faintly distinguishable from the general noise. Looking down at the edge of the door frame, Karen stepped back. No way she was walking in there.

Outside things continued to escalate. More stores were

now on fire, and there were gunshots cracking off. The next complex over from the Target building contained a Subway sandwich shop. That was where Karen headed. It was flanked by a shoe store and a Verizon shop. The shoe store had already been broken into, but only a few people were milling around in there, searching for their perfect fit. The Verizon store was untouched. 'Lets hadn't been very useful lately, with the power and service shrinking.

The Subway door was locked. Peeking through the windows didn't offer much, but it did look like there were loaves of bread on one of the shelves. Honestly, food was the only thing on Karen's mind. Food over the past couple weeks had been hard to find; that was what had driven most people on this riotous march, even if they got caught up chasing shinier objects once they got here. Finding a baseball-sized rock on the ground, Karen heaved it against the glass doorway, but the rock just hit with a loud crack and dropped to the ground. Only a chip of glass marked its impact.

She bent down to pick the rock back up, but a foot appeared and sent it spinning out into the parking lot before she could grab it. "Ahhh!" Karen exclaimed, jumping back. The silent stranger stared at her for a moment, then swung his sledgehammer full-force against the glass. It shattered completely, leaving a full opening. The stranger looked back to Karen, giving her the universal hand gesture of *after you*.

"Uh, thanks." She stepped past him onto the cracking glass. With a nod of his head, he continued towards the next complex, sledgehammer in tow.

Inside the Subway there was still food, chips, warm Coke bottles, and stale bread. It also smelled terrible from the food that had started rotting since the power had gone out. Collecting her loot, Karen took a seat in the first booth and had a bit of a picnic with a view of a full-fledged riot before her.

The first night had been a party. Those who made it through the mad rush of bloodlust now settled down to enjoy the fruits of their conquests. Furniture was dragged out to the parking lot, TVs piled high, like buffalo carcasses from the Old West. More important was the access to whatever liquor had been found, and it was a lot. The musically inclined found instruments and got a band playing out front of the Dicks Sporting Goods. It was hard to hear unless you got close enough, but it added to the party vibe. The gunshots continued throughout the night, even though Karen didn't actually see anyone shooting. It was a good time and Karen made a few friends, mostly people with gin who were willing to share. The party was still going when the sun returned, and the burning heat of summer drove the partygoers from the parking lot and back into the buildings. The luster of the new reality was beginning to wear off as people started slipping away. Still, the party started back up at sundown the second night, because there was still plenty of liquor left. Even a few more buildings got burned to light the place up.

Karen had appropriated a couple of cushions and set up the storage room in the Subway as her own. It was cramped, but at least she had her own space. When she crawled out of her sleeping spot at dusk on the third night, it was obvious things had changed. The music was gone, and the large groups of happy drinkers had been replaced by sullen small groups who were sucking on anything that had survived this long. Giving the creepier groups a wide berth, she toured the area farther than she had so far. The next building over was a Home Depot. It had been given an even rougher treatment than the Target had. It looked like the raiders had literally pulled everything out of it just on principle, including the shelving units. The next building was a Bed Bath and Beyond. It was sorta tucked away from the rest of the stores, up a small hill and facing away from the rest. It hadn't been fully ravaged yet. The windows were broken and everything inside had been thrown all over the place, but not gutted. Stepping in carefully, she looked around. The store appeared deserted, and there wasn't anyone hanging around in the front of it, like there was at all the other buildings.

She ventured in. It took a while, but she inspected enough of the store to believe it was devoid of people. In the back were several display beds that had been overturned. She dragged a mattress against the wall and with a solid effort stood another one up over it, so that it resembled a lean-to. Crawling into her fort, she got comfy and passed out again.

After that night, the Bed Bath and Beyond was Karen's home. Emptying out the manager's office, she had forced the best mattress through the door and then piled the comforters around the rest of the room, layering the sheets and coating the floor in pillows. It was an entire room dedicated to comfort, or as much comfort as was possible without electricity.

For the next few weeks, Karen roamed around the wreckage of the Centennial Plaza shopping district. There was plenty of food and drink to be scavenged from the stores, but most of it was candy, chips or other less filling foods. From rumors she picked up from the random strangers who passed by, she found out about the food delivery trucks that were supplying rations to the neighborhoods, and also the rules that came with them. That suggested that she wouldn't have much luck if she headed back to her actual home. She had to make do where she was for the time being.

The neighborhood directly behind the Home Depot was where she started, and after a few inquiries she made some friends who were willing to share, for a price. They gave her lists of things they wanted from the stores. She searched through the debris and brought them what she could. They gave her some of their government rations. There was a very strict system for getting the food deliveries. Every person from every house had to be present and out front of their house, with proper identification. But there were ways around it, and some of the delivery people could be persuaded to help out. So extra food was available and a little black market hummed. Even when Karen couldn't find what her partners wanted, or just couldn't be bothered to look, she had other ways of satisfying their demands, and pretty soon that became the preferred method of repayment. She lived in her cushy room, surrounded by all the trappings of a well-furnished lifestyle, and she only had to work a little bit to produce food. It was an easy life.

It took about six weeks for Karen to tire of her new situation. Her room was comfy, but it was hot and stuffy, and there was no way to clean anything. Her business partners were increasing their demands and gradually growing more difficult. The food that could be found had mostly dried up, and now she was reduced to drinking half-full bottles of Pepsi or slathering ketchup all over peanuts when she exhausted her purchased rations. Every day she watched the brown school buses as they drove past her in the morning and returned every night. They were filled with people, and a few times they stopped within sight, the spilled-out workers all in matching brown uniforms cleaning up some of the mess that had been left behind, towing some of the burned-out husks of cars. Karen watched them, but never let herself be seen. She knew they were the Dirts, or at least that was what she knew them as, but she couldn't remember their official name. It was kind of a civilian army for reversing humanity's stain on the earth or something like that. They had gotten started literally the day after the Inauguration, putting people to work, basically doing busywork. Once the troubles had begun, they had expanded rapidly, filling every role imaginable. But the majority of the work was focused on the massive garbage cleanup operation. In this case, the garbage was humans.

One particularly hot morning, Karen woke up soaked in sweat, the entire day ruined already. It had been awhile since she had even seen enough water to take a bath in, so there wasn't any rinsing the stickiness off. Her business partners were sure to whine if she smelled too bad, not that they smelled great either. However, they didn't seem to factor her opinions on their cleanliness into consideration very much.

That was when she decided to move on. The rest of the day she spent enjoying the small pleasures of her habitat, digging deep through the wreckage to find a couple of candy bars. Picking out the best pairs of socks, shoes and underwear that remained, she packed them into a small backpack with a couple of books and headed out to the road. It was around five o'clock, she estimated, when the buses made their return trip. Karen was waiting for them when they puffed around the corner and into sight. Standing at the side of the road watching them closing the distance, Karen was excited. She had tried the loner lifestyle and had enjoyed it, but she was ready to be around people again, a new group of friends to deal with, and maybe a shower.

The first bus slowed down and coasted to a stop where Karen was standing, all the other busses gliding to a stop behind it as well. Swinging open, the door revealed a young guy behind the wheel. He didn't say anything, just nodded to Karen, and she climbed aboard.

CHAPTER FOUR
HOUSE

At 4 p.m. on the dot, Eric joined us in the break room. We had been lounging around listening to him do his end-of-day routine for a while. "We are all locked up now," he announced. "I always leave a note on the front door saying when I'll be back, in case anyone stops by after hours. I can't be expected to be here 24 hours a day, every single day by myself, can I?"

"No you can't," Sami answered first, shooting me a look.

Eric gave our new luggage a lookover, but didn't say anything about our new Land Rover swag. "Well, let's get a move on. It's a bit of a hike." Throwing the bags over our shoulders, we followed Eric to the back door.

"At least the weather is nice for a stroll," Sami said once we got moving.

"Oh yes," Eric said merrily. "I think it's been a very nice summer so far, except for the occasional storm."

"Yeah, those storms have been keeping me up at night," I said, adding my wit to the banter. Eric missed it and Sami, as usual, wasn't impressed.

For a while the trip was uneventful. We weaved in and out of parking lots, over roads and around buildings. Walking as the crow flies, as is said. That was during the stretch through the more commercial spaces that surrounded the dealership. The evidence of the disruption to the previous order was apparent, but understated. Instead of cars filling the roads, everyone on their own path of errands, the streets were open and parking lots bare, even if that didn't stop me from looking both ways when we crossed the street. We passed the smaller storefronts first. They looked normal from a distance, but up close they looked like what the stores always looked like after hurricanes down in Florida or somewhere. Broken windows, shopping carts overturned, and junk strewn about out front, as if it was the lair of some monstrous dragon who made its nest out of trash.

"I thought there'd be more people around this area," Sami said as we wandered through one of the massive parking lots towards some large big-box stores.

"Oh, it was crazy for a while," Eric answered casually, as if he was an RA giving us freshmen a tour of the dorms. "There's still a few around here, hiding in the buildings, but most of the people moved on pretty quick once everything was gone."

The larger the parking lots, the larger the store, and the larger the mess that appeared out front of them. Piles of junk were everywhere now, including multiple burned-out cars that dotted the parking lots like empty husks.

"Looks like things got pretty crazy here," I said, pointing to a building that had been set on fire. It was still standing, but had been blackened to a crisp.

"Oh yeah, those first few days they were setting things on fire every night. Not sure if it was because the store offended them for some reason or just for fun."

"Were you here for all of this?" Sami asked now.

"Oh, I saw a bit of it when I was on the way to the office, you know. Though things were usually a lot calmer when I would pass through in the early morning hours. They all would sleep during the day, and hadn't really gotten stirring again when I was on my way back in the late afternoon. I missed their big hullabaloos, but I could hear it going all night."

We counted ourselves lucky that our neighborhood had remained peaceful during the initial crash of society. Sami and I had stocked up on food before the shortages had gotten too bad, and the garden had gotten started around then. Most of our neighbors were paranoid enough to stock up as well. That kept everyone pretty even-tempered when the shutdown happened, then the food deliveries started happening before any of us really ran out of supplies. That kept everyone happy and inside the walls of the subdivision for the most part. There had been some people who had ventured out, mostly for curiosity's sake, but that was about it. Last night was the first time Sami and I had been away from home in quite a while.

Eric came to an abrupt halt. Even though we were in the middle of an empty parking lot, I still bumped into him. "What is it?" I asked as I bounced off of him.

"I think the buses are coming. Do you hear them?"

"I don't hear anything."

"I do," Sami cut in.

"This way." Eric motioned to a couple of couches that were sitting in the grass-covered island in the parking lot. Scurrying over to them, he crouched down to shield himself from sight of the road.

"What's going on?" I asked, plopping down next to him. "What buses?"

"The Dirt buses. They drive through here in the evenings while going back to their camp."

"Okay." The sound of the engines was unmistakable now. They were getting close, though still out of sight.

"Aren't they just for the clean-up crews?" Sami questioned. "I've heard them being talked about. Why do we need to hide from them?"

"They don't really like people out on their own. Think they're up to no good and they grab them."

"Grab them?"

"Oh yeah. I've seen a few people get snatched up by them now. Just out minding their own business and away they go."

The busses became visible now, about six of them snaking down the road in a convoy.

"Look over there." Sami directed our eyes farther down the road. There was a woman standing under a tree. Once she saw the busses, she got up and stepped off the curb, into the street.

"Is she hitching a ride or something?" I guessed.

Eric didn't answer, but just watched the scene intensely. The busses slowed down and the lead bus pulled over, the door swinging open when it reached where the lady was standing. It looked like a few words were exchanged and then she climbed on, the door closing and the convoy proceeding on as if nothing had happened.

"Okay, we can go now," Eric announced once the last bus disappeared.

"That was weird," Sami said as our hike resumed.

"Guess she wanted to join the Dirts," Eric answered indifferently.

"Do you know anything about the Dirts out there? You said they had a camp?" Sami continued.

"Just some rumors. I know they have a camp on the other side of town, though." His tone was flat, not interested.

The rest of the walk to Eric's house was uneventful. His house was somewhat secluded from the rest of the houses on his street, since it was set back off the road a good bit. "Please leave your shoes by the door," he said in a sing-song voice after he unlocked the door, letting us inside. "The guest room is down this way." He pointed down the stairs. The house was a split-level, with the steps immediately inside the door.

On the bottom level, he opened the first door and motioned us in. "This is it."

"Oh, it's very nice, Eric," Sami said pleasantly, looking around the room.

"Thanks for letting us stay here, Eric," I said, stepping into the room and setting my bag on the bed.

"Dinner will be in about an hour."

"Is there anything we can do to help?" Sami asked. "Does Debby need any help in the kitchen?"

"I'm afraid Debby isn't feeling very well, so I'll be cooking dinner."

"Oh, I'm sorry. I hope she feels better. Do you need any help with dinner?"

"I'll let you know about that," Eric responded as he turned to go back up the stairs.

"Thanks again," Sami called after. "He seems weirder than normal," she whispered once the sound of his steps were safely overhead.

"I don't disagree, but what can we do about that?"

"It just makes me nervous sleeping here when he's obviously not right."

"It's better than the couch at the dealership."

"Yeah, I'll let you know about that." She poked me, but a little harder than a joke poke would be.

* * *

Eric had dinner ready about an hour and several refusals to let Sami help later. It was simple, just a couple pieces of chicken and some tomatoes, but it was much better than vending machine food.

"How long has Debby been sick?" Sami asked once the three of us were seated at the table.

"That's a personal question, and I don't think any of your business," Eric responded.

Catching my eye, Sami gave me the universal wide-eyed look you make when you encounter a crazy person.

"Uhh, have things been good around here since all the trouble began?" I asked to try and defuse the awkwardness.

"It's been fine here. Just less cars now."

"At least there's a bright side."

"I sell cars," Eric answered.

"Yeah, I know. Still, it must be nice not to have strangers cruising down your street all the time." Eric just shrugged.

"Anything on the agenda for tomorrow?" Sami asked, trying again.

"Just work. We can leave around 7." Eric looked back and forth between us.

"Oh, you want to go back to the dealership?" I said. I guess it made sense in his mind.

"That's where work is."

"I kinda thought we'd stay here tomorrow and figure out our next step," Sami interjected.

"You can't stay here. We have to go to work."

"Are you sure? We could help Debby if she needs anything. Maybe help her feel better."

"I didn't let you come here so you could help Debby. Your job is at the dealership. Considering how much time you took off, you're lucky I haven't fired you already," Eric shot back.

"Okay, we'll go to the dealership in the morning, leaving at 7 a.m.," I answered.

Silence followed, an awkward silence for sure. Luckily there was so little food on our plates that it didn't take long to finish eating. "That was really good, Eric. Thanks for making us dinner," Sami said, cleaning the plates from the table.

"There's no running water, so just leave them in the sink," he responded.

"Oh, okay."

Standing up and stretching a bit, he said, "I guess it's time for bed now." Since the electricity was gone, bedtime always came earlier than we were used to. "Just be ready at 7 a.m." He got up from his chair and headed towards his bedroom.

Sami and I went back downstairs and got undressed for bed. "Did you lock the door?" she whispered.

"Yes, you already asked me that."

Still looking at the door, she bit her lip. "Does the lock seem strong?"

"What are you worried about?"

"He could have a key or something."

"Fine." Climbing back out of bed, I grabbed the end of the dresser that was next to the doorway and pulled it in front of the door, blocking it from opening. "Is that enough?"

"Yes." She smiled. "I think that will keep everyone out."

"Okay. Anyone can come in as far as I'm concerned, as long as they don't wake me up." I got back under the blankets.

"Kyle." She was whispering in my ear.

"Yes, dear?"

"Eric is creeping me out. He was odd today, but he got even weirder when we got back to the house."

"He's always been kinda weird. I guess all this is just making it more obvious."

"What do you think is wrong with Debby that she couldn't even come out and say hi to us?"

"I dunno. Maybe lupus."

"That's really the joke you're going with?"

"Ugh, leave me alone. My house got burned down yesterday." I rolled over and pulled the sheets over my head.

"*Our* house got burned down, baby. *Our* house."

"That's what I said. Now hushy."

* * *

BANG BANG. "Are you two up in there?!" the voice shouted.

"Yes!" I shouted back before I was even really awake. "We're getting ready!" I sat up.

"Good, we need to get going soon."

"Alright, we'll be out in a minute."

"What are we gonna do at the dealership all day long?" Sami moaned.

"We can nap on the couches."

"Let's just nap here. I'll start," she mumbled while rolling over.

"Come on, get up." I pulled the blankets away from her.

"Uuuunnnnnnrrrr."

"You don't want him coming back. Let's go." I slipped out of bed and grabbed my pants.

A couple minutes later, the three of us were trooping out of the house and on our way to work at a car dealership, in a world were owning cars was illegal. A fact that Sami felt was important to remind Eric about. "Don't you think you should mention that to him?" she asked me in a quiet voice.

"I mentioned it."

"You told him that our house got burned down because we

owned a car. And we're now walking to…"

"I get the irony, dear. But he's obviously not right at the moment, and he's the only friendly face we have."

Rolling her eyes, Sami stepped up the pace and pulled back up with Eric. "So you know that owning cars is illegal now, right, Eric?"

"That's unfortunate," he responded gravely.

"It just seems like a waste to keep the store open if people can't actually buy the cars…that is, if there were even any in stock."

"Well, I didn't want to spoil the surprise, but I guess you two can hear it now." Excitement was creeping into his voice.

"What's the surprise?" I asked.

"So, just before we started having this trouble with the internet, I received a very important email from England. They were working on getting us a large shipment of the brand-new Nature Rovers. That's top-of-the-line Green tech and is completely compliant with the new regulations." He was smiling widely. "Once those new cars get here, we'll have customers beating our doors down trying to get them. Our dealership is the only one in the whole state getting them. We'll be sold out in a couple hours."

"How long ago did you get this message?" Sami questioned.

"About two months ago."

"Any guess when these brand-new cars are going to get here?" My turn.

"Oh it should be any day now. That's why I'm so glad you came back to work. It's going to be too much work for me to handle myself."

"Eric, people aren't getting enough food to eat, all the power is shut down, and they're burning homes down to appease angry rainstorms," Sami said as gently as possible. "I don't think those cars are coming. Even if they do, there isn't anyone to buy them anymore."

"Nonsense. They'll come, and then we'll be back in business, you'll see."

"I guess I will." She fell back again, to a few steps next to me.

Once we arrived at the dealership, Sami and I set up in the break room as Eric wandered off to his office to work on his papers and await the new shipment of cars. Sami napped for a while. I couldn't fall asleep, even though I was tired. Once I'm awake, it's so hard for me to sleep soon after.

After her nap, Sami was more than awake and antsy, demonstrated by throwing one of the magazines after just a moment of reading. "Nothing good in that one?" I asked, eyebrows raised.

"I'm sick of being here."

"Any suggestions on other activities?"

"No."

"Well…"

"Actually, yes," she cut back in. "I'm going to tear this place apart." Jumping up and rushing out of the room, based on the sounds I gathered she had headed back to the rear of the building and begun rummaging through one of the office spaces back there. I stayed in my seat.

About an hour later she returned carrying a prize, a small radio. "Where did you find that?" I asked.

"It was in the bottom of one of the drawers. I think it's older than we are, but it might work."

"What size batteries?" I asked, grabbing my backpack that held our finds from the day before.

"Four double-As."

"Here." I handed them to her and she shoved them in. The front of the radio lit up immediately. First it was just the usual static, but Sami spun the dial until we heard a male's voice speaking over the static. "We will soon be hearing from our beloved President Rodriquez with an important update on the severe weather that has hit the Chicago metro area."

The female voice took over now. "I really can't imagine the strain the President is under. She's been working to save this planet from the moment she took office, and it just hasn't stopped for a single minute since then."

"It really hasn't," the male voice cut in.

"I just hope everyone out there is keeping the President in their thoughts. The work she's doing for us is unprecedented. I actually have a picture of her hanging over my desk. You remember, from when she toured the floods?"

"Oh yes. What a powerful image."

"Whenever the world seems to be too much for me to handle, I look up at it and just remember what she's going through, yet how much she perseveres in the face of such challenges."

"We've been waiting a very long time for a leader like her, one who really cares about the people and leads by example," the man answered.

"Absolutely. We're lucky to have her. And speaking of which, we're now going live to the White House to hear from her."

"Change the station," I said.

Sami gave me a look, but spun the dial, finding static and then the President's voice on a different station. "They're all playing the speech," she said, spinning the volume knob until it turned off.

"Of course they are."

"I guess the storm really freaked people out."

"Storms have been happening my whole life, and no one burned any houses down because of them before," I said tersely. "But now, our house gets murdered because someone has to be blamed, and then turn on the radio and there's the President, saying that we're killing the earth because there's a car in the garage or we have some plants in the back yard."

"I know, honey."

I gave a long sigh. "It's just frustrating. What are we supposed to do?"

Sami didn't answer. She had known me long enough to just listen when I got angry. We hadn't ever been in this exact position, but the same rules applied.

* * *

The rest of the day was spent waiting. Sami dug around

every corner of the building, but didn't come up with anything else interesting and gave up. Each of us avoided talking about the black abyss that stared us in the face. Eric came and got us right on the dot at 4 p.m. again. He had spent the entire day in his office without coming out once. "You guys ready to go home?" he asked casually, like it was just another Thursday.

"Yep." We were already holding our bags.

The trip home was easy. No bus convoys passed us this time, and we only saw a few people out wandering around. We gave them a decent berth, even if they didn't look threatening.

"Take your shoes off," Eric said when we reached the front door, exactly like yesterday. His voice sounded flat again, different than it ever sounded while we were at the dealership.

"Can we help you with dinner tonight?" Sami asked. "Or does Debby need anything from us? We'd love to say hi."

"No, I'll come get you when dinner's ready. Wait down there." He pointed to our room.

This time, dinner was just a collection of raw vegetables and crackers. Eric hadn't bothered to call us this time, but just stomped on the floor to signal us to come upstairs.

"Looks great," Sami said brightly when we got to the table.

"It better," Eric growled.

"Is there anything we can do around here to help you two out, Eric?" I asked. "It's very nice of you to let us stay here."

"No, we don't need anything from you."

"Maybe we could try and find some medicine for Debby? Do you know what's ailing her?"

"No." He bit into his carrot.

"Even some Advil or something like that could help."

"She doesn't need any medicine," Eric said, turning his attention to the cucumber.

"We're just worried about her. We haven't seen her at all, and she's always been so friendly to us."

Eric suddenly slammed his fists down on the table hard enough to make the flatware rattle. "You're *worried* about her? You're wondering where she *is*? Then by all means, I'll go get her for you." He stood abruptly and stormed off to the bedroom.

"I think something's really wrong," Sami whispered.

"No need to whisper, dear. I think we all know something is really wrong." I turned to face the door to the bedroom that concealed Eric and Debby.

The noise in the room died down after a couple minutes, though we could still hear him moving around in there. "Maybe we should just leave…" Sami started saying, but her voice trailed off as the door opened. Eric stood in the doorway in a dress hideously too small for him, yanked down over his lumpy body. The entire neckline was covered in dry blood, and red spatters streaked down in vertical lines all the way to the beltline. His legs were covered by stockings marred with excessive runs, standing atop of a pair of red high heels. His face was smeared with makeup, as if a toddler had tried his hand at face painting, with a blonde wig that I remembered Debby wearing during a fancy fundraiser we had all attended a few years back.

"*Here I am, Sami!!!*" he squealed out in a hideous, blood-curdling falsetto. "Sorry you haven't seen me! I haven't been feeling myself lately!" He emitted a grotesque tittering of a laugh. "Why, I almost thought of killing myself the other day, but thank goodness Eric was here to save me! Now, give your friend Debby *A BIG HUG!!!*" He lurched forwards towards her, stomping on top of the too-small shoes that were strapped tightly to his ankles.

"Eric, stop it!" she screamed, jumping out of her chair and holding it between them like a lion tamer.

"What's the matter? Don't you want to see Debby? You won't stop *FUCKING ASKING ERIC ABOUT ME!!!*" He rasped heavily, seething between sentences. "You wanted to help me with my medicine? Well, come take your medicine!"

"Hey!" I pushed the table into his path before he could get around to Sami. "You need to calm the fuck down, Eric. This is insane." Scampering around the edge, Sami got behind me, and I took the lion's-tamer chair from her and held it out myself.

"I'm Debby! I'm Debby!" Eric was laughing like a maniac as he started grabbing at the food on the table.

"Go get our bags," I ordered Sami as we backed down the hallway towards the stairs.

"Where are you going? You aren't afraid of poor little sick

Debby, are you?" He followed us down the hallway with his insane laughter.

At the landing, Sami rushed into the bedroom and I kept the chair pointed at him as he inched down the steps. "Stay there, Eric," I said. "Don't come down here."

"What do you mean? You want to stay here with me, don't you? I remember how you used to look at me at the parties." He was running his hands over his body like that scene from *Silence of the Lambs* with Buffalo Bill admiring himself in the mirror.

"You're insane!" Jabbing forward with the chair, he tried to bat it away.

Sami came running out of the room, all of our bags in hand. Eric reached over the handrailing, trying to grasp for her. Slamming the chair forward this time, I struck him hard in the chest with the legs, sending him falling onto his back with a whimper. Ducking to avoid his reach, Sami slipped behind me, pulling the door open and escaping without looking back.

"I gave you food and now you're leaving me too!" Eric screamed at us, pure male again and now pure rage, still laying on the stairs where he had fallen.

"Kyle!" Sami yelled at me from outside. "Get our shoes!"

Keeping the chair pointed at Eric, I grabbed the shoes in my right hand and backed out the open door. Eric didn't move, just watching us through his smeared makeup as I closed the door and left the chair in front of it.

"Here." I handed Sami her shoes when I reached her at the curb.

"Thanks." She sat down and pulled them on. Once she was back up, I sat down and did the same. Defensive tactics were starting to come naturally to us.

"You don't think he'll follow us, do you?" Sami asked once we got moving.

"I don't think so." I paused. "But I didn't think he was going to try to kill us while wearing his dead wife's dress, either."

CHAPTER FIVE

RIAN

Rian Elliot's life changed one night in October 2028. It was a rainy, crappy day at the coffee bar where Rian was a barista. Getting off work at 5 p.m., he headed out with his friends to a couple of actual bars and spent the next five hours bitching about the general state of the world while getting drunk. Of course, by "the world" he meant the things that directly affected his life: his dick of a boss, his student loans, and his poor credit score. A little after 10 p.m., Marissa finally responded that she was down. He had made a match with her a few weeks ago on Feelerz, and they had been hooking up once a week or so since then. "I'm out!" he said, slamming his beer and leaving less of a tip than those Athleisure-wearing MILFs who he was always whining about at the coffeehouse.

It took two tries to get the keys in the ignition, but once he got rolling, he was in the midst of a perfect buzzed driving frame of mind. The kind that makes it seem like your reflexes are faster than reality. The best thing about Marissa was that she's a straight-to-business kinda girl. Even with strangers from the internet, that was hard to find. Most of the chicks expected some kissing or foreplay before they were ready for action. Marissa wasn't about that life. The worst part about her was where she lived, just beyond the edge of town and into the cornfields. It was annoying, but not far enough to affect the math of the transaction.

Rian focused less on staying between the lines once he was off the big road and now cruising down the small ones through the cornfields and grasslands. No wonder farmers drank so heavily; it was easy to drive drunk out here. Probably even easier if you were driving one of those tractors people always got stuck behind on the country roads. Who cares if you end up putting some wheels in the grass when the wheel is four feet tall? The weaving back and forth is what saved Rian when the deer stepped out of the corn stalks. He was already drifting to his left when the deer appeared. Slamming on the brakes, he came to a full stop at a crazy angle in the opposite lane.

With panic and adrenalin pumping through his veins, he jumped out of the car, fearing he had clipped the deer in the confusion. It was completely silent on that road, only the wind rustling the leaves and the blood pounding in his ears. The deer still stood its ground, bathed in the moonlight, looking directly at Rian and the car that had almost splattered it. Their eyes connected for a moment that felt like an eternity. Rian's intoxicated state dissipated instantly. All that mattered in the world was what the deer was trying to communicate to him. He blinked and the deer turned around, returning to the cornfield from where it had come.

In the time that followed, before he mustered up the strength to climb back in the driver seat, he sat on the asphalt reliving the experience. Nature had warned him. He was speeding towards his doom, and nature had stepped out in front of him and told him to get his act together. His problems were the world's problems. The world was speeding to its doom and this was a warning—change course now or suffer the consequences.

The drive home was slow. Even though he had sobered up, he drove as carefully as an old lady on her way to church in a snowstorm. Collapsing onto the foot of the bed, he grabbed the remote and clicked on the TV. The commercial break wasn't even over by the time he was asleep. The face of the deer and the omen of the future danced in front of him all night long. When he woke again, it was the middle of the day, and the TV was still on. In his daze he focused on the face of the angel on it. Clearing his eyes he recognized her, Alyssa Rodriguez, candidate for President. It was one of her campaign ads, something he'd probably seen dozens of times already during the election season and never paid any attention to. This time, though, she captured his heart. She spoke about the damaged planet and the sins of those who polluted, those who consumed, and those who turned a blind eye to the damage being done to Mother Earth. Something must be done. If we didn't act, the planet would.

She was right. Rian had seen the planet act. It had sent an angel to confront him last night. He was a nonbeliever no more. Falling to his knees, he said his first prayer to Gaia, pouring out his transgressions, his sins and his abuses. After that, he set himself to the task of perfecting his existence in harmony with the earth. In the garage he flipped all his circuit breakers off. Pulling his car keys from his pocket, he stuck half the key into the ignition and then tried to snap it off, but leaning on it with all his strength did nothing. So grabbing the hammer out of the tool kit his dad had bought him last Christmas, he slammed down on the end of the key, which finally snapped it in half, leaving the ignition perfectly jammed and the car rendered inoperable.

Next he pulled the bike down from its hooks and took a look at it. The tires were flat, but he had a pump on hand. Back in his bedroom, he found his 'Let where he'd dropped it the night before, the only thing he had managed to remove before he passed out. He had intended to charge it, but charged himself instead. The 'Let was dead in his hands, since he had already committed to this lifestyle by killing all the power in the house. So the 'Let got left on the floor where he found it.

The peddling to the coffeeshop lost its sense of excitement by mile two, but Rian pressed on. By the time he reached work, his thighs were chafed and he was soaking wet. But the exhilaration returned. "I'm here," he announced, bursting through the doors. The shop was fairly crowded; rainy days always brought out the coffeeshop types, the aspiring writers and soggy hipsters having been driven indoors to practice their craft.

"Rian, where have you been?" Rachel was behind the cash register, looking at him with confusion.

"I've had an unbelievable night!" he exclaimed, rushing up to her.

"Mike's pissed. You're like two hours late. Where's your uniform?"

"No uniform for me anymore. The earth is my uniform."

"How much have you been smoking?"

"Rian!" Mike had appeared out of the back room, looking agitated. "Get back here."

"No!" Rian shouted back, loud enough to get the attention of the whole shop. Climbing atop the chairs that were arranged for people waiting for their to-go cups, he launched into his sermon. "Fellow humans, I've seen the light. We're wasting our lives, and we're wasting the planet's life. We aren't meant to consume like this. We must return to harmony with the earth and it'll provide everything we need. Turn off your phones, your tablets, your homes, and hear what Gaia is saying to us, before it's too late. I didn't listen and I almost died last night for my sins. But I've been reborn! And now it's time to do something about it!" Rian had been raised as a Southern Baptist, so his pleas carried the earnestness of a preacher addressing his flock.

Silence met his oratory, most of the people looking like they were annoyed they had bothered to remove their headphones to hear what he had to say. "What the hell are you talking about?" Mike shouted back.

"I think he's just really high," Rachel interjected.

Jumping off the chair, Rian lunged forward, grabbing ahold of Rachel's hand. "I'm not high, I'm completely sober. I've just seen the truth. Gaia spoke to me last night, and then I heard Alyssa. It spoke to her too."

"That's enough!" Mike had moved around the counter while Rian was talking and grabbed him by the shoulder. "Rian, you're fired. Now leave before I call the police."

"I beat you to the punch, Mike. I quit last night. I'm pledged to the planet now. I am one with it!"

"Cool, now get out." He pushed Rian towards the exit. He didn't resist, letting himself be propelled out the door.

"You'll all see! There's a reckoning coming, and Gaia will know whose side you're on!"

Outside Mike gave him an extra shove towards the street. "Get out of here, you piece of shit, and don't come back!"

"You can threaten me all you want, but Gaia is on my side."

He rolled his eyes as he headed back inside. "I'll keep that in mind."

Picking his bike up, Rian set his path to the local Gaia headquarters. He had passed it a couple of times when they first set up shop there last summer. Prior to their arrival it had been a defunct office space that had been built but never put to use. The developer had overextended himself, only realizing his mistake once it was completed and uninhabited. For a few years the building had stood with the grass growing wild around it, the large empty parking lot collecting various junk that people decided would look better there instead of in their homes. When the Gaia Party popped up, they laid claim to the place, claiming "squatter's rights," though the legality of the move was never established. Once they set up shop, the exterior of the place took on a marked improvement, even if they didn't trim the grass or bushes. But the paint, cleaned windows, and life they breathed into the building looked good.

The other addition that came were the tents that started appearing in the parking lot. That was where Rian was heading. The road in front of the headquarters was deserted as he came up to it, allowing him to ride his bike in the middle of the street. It had been devoid of traffic ever since the party faithful had arrived and started protesting every passing vehicle. They had done so at first with signs and the hurling of insults at the passing automobiles. That was the method back when Rian had last used the street. After that, their tactics had become more aggressive—throwing rocks turned into improvised spike strips, and then they just decided to close the street themselves, blocking it with whatever nature provided them. The junk that had littered the parking lot was re-purposed into roadblocks, and after a few days of that, the word got out to just avoid the street in general to avoid the hassle.

The impediments still stood, even if they were no longer necessary; the humans had altered the behavior. The bike weaved through the openings, bike traffic being the preferred method of travel with the Dirts. It appeared that all the residents of the campsite were sitting cross-legged in the spaces between the tents, looking up to the sky, holding their hands out as if singing to the rain. The slight squeal of Rian's braking tires attracted the attention of a few of the worshipers. A clean-cut young man rose up to greet him. "Hello, fellow creature."

"Uh, hey," Rian responded as he dismounted from his bike.

"What brings you to this habitat?" He was wearing the usual uniform of the Gaia Party, the shapeless burlap they had fashioned into clothing. The outfit looked like a cross between a scarecrow and monk.

"I guess I'm here to join up."

"Join up?"

"Yes?"

"This isn't a company softball team or a rewards program at your local convenience store. This is a movement, an ideal, a group of creatures dedicating the time nature has allowed them to exist to the pursuit of living in harmony with Gaia." The man paused and looked Rian up and down. "Is that what you're here to join?"

"Yes. Yes I am." Rian looked directly back in his eyes.

"What's your name?"

"Rian."

"My name's Kale," he responded with a bow of his head. "Now, come and join us here." He motioned to the people still sitting on the ground. Squatting down, Rian joined them. "In order to fulfill Gaia's desires, we must be at peace with her. Every molecule of dirt beneath our feet is speaking to us. It cries out for us to obey the rules of nature. Do you hear it?"

"No," Rian admitted.

Kale reached out and slapped Rian across the back of his head. "Did you feel that?"

"Yes," he answered through gritted teeth.

"That's how I feel when I see a building that blocks out the sun, or concrete that suffocates the earth. Gaia speaks to us, but only some of us actually heed her commands."

"Okay."

"Can you feel the rain on your face?"

"I can."

"It's a message," Kale whispered.

Rian had already gotten soaking wet on his ride to the coffee shop, and since then had only become more wet, so feeling the rain wasn't a problem on his already numbed skin. The wind and cold were combining to make themselves felt in the wintry air. The touch of nature was reaching through him, the way it had the night before when the deer had looked in his eyes. Gaia was searching for a reason to let him live, a reason why he deserved its sanctuary. He pleaded with it to understand his plight.

For two more hours they sat there as a group, until Rian's legs ached and his face screamed with pain from the frosty wind. The rain had finally stopped and just a damp mist hung in the air around them. "Who has heard Gaia's message today?" Kale finally asked, breaking the long silence. All the other people raised their hands. Rian didn't know what to do. He had felt the cold and rain, but it felt the same as it always had to him.

"Daphne, what did you hear today?" Kale asked one of the women.

"It was wonderful. Gaia told me I'm doing my best, that I deserve to be here, and that she's proud of me."

"Very good," Kale answered. "We're all very proud of you as well. Ryder, how about you?" He addressed the man seated next to Rian.

"I think Gaia forgave me today. She saw my weakness and accepted that," he answered, tears streaming down his face.

"And Rian, how about you?"

"Um, I don't know if I heard anything. I guess I'm just glad I'm here."

Kale smiled. "Rian is new to our group. Tell us about yourself."

"Oh, okay. Well, I'm Rian. I'm twenty-three. I went to Joliet Junior College. I work…uh, worked at a coffee shop."

The crowd hissed its disapproval. Holding up his hand, Kale quieted the crowd. "Rian, you're no longer those things. That's the Polluters speaking through you, defining your existence in jobs or accomplishments. Those aren't what we're interested in."

"Okay," Rian started again. "I was, uh, driving last night, and this deer came out of the cornfields and just stared at me. I almost hit it, but something saved me. But the deer didn't run off. It just stayed there and looked at me. The deer spoke to me. I don't know how, but it did. I realized everything I was doing was wrong. So I woke up this morning, turned off all the power to my house, quit my job and came here."

Kale nodded and stood up. "A moment ago you said you couldn't hear Gaia speaking to you, but last night she told you everything you need to know. She told you that you're our brother!" Everyone cheered and started getting to their feet, stretching out their limbs. They had all been sitting in lotus positions for at least the two hours Rian had been there, and maybe more.

"Let's go inside, Rian," Kale said, taking him by the shoulder and leading him into the main building. "Let's get you dressed and get some nourishment inside you."

* * *

"Sun is up." A young girl shook Rian's cot, bringing him back to the world.

"What time is it?" he muttered, still half-asleep.

"Sunrise," she answered sweetly, walking off.

Once they had finished with the prayer session the previous night, events had moved swiftly. Everyone had some words of welcome while Kale showed Rian around the Hatchery, the name for this particular Gaia site. It suggested that all the creatures inside it were being reborn as children of Gaia. Kale had taken him to the back room, where all the sewing and mending was done. An old hippie-looking woman named Hilda took his measurements and dug out a uniform that fit him well. He now looked like he belonged there. After he was dressed, they went out the back of the building where dinner was presented. A large wooden table was sitting there covered in fruits and vegetables. Everyone helped themselves to a handful and took a seat on the ground nearby.

"Our food comes from the ground," Kale said. "We should never forget that. Gaia provides for us if we're patient. Therefore, when we eat, we're as close as possible to harmony with nature. Feel it beneath you as it nourishes your body," he encouraged while they sat down on the wet dirt.

After they finished eating, it was bedtime. Kale took Rian to the "Mist" room. It was one of the office spaces that had been converted to a bunkhouse. There were already five other "creatures" sleeping in there by the time they arrived. Kale pointed to an empty cot and bade him good night. Now it was morning and sunlight crept in through the blinds. The rest of the cots were empty and neatly made. Having not made his bed since childhood, Rian was taken aback by that. But, like riding a bike, it's not a skill easily forgotten.

Following the sound of voices, Rian wandered out to the back door where they had eaten dinner the night before, and found most of the people already enjoying breakfast. Kale motioned him over after he grabbed a couple of apples and a handful of pistachios. "What a beautiful day Gaia has given us!" he said joyously. "Sit with us, fellow creature. You've brought the sun with you this morning."

"Thanks," he mumbled as he sat next to Kale and an older man sitting watchfully next to him.

"Rian, this is Creature Derek. He's the leader of this Plot."

"Nice to meet you," Rian said, unable to extend his hand due to the food.

"And you, Rian," Derek responded. "Welcome to the cause."

"We're just getting a plan of action ready for today," Kale was saying. "Yesterday was a day of rest, reflection and atonement. Today Gaia guides us on our endeavors, and we shall not fail her."

"Let's get everyone moving," Derek said, rising to his feet. The rest of the people fell silent, waiting his instructions. "Today is destined to be a great day. Gaia's inspiration flows over all of us, and those who are at peace allow her to guide their hands and hearts. Bask in the beauty that Gaia provides us and let her guide your hands and your hearts." With a bow of his head, he went back into the building. Everyone else began following suit, climbing to their feet and moving about.

"What are we doing today?" Rian whispered to Kale.

"Just business as usual." He was also standing up. "Saving the earth might be the cause above all other causes, but we still have campaign legwork to do, like everyone else. Phone calls, registering people to vote, and handing out literature. I think you'd be best suited to start with our outreach pack. Go out, meet people, and let them hear your story. Bring them home to us." He led Rian over around the side of the building, where a group of people had gathered. "Georgia!" he called out.

"Hello!" A pretty blond girl stepped out from the group and towards them.

"Georgia, this is Rian. It's his first day. I want him to go with you."

"Of course!" she squealed, grabbing Rian's hand. Even before her attractiveness, the first thing you noticed about her was her accent. It was British, but like a fake version of it. A British accent with a Southern drawl mixed in. "Come, Rian, let's get set up," she cooed, pulling him away from Kale. "I think we're going to go to Crushit today. Do you know that place?"

"No."

"It's a gym. Pretty fancy. I used to go. A bunch of bitches with no cares in their lives other than trying to get some trainer to look at their ass. At a certain point I just couldn't take it anymore."

"I see." He noticed that Georgia's burlap was cut a bit shorter than the others. She had even wound some twine through it to make it follow the curves of her body better.

"I know we can help them. Maybe some of them will listen to the truth. We can change lives!" She dug her nails into Rian's arm excitedly.

They walked about thirty minutes to get to the gym, Georgia talking the whole way, in between frightful shudders anytime a car passed us by. "I can't stand them!" she yelled once, shaking her fist at a Jeep as it cruised by. "All of them deserve to burn in hell for what they're doing to the planet, to us. I feel sick all of a sudden. The exhaust is getting to me. I have very sensitive lungs." She dropped to the ground in a coughing fit.

"Those bastards," Rian swore in agreement, holding her hand as she struggled to recover from the attack.

"I know. They aren't like us. They just abuse people. They abuse the world. We're the victims. They're always taking advantage of us," she said tearfully, pulling herself up. "Let's keep going. It's the least we can do." So they soldiered on.

The gym's parking lot was still full of cars; not as many as before the introduction of the Turtles, but still too many. "Oh, it's horrible," moaned Georgia. She collapsed on the curb in front of the entrance. "I can't go any farther. These cars are giving me a migraine."

As she settled down, the door to the gym opened and a couple of jock types walked out, their keys jingling in their hands. "Yo, let's grab a shake," Shaved Head Jock was saying to Ballcap Jock.

"Hey!" Rian shouted, stepping in front of them. They stopped, noticing the two for the first time. "Your cars are killing my friend." Reaching out before they realized what was happening, he snatched the keys out of Shaved Head's hands and shook them in his face.

"Bro! What's up?" Shaved Head said, reaching for them back.

"The monsters you're driving around are spewing death into the environment, just so you can come here and sweat, when you can do that outdoors for free. Maybe you should try sweating for the planet!"

"Look, dude, just give me my keys back," Shaved Head said, stepping forward.

"Never!" Rian screeched. Throwing them with a mighty heave, they went sailing into the bushes.

"Are you shitting me right now?!" Ball Cap yelled, looking between the landing spot and Rian. He jabbed a fist into Rian's ribs, knocking the wind out of him. Georgia wailed as Rian stumbled back, the violence taking him by surprise. "Want the next punch? It's only *fair*." Ball Cap taunted, taking a step back and holding his arms in the air. . "No? ...Pussy." He spat out at Rian and Georgia stumbled farther back. "Come on, bro, let's go find your keys." The two walked off towards the bushes.

"Oh my God." Georgia crawled over to Rian, tears streaming down her face. "Did they hurt you?"

"I'll be okay." He groaned as he stood up. "Just surprised me."

"One day they'll get what's coming to them." She was shooting daggers at them as they kicked the bushes around. "Look at them, destroying everything in their path."

"That's what those types do," Rian answered.

They spent the rest of the day working through the shoppers, employees and random pedestrians on Maple Street. There was a bunch of stores, restaurants and coffee shops clustered together there, and since it was the first sunny day in a while, it was a prime area for pedestrian traffic. Georgia had a field day, milking everyone she targeted for pity and an agreement to attend the next rally. Rian wasn't ready to solo yet, but he was getting the hang of it after a couple of hours. Of course, he was lacking the "pretty girl in distress" angle that worked so well for Georgia, but she had ideas about how Rian could play his own angles, and they had a good racket going by late afternoon.

The rally started taking shape later that day. It was much looser in form than one would expect. It started with an impromptu marching band moving through the street as a call to attention, really just a bunch of Gaians playing various instruments with varying skill, roaming back and forth in the street. They weren't even trying to play the same song. After the music, everyone grouped up. Derek climbed up on top of a parked car and started speaking. He talked about all the change that needed to happen and why supporting Alyssa Rodriguez and the Gaia Party would help save the planet. Kale was up front, leading the cheering at the appropriate spots.

Once the speaking was over, the crowd just started milling about chatting. "Find someone to talk to," Georgia said to Rian, suddenly reappearing at his side. "Get them worked up. We need to raise the temperature."

"Alright." Looking around, he spotted a couple of the people he had talked to earlier in the day and moved in on them, but his attempts to engage fell flat. They had been happy to observe the rally and listen to the speeches, but they weren't being won over by any of it.

"THIS WAY! THEY'RE OVER HERE!" The sudden amplified voice echoed over the crowd, causing the voices conversations to peter out. "LET'S SHOW THEM WE MEAN BUSINESS!!"

The voice continued to cajole the crowd forward as they moved off of Maple, down a side street and towards Douglas Avenue. Shuffling along with the crowd, Rian that the people he had talked to had left for good. They didn't deserve to see whatever was about to happen with that attitude of indifference to the plight of the world. The people around him looked on edge. The rally was taking on a darker vibe as they moved farther away from the business district.

Once they cleared the surrounds of the side street, they found what they had been looking for, the local office for one of the major political parties. The people who had brought the vengeance of the planet upon us. The people who littered, polluted, and abused the planet for their profit. The mass of people shouted their insults while gnashing their teeth. Within moments the quiet day on Douglas turned into a full-on siege. Pushing forward, Rian made it to the edge of the building, screaming his voice hoarse with rage. You could see people moving around inside the building, scurrying around, covering the windows and locking what they could, like rats on a sinking ship.

The unfettered rage lasted for a while. It was hard to tell how long they stood, shaking in their anger. Finally, Kale pushed his way through the crowd, making it to the very front. This time he was carrying an old-fashioned megaphone in his hand. The crowd fell silent when he spoke. "LET'S MAKE SURE THESE PIGS KNOW WE'RE HERE!" The crowd let out another whoop and started screaming obscenities at the docile building. "HOO HOO!" he began, the crowd mimicking his chant. "HEY HEY! IT'S GAIA ALL THE WAY!" Now that the chanting had started, the group balanced itself out a bit, focusing on the tried and true rituals of protest. Picket signs started making their way over their heads as their voices cried out in unison.

Out of the corner of Rian's eye, he saw Kale hand the megaphone off and push his way back through the crowd. Rian left his post at the barricade, heading in the same direction. Behind the mass of people, Kale and he popped out fifty feet apart. Derek was standing with a small group in the side street, most of them wearing Dirt tunics. "What do you think?" Kale asked once he reached the group. Rian hung back a few feet, trying not to get in the middle of the leadership meeting, but clearly listening in.

"Good work," Derek mused, searching the sky as he spoke.

"Should we push it?"

"I think it's going to rain again." They all turned up to look at the sky. It had been clear and beautiful all day long, but here in late afternoon it had started to turn gray at the horizon.

"It might," Kale answered.

"Keep everyone going for a while longer. If it starts to rain, you know what to do." Derek turned back to where they had come from and retreated towards Maple with the rest of the group.

"Have a good first day?" Kale asked in his pleasant voice.

"It's been interesting to say the least," Rian answered. "What's next?"

"Well, we're going to keep demonstrating for a while more, then we'll see where Gaia guides us. Hang back here for a bit and rest up. I'll send you in with the guys if needed." With that, he walked off into the crowd.

Leaning back against the buildings on the opposite side of the street, Rian kept an eye on the protesters. The crowd was continuing to grow as people wandered in, joining ranks with the original marchers. His other eye was on the sky that was beginning to get undeniably darker. The telltale smell of rain crept into the air, soon followed by the first raindrop. He watched it hit a leaf on the street. It shuddered slightly from the impact, as did he from all the excitement. A few more drops and the crowd was suddenly noticing it as well, their heads turning up, the rhythm of the chants breaking down, as everyone wondered if the rain had really come.

Kale emerged from the crowd. As he did, several other men on the younger side appeared from different spots. Georgia was among them as they all followed Kale to where Rian was standing. "Gaia has sent us her message. It's washing away the filth, which means it's time for us to as well." He spoke softly, but his voice felt like steel.

No other words were spoken as they turned back to the crowd. Moving forward at speed, they hit the back of the people, forcing their way through roughly. Once Rian reached the building, he roared to the crowd, "Come on!!" He picked up one of the wooden sawhorses the police had scattered around in a facile attempt at crowd control, and ran full-speed with it at the building's large front window. The glass shattered into safety pebbles, and then the crowd was surging forward and through the hole, the defenses now breached and the invaders pouring in. It was the eternal law of siege warfare; once the walls are broken, the city will fall. There's no stopping it.

CHAPTER SIX

EXPRESS

"I'm glad you remembered the shoes," I said.

"Would you have been brave enough to go back for them if I hadn't?" Sami asked playfully, some of the tension draining away now that we had made it well out of sight of Eric's house.

"Maybe you could've distracted him with makeup tips."

Coming up to our first four-way stop, our pace slowed. A right turn would take us on the familiar path towards the dealership. Going straight would lead us in the direction of the remains of our house. A left turn took us towards downtown. "So, where are we going?" Sami finally asked.

"I don't know. What are we looking for, just a place to sleep for the night?"

"That'd be a good start. I'd rather not sleep in the woods."

"Probably shouldn't head back to the dealership. Might be an awkward morning when Eric shows up."

"Yeah, the dealership has run its course."

"Alright. Well, ahead of us and to the left are just houses and then downtown, but I don't know what we'll find down there."

"Maybe hang right and find a hotel?" she suggested,

pointing to the right.

"If we check into Doubletree, we'll get free cookies," I respond dryly.

"Are you done?"

"Probably."

"I bet the hotels are empty. There isn't much to loot, and it's not like there's any out-of-towners stopping by now."

"It's worth a shot. So where do you think a good one is?" I checked our surroundings.

"That's I-80 up there, isn't it?" Sami answered, pointing down the road to some green highway exit signs glowing just enough in the darkness to be visible.

"Yeah."

"There's an Express at the Houbolt exit. That should be two or three miles from us at this point."

"Okay. Sounds like a plan."

* * *

"What do you think?" Sami whispered as we crouched behind the bushes around the perimeter of the hotel, scoping out the building.

"I don't know. I can't see much."

The parking lot had a few cars left sitting around. All of them appeared to have been sacked at some point; broken windows and dented doors were visible in the darkness. The rest of the area seemed deserted. Even most of the windows seemed to be intact.

"I guess it's worth a look," I continued as I pushed through a gap in the bushes and slipped across the parking lot. Edging around the corner of the building, we made it to the automatic glass lobby doors, currently shut. "Wait here," I whispered to Sami. Creeping up to the glass, I looked in. Nothing but blackness could be seen. Motioning my intentions to Sami, I moved to the door and dug my fingers into the gap between them, prying them open. They moved easily and noiselessly. Five steps into the lobby, I fished for my flashlight from my pocket, pulling it out and aiming it towards the reception desk.

"Don't turn that on," a voice suddenly called out from the darkness. I nearly jumped out of my skin before I stumbled back, tripping over my own feet and falling flat on my butt. "Calm down," the voice continued. "I'm not going to hurt you if you don't hurt me."

"Where are you?"

"I'm in the corner, but I don't want you to ruin my night vision by turning that flashlight on."

"What are you doing here?" I said, climbing back to my feet.

"I'm the night watchman."

"The night watchman?" His tone made it sound like this was the most obvious thing in the world.

"Yes. There's a group of us here. It's my turn to make sure no one wanders in and disturbs us while everyone's sleeping."

"I'm not trying to disturb anyone. I was just looking for a place to spend the night."

"Fresh out in the wild, huh?" the voice asked.

"Uh, yeah, I guess. We had a house but it got burned down."

"Yeah, that's been happening a lot. That's your wife outside, then?"

"Yes," I answered sheepishly.

"Well, since it's late, I can give you a room here on the first floor. That's where we keep the temporaries. But you'll have to pay."

"We don't have any money."

"Wouldn't help if you did. What *do* you have?"

"Not much. Just some candy, flashlights and a couple knives."

"That's too bad," The voice answered.

"We have a bottle of liquor." Sami's voice made me jump when it spoke up from the doorway.

"That's more like it," the voice said. "Let me see it."

Sami pulled her backpack off, yanking out the bottle of peach schnapps we had found at the dealership and handing it over to me. Holding it forward, I inched towards where the voice had been coming from.

"That's good, right there," the voice said before the bottle was grabbed from my hands. We heard the sounds of the cap unscrewing and then a deep whiff being drawn in. "Yeah, this is good for a couple nights here at the Express," the voice said with delight. A click followed and a faint red light appeared, pointing at the ground. "Follow me this way and I'll get you in a room." The voice motioned with the light, deeper into the blackness. Sami slipped her hand into mine as we started forward, following the bobbing light ahead of us.

"We have just a couple rules here for the temporaries. First, once you're in your room, stay in there after dark. If something comes up, holler for me and I'll come down. Don't go wandering around the place."

"Okay." Silence ensued as we slid past the doors of hotel rooms. "What's the second rule?"

"No shitting in the toilets," he answered with a laugh.

"Got that, honey?" I asked. Even in the dark I could feel Sami glaring at me.

"Nah, I'm just messing with you. You guys'll be fine. Just stay in your room until morning and then you can do as you please. Come on out and meet the group in the morning and we can get you squared away."

"Alright."

"This is it." The man turned around. The red glow finally revealed his bearded face, giving us a smile before he pushed the door open. "The keycards don't work anymore, so you can't lock the rooms from the outside. But the deadbolt on the inside works fine."

We followed him into the room. The red light swept the space. It looked like just a normal hotel room; even the bed was made. "Alright, have a good night," the bearded man said, walking back to the door. "You can use that flashlight once I'm gone."

"Wait, what's your name?" Sami asked.

"Oh, I'm Carl."

"I'm Sami, and this is my husband Kyle."

"Nice to meet y'all. See you in the morning." The door slammed closed behind him and I clicked the deadbolt into place.

* * *

Hotel curtains never stay all the way shut. You'd think they could figure out a more effective method for keeping the light out, considering that providing a good sleeping experience is really job number one for a hotel. This time, though, it didn't matter. Sami and I stayed asleep far past sunrise, even if the annoying sliver of light kept poking through the window.

"We should get up," I mumbled, shaking Sami's shoulder.

"Nnnnmmmm," she moaned in disagreement.

The sudden rush of the unfamiliar surroundings came upon me, waking me fully. The room was basic-looking, just like it had looked with our flashlights last night, only now dimly lit by the creeping light of morning. If I didn't know better, it would be like everything was perfectly normal. The voices outside caught my attention. Sami stayed motionless as I climbed out of bed and over to the window. It took my sleepy eyes a minute to adjust to the glare of the outdoors. Once they did, I could see a fair bit of the parking lot, but the sources of the voices remained out of sight, around the corner of the building.

"Babe, we should get up." I shook her foot. This caused her eyes to open. A lack of amusement was clear. "It sounds like there's a lot of people here."

"Okay." She was agreeable, but not willingly so.

We didn't have any clothes to change into, so getting ready in the morning remained a pretty quick affair. "Bring your bag with," I said once we had our shoes on. "He said the rooms don't lock from the outside."

Retracing our steps, we made our way to the lobby and the voices. The lobby had been arranged like a giant living room; couches, chairs, tables and some mattresses were scattered about, even extending out underneath the roof overhang. About fifty people lounged around in the comfort, reading books, flipping through magazines, or just chitchatting.

"You must be our new guests," a voice said from behind us. Turning around, we found a group of four men sitting in a semi-circular booth built into the wall, some kind of niche sitting spot for hotel guests.

"Yes, I'm Ky.."

"Kyle and Sami," the man closest to us answered before I could.

"Yeah, that's us."

"Are you leaving so soon?" one of the other men said, pointing to our bags.

"We, uh, we weren't sure we should leave them in there. Carl said the doors don't lock."

"That's true, they don't, but you don't have to worry about any theft here at the Express. Everyone here is trustworthy. Other than yourselves, that is."

"We're trustworthy," Sami answered, sounding slightly offended.

"Don't mind Don," the first man said. "He's just grumpy in the mornings."

"No, we understand," I answered.

"Would you like a drink?" The first man produced the bottle of schnapps from behind him and set it on the table.

"Ha, no, it's a bit early for me for the hard stuff."

"Fair enough. You wouldn't happen to know where there's any more of this particular product, would you?"

"No. We just randomly found it in someone's office a couple days ago."

"Figures. Everyone wants something to drink, and the fucking casuals burned through everything in the first couple of nights," the third man said.

"Why don't you grab a couple of chairs and sit with us for a few minutes?" the first man said. There were a couple of folding chairs leaning against the wall. Sami snagged them before the man finished speaking and we were soon seated at the table with them. "I'm Jasper. This is Don, Mike and Nick." We all nodded around before Jasper continued. "We took a vote and decided that four nights of room and board is a fair payment for the bottle. Do you agree?"

"Oh, yeah, that's good for us," I answered awkwardly. Three more nights in the hotel were an unexpected windfall for a bottle of schnapps.

"Meals are served at 7 a.m., noon and 6 p.m. You're welcome to partake as part of your payment."

"Guests are also required to leave any firearms with the front desk," Don said this time. "Seems Carl forgot about that last night."

"We don't have any guns, just a couple of box cutters."

"You sure?" he pressed aggressively.

"Yes. You can check if you want." I started to pull my backpack off.

"That won't be necessary," Jasper said. "Just know that we value truthfulness above all else here."

"We don't have a gun," Sami chipped in.

"Very well. I hope you enjoy your stay here," Jasper said with a smile, putting the bottle back down on the seat. "Nick, why don't you give them the tour."

Nick, at the other end of the table, stood up. "Sure thing. Come with me and I'll show you what's up."

"Thank you," I said as Sami and I stood up.

"Actually, let's put your bags back in your room to start with," Nick suggested. After we did so, he led us farther down the hallway and out a stairwell exit. "So the hotel has a fence around most of it, covered by the bushes. Only the front side doesn't. I assume you discovered that for yourselves last night."

"Yeah," I answered sheepishly, not caring to admit we hadn't inspected the perimeter.

"Anyways, it's pretty secure from any intruders, not that we've really had any problems with that yet."

"How did you end up here?" Sami asked as we walked around the side of the building and onto the main road.

"About half of us were staying here as paid customers when things got really bad. We're too far from home to get back, so we just sorta took over once the staff stopped showing up to care for us, ha." He came to a stop, looking across a retention pond at a Walmart. "It was our good luck that Super Wally World was right across the street. We got started in there before things got really bad. A nice head start."

"Oh, really?"

"Yeah, we hit that place before the masses started moving around. We had a bunch of battery-powered tools from the hotel's maintenance room. Used them to cut through the back door and got in without making a scene. There were actually people milling around out front, trying to work up their nerve to break the glass while we were inside gutting the place," he said with a laugh.

"What all did you get?" I asked as we turned and headed down the street, angling around the hotel.

"Oh, you wouldn't believe. Those supercenters really do have everything. We started with the obvious, survival-type supplies, canned food, medicine and such. Then we expanded out. It's really worked out nicely, since we've been able to barter a lot of things that we took for no other reason than they were there."

Once we got around the corner, we faced a long row of low-rise office buildings, the kind that double as small warehouses and shop fronts. "After we finished with the Walmart," Nick continued, "we went to work over here." Lined up on the road was a giant mass of blue shopping carts, with a bunch of wheelbarrows and other rolling tote devices scattered around.

"That's a lot of carts," Sami commented.

"Yep. The Picker crews use them. Here they come now." From behind the hotel a pack of people emerged, mostly men, being led by Don. They were all dressed roughly, like miners heading down the mouth of a shaft. They also all carried some kind of bludgeoning tool, whether sledgehammer, axe or prybar. There were several guns in the mix too, deer rifles or shotguns slung over shoulders or pistols strapped to hips.

"Good hunting, boys," Nick said cheerily as they passed us. Don just grunted, but several other men replied friendly enough to Nick. A couple of the women shot us smiles or waves on their way through. They broke into smaller groups, about five people with three carts between them, and pushed off. Each group took a different path, heading in different ways but all in the same direction, into the mass of buildings.

"Pretty organized," I said once the Pickers had moved out into the wild of the industrial park.

"Oh yeah. That's Jasper for you." We were heading back to the hotel now.

"Is he Army or something?" Sami asked.

"No, but Don is. That's why he's in charge of the Pickers. He runs it like a military operation. Jasper's a smart dude who sees the big picture."

"You said only about half of you were staying here when things got bad?" I asked. "Where did the rest of the people come from?"

"Oh, they wandered in or latched on to us while out picking. There's lot of people out there looking for a good group right now. Safety in numbers, you know."

"Sure, makes sense."

"How about you two?" he asked us as we reached the front of the hotel again. "Where have you been all this time?"

"We've just been in our house. Didn't even really leave when the rioting started. We just stayed around our place to wait it out."

"Most people did that. It's like the Balkans out there, each neighborhood facing off against the others."

"Pretty much."

"So what happened? From the looks of it, you left in a hurry."

"They burned our house down," Sami answered flatly.

"The Dirts?"

"Just one supervising," I said. "It was the neighbors who did most of it."

"Those bureaucrats." This was the intro sentence to several minutes of Nick's feelings on the government, the President, and the lack of masculine values that resulted in this crisis. By the time he was done, we were back to the stairwell we had passed on our way outside.

"So the first floor is pretty basic, eating and guest rooms," he said once we were on the steps. "Second floor is pretty empty."

All the walking the past few days had been wearing on our

legs, but the stairs were another thing all together. We were lagging badly behind by the time we got to the third floor. "You get used to the stairs after a while," Nick said, noticing our struggle.

"You didn't find an elevator over at Walmart?" I asked.

"Ha, no. We did do some rigging to ours, though, and got it to drop to the basement and out of the way. Now we have ropes and pullies mounted in the shaft, so we can move things up and down easier. We call it our Edivator." He said this with a smirk, and then when he saw that neither of us were going to take the bait, further explained, "Ed's a guy who fell down the shaft in the first week." He didn't seem too concerned.

"What are you moving?" Sami asked, changing the subject once we reached the third floor.

"Our stockpile. We keep it on the third floor, just in case we might have problems with casuals." The rooms had all had their doors removed and were stripped of all their furnishings, filled to the brims with loot. We walked by a room stacked to the ceiling with blankets in packages or folded up nicely.

"Wow, that's a lot of bedding," Sami said.

"Yeah, we brought all of them we could find at Walmart. Of course, no one put it together that we were already in a building with more blankets than we needed. But now we have plenty to barter with. We think they might be more valuable once winter starts up."

He led us back to the stairwell. "The fourth and fifth floor are more storage. We try to keep everything organized, so we use a whole room for single items."

We kept moving up the stairs. Floors six to ten were living quarters. We poked our head in on the sixth floor, but it just looked like a normal hotel hallway, so we pressed on to the roof without stopping at the other floors. Our pace was now at a crawl, but Sami and I found the energy to soldier on.

"Here we are!" Nick said grandly, opening the doorway to the exterior. The brightness and breeze greeted us warmly. Six large garden beds were the most obvious landmarks. They were about twenty feet long and ten feet across, encased on all sides with wooden planks, the dirt spilling over the edges as the plants bloomed forth. The rest of the roof was unremarkable. There were about a dozen people tending to it, mostly women.

"Morning Nick!" an older lady greeted us, taking her gloves off.

"Morning, Michele. This is Kyle and Sami. They're spending a few nights with us."

"Welcome, welcome," she said with a big smile. "Are you enjoying the tour? I remember when I took mine. A lot has changed since then, ha." She talked in a rushed manner, like if she didn't get all the words out, they might be forever forgotten.

"It's very interesting," Sami answered.

"Yes, your organization is impressive," I added awkwardly.

"And this is just phase one. We have big plans about adding more growing space. Might even try and find some space for some animals. Might as well try and grow us some protein."

"Urban farming at a hotel," Sami said. "Talk about farm to table. Or roof to table, I guess."

"You can stay up here until lunch if you want, and I can show you our process."

"Sure, that sounds like fun."

"Okay, then, I'll see you guys at lunch," Nick said, flashing us a smile and heading back to the stairwell.

* * *

A couple hours later we were heading down the stairs with the farming group. They had welcomed us in warmly, even though we hadn't done much actual work because of Michele's constant talking. After a while it seemed like the rest of the group was glad that we had shown up to soak up the words that flowed effortlessly from her.

"Anyway, that's how we get the water up to the roof…" She was finishing giving us a detailed rundown on the irrigation system they had installed as we approached the second-floor landing. Just then, the door opened and a woman stepped out, wearing a loose t-shirt and sweatpants. "Hey, Courtney," Michele greeted her as we came down the steps.

"Hi," she said shortly, just giving us a glancing once-over

while she waited for us to pass. Her eyes seemed glassy, like she was high.

"She okay?" Sami asked Michele in a low voice once the distance between us had grown.

"Oh yeah. She's just on second-floor rotation right now."

"What's that mean?" I asked.

"Well, we have this schedule where we rotate through all the different projects and areas around here. That way we're all trained on everything, and we know how everything gets done. Like, what if I was the only one who knew how the irrigation pump worked, and then something happened to me? Everyone would be lost."

"That makes sense," Sami answered. "So what do they do on the second floor?"

"Oh, there's a bunch of stuff going on there. You'll learn all about the rotation schedule if you end up staying. Anyway, I hope you like corn. It's the main staple for most of our meals right now. Jasper reached out to some of the farmers out on the edge of town, and now they trade us corn for mechanical supplies they need."

"It'd be hard to live around here and not like corn," I said.

"That's the truth."

* * *

"How'd you like your first day?" Jasper asked, taking a seat at our table. It was dinnertime and most of the residents were crammed into the lobby and bar area. Dinner was creamed corn, light on the cream, lettuce and a piece of fish. A very simple meal, but clearly made with care.

"It was awesome." Sami answered first.

"The food's really good too," I followed up. "We've been living mostly on junk food for the past few days."

"Oh, don't worry, you'll get sick of corn pretty soon," he said with a smile. "So how would you feel about going out with the Pickers tomorrow and seeing how it goes?" The unspoken implication of perhaps extending our stay hung over it.

"We could do that," I said, nodding. Sami nodded along with me. "It'd be nice to see how the professionals do things."

"Good. You know, we're always looking to expand our group here, but it takes some time to get a feel for people."

"Yeah, we understand. We've had some pretty bad experiences with people lately ourselves."

"Are you finished eating?" he asked, pointing to our completely empty plates which we had practically licked clean.

"Yes, it was very good," Sami said.

"Alright, then follow me. We have one more surprise for you today."

Leading us out of the lobby, we took a right turn towards the opposite side of the building from our room. Through a couple of glass doors we walked into the indoor swimming pool area. The large pool was drained of water, but what caught our eye was the hot tub. A large frame had been built around the edge of it, holding a large metal basin above, with a bunch of pipes and hoses running back and forth. "How long has it been since you took a shower?" Jasper asked proudly.

"Oh my God, are you serious?" Sami said with astonishment.

"Yep. Another marvel of our boredom. It's even got hot water."

"How does it work?" I asked, wandering around the contraption. It looked like the showers they used in *M*A*S*H*.

"We use car batteries to send electricity to the resistance coils, and they get warm and heat the water up. It's never going to be as hot as we were used to, but it's better than cold. We fill the basin up every couple days, then the used water's collected and piped up to the farm for them to use. That way the water gets used twice."

"It feels like a year since I've had a proper shower," Sami said.

"Well, keep in mind there's a ten-minute time limit. Soaps and shampoos are over there." He pointed to a table overflowing with little hotel shampoo bottles. "When you're done, we got you some new clothes too. They're over there on that table. Looks like you've been in those for a while."

Seeing the new clothes, Sami grabbed Jasper in a bear hug. "This is like Christmas morning!" she cried.

"Thanks, Jasper," I said, extending my hand out. "It's really appreciated." I tried to keep it together during the happiest moment I've had in several months.

"It's my pleasure." He shook my hand firmly. "You two enjoy yourselves, and we'll see you in the morning for breakfast and your day out with Don." He left us alone in the big room.

"I don't think I remember even how to take my clothes off," I said.

"You've never had that problem before," Sami said, already getting started.

"I think I have to peel them off of me by this point."

"Don't ruin this," she said, throwing her shirt on the ground and almost skipping with delight naked into the hot tub. I smiled as I kicked my shoes off and got ready to join her.

CHAPTER SEVEN

PICKERS

This time we left the curtains open purposely. The morning sun is an unsnoozeable alarm. Sami woke up easily. The anticipation of actually having a purpose for the day was invigorating, something that had been lacking from our lives for the past few months. Unless you count getting up to go to work with Eric, there hadn't been many reasons to get out of bed and start the day.

Sami's new clothes consisted of a pair of loose-fitting blue jeans, a black t-shirt, a couple of pairs of socks and underwear, and a sports bra. Mine was a pair of khaki cargo pants and a long-sleeved black shirt. We each were sporting a new pair of Asics sneakers. Walmart chic.

"I feel like I'm getting dressed for a wedding," I said, tying my laces.

"Ha, it's like the first day of school when you get to show off your new wardrobe," Sami replied.

"Come on, let's not be late to our first day of work." I led us out the door.

We weren't the first people in the lobby for breakfast, but we weren't the last, so we just blended in. Now that we were freshly tailored, everyone else's clothes stood out. Most of the people wore similar outfits to ours, just different colors, though people had different styles of shoes on. A lot of them went with sneakers like ours, but there were numerous work boots being worn as well. Breakfast was a small bowl of fruit cocktail, a piece of toast, and rehydrated beef jerky standing in for sausage. Never been a fan of beef jerky, but it'd become a staple in our post-apocalyptic diet.

It took about thirty minutes for the eating to wrap up and the people to start splitting off, heading to their respective rotational spots. Don came up to our table. "I guess you two are with us today."

"Yes, sir," I responded. His entire demeanor was of an annoyed drill sergeant.

"Come on." He motioned for us to follow him. We walked with him to the side of the hotel we had visited when we had showered the night before. This time we went into the guest room portion of the building. The first doorway was open and marked "Picking." The room was full of barrels and large trashcans, each bursting with various tools like we'd seen the pickers carrying the day before. "Find something you like and grab a pair of gloves," he said from the doorway, picking up two duffel bags that were sitting just inside.

"Any suggestions?" Sami asked, looking over the many options.

"The girls usually have luck with one of the big hammers, or a prybar." He looked me up and down. "You should bring a sledge."

"Copy that." I pulled one of the sledgehammers with a wooden handle out of the bin, while Sami grabbed a large construction-type hammer and a two-foot-long crowbar. "Can you grab me some gloves too, babe?" I asked as Sami reached for the big pile on one of the shelves.

"Grab a bag as well," Don ordered before leaving the doorway, heading back towards the lobby.

Hanging on the wall was a huge assortment of large backpacks. Most of them looked pretty worn. Picking through them, I found a couple that looked the freshest and slung them over my shoulder before we scurried after Don.

The lobby was already mostly empty, so we continued following him out to the shopping cart-filled parking lot we saw the day before. The other pickers were already there, preparing for their missions. "Chucky, Mike, Nicole, you're with me and the new ones today," Don announced. The three whose names had been called separated from the group, moving over towards us and introducing themselves. Chucky was a skinny kid with a scraggly beard, the kind of guy you see working the graveyard shift at a convenience store. Mike had been at the table with us the morning before, another military-looking guy, though his beer belly and shaggy crewcut probably made him a cop. Nicole was thirtyish and rather severe-looking, the kind you'd find on a softball team or in the gym, but a serious gym, not the "doing yoga in candlelight" gym. They were all carrying guns of varying sizes.

Don spoke to the rest of the group for a minute before they started dispersing. "Grab some carts," he then said to us, the five of us grabbing what was left. After dropping one duffel bag in my cart and the other in Sami's, he faced the group. "Alright, we have two rookies with us, so let's be smart today and try not to find any trouble." He eyed Mike a little harder than the rest of us. "We're heading out to the Highway 7 business district today. A lot of business fronts down there, plus some private homes. Not sure what we'll find, so stay frosty." He took the lead, Mike dropped back as the rear guard, and the rest of us were strung out in the middle, pushing our carts like some very confused shoppers or unsuccessful homeless people, a description we actually fit quite well.

It was a hike, well over an hour. Once we started getting into a denser part of the town, I noticed that most of buildings had broken doors or windows, with a large "E" spray-painted on them, which Jasper had mentioned yesterday was what they marked on buildings once they'd been emptied out. Eventually holding up his hand, Don brought us to a stop. We were at the first buildings in a while that didn't have any visible spray paint on them. "Let's start here," he said. "Chucky, Mike, Sami, check that one." He pointed to the building on our right, a lawyer's office. "Us three will work on this one." Across the street was a tax accountant's office.

Sami shot me a concerned look before walking off with her group. Turning my attention to Don, we pushed the carts up to a solid wooden door. "Go on," Don said to me, stepping away from it. Picking my sledgehammer up from the cart, I took a step forward and checked my grip. It'd been awhile since I had swung one, but I figured I'd remember.

"Is there a certain place I should aim for?" I asked.

"Yeah, the door!" Nicole answered, still standing in the grass.

"Alright, then." Heaving it back, I let the hammer fly. It connected with the door and about jumped out of my stinging hands as the reverberations echoed up my arms. Other than a dent, the door looked fine. Nicole snorted loudly as I reloaded. This time I aimed for the lock and door handle. This blow connected fully and resulted in a satisfying crack. On my next swing, you could see the wood begin to shatter around the handle. The fourth swing almost got us all the way in, and with the fifth swing the door snapped open, the lock and handle hanging loosely from the splintered wood.

"First we check every room to make sure the place is empty," Don said to me, his hand resting on the butt of his pistol. He led us in as we started searching room by room. The building did end up being empty, and looked like it had been since before the shutdown had started, no signs of anyone sneaking in at any point. Once Don was sure we were alone, we headed back to the entrance and started our detailed search.

The small lobby-slash-waiting room didn't need much of a lookover, just magazines and chairs. The next few rooms were offices. We pulled the drawers out of the desks and file cabinets, but nothing much other than paper and folders appeared. Even in the drawers with personal items, nothing interesting was found. The next offices were the same.

In the very back was the break room-slash-kitchenette. Once we reached that room, I went straight for the refrigerator. "Don't," Don said quickly. "Anything in there has long spoiled. It'll smell like a rotting corpse and be inedible anyways. Check the cabinets instead." We rifled through them, coming out with some coffee grounds, a couple bags of sugar, and an open container of stale Oreos.

Lastly was the bathroom, unremarkable except for a full package of toilet paper, officially our biggest score of the hunt. Dropping our loot in the cart back outside, we watched as the other team exited their target, with not much more to show for their efforts. "Okay, let's get started on the next ones," Don said as he dug a can of spray paint out of the duffel bag and started marking the first two buildings.

We worked through six more small business fronts during the next couple hours. We stayed separated in our groups, Sami seemingly getting along fine with her two partners. It was weird; since we hadn't been apart this much in so long, even just being on the other side of the street from each other felt like we were in different states.

By noon, the picking experience was already starting to slip into dullness. None of the buildings had given up anything interesting, just more toilet paper, boxes of cereal, candy, packaged meals like an office worker might make for lunch, and a few other knick-knacks Don deemed worthy of adding to our cart.

"This one looks like a bakery!" Mike shouted across the street as they moved on from the nail salon they had just picked over.

Looking over the used bookstore we were about to break into, Don grunted, "Let's go check that one out with them." Our team moved across and linked up with the other task force right as Chucky shattered the glass door with his ax.

"I've been here before," Sami said as we stepped through the glass. "They have really good cupcakes here."

The Coke-branded fridge in the corner was empty. All of the display cases that normally housed the sweets for sale were empty as well. "No more cupcakes," Nicole said.

"The back door's busted through," Mike reported, coming back from the rear of the building.

"Look for the baking supplies," Don ordered, pulling open cabinets behind the counter. The rest of us spread out and inspected the rest of the bakery, but to no avail. All of the ingredients were gone, and judging from the empty spaces, most of the cookware had been requisitioned as well.

"There isn't enough left in this place to make a damn hot dog bun," Chucky swore, kicking a stack of buckets that went flying across the storeroom.

"Kyle," Don said. "Go grab the duffel with the food in it." I didn't realize that one of the duffels had food in it, but I thought that was better kept to myself. Outside, I went for the duffel that had been in Sami's cart. Sure enough, there were sandwiches in Ziploc bags, a couple family-sized bags of chips, and a bunch of bottles of water.

Inside everyone had taken a seat around the tables. Sami had kept an open spot for me next to her. "Peanut butter sandwiches again?" Mike moaned as I passed the bounty out.

"At least it's not corn," Nicole responded.

"That's gonna be engraved on my tombstone," Mike answered back.

Lunch proceeded silently as every crumb got sucked out of the bags. Using my finger, I wiped the smudges of peanut butter from the baggy, before it went in the pile with the rest of them. Ziploc bags were considered valuable, so they were kept and cleaned back at the Express. My last morsel was a potato chip I had saved, the biggest out of the handful I had been given, so it sat there waiting as I worked through the half-pieces and crumbs, a final satisfying bite. Looking at the chip, I felt I wasn't the only one paying it attention. Glancing over to my wife, her eyes were focused on the chip, no doubt dreaming of a whole bowl of them. Picking it up, I held it out for her. With a slight smile she ate it out of my hand, while slipping her hand into mine under the table.

Chucky jumped up from the table suddenly. "I hear them," he said, panic creeping in his voice.

"Hear who?" I started to ask before Don and Mike held their hands up, ordering silence.

"Shit, I hear them now too," Don said. With that, the rest of the group sprung to their feet, knocking the tables and chairs over, sprinting out the door towards our collection of carts in the middle of the street. Sami and I followed in confusion.

"Get those two in!" Don shouted, pointing to the two fullest carts. Sami grabbed the one that had been hers, chasing after Nicole who was already pushing one of the carts at a full run back into the bakery. Chucky and Mike each grabbed an empty cart and flung them as far as they could in random directions, the carts bouncing into the grass. Pulling the duffel out of my cart, Don kicked it over where it was. "Come on!" he yelled. They were running back to the bakery before I could get a grasp on what was happening. Sami and Nicole were fighting the carts behind the counter of the bakery as we passed them. Mike led us to the kitchen before he stopped, dropping behind a cabinet. Moments later we were all crowded into the room, kneeling on the floor.

I finally picked up the sound of a car engine as it drove down the street in front of us. Laying on the floor, we could see down the hallway through the glass of the display cases and the front windows as a black SUV came to a stop right where our carts had been sitting a minute ago. The vehicle had the large DERT emblem crudely painted on each of the doors. The side doors opened and out popped a couple of men, wearing military-style tactical vests on top of their collared brown shirts to go with their AR-15s. "ATTENTION! ATTENTION!" the speaker on top of the SUV blared into the air. "THIS AREA IS A RESTRICTED ACCESS ZONE. TRESPASSING IS A VIOLATION OF THE FAIR WEATHER ACT. PLEASE SUBMIT YOURSELVES FOR REMOVAL."

There was a pause. No one in the room moved. The Dirts outside the car just looked around, not really expecting anyone to turn themselves in. Another voice echoed over the speaker. This time it didn't sound recorded. "WE KNOW YOU ARE HERE. SURRENDER YOURSELVES OR WE WILL OPEN FIRE." Still no one moved in our room. Everyone was breathing quickly and watching the men outside.

The driver's window rolled down. The driver stuck his head out the window for a moment, speaking to the guys standing outside. They responded by lifting their guns. Everything was overtaken now by the oppressive sound of automatic weapons firing indiscriminately. Swinging their guns around at the buildings in front of them, they poured bullets into the structures without bothering to aim at anything in particular. The bullets whistled through the air over our heads, glass shattering and shrapnel flying about as the lead ricocheted around the room. Sami dug her head into my side, shielding her face from the hellfire. The firing only lasted a few seconds, until their magazines were emptied. After their guns started clicking, the men took a final look around, then climbed back into their SUV and continued on their way, the black beast crawling slowly down the road.

"Go take a look," Don whispered to Chucky. He crawled forward slowly until he was peeking through the shattered glass of the front windows. "Nicole, go out the back and see how things look." She slipped off behind us and to the back door.

"What was that?" I finally asked as Sami and I crawled over to the wall, her face white and eyes wide.

"Just Rodriguez reminding us she's still in charge," Mike said. "They can paint flowers all over their tanks if they want, but they're still the same bunch of trigger-happy Nazis they've always been."

Nicole reappeared from her trip out back. "It looks quiet out there. The Dirts kept rolling down Maple."

"Alright, then let's move the other way, since they probably scared everyone else off," Don announced, climbing back to his feet. "Girls, get your two carts and move that way. We'll get the rest."

Our group started moving forward. Sami and Nicole got to work unjamming the carts they had just crammed behind the counter. The men went up to the front windows and took a look around. "Looks fine out there," Chucky said.

"Get your carts and use the alley three streets over," Don ordered. The four of us ran out to the carts that we had sent in every direction. Mine was still sitting in the road, tipped on its side. Flipping it over, I scurried after the others down the alley and away from Maple Street.

Our two groups reunited in a small alley in between two houses. Don broke open the gate to the backyard and we filed through, then into a house once the door was busted open. "Clear it," he instructed from the back of the group. The rest of us split off and searched the house top to bottom for lifeforms. None being found, we reconvened in the dining room where our carts were piled up. "Nicole, you watch the front. Mike, you watch the back. See if anything moves out there. We'll pick this over in the meantime."

Sami and I climbed the stairs and started rooting through the bedrooms as Don took the kitchen and Chucky worked the rest. "Where should we start?" Sami asked, looking around the master bedroom.

"How about the closet?"

The closet was a walk-in, though on the smaller side. The clothes didn't offer much of interest, mostly dressy-looking stuff for old-lady types. Grabbing a stool from the bedroom, I stepped up so I could search through the boxes stored on the top shelf. The first box was pictures, the second assorted papers, then a box of letters and birthday cards. The next box was the ticket; it contained a snub-nosed .38 Special and two boxes of ammo. "Well, this is better than toilet paper," I said, handing the box down to Sami.

"Why wouldn't they take this with them?"

"I don't know." I climbed down from the stool. "Put that in the hallway and let's check the bathroom."

Don's standing orders were to collect any form of medicine we found, from prescription stuff to acne ointment and everything in between. This bathroom yielded a good amount, including a bottle of antibiotics, which apparently was like finding a diamond in the picking world. Pulling the bag out of the bathroom's tiny wastepaper basket, we threw everything we found inside it. Back in the bedroom we flipped the bed. Not even dust was under the mattresses. The dressers were boring, so that left just the bedside tables. The side that appeared to be the man of the house's contained a few paperback books, some other trinkets, and a gold Rolex in the top drawer.

"That looks expensive," Sami said when I held it up.

"Not super useful now, but probably worth something," I answered, putting it in my pocket.

There were two other rooms on the top floor. One was a guest bedroom, even less interesting than a hotel room, nothing but cheap bedding and a stack of towels. The other room was an office space. An old beige desktop, circa 2005, occupied the space, along with a cheap laserprinter. A thorough search of the room revealed nothing that seemed useful. "I think that's it for up here," I said, picking up the box with the gun in it. Sami grabbed the bucket of medicine and we headed back down.

The rest of the rooms had been tossed already. Don and Chucky were sorting through what they had found on the dining room table. "What did you find?" Don demanded, his mood having gone rapidly downhill since the encounter with the Dirts and their AR-15s.

"A bunch of medicine from the bathroom and a gun."

Holding the box forward, Don snatched the gun box from my hands. "Was there any more?"

"Any more guns?"

"Yes, any more goddamned guns!" he suddenly shouted. "Did you take one for yourself? What's that in your pocket?"

"I found a watch up there too, that's it." I pulled out the Rolex.

"And you were going to keep it?" Don snarled.

"Mine," Chucky said, snatching the watch out of my hand and sticking it in his own pocket.

"I wasn't trying to keep it, and we didn't find anything else. Just this gun and the bullets."

Sami was still holding the basket full of the bathroom drugs in it. "Do you want these?" she asked Chucky.

"Put them in the carts and let's get out of here," Don said, examining the pistol.

Sami set the basket down and backed out of the room, me following. The other rooms on the ground floor were occupied as Mike and Nicole kept watch, so we retreated to the stairwell, sitting on the steps halfway up.

"Not a big fan of Sergeant Fury right now," Sami whispered.

"We did just get shot at by automatic weapons," I whispered back.

"That's wasn't our fault."

"We *are* the new guys. That would put me on edge too."

"I guess so. They're just making everything more difficult." She leaned her head against my knees.

We rested there for a few more minutes, contemplating our

situation. Don, Mike and Chucky were the kind of guys I had avoided before the world went to shit. They were the kind of arrogant assholes who openly wore a pistol on their belts in public just because they could, who drove lifted trucks and hunted deer with compound bows and bragged about their knowledge of mixed martial arts. Now in this world they had been given free rein, only the occasional government agent to spray bullets in their direction to keep them in check but otherwise a bunch of Jesse Jameses in a lawless world. Society might have broken down to that point now for them; but for us, we had been living in our own house four days ago, doing nothing more illegal than growing a couple of scraggly tomato plants.

"I don't know what else to do, honey." I ran my fingers through her hair.

"I know, me either," she whispered back.

"Alright, let's get going," Don's voice commanded from the lower level. Heading down, we found the full group assembled in the dining room. "Everything looks like it's calmed down and the Dirts have moved on. We've got a couple more hours, so we'll work the houses on this street as a full group." He looked around at all of us. "Any questions?" Nobody said anything. "Get the carts." He walked out the front door.

I grabbed my cart, my sledgehammer still sitting in with the duffel bag. It made me realize I'd never seen a shopping cart in a house before, which then made me quickly realize that they're not meant to be pushed around the narrow corners of private homes. It took a few minutes, but we finally dislodged them from the dining room and got through.

Outside, we left the carts lined up in the front yard. Nicole was tasked with keeping watch over them and the street as we searched the next house. "Kyle, get the door open," Don said. Pulling my sledge out, I went straight for the lock this time and burst it open on the first hit. "Nicole, you keep watch out here. Everyone else, clear this place and get to work."

The initial sweep of the house revealed nothing out of the ordinary, just a standard abandoned home. Sami and I headed up the stairs again. The layout was identical to the last house we had searched. "Let's check this one first," I said, taking us into the what had been the guest bedroom in the other house. This time it was a craft room, which didn't look promising.

"I wonder where all the people have gone," Sami pondered out loud. "Everyone in our neighborhood pretty much stayed put."

"That family with the three girls left pretty early," I reminded her as we kicked through the craft supplies, rifling through the drawers.

"They were going to his family's place in Indiana, right?"

"I think so."

"We could always go that same route," she said hesitantly.

"Why, do you have family in Indiana?"

"Kyle."

"I know. That's a long walk, though."

She was talking about her father's place. Sami and her mother had been very close before she had passed away when Sami was thirteen. Soon after that, her father Daniel got remarried to a woman named Carla. Carla and Sami fought every day until she was finally able to leave for college. That had apparently been what Carla had been waiting for, since they sold Sami's childhood home immediately and moved out to a town called Dakota near the tri-border area of Illinois, Iowa and Wisconsin. The town was tiny, but they didn't even live in the city limits, instead owning a farm deep in the corn fields nearby. It was part of a four-plot grid, a house on each corner so that they were all neighbors of a sort, where Carla dominated the other three families nearly as badly as she did with Daniel and Lincoln, Sami's half-brother, born on the farm and practically invisible whenever we visited.

Their homestead was about a two-hour drive from us. We had only been out there twice since becoming a couple, and it was terrible both times. The seclusion hadn't been healthy for any of them. Daniel barely spoke to anyone, floating through our time out there like he was adrift at sea, and yet seemed angry at everything. Carla had turned the place into her own little pastoral Eden, preaching the sins of city living as if Joliet was Sodom reincarnate. It'd been three years since our last visit, which had ended with raised voices as Carla denounced our urban lifestyle and goaded Daniel until his temper snapped and he started lashing out at everyone.

"I'm sure they have plenty of food out there," Sami mused.

"That's probably true. Though everyone around here seems to have enough corn to eat."

"There's probably still enough wildlife running around out there to keep them fed, too."

"Yeah."

The silence crept up as we shifted through the mess, nothing standing out as being useful in any situation. Going to Dakota was a last resort; it would take days and days to get there by foot, and even once there, our arrival could be received a hundred different ways. And even if everything went great, we'd just be living with people we couldn't get along with even when the world was normal.

CRACK. The rifle shot broke the silence between us, I dropped the box I was holding as three more shots rang out in rapid succession and the shouting started. The cries were indistinct as we ran back to the stairs, but then I heard Nicole screaming in a shrill and panicky voice, "RAIDERS! RAIDERS OUT FRONT!!!" Halfway down the steps we saw her. The back of her shirt was stained wet with blood, smeared on her hands and against the door she was using as both cover and a crutch to support her body weight, as she returned fire into the front yard.

Mike reached her first, pulling her fully inside and spraying bullets out front before he slammed the door closed. Grabbing Nicole from the back, I pulled her into the dining room. "Four of them," she sighed out, obviously in pain.

"Check the back!" Don yelled, he and Chucky running towards the rear of the house.

"How bad is it?" Nicole asked, panting, as I dropped her onto the chair in the kitchen. The whole right shoulder of her shirt was sticky with blood. "Get some towels or something!" she yelled out to Sami, who had followed us into the room. I'd never seen an injury like this before; probably a broken nose was the most traumatic thing I'd ever been personally involved in before today. Looking around the room, I spotted a pair of scissors on the countertop. Snipping through her collar revealed a small round hole pulsing blood on both sides of Nicole's shoulder.

"It looks like it went all the way through," I said, grabbing the hand towels Sami had found and pressing them against the wounds.

The sound of fresh gunfire broke out from the rear of the house, mixed in with Chucky's screams. "THEY'RE OUT BACK TOO!" Don was still running around, trying to look out every window. Considering that the houses were close together, there wasn't much to see out the side windows, but Don kept looking out of each of them as the shots picked up from both directions.

"Hold these here." I handed the job of compression over to Sami. "We need to get her on the floor." Sami held the makeshift bandages in place as we slipped Nicole out of the chair and onto the linoleum floor. With Sami tending to her, I crawled over to the defensive positions Don and Mike had taken just outside the kitchen. With the entire living room between them and outside, they were firing through the walls or blindly out of the windows at our attackers.

"We have to get out of here!" I yelled.

"They've blocked both sides!" Don shouted back.

"We're trapped, man, we're fucking trapped!" Chucky continued to holler from the back of the house.

"Can we get out the sides?" Sami shouted over. "Maybe a garage door?" It didn't seem likely, but we weren't going to gain any ground by using the front and back doors. Scrambling away from the cluster of people, I tried searching for another way out. Behind us, the dining and utility rooms were a warzone worse than the front of the house. Chucky had overturned the table, put it against the wall and was firing wildly out the window. Broken glass was everywhere. No escape back there without going straight into the bullets.

The only other door to be seen was located under the stairwell. Pulling it open revealed a guest bathroom, not very big, but with a window of frosted glass. "In here!" I yelled, sticking my head back into the hallway that connected our two little groups.

"Fuck that! We're shooting our way out of here!" Mike screamed maniacally, standing up and moving towards the front door before anyone else could speak. As soon as he reached it, a bullet went through his head with a dull *thunk*. If you've ever heard someone really hit their head and you hear that hollow echo sound, it was like that. Like drumming on a watermelon. The brain matter splattered across the wall as the body fell sideways towards the doorway.

"NO! MIKE!" Nicole shrieked, woken up now from the daze she'd been in since getting shot. She tried to go after Mike, but Sami kept her from standing up into the crossfire.

"GODDAMNIT!!" Don poured fire back at the unseen attackers. Looking at Mike's body sprawled out in front of us, my eyes finally focused on my sledgehammer laying on the floor in the middle of the living room, where I had dropped it when we dragged Nicole out of the doorway. Crawling forward, I stayed under the bullets and snagged it, dodging Don as he returned fire with a vengeance.

In the bathroom I hit the center of the window frame with everything I had. The glass shattered immediately, but it was too small of a hole. The whole window had to go. Another whack and the center of it buckled. The third hit sent it flying into the yard. Climbing onto the toilet, I stuck my head out and into the air, not knowing if there was someone waiting to watermelon my head as well. This side of the house looked calm, even if the sounds of the battle still overwhelmed the scene. There was two feet of open space and then a row of hedges separating the yards. This was the best escape route we were going to get.

Back in the fight, Nicole had pulled free of Sami and had taken Mike's spot on the firing line. Sami was laying flat on the floor, hands over her ears, looking directly at me. Waving her forward, she crawled across the floor towards me in the bathroom. "We can get out the window!" I shouted at Don and Nicole, but they couldn't hear me anymore. The fog of war had settled into the front of the house.

Picking up the bathmat, Sami threw it across the jagged glass at the bottom of the window opening. "Go on, get up there," I shouted.

"You go first."

"I'm not leaving you in here. You have to go first."

She set her face and stepped up on the toilet. It was an

awkward squeeze to get through the window, upper half through and upwards. I held her legs so she could twist and kinda fall through the rest of the way. Once she was through, I tossed my sledgehammer through, then followed. It was harder to get through the opening by myself, but Sami caught me as I fell through to the outside. We were out of the house and there was no one in sight. The gunfire was focused only on the front and rear of the house.

"Through the bushes," I said, pushing into them on my hands and knees. The bushes weren't made to be crawled through, but we were determined, getting my head through to the other side with only a few scrapes. There wasn't anything in the direction of the front of the house, no people in sight. However, if we went that way, it would expose us to whoever was out there with the guns. The other way, as I turned my head in that direction, was even more dangerous. About fifty feet from us down the hedge line was a large tree, right in the middle of the bushes. Using it as cover was a man. He was holding a rifle and firing it into the house we had just left. In our favor was that he was looking around the opposite side of the tree, so his back was facing us. Freezing, Sami and I shot glances at each other. The back yard was the best way to go; however, if the man at the tree turned for just a moment, he would see us standing in the middle of the yard with just the overgrown grass as cover and no weapons.

"Stay here," I said. The decision wasn't made lightly, but it was made quickly. There was only one choice—eliminate the obstacle. Pushing through the last of the bushes, I gripped the sledgehammer firmly and moved forward. Running crouched to stay below the bushes, I covered the ground in just moments, though it felt like running up an escalator, every step feeling like I was sliding backwards. The man didn't move, just his shoulder rocking back from the recoil of the rifle firing. Two steps away, I turned my body, bringing it to a stop in a batter's stance. The sledgehammer was already cocked when I stopped. Swinging it harder than I had all day, the center of the head connected with the man's back, between the shoulder blades. I could see the indention the iron left in his flesh.

The man grunted as the wind left his chest, crumpling to

the ground at the base of the tree. Ending up on his back, his eyes locked onto mine as he struggled to find his breath in painful gasps. Blood glittered on his lips. Even though he was clearly fighting desperately to move, his brain had lost its connection to his extremities. The only movement was the involuntary motion of his arm. It bent slowly at the elbow, index finger pointing aimlessly at the sky. It was the same movement you see in the tail of a snake or lizard when you chop a piece off. Mindless and reflexive.

Pulling my eyes off of the crippled man, I saw the pistol tucked into his belt, a black semiautomatic. Without thinking, I took it and slipped it into my pocket. His rifle laid half against the tree where he had dropped it when he got hit. It was a black AR-15. Picking it up, I took his spot against the tree, finding my footing around the still shaking body at my feet. Looking down the rifle barrel, I saw two other men on the other side of the yard, in mirror positions from where I was now at. They were firing into the house still, not having noticed the fall of their counterpart. The gun recoiled against my shoulder as I put the sights on them and pulled the trigger. The first few bullets kicked up dirt around their position, getting their attention in a hurry. They fell over themselves retreating as I fired the next salvo. Letting go of the trigger, the air was silent for a moment, just the flashes of our retreating attackers running through the adjacent yards, the tide having been turned in the back yard.

"Come on, Kyle!" Sami grabbed at my elbow, pulling me away.

"Wait, the rest of them can get out now." I leaned around the tree so I could see the back of the house where Chucky was dug in. "CHUCKY!" I screamed. "THEY'RE GONE! COME ON, IT'S CLEAR!"

Chucky's head appeared over the window ledge, seeing for himself what had happened. A moment later he was standing, yelling back into the house. It took just a few seconds for the three survivors to come bursting through the door. Chucky was in the lead, Nicole in the middle, and Don as the rearguard, still firing back into the house they had just fled.

I fired a couple parting shots where I had last seen the

ambushers before they ran out of sight. Turning with Sami, we sprinted across the yard and out the back gate into the alley, the rest of our group following behind us. We kept running for about a mile, the tempo falling as we put the battle site farther behind us.

"Stop, stop," Nicole gasped as we turned a corner. Collapsing against the wall, Nicole sucked for breath. The rest of us were heaving as well. The adrenaline of the battle was draining out of us now that we were out of immediate danger. Sami slumped down next to Nicole, trying to catch her breath as well.

"Give me that." Don ripped the AR-15 from my hands, giving me a shove with it once he had it.

"What the hell?" I shot back, my surprise and exhaustion fueling my confusion.

"Climbing out the window and trying to leave us like that? You're lucky I don't execute the both of you right here." His clothes were soaked with sweat and blood, and his face shone bright red under the perspiration.

"What are you talking about? We saved you!" I screamed back, my voice cracking with rage. I moved forward at him, jabbing the air with my finger. "You'd still be in there waiting to die if it wasn't for me." Chucky caught me by the shoulder and pushed me back, away from Don who was snarling like a mad dog, too angry to speak.

"Everyone calm down," Nicole spoke up. "We aren't out of this yet."

"Let's just get back home first," Chucky said, now the voice of reason.

Don just gave us a long look, then walked off silently, my rifle still in his hand.

CHAPTER EIGHT

ROTATION

Our adventure earned us another date with the shower. Surprisingly, a post-gunfight shower isn't as relaxing as it sounds.

The rest of the hike back to the Express had been conducted in sullen silence and at an easier pace than the first bit had been. Halfway home we ran into another Express armed squad, on their way out from the hotel to look for us, the gunfire having been heard and noted that it was coming from our search area. There had been ten of them, all heavily armed and wearing an odd assortment of body armor, looking like a SWAT team outfitted at Goodwill. (They were right; those supercenters really *do* have everything.) They took Nicole and carried her back quickly, while the rest of us trudged onward.

Back at the lobby there were a bunch of people watching us. Word had spread around the hotel about the battle and casualties. Pushing past them, Sami and I went straight to our room. "Watch the door," I said as soon as it closed behind us. She stood in front of it, watching me carefully. The bathroom had a drop ceiling. Standing on the toilet, I pushed up one of the tiles. The space above was dusty and unfinished, wiring and pipes running around between the rooms. I fished the gun out of my pocket and set it in there. Gently letting the tile fall back in place, it was hidden for the moment.

Stepping out of the bathroom, there was a knock on the door. Sami hesitated, looking at me with worry. I held my hand up for her to wait, so it wouldn't look like we were standing directly in front of the door. After a moment I nodded and she opened it. Nick was standing out front. "Hey, guys, Jasper'd like to talk about today with everyone."

"Alright. We were just taking a minute to lie down."

"Of course. It's been a rough day. Jasper just likes to do a kinda debriefing after something like this, and then we can get you cleaned up." He eyed the bloodstains on our clothes and skin. "Did either of you get injured? Cuts, bumps or such?"

"I don't think so," I answered, looking over my hands. There were a couple of scrapes on them, but nothing to be concerned about.

"I'm good, just other people's blood on me," Sami answered. Her hands and arms were stained badly from helping Nicole.

"Looks like we'll have to get you some new clothes again. These only lasted a day." He chuckled. "Are you ready or do you need a few minutes?"

"We're ready," I said, following him back down the hallway.

Back in the lobby, there was a room off the main space, probably an office, probably once with a computer and printer in it. Now it was re-purposed as a briefing room. Several maps hung on the wall showing the surrounding area, with marks and colored pins stuck in it, tracking their progress of searched areas. "Let's make this quick," Don growled. Our entire group was now there, minus Nicole. The meeting lasted about half an hour. Don outlined where we were, how we had gotten there, and how we got out. Reasons for the battle, what we had found, and anything else we could think of that influenced the incident. The common thought was that we had wandered into someone else's turf unwittingly and they had jumped us.

Once the meeting broke up, we were ushered back into the lobby where we waited for our turn to use the showers. Don went first and then Chucky. We waited quietly at a table, nibbling the food they'd brought us. More desirable than the food was the water. We hadn't drank much before the battle started, and the shooting and running only parched us more. We finished off a full gallon jug while we waited.

After the shower we were given a set of fresh clothes, identical to the ones that we had been given the night before. "You killed that guy?" Sami asked, breaking the silence once we had gotten back to our room.

"I think so," I answered as I joined her on the bed.

"Hope he didn't suffer very much," she said, crawling into her usual position on my chest.

"Me too."

"Do you feel different?"

"Not really. It just happened so fast. I didn't have much time to think about it. I had to do something to get us out of there. We wouldn't have made it to that gate without being seen."

"I know."

"I don't think I'll feel different, but I think I'll always feel it. The way it felt when it hit his back, the sound, the taste of the moment, it's in there now. It's not going away."

She patted my chest as she spoke. "Things like that aren't easy."

Tears welled in my eyes. "I didn't know what else to do. I had to get us out of there."

"You did, Kyle. You saved us."

The silence returned for a while as we struggled with the implications of that on our own.

"What do we do now?" she finally asked.

"I feel like we keep asking that question every day or so."

"We used to do it before. Just then it was about where were we going to eat or what we should do until the movie starts." The lightness was beginning to return to her voice a bit.

"I could go for some Chick Fil-A right now."

"Eating Jesus chicken right after you killed a man won't absolve you." Not saying anything, I just gave her a look. "You would have said the same thing if you were in my place." She pushed my chin so my face aimed away from her. "You think they'll offer to let us stay here with them? Become part of the Express?" she continued.

"Probably. Despite Don's bitching out there, I think we proved helpful, able to handle ourselves. Mike got panicky and got shot through the head for it."

"I agree."

"So the question is, do we want to stay?"

"Correct. That's the question." It had been lingering over us since we arrived the other night. Is this a place we could call home, or at least a home for a while? Everyone in our neighborhood had assumed the trouble would pass and things would get back to normal before long. That we would go back to our regular jobs and carry on as we always had, maybe with just less driving or something. We had clung to that hope too, until our house got burned down by the very people we had discussed that hope with. Now we were on the outside and it didn't seem very likely that things were going to go back to normal anytime soon. When government agents are spraying automatic fire at random, and shootouts are happening in subdivisions in broad daylight over some shopping carts, it's hard to imagine things being normal anytime soon. So if it wasn't going to just slip back to the way things were, what should we do about it?

"If we leave, we don't have anywhere specific to go," I spoke, thinking out loud. "We could go to Dakota, but that would take a while on foot. With no sure food or water, who knows how long 140 miles would take. So if we do stay here, do we do it at the Express? How do we know there aren't any better ones out there?"

"We don't. But they could also be worse. Like those people we ran into today, killing others for crossing some invisible line. We might get shot just walking around out there."

"So we don't really have a choice, I guess. Stay here or wander in the jungle."

"We could try one of the camps."

"The Dirt camps?"

"Yes. They probably aren't bad. Eric was just making them seem that way because he'd already had his psychotic snap."

"We don't know that. Remember, we got shot at by some

of those people today, too."

"I know. It's just the only other option."

Silence ensued again as we thought through what was left.

"I guess we're staying, then," Sami said, breaking the quiet after a few minutes.

"I guess so."

The day's events overcame us now and we drifted off to sleep.

* * *

"Someone's at the door." I mumbled, the knocking invading my dreams. Sami just moaned and shifted her position as usual. The next knock brought me back to awareness. The light from the window was nearly gone. It was dusk.

Stumbling to the door, I found Nick waiting there again. "Hey, are you coming to dinner? It's almost over."

"Yeah, yeah, we'll be there. We fell asleep," I answered, trying to smooth the hair on the back of my head I could feel sticking up.

"Oh yeah, we figured. But Jasper and them would like to see you again."

"Alright, we'll be there in just a minute." I let the door close.

Sami resisted for a few minutes, but eventually conceded to wake up, and soon we were on our way. The lobby was full of people again, lounging around and enjoying dinner. Jasper waved us over before we could get plates. There were already two chairs waiting for us at the table. "Welcome to dinner," he greeted us brightly.

"Thanks. Sorry we're late." We took our seats.

"That's fine. I'd be late too if I had had the kinda day you guys did."

Don grunted in response to this as Nick put two plates of food in front of us. "Thank you," we said in unison.

"Anyways, the council has been talking, and we feel like you both would be a welcome addition to our family here at the

Express. How would you feel about joining us?"

"Uh, well, we talked about that today, and I, uh, think that's a good idea," I answered.

"Excellent." Jasper smiled broadly.

"Don't really have a choice," Don growled. "You go out there alone, you're gonna get yourself killed quicker than you almost did today." Everyone shifted uncomfortably. "What? Two of my people got shot looking after them today."

"That's not true," Sami shot back. "We did everything you told us to do. We didn't lead you into that house, but we did lead you out of it."

"You're going to learn a thing or two about that mouth, lady," Don snarled back.

"That's enough!" Jasper cut in before I could tell Don where to shove it. "Today was unfortunate, but it's nobody's fault. These things happen in this world. All we can do is be prepared." Don mumbled under his breath, looking away from the rest of us. "We're happy to have you here with us. Even if some people are being difficult. We all know you were of help today, and will be so in the future."

"We'll do our best," I answered.

"That's great. It was a hard day for all of us. Mike was a good man. He'd been with us since the beginning. We need to stay focused on the fact that the enemy is out there, those who wish us harm and the chaos that ensues. That's our common foe," Jasper said, looking pointedly at Don. Don sat back up straight, looking grumpy, but slightly reconciled. "So normally we'd move you upstairs to one of the actual resident rooms, but since it's late, we might just leave that for tomorrow?" Jasper asked, the lightness returning to his voice.

"That sounds good," I answered, digging into my food.

"Tomorrow, Kyle, you'll go back out with Don. You'll be doing kind of a routine we like to run the new guys through, get a feel for how we do things."

"Alright," I answered, looking at Don. He was staring hard at me. "Anything I need to prepare myself for?"

"After what you went through today, it should be a

breeze," Jasper said with a smile. "And Sami, tomorrow we'll start you in the domestic rotation."

"Oh good," she answered with a smile. "Where at?"

"The second floor is always the starting spot."

"Okay. What kinda work are they doing there?"

"It's a little too detailed to describe. You'll just see tomorrow." He smiled again.

"Alright, can't wait." She smiled again.

Our first acquaintance at the Express, Carl, walked up to us. "So are you guys in?"

"Yeah, I guess so," I answered, shaking his offered hand.

"That's great. Glad you two wandered in the other night." He gave Sami a hug. "Especially you, Sami. I think we'll have some fun."

She laughed. "I get that a lot. Kyle doesn't look like the fun one."

"No he doesn't, but I'm sure he's used to it." He slapped me on the back. "Alright, I'll see you tomorrow." He headed off to the stairwell.

We finished our dinner with idle chitchat, just the usual getting-to-know-you stuff. More residents stopped by our table to greet the newest members of the club as they headed off to bed. "I think that's it for me," Jasper finally announced, a few minutes after we finished our food.

"Yeah, I think I could use a nap again," I said with a laugh.

"Yep, busy day tomorrow for all of us," Jasper answered as we all got up from our seats.

"Thanks again so much for letting us stay here," I said, shaking his hand again, then Nick's, then moving to Don's.

"We're glad to have you," Jasper said, heading away from the group.

"I'll see you tomorrow," Don said, squeezing my hand harder than was necessary. "And I'll see you too," he said over my shoulder to Sami.

"Alright, see you then," she answered uneasily as we stepped away and back down the hallway to our room.

* * *

We slept as hard that night as we had during our afternoon nap, awaking only when the sun was shining directly in my eyes announcing morning. Sami was already awake, looking at me from her pillow. "Morning, dear."

"Hi. How long have you been up?"

"Not long. Just thought you could use a few more minutes."

"I've never complained about more sleep," I answered, pushing myself up to a half-sitting position.

"What do you think you're going to be doing with Don today?" she asked.

"Oh, I dunno, probably just some starter course on survival skills or something."

"Are you going to bring the gun?" she said. I realized that her eyes were bigger than normal.

"I hadn't thought about it. Why would I?"

"Why wouldn't you?"

"I dunno."

"After yesterday, you might need it…" Her voice trailed.

"You're worried about Don?" She just nodded. "I don't think he's like that, but I guess you're right, better to have it and not need it than to need it and not have it."

"I'll feel better if you took it."

"You sure you don't need it here?" I asked lightly.

"I think I can manage here without any projectile weapons."

"Okay then."

We pulled our Express-issued clothes on and got cleaned up the best we could for the morning without any running water. We rubbed the sleepiness out of our eyes and smoothed our hair down as much as we could. I put the gun in the lower pocket of my cargo pants. It bulged a bit but wasn't really noticeable. I was planning to move it to my waistline once we finished with breakfast. Sitting down with the un-holstered gun in my belt wouldn't be comfortable.

The lobby was its usual scene of everyone preparing for the day. We settled into a nice spot after getting our plates of food. Several people stopped by to greet us as the new people in town while we ate. Michele was the last. "Happy first day, guys!" she greeted us, taking a seat at our table. "Have you moved into your new room?" she continued without pause.

"No, we stayed in a guest room down here last night," Sami answered.

"Hopefully it's near mine on the seventh floor. We have so much fun up there."

"Hopefully," I answered. Sami gave me a sideway glance.

"I heard about yesterday. That must've been really scary. I can't believe things have gotten so bad out there."

"It was pretty rough."

"It's sad how terrible people have become now. It really makes you lose faith in humanity, doesn't it?"

"Guess so."

"I just take comfort in the fact that we're safe here. We all look out for each other and take care of everyone. Even if we have our disagreements or adjustment problems, we're still lucky to be here and be safe. You should never take that for granted, that we're taken care of here and sacrifice for this place."

"You're right, it's nice to feel like we have a home here," Sami responded.

Michele squeezed her shoulder. "How right you are, dear."

Don walked up to our small group. "You ready?" he addressed me, looking a bit happier than he did the day previous.

"Yep, I'm ready." I stood up from the table.

"We should get going as well, Sami," Michele said.

"Oh am I with you today?" she asked.

"Oh yes. I'll show you the ropes today, honey." She smiled brightly.

"Okay, well, have a good day, honey," Sami said, giving me a hug.

"You too, babe. I'll see you tonight." Michele led Sami off to the back as I turned to face Don. "Do I need to get any tools?" I asked him.

"Nope, I got you covered." He patted the bag slung over his shoulder.

"Alright," I answered, following him out the door.

Outside, the Pickers were getting their usual start to the day, picking out their carts and wheelbarrows. Don gave a quick rundown on the plan for the day and sent them on their way. "Do I need a cart?" I asked as the groups moved away.

"No cart today. Let's go."

We walked in silence for a while. I wanted to know where we were going and what the plan was. However, Don had made it clear he didn't care to share the details of our day trip together, and that pestering him would only make the situation more difficult. He was predisposed to dislike me already. When we came to a stop, it wasn't too far from home base, just a few twists and turns down some forgotten industrial service roads. It was a relatively small building, built out of cinderblock, low-slung with several large rollup doors on the front side. It looked like an old car repair shop. "Wait out here," Don said, pointing to the curb. "I'll come get you in a bit."

"Okay." I took a seat on the curb.

Don went to the front door. It had a heavy chain on the handle. He fiddled with the lock for a minute before getting it off and entering, shutting the door behind him.

This was not the start to the training day I had expected. I had thought it would be a day of drills and strategy, some tricks of the trade to avoid trouble and get out of tight scrapes However, it didn't seem to be the point of today's field trip. Keeping an eye on the featureless building front, I noticed there were no windows, just the metal front door and the rollup doors. Turning so my body blocked the view, I pulled the gun out of my pocket and slipped it into my waistband as I stood up. The safety was on and there was a bullet in the chamber; I had checked it before we left the room this morning.

After a bit, the door opened behind me and Don returned. He didn't have his bag with him, though. Joining me at the curb, he took a seat next to me. "Joining the Express is a commitment. Do you understand that?" he asked.

"I do."

"This isn't like joining some pickup softball team. This is the real deal. Lives are on the line. We have to know you're committed. We have to be able to count on you always."

"You can do that. We're serious about this."

"A number of people have sat here and said those same words, but when things got tough, they failed us. They weren't committed to the cause. This is like the military; it's for life."

"I understand. I think I showed yesterday that I can be counted on."

"That's true, you did. Taking another life is a big choice. But taking it in the heat of battle is like a reflex. It's automatic. You know what I mean?"

"Sure."

"Alright. Let's go inside and see what you're really made of."

I led the way into the building. Before I even got through the door, the smell hit me. The stench was nearly unbearable. It smelled like an overripe dumpster, thick and sweetly poisonous, crashing through my ability to think. "What is that?" I asked, coughing as we entered, putting my shirt sleeve over my mouth to try and buffer the smell.

Don didn't answer, but just nodded me forward down the hallway. The walls were unmarked, giving no impression of what this place used to be. Passing several doorways, the hallway turned left and brought us to a door blocking our path. "Go on," he instructed.

I was hesitant. Surely nothing good could be found in a place that smelled so bad and was so cut off from outside life. It felt like a prison, a concentration camp hiding in a nondescript building in an industrial park. And in fact, that's exactly what I found when I opened the door. It was a large space, taking up most of the total square footage of the building. It felt like it'd been a large garage, able to fit about ten cars. In between the rollup doors on the backside of the building was a normal-sized door as well, standing wide open. The light coming through brightened the scene, giving clear light in contrast to the clouded light coming through the panels on the roof.

Around the room was a multitude of people. Some were

chained to the walls, others tied to posts in the open spaces. There were also cages, most of them only big enough for a single person to be squeezed into it. There were a few bigger ones too; they looked custom-built, made out of scrap pieces and awkwardly joined, housing several people each. They were all starved-looking, ribs poking out, their faces drawn and gaunt, lacking the human spark. They all stared in silence as we entered the room. Their faces may have lost the human look, but their eyes lived when they saw us, eying us like a stray dog eyes a human.

"What the hell," I whispered, my voice barely registering.

"Whaddaya think?" Don's voice flickered with enjoyment.

"What is this?" I asked, looking around at the misery chained in place.

"This is a prison and these are the prisoners." He said it as if it was perfectly obvious.

"Why?"

"These people caused trouble. Stealing from us—" he pointed around the room as if accusing specific people— "attacking us, spying on us, sabotaging our facilities. They've been found guilty, so now they're here. We have uses for them from time to time, so we keep them alive and put them to work when we need them." Don gripped me by the shoulder, leading me towards the open doorway. The prisoners all cowered slightly as he neared them.

Walking out the door, the breeze brought new life to me after the suffocating thickness inside. The back was fairly large, an empty field surrounded by cinderblock walls and topped by barbed wire. It definitely had the look of a prison. Directly behind the building the ground was concrete, but everything behind that was grass-covered. Sitting in the middle of the grass among several dirt mounds was a man, kneeling and facing the ground, looking at what was stuck in the ground in front of him. A machete.

"Everyone at the Express has to prove their loyalty at some point," Don said as we stepped onto the concrete. "There's no such thing as a free lunch, even if it's just corn." He chuckled at his timely reference.

Focusing on the scene in front of me as we crossed the yard, what was about to happen became clearer. The man was youngish, probably a few years younger than me, but the recent ordeal gave him the look of someone in his fifties at least. He was dressed in what was a couple of months ago a pair of blue jeans and collared shirt, but now practically black and paper-thin. He was watching us now that we had closed the distance. His hands were tied together and hooked to a stake in the ground. His feet were tied together as well. There were more mounds of dirt around him than I had realized; I had only seen the recent ones at first, where the dirt was still bright. The rest of the yard was filled with smaller mounds that had settled in with grass now growing on them. The chained prisoner wasn't sitting directly next to the mound; there was a hole in the ground separating them, a grave-shaped hole. In front of him was a machete, stuck in the ground with a shovel laying next to it, its edge still coated in the dirt it had just moved.

"This is simple," Don said once we were about five feet from the prisoner. "You have to kill him if you want to join the Express."

"I already killed somebody. I practically broke him in half yesterday with a sledgehammer!" My voice was unstable.

"Killing in battle isn't the same. This is about tribute. Kill this man because it's your vow of commitment." Don pulled the machete out of the ground, forcing it into my hand. "You're going to chop his head off, push it all in the hole, and then bury it all." He pushed me forward, into striking range.

The prisoner stared at me, his eyes were blank, having accepted his fate. "No, this is crazy," I said. "I'm not killing people for no reason. You know I can be trusted. We proved it yesterday!"

"Look around you. Do you see all the other mounds? Everyone else has done it. Every single man you see at the hotel. You aren't getting out of it just because you're a whiner. Now get on with it. This is your last chance." He spoke softly.

I looked back at the prisoner and saw that his expression had changed. He looked like he was just waiting for the blow, his mind having made the logical decision that I would realize it was in my best interest to kill him, so I would do it, just like all the others had done who had been brought here just like this. I felt the weight of the tool in my hand. The handle was hardened plastic, one of those carbon alloy things, and the blade was curved. It was more of tactical-style machete popular with survivalist types instead of the straight-bladed yardwork style. Its edge gleamed silver, sharpened to a killer point. I had always wondered how easy it would be to chop through someone. It looked easy in the movies. The blades always went straight through the enemy. But I doubt any of those people had ever actually seen it done in real life either.

I dropped the point of the blade back to the ground. "No, I won't do it. We'll just leave."

I turned around to see Don holding his gun. It wasn't currently pointed at me, but it was prepared to be. "I don't remember saying you had that option." He smiled now. "Put him in that hole, or I put you in it."

"Just let us go. I'll go get my bags right now and my wife and I will leave with no trouble." I took a half-step forward, causing him to raise his gun fully at me.

"No can do, amigo." He motioned at the pit again with the gun. I looked into the hole that had been dug with a single specific purpose in mind. The weight on my waist beckoned. My hands had been at my side, so turning my left side to him a bit, I shielded my right hand as it inched towards the gun handle. "And speaking of your wife," he continued, "I guess I forgot to mention how the womenfolk prove their loyalty. Do you not know yet what happens on the second floor?"

"No."

"Every woman spends a few days per month being of use to all the men." He paused again, watching his words sink in on me. "Then they get rotated to other jobs for most of the rest of the month. That's where your wife is right now. It's always the first stop of the domestic rotation. Jasper gets first dibs on the new girls, then Nick. I don't mind waiting, though. I'm going to enjoy this here with you just as much. I'll tell her about it afterward. I like to be there when they realize how things are now. Hopefully she isn't too doped up to understand."

"Fuck you!"

"Yeah, that's exactly what she's gonna say!" he laughed, casting his eyes upwards, enjoying the thought. "Then she's gonna say th…"

His voice was drowned out by the gunshot. The moment his eyes came off of me, I had gone for it. Drawing a gun feels like an eternity. When you think about drawing a gun, it seems like such a deliberate slow motion. In reality, it happens in a blink. Don's eyes were still looking up in the sky when I fired. He didn't even see it coming. He stumbled a couple of steps backwards, grasping at the hole in his chest, the blood soaking through his shirt already. His eyes were on me as he fell to the ground. Landing on his butt, he sat there awkwardly on the ground, flicking his eyes between me and his bloodied hand for a moment. Realization is slow-moving once there's a hole in your body.

Setting his face, he lifted his right hand, still gripped firmly onto his pistol, raising it halfway. It was reflexive, his mind finding only one action worth attempting with his final moments. Halfway was as far as he got. Our eyes locked for a heartbeat as I squeezed the trigger again, obscuring our view. This time the bullet found his head, penetrating through his cheek. His body went limp and collapsed backwards in the grass, his gun dropping harmlessly to the side.

Stepping forward, I picked it up. It was warm from his grip, but clear of any blood. He carried his pistol in a holster that was attached to a belt with several other pistol magazines on it, each fully loaded. The buckle was a simple latch. I popped it and pulled the belt free from the new corpse. I didn't have time to figure out how to tighten the belt. Buckling it together, I slid it over my shoulder in sort of a bandolier as I headed for the exit.

Two pistols and a couple spare mags; that was what I was taking into battle. Sami was the only thing I had been able to see once Don started telling me his story. First it was what would happen to her if I was dead, where she would go. I had sworn to protect her in our previous existence when the biggest danger was flat tires or an unresponsive internet router. Our current life required a much larger commitment of protection, but that was a challenge worth living up to. Getting to the second floor was the only object in my mind.

"WAIT! WAIT!" The voice jolted me back to the current location. "Please don't leave me here. Shoot me or cut me free, but don't leave me here," the voice pleaded. Looking back, I saw the prisoner staring at me, the pain of life having returned to his face. The prospect of being beheaded hadn't fazed him, but being left alone in the yard, chained to the earth, was too much to remain stoic about.

There wasn't a moment to lose, but he was right, I couldn't leave him there either. I swiftly grabbed the machete from where Don had dropped it and held tantalizingly close to the restrained man, but still fully out of his reach. The shiny blade slipped through the rope easily, releasing his hands from their binds. "Will you help the others?" I pushed the blade into the soft ground in front of him.

"Yeah, I will," he answered, rubbing his wrists.

"I'd help, but I have to go save my wife. Good luck." With that I left him where he was, wondering if he would bend to the allure of irony and throw Don's body into the hole that had been meant for one of us.

The path back to the Express wasn't hard to follow, though the trip did put my physical fitness to the test. Alternating between running and aggressive jogging, I pushed myself to cover the distance as quick as possible and still be ready once I made it there. Nearing the building, I veered to the right. Though I had no idea what the second floor looked like, I could guess it was about the same as the rest of the hotel. The stairwell near our room was the most active path for transit between the floors. It was my assumption that the room containing Sami would be located closer to the entrance of that stairwell than not. That side of the building was on the opposite side of where I was currently at. Wanting to enter the hotel from that side, I moved around the backside of the building, using the cover the best I could to avoid being seen and then sprinting across the road to the cover provided by the tall hedges that hid the fence along the property line.

I got to the far side quickly, with minimal time spent in the open. Peering around the corner of the hedges, everything at the hotel seemed normal. There were a few people in sight around the lobby area, but they just seemed to be going about their duties, preparing for lunch. There was no one visibly keeping watch.

Even the rooftop didn't seem to have any watchmen. My final preparation was to slip Don's gun into my waistline on the back side. It would be the backup. My own gun I put in my right pocket, still holding it tightly, but concealed from casual eyes. Pulling the three magazines out of their pouches on the belt, I put them in my left pocket, pushing the belt into the bushes at head level. If luck was on our side, I would snag it on our way out.

With my tools in place, I stepped out from the hedges and into the parking lot. Moving as quickly as I could without being suspicious, I crossed the parking lot and reached the side door. It opened as normal. More people were visible at the end of the hallway in the lobby area, but no one was close or paying attention. Through the exterior door and directly into the stairwell, the space was silent. Bounding up the steps, I reached the second floor. Easing the door open with my left hand as the right pointed the gun, I peeked into the new hallway. It was empty.

Stepping into it, it looked like all the other floors of the hotel. The doors to most of the rooms had been removed and the rooms stripped bare. There was an elevator bank in the middle of the hallway, and then the last four rooms still had the doors on them. Each had a locking device attached to the outside of it, a hook and a ring to keep the door from being opened from the inside. The second door on my right was the only one unlocked. Reaching for the handle, I heard the voices inside. Indistinct, but a man and a woman were in there. Repeating my slow opening of doors, I led with my left, gun tight in my right.

"You can fight it all you want, but it won't change what's going to happen to you." I heard the voice as the door swung open silently. It was Jasper speaking. This room was also stripped bare with the exception of the bed. Jasper was standing directly in front of it, looking down on the ground where Sami laid, arms shielding her face, dressed in the same loose t-shirt and sweats we saw the other woman wearing during our tour. He was shirtless, holding the two ends of his belt in his hand, the leather loop creating a makeshift whip. His attention was focused solely on my wife, curled into a fetal position against the wall.

"Fuck you," I said, the door firmly shutting behind me. My voice caused both of them to jump. Sami sat up suddenly when she saw me through her defenses. Jasper turned his head in surprise.

"What are you doing here?" His eyes flickered like Don's had, the confusion of death impending.

"Fuck you. That's what Don said my wife would be saying today to you while you were raping her. 'Fuck you.'" I stepped closer.

"I don't know what Don told you…" He was scrambling.

"Sami, say it. Say it to him."

"Fuck you." The hardness of her voice cut through the room. He scowled at her words as a bullet put a hole through his heart. He didn't even have a chance to change his expression before he toppled onto the bed.

"I knew you'd come." Sami rushed into me, burying her face into my chest. "I prayed you'd come. I knew you would."

Kissing her forehead, I tilted her head back from her chin. "Babe, where are your clothes?"

"In the bathroom."

"Then grab them and come on." I peeked out the peephole, which revealed no one in sight. "Let's go," I hissed louder. Footsteps could be heard above us.

"I'm trying to get my shoes on."

"Just carry them. We have to go, now!"

"Alright." She pushed out the door past me, wardrobe in hand.

Sprinting to the end of the hall, we were back at the stairwell. "Wait," she said. "What's our plan?"

"Down the stairs, out the exit door, straight over to the corner of the parking lot, and then as far as we can go," I said, putting my hand on the door handle.

"What about our bags?"

"Do we need them?"

"Maybe. I don't know."

Pushing the door open revealed us to be alone in the stairwell. At the first-floor door I cracked it open. The hallway looked empty. No one had seemed to react to the sound of the gunshot. "Go get the bags, I'll watch from here," I whispered.

Sami slipped through the doorway and into our room. Above me I heard the sound of doors opening several floors above us. Several agitated voices carried down the stairwell, people coming to check on the noise. Looking up the center of the stairs, I could see their hands on the railing, probably around the fifth floor, but coming fast. Pushing through the door, I was back in the hallway. Sami came out of our room, bags in hand, only to be bowled over by Nick. He had been sprinting down the hallway in our direction, on his way to investigate the disturbance above him. He didn't even see Sami before they collided. She went sprawling across the carpet.

"What are you doing?" His voice was filled with rage, looking at her on the ground as he steadied himself against the wall.

"We are *leaving!*" I said. Nick hadn't seen me before I spoke, his attention taken by Sami. His eyes darted to me and the gun I had leveled at him. He read the situation instantly, quicker than his partners had.

"What did you do?" he snarled, stepping towards me.

The gun jolted in my hand for the fourth time that day. Nick fell against the wall, sliding down it from the slickness of his own blood, his face still contorted in rage.

Sami burst past me on her way to the door, blowing it open on her escape to the outdoors. I realized as she passed that I was still holding the stairwell door open with half my body. The pursuers might have been originally heading for the second floor, but with the additional gunshot down here they would head straight for us. Since the door was already open, I stuck the gun through and fired several shots upwards. There was zero chance of hitting anyone, but the sound of the bullets ricocheting around the walls might slow them down. We needed every second to clear the parking lot.

I hit the exterior door at full speed, racing after Sami. Around the halfway mark I heard the cracks of rifle shots and the peppering of flying asphalt on my legs as the bullets bored in on me. I made it back to the hedges without being holed. Swinging my right arm out, I caught Don's belt from the branches as I passed. Sami was ahead of me. She hadn't slowed down, trusting me to follow. It took a minute, but I caught her before we reached the corner. I pulled one of the backpacks from her hands and onto my shoulder even as we ran. Our flight from the battle yesterday was laggardly in comparison. We sprinted until my legs felt like they were going to explode, my legs going numb from the heavy steps. Glancing behind us, we appeared completely alone. We had pushed through the retail area extended around the Express, the space now narrowing to country roads surrounded by small patches of forestry.

Pulling Sami's arm, I aimed us into the woods. Several feet in, we collapsed in a heap. Sami ended up on all fours, dry heaving in exhaustion. Rolling over, I found a spot behind a tree where I could keep watch on our trail while I struggled with my breathing. My throat was raw, and my entire chest felt like it was seizing in protest. We just stayed in that position for a long time.

CHAPTER NINE

GYM

The sun was low in the sky when I shook Sami awake. She had curled up next to me behind the tree once the convulsions had gotten out of her system. Without delay she had dozed off. "Babe, we need to go." I shook her arm gently, but the gentleness didn't help from her waking up with a start.

"What's going on?" she demanded, looking around wildly.

"Nothing, it's just getting dark and we need to find a spot for the night," I said, pulling the backpack fully over my shoulders. During the waiting period of my lookout position, I had figured out how to tighten Don's belt so that it fit snuggly around my waist. "Come on, it'll be dark soon." I urged her to her feet.

"Let me get my shoes on," she protested.

"Alright, I guess we can wait on that."

We both wobbled a bit once we were up, our legs unamused with their continued use. "Where are we going?" she asked as I led us deeper into the woods.

"There's that gym just around the corner here. The gym and bowling alley. Remember?"

"I guess so."

"I don't think a gym's a very likely place for anyone to be camping out in after all this time. I'm hoping it's empty."

"I vaguely remember you saying that the last time we were looking for a place to stay."

"Do you have any better suggestions?"

"No, we can try the gym, babe."

Stopping before we reached the edge of the woods, we took a careful survey of the area in front of us. It was a normal small commercial space. The low-slung gym building sported its franchise's purple branding, while next to it stood a taller building that was the bowling alley, a pizza restaurant attached to the far side of it. The parking lot was mostly empty. Three cars sat randomly through the space, which had been clearly junkers even before the shutdown, but had been picked over and stripped apart even more by now. Pulling my backpack off, I handed Sami my gun, choosing to move forward with Don's piece that came with a holster and extra magazines.

"I'll go down and check it out."

"You want me to just wait here?" She asked a little perturbed.

"Yes, you're covering me." I nodded to the gun in her hand. "If you see people coming, take a shot, or if I come running and it looks like I need some covering fire." I pulled a flashlight out of the backpack.

"Okay."

"It'll be quick. This place looks deserted already. There can't be much of use in any of these buildings. No reason for people to set up shop here to begin with."

"Alright. Good luck."

"Love you, honey."

"Love you too."

The glass front of the gym was broken completely, though that looked like the extent of the vandalism. Windows were meant to be smashed in times like these. The gym proved to be empty of people. The vending machines were emptied out, but the rest of the space seemed like it had been unspoiled by man for months. The bowling alley and the pizza place looked the same, except for the kitchen spaces that had been cleaned out of salvageable food items.

Sami joined me in the gym, taking a seat and starting to care for her feet. Using the disinfectant and paper towels that we dug out of the storage closet, she tried to get them cleaned up. Our fleet-footed escape had left them dirtied and scraped up, but only superficially damaged. I set to work setting a room up for us. Emptying out one of the back rooms, I was able to fit the lobby's couch, a bunch of yoga mats, and every other cushy thing I could find in the building into it. It made for a decently comfy room. Most importantly, under the front desk I discovered a full case of unopened water bottles. "Sami!"

"What?"

"Look what I found!" I held the case up.

"Jesus, don't scare me like that."

"Sorry."

"Now give me a couple of those."

We sat for a while, watching the sun fade away, drinking our newfound water. I had been worrying that we were on the verge of dehydration after our marathon today and no drinkable water in sight.

"So, you shot Don?" she asked casually.

"Yep, once in the chest and once in the face."

"What was he doing?"

"He took me to some kind of prison and wanted me to execute a guy to prove myself. When I wouldn't, he was going to kill me instead, and he started telling me about what was going on with you at the hotel. So I shot him and ran back."

"Just in time."

"I'm sorry." I squeezed her hand.

"It's not your fault."

"I took us there. Decided to stay even when it started getting weird."

"You had no idea. I wanted to stay too. All that matters is we made it out safe and alive."

"And now we own a gym," I answered.

"And now we own a gym."

* * *

We slept fairly well that night in our slumber party manner, not as comfy as the hotel bed of the past few nights, but with less insane rapist murderers around. We both awakened to the sound of vehicles approaching. Watching through the broken windows, we saw it was the Dirts' bus procession heading out into the town.

"The camp must be over that way, then," Sami said, nodding down the road from where they came.

"I didn't think there was much over that way, but maybe there is now."

"We should check it out, so we know how close we are to other people."

"That's a good idea. I'll go take a look that way."

"I'm coming too."

"Are you sure? You should stay off your feet, not go hiking through the woods," I countered.

"Well, I'm not leaving your side, so I guess I'm going with you."

We repacked our bags a bit, designating a single backpack for this trip, stocking it with just a bit of food, water and a flashlight. I also reloaded the magazine on the first gun completely, emptying some of the bullets out of the spare mags for Don's gun. The first gun got handed over to Sami as her own. Moving into the woods, we stayed within sight of the road, but far enough into the trees that we were well hidden. Though that path did slow us down as we picked our way through the brush.

"Damnit, damnit, damnit!" Sami swore from behind me.

"Another spider web?"

"It's in my eyes." She leaned against a tree while trying to wipe the strands from her face.

I grabbed a stick from the ground. "Here, use this. Flick it ahead of you to knock them away before you walk into them."

"Maybe I'll just stay directly behind you." She took the stick from me.

"Whatever makes you feel safe from the spiders, dear."

The woods thinned out into a couple of large fields. We skirted the edge, staying in sight of the road.

"Kyle."

"Yes, honey?"

"Why are you still wearing your Bracelet?" She pointed to the thing on my wrist.

"I don't know."

"It hasn't been charged in months."

"I like the look of it."

"Oh really? Is it fashionable to wear dead 'Lets on your wrist in this post-apocalyptic world we live in?" She rolled her eyes as she was prone to do.

"I don't know what the other homeless gym owners are wearing, but I like mine."

"Alright."

"Besides, it looks like R2-D2." I was referring to the retro-looking blue and white case and band I had purchased for it.

"Hoping it'll be useful in case we get stuck in a trash compactor on the Death Star?"

I smiled at her surprisingly correct Star Wars reference. "You never know. He always saved the day in the movies."

"Ugh, how much farther do you think this camp is?" she groaned as we approached the end of our current field. The horizon was blocked by a slight ridge running in front of us.

"Let's get to that and take a look. If it's far out, it won't really be a problem for us at the gym."

"True."

At the top of the ridge, we both dropped to the ground. The other side revealed the camp. It was still a couple hundred yards ahead of us, but we were close enough to be seen. In the fields ahead of us was what looked like a high-school complex. You could see the football bleachers on the far side. The area surrounding the school was covered in military-style tents, long rows of them covering the entire parking lot. It looked like a refugee camp after a natural disaster, which we were sort of in the middle of at the moment, just a really slowly developing version of one.

"They were in the middle of building this school before things shut down," Sami said as we laid in the grass.

"That's why I didn't know it was here. I thought it was just fields over this way."

We watched the people moving around the camp. They were all wearing brown clothes, some looking like uniforms and some just a brownish blob.

"Doesn't look like much is happening," Sami said.

"Yeah, looks like they're just hanging out. Over there it looks like some kind of meeting or something." On the far left side where it was mostly grassless dirt, there were several groups sitting in circles.

"Probably a drum circle."

"Or hacky sack strategy session."

"Either way, it doesn't look very threatening. I don't see any guards."

"Yeah, I don't see any guns either."

"They probably wouldn't let us bring these in, then." She nodded to the guns we had.

"True. Probably best to leave them somewhere if we're going up to it."

We looked for a few more minutes before we were satisfied we'd seen everything. It was pretty straightforward from the outside, just a refugee camp for the displaced. Even though there wasn't anything outright threatening, we jogged back across the fields, only slowing down when we were back in the tree line.

"Let's have a snack before we get going again," Sami said. "I don't want to battle the spider lords on an empty stomach."

"You wouldn't stand a chance in the Forbidden Forest. You would've been sobbing with Neville at the sight of all those big spiders."

"I don't have a problem with spiders, just their damn webs."

We stumbled back into the gym around midday, tired, sweaty and hungry. "You said the bowling alley and pizza place were completely cleaned out already?" Sami asked as we took our seats in the lobby of the gym.

"They looked that way. At least everything noticeable had been grabbed."

"But it couldn't hurt to check a bit deeper, could it?" The hunger was catching up with us again. We hadn't eaten an actual meal since breakfast the day before. Since then it had been a lot of exertion with just water and candy bars to sustain us.

"We might as well be sure," I answered, standing up.

"Let's wait a few minutes." She put her hand on my arm. "It's hot out there."

We started with the pizza restaurant. It turned up nothing. The entire kitchen had been cleaned out and all of the nooks and crannies had been scoured. In the bowling alley we started quickly with better luck. A bag of tortilla chips had been left sitting on top of a shelf. We split up; Sami searched the rooms and I went behind the lanes. Partly I just wanted to see what it looked like back there, and I also thought it might be a good spot for an employee to stash some snacks for a long shift. My hunch played out correctly—two bags of chips, a bag of Skittles, and a stick of beef jerky.

"Kyle!" Sami's voice echoed through the machinery.

"What?" I shouted back.

"I fo…me…it…" Her voice dipped in and out over the distance.

"I can't hear what you're saying!" I shouted in her direction. I continued my search through the back of the bowling lanes, but there wasn't anything else that caught my eye by the time I reached the far end, exiting out that side.

"I said I found something!" Sami was standing in front of a doorway, screaming in the direction I had left.

"Okay, I'm here," I answered, much closer than she expected.

"Why didn't you answer?"

"What did you find?" I demanded, joining her at the open door. In the darkened room, I could make out the long row of cabinets against the opposing wall. The drawers were all pulled open. The flashlight revealed the first one to be filled with about six bags of pretzels, the next bags of potato chips, then a couple boxes of microwave popcorn and several packages of Oreos. Sami shined her flashlight into the final drawer. It had four twelve-packs of soda, two Coke and two Sprite.

"Oh my," I exclaimed. I hadn't seen a can of Coke in far too long.

"They're both completely full," she said, taunting me.

"Looks like we're getting Coked up good tonight," I said, pulling one of the shiny red cans to admire it.

It took two trips to haul the loot back to our new bedroom. We were even diligent enough to search the rest of the building carefully, but there was nothing else to find. Settling into our chairs, we portioned out a meal for each of us. The joy of finding something substantial overrode the knowledge that even at its best, it was still just junk food. Pretzels and Coke wouldn't keep us in good health for very long, even if it did ease the pain.

"I think we should keep looking after we eat," Sami said.

I paused, enjoying the first crisp taste of my favorite drink. "What I wouldn't give for some ice right now." Warm Coke was better than no Coke, but it was also heartbreaking, knowing how good it could be if only it was cold.

"If we're wishing for things, we could aim a little higher than ice cubes."

"Meh, that'd be enough for me."

"Anyways, I think we should go back out today."

"Where should we go?"

"Some of those buildings we passed before we got to the woods yesterday looked kinda undamaged. I think a saw a little medical clinic."

"I wasn't looking at the buildings we were running past."

"Well, I wasn't really looking either, but there were some that felt like they might've been overlooked."

"That's fine. We just have to be careful. We don't know whose turf we might be stepping on." I mulled her proposal over. We couldn't live forever on the two armfuls of food we found today, so venturing out and getting the feel for the land was bound to happen. That is, if we were planning on living here in our gym long-term.

"I thought you wanted to go to the camp."

Leaning back, she thought for a moment. "I don't know what to do, Kyle. I know we keep saying that, but it's not getting any clearer."

"Staying here, we're at least with people we trust, but I don't know how we're going to survive. Finding actual food seems pretty tough. Trying to grow our own will take longer than we've got, if it works at all. We can try hunting, but pistols aren't really hunting weapons, and I'm sure everyone else is out there looking for something big enough to eat as well. Then if we run into trouble or someone comes looking for trouble, the two of us aren't going to win many gunfights."

"So, you think we should go to the camp?" she asked, turning the question around.

"Like you said, I don't know. I know what we face out here, it's been catching up with us for awhile, and now we're sorta up against the wall. If we go to the camp, we're trusting other people, the government, to take care of us. It was the government that got this whole thing started. They let this happen. They authorized people to burn our house down. Not exactly inspiring work from them lately."

"So, what are we going to do?"

"Can I finish my Coke?"

"Sure."

We ate in silence for a while, munching pretzels and sipping our bubble beverage.

"Do you want to talk about what happened yesterday?" She broke the quiet.

"Which part?"

"All of it. You didn't say much after the sledgehammer thing, but it was there in your eyes. Then you had to do it three more times, face to face, people whose names you knew." Her voice was soft and caring.

"You almost got raped yesterday. Do you want to talk about that?"

"There isn't much to say about it. I was terrified, angry, confused and worried about you."

"Worried about *me*?"

"Yes. When I realized what I was in for, all I could think about was what they were going to do to you. If you'd ever come back. I knew I'd survive, but what if you didn't?"

"I almost didn't. It was close. But you said I needed to take the gun. I had it with me when I needed it, because of you." I stared at the floor. "I just keep thinking about how things could have gone differently so easily. Just one decision made differently, one step in a different place, and I could be in that hole. I've always thought about things that way. What if that one tiny detail was different? How would things have changed? If the outfielder was one step to his left, would he have caught the ball? The amount of things that worked out to get us to right here, right now is staggering. It scares me how easily we could both be dead right now, or even worse. Will we keep being this lucky? Will our foot be in the right place next time?"

"Normally you'd say that worrying about stuff like that is a waste of time," Sami answered. She was right. A lesson I'd learned over the past few years was that most things are out of my personal control, and worrying about them didn't make a difference one way or another. It was best to just face the situations when they arrived instead of trying to weave through the traffic of life, only to end up at the same stoplight as everyone else.

"But this isn't normal anymore, is it?" Sami finished her trailing thought.

"No, it isn't. We have to worry about things like that. It's been keeping us alive so far. A constant assessment of our decisions, past, present and future. This time we were only a half-step ahead of fate, so maybe next time we'll have a full step on it. Don didn't think for a minute that he wasn't in complete control of the situation. That got him killed. Almost got him killed the day before too. Jasper and Nick just assumed they were better than us, and the same thing happened to them. Even if they were right, they weren't right enough."

"So," she posed the question again, "what's the right enough thing to do now?"

"That I don't know."

"We can stay here, try for my Dad's, or go to the camp."

"Yeah, I agree, I think those are the only options."

"What do you think we should do?"

"I'm deferring to your judgment. My past few choices haven't led us to the promised land. Maybe yours will."

"I'm leaning towards the camp," she answered. "But you know that."

"I do, and I can't say I'm enthused about the idea, but there isn't a better option as far as I know."

"Okay, let's try it, then," she said firmly.

"Alright. Now or in the morning?"

"The morning. We can handle a few more hours on our own, I think."

"Do you still want to go out picking at your virgin buildings?"

"Seems pointless if we're going to abandon it all tomorrow."

"Alright. I guess this is our cheat day."

CHAPTER TEN
CAMP

The noise from the buses woke me up for a moment, but I rolled over and went back to sleep. Ain't nobody got time for that. It was mid-morning by the time we got up and moving around. Apprehension could be felt in the air as we went about our final tasks. Trusting other people hadn't been a good bet recently, and going to a government camp might be like walking into the dragon's lair. Or it could be boring, simple and the best thing we could do—stop listening to the crazy people we were meeting hiding in abandoned buildings, and get our life reorganized.

Either way, we prepared the best we could. The guns, our bags, and all the food got hidden away. I found the attic access in the pizza restaurant, and we bundled our stuff into some trash bags and started burying them in the insulation. "You should put your 'Let in there," Sami said as we started on the last bag.

"You think so?"

"I can't imagine they're big on electronics in there."

"Fine." I slipped it off, revealing the white band of skin on my wrist where it had lived. Into the trash bag it went and we covered it up, leaving all of our worldly possessions there.

"What about our shoes?" Sami asked as I slid the door

back into place.

"What about our shoes?"

"Should we leave them here, too? What if they want to take them away?"

"You want to walk all the way there barefoot?"

"I've gone farther without shoes," she answered, having been waiting for me to walk into it. "But there's a bunch of bowling shoes next door. We can wear those to the camp. Keep these ones safe in case we need them later."

"Alright, go grab us some." I pushed the door to the attic open again.

Once our shoes were safely buried and our bowling shoes laced up, we were on our way, with just a candy bar each to fuel our march. This time we walked on the road itself instead of through the woods. "These shoes are a pain to walk in," I said. The flatness and slick nature weren't made for walking outside.

"I think this is the longest I've seen you wearing bowling shoes without trying to moonwalk in them."

"They don't work so well out here. If we go back to the alley I could show you a thing or two." I tried to slide my feet, but they just ground on the asphalt.

"That's alright, I've seen enough before."

It was around a three-mile walk on the road to get to the camp. We paused when we reached the slight ridge we had hidden behind during our recon yesterday. Sami nodded me on and we moved forward to the camp gate. It was manned by two bored-looking men dressed in the baggy brown clothes everyone here seemed to be wearing. Up close they were revealed to be jumpsuits, like something a painter would wear except they were a burlap material with the "DERT" logo branded into it. "Hello," I greeted them. They'd been watching us for a while as we approached, but didn't seem to be interested enough to respond to me. "Uh, yeah, we're looking for a place to stay. Is this the right place?"

"Yep," the one on the left grunted. He was older than us and bearded, giving off the look of a businessman. Perhaps in the previous world he was, but now he looked like a businessman on the verge of suicide, or at least an alcohol-related death. The other guy didn't look much different, just older still.

"Do we need to check in or something?" I asked. It didn't look like a seat-yourself kinda establishment.

"Go to the school," the guy on the right said, jerking his thumb over his shoulder.

"Thank you," Sami answered as we passed through the open gate and indifferent guards. We followed the road forward as we entered the tented area. The road seemed to be the main avenue for traffic, all on foot of course. The tents were arranged just off the road with paths leading between them to the rows that were set deeper. Once we turned off the road and into the parking lot of the school, the scene changed a bit. These tents seemed to be for specific purposes. Most everyone who was dressed in the brown jumpsuits kept their eyes down, avoiding the sight of us and the gaze of the others; though there was a different class of people as well, wearing button-up brown shirts and slacks. Their hair was combed and generally cleaned up well. They looked us in the eyes as we passed, taking measure of the newcomers.

"I've got a bad feeling about this," I whispered once we reached the school building's steps and were temporarily out of earshot of anyone.

"Should we leave?" Sami queried, scanning the area behind us.

"You must be new!" the chipper voice came from inside the open school doors. It belonged to a younger woman, probably still in her teens actually. She was wearing the button-up uniform, her hair pulled back tight, her big blue eyes taking us in.

"Uh, yeah, we just wandered in, I guess," I answered.

"Well, welcome!" She threw her arms around me first than Sami. "My name is Kelly and I'm kind of the greeter here at Camp Meadow. So welcome! We're so happy to have you here with us."

"Thank you."

"Are you ready to commit to helping your fellow creatures and most importantly Gaia?" Her eyes were still noticeably big, taking us all in, her voice so earnestly innocent.

"Yeah…" Sami answered, looking at me as she said it.

"That's great. We're just so happy to have you here." She

put herself between us and, grasping both of our hands, led us forward into the school. "What's your name?" She looked at me.

"I'm Kyle."

"And I'm Sami."

"And you're married?" she asked, still smiling at both of us.

"Yes, we are."

"That's awesome. How long?"

"About five years now," Sami answered as we turned into a classroom. It was still arranged as if school was happening today. The teacher's desk sat at the head of class with two chairs pulled up to it.

"If you would take a seat here, I'll start the processing," Kelly said happily, taking the seat behind the desk and reaching for the laptop sitting on it.

"Oh wow, a computer. Haven't seen one of those in a while," I said, somewhat jokingly but also somewhat sincerely. Most computers, even lightweight laptops designed for traveling, proved to be useless without constant access to electricity.

"Computers help us organize our efforts here to minimize our impact on the planet. It would be irresponsible not to use everything in our power to better Gaia," Kelly shot back stiffly, her smile cracking a bit.

"Of course, of course. I just haven't seen one powered up in a while." I took my seat.

"Can I assume your full name is Samantha?" She turned to Sami.

"You can." Sami gave me a look once Kelly turned her eyes to the computer. *Don't antagonize the new hosts*, I was ordered.

Kelly muttered to herself as she typed and clicked her way through the computer for a few minutes. I surveyed the room as we waited. The walls of the room were completely bare, stripped of the educational material you would expect to see in a school building. The only feature besides the desk and chairs was a large projection screen hanging behind Kelly's desk, the projector still hung from the ceiling in the middle of the classroom. "Okay, I think I got you set up," she finally said, her eyes flicking up to us.

"Kyle and Samantha Harrison, that's you, yes?"

Sami shifted in her seat, as my back straightened. "Yes, that's us," I answered.

"Very good. So I see you were displaced a few days ago because of several rather serious violations of the new regulations. Is that also correct?" Neither of us answered. "That's okay, I understand it's hard to talk about, especially it being so recent. I'm sure it was very traumatic for both of you."

"It was unexpected," Sami answered finally.

"Yes, well, here at Camp Meadow, we aim to help people like you understand what you did wrong, and how to atone for it here in a safe learning environment. We have many people like you who are here. They committed crimes, violated Gaia's trust, and have had trouble adapting to our evolved understanding of our purpose on this planet. This is a place to learn, about yourselves and about our glorious planet."

"Alright," I answered. This situation was not looking promising.

"Okay, so you've been assigned to tent group ten. But before we go any farther, we have a video we like new members to watch, so they can get an idea of what to expect while they're here." Pulling a remote out of a drawer, she clicked the projector on, and the screen filled with images. "I'm going to step out and finish the rest of the processing while you watch this. Have fun!" She left us alone with the projector.

It was a simple welcome video, like ones at amusement parks about keeping your arms and legs inside the vehicle at all times. Starting out it had a map of the camp, then a walkthrough of daily activities. There were work parties; they were the ones we saw riding the busses every day. Talking circles, meditation and yoga sessions, and harvesting. The smiling people in the video seemed to be enjoying themselves, goaded on by the good-looking young man who was our tour guide throughout the video.

The video ended, the screen going black, leaving Sami and I alone in the room. "What do you think?" Sami whispered.

"I'm not sure. It seems a bit off. None of the people we saw out there look as happy as the people in the video."

"That's true..." But before she could finish her thought,

the door opened and Kelly returned, carrying a bundle of the brown burlap jumpsuits. She was followed by the young man who had been in the video. He was young, in his early twenties, and also wearing the button-up uniform.

"Kyle, Sami, this is Rian. He's the leader of tent group ten, so he'll be looking after you from now on."

"Hello. Nice to meet you, Rian." I held my hand out.

"You too, Kyle and Sami!" He shook our hands enthusiastically. "I can't wait to get started. I think we're going to have some real fun."

"Hope so," I answered.

"Alright, grab your uniforms and follow me," he said, still smiling broadly.

"It was great meeting you two. I'll see you around, I'm sure," Kelly said, holding out our new clothes. The burlap felt even rougher to the touch than it looked.

"Thank you," we both said, following Rian down the hallway.

Rian led us into another room. This one was devoid of chairs. Instead it contained just large plastic containers, each with a sign above, indicating what went inside: shoes, shirts, watches and so on. "Time to strip away the old life. Please put everything into the proper bins," Rian guided from behind us.

Our new bowling shoes came off easily. They hadn't enjoyed the walk through the outdoors. Stripping down to our underwear, we were at least allowed the dignity of keeping those, since our provided clothes seemed to only consist of the jumpsuit.

"Don't forget your rings," his voice sounded from behind us.

"Our wedding rings?" Sami demanded.

"Yep. Everything must go."

"These are our wedding rings. They mean something to us."

"And the preservation of the Gaia means something to me," Rian snapped. "Do you have any idea how destructive to the world those rings are? The mining operations alone nearly ruined this planet, just so you can have something pretty on your finger.

Put them in the bin." His voice sharpened.

"Okay," I answered meekly, slipping the band off my finger. Sami did the same, hiding her fury. They clinked as they landed in the bin, joining the other discarded rings.

"Now put on your uniforms," he ordered. The jumpsuit did not like me, judging from its resistance to me getting into it, and I didn't like it by any measure back. Instead of zippers or buttons, the front was held together with pieces of string, so you had to lace yourself up into it. Sami and I eyed each other once we were fully ensconced inside them. It wasn't flattering.

"This way." He ordered us out of the room again and farther down the hallway. At the end there were two open doors. "You, in there." He pointed at me and the first door. "And you in there." He pointed Sami at the other one.

"What is this?" I asked. The last time we'd been split up hadn't gone very well.

"This is your time to write out your confessions, admitting your past mistakes. It's a very personal experience, best done alone."

"It's okay. I'm just in the other room," Sami said, stepping into her doorway.

"Fine." I walked through mine. The room was bare except for a table and chair in the middle of the room. It had a manila folder, a pencil and a lamp sitting on it. Rian followed me in, closing the door behind him and flipping the folder open. There were several blank pieces of paper in it and one official looking one. He picked that one up, starting to read. "Violation one, storing and maintaining a fossil fuel motor vehicle with the intent to drive. Violation two, unnatural collection of precipitation. Violation three, illegal cultivation of the earth. Violation four, failure to submit to an inspection. Violation five, failure to provide a sustainability plan. Violation six, disregard of the natural order of the earth. Violation seven, intentional disregard of the climate safety of the area. Violation eight, neighborhood endangerment." He read slowly, emphasizing each violation as if he was a TV courtroom judge. "These are the charges brought against you by Arborist Rachel MacMillan, operating under the authority granted the Department of Environmental Reclamation and Trust by the Fair Weather Act and President Rodriguez's emergency decree of July 4th 2029. You've already been convicted of these crimes, so there's no use arguing with me about them."

"And sentenced, I believe," I shot back from my seat.

"Some have paid a much dearer price than their house for crimes like these," he sneered. "You are to use these pages as a confessional." He jabbed his forefinger onto the blank pages. "An admission of guilt, a clearing of your conscience, so you can start off your rehabilitation honestly." Picking up the pencil, he handed it to me. "I'll be back later to check on your progress."

I read before that children have a very hard time admitting guilt, because their undeveloped minds can't process the conflicting ideas that they did something bad but are not a bad person. As your brain matures, you learn to handle the competing notions—I did something wrong, but I'm still a good person who will do better. Of course, that's much easier said than done, even for the most aged minds. Admitting fault is a hard pill to swallow no matter your age, but some of us can do it. Admitting you've sinned by standards you don't recognize, that you view as unfair, arbitrary and misguided, is an entirely different concept. I've never read anything that could prepare me for such an experience that I found myself facing, staring at the blank page next to a sheet with my picture, my information, and a long list of my infractions. A rap sheet fabricated after the punishment had been doled out. I don't know what stage of development my brain's currently in, but it was not prepared for this exercise.

After a good long staredown with the paper, I started writing. It's in my nature to withdraw when I'm angry, so attempting to write an explanation to the charges leveled against me resulted in very short statements. I basically repeated the text of the charge and added a couple "I"s to the sentences. The briefness of my writing didn't mean it was a quick process, though, each charge bouncing around my head like popcorn being cooked.

How long it took, I can't say; my internal clock was frozen. Still, it was at least an hour after I finished my homework before Rian returned to check on my work. "How's it going in here?" he spoke as he came through the doorway, his smile having returned instead of the sneer he'd worn previously.

"Fine." I watched him as he took a seat.

"May I?" He reached for my confessional page.

"Sure."

He read it slowly, shaking his head as he finished, placing it on the far side of the table. "That wasn't very good, Kyle."

"Sorry, I've never wrote a confession before."

"Your wife's doing a wonderful job in the other room. She's very open and thoughtful about the world around her and why she needs to do better."

"That's why I married her," I answered sharply.

"No doubt, but that begs the question, why would she marry someone like you? Or remain with someone like you? A unreformed Polluter like you, using the world like a cheap prostitute. Apparently you were a car salesmen, the smiling arms dealer in the war against Gaia, against humanity. Profiting from destruction and selling other people's souls so you could tool around in your fancy weapon of death. You've never cared about anything before in your life, not the people around you nor the ground on which you walk. What kind of woman loves a man like that?"

"I care about my wife!"

"Then maybe you should try writing another confession, a better one. Show people that Sami wasn't so misguided when she married you." He slid a fresh piece of paper towards me. "Be better." He left the room again.

This draft took even longer to compose, partly because of the amount of time I spent staring at the empty seat once Rian had left. This version was formed slowly, but with more tact. I never enjoyed telling people what they wanted to hear. It's part of my philosophy that if someone wants to hear me say something specific, I shouldn't say it. Some might call it spiteful, but I view it as a healthy dose of self-care medicine. People who fish for compliments are weak-minded. People who want you to agree with them about everything are weak-minded and also insecure, begging for someone else to affirm their self-worth or validate their opinions. These Gaia nuts were no different when they started making themselves known. Touting their good works, expecting all to honor them as heroes for planting some trees or riding a bicycle. Trying to get me to agree with their beliefs because they needed others' approval for their thoughts. I'm sure they'd be laughing now if they could see me, hunched over a table scribbling away about how I had violated the planet, telling a Dirt what he wanted to hear and seeking his forgiveness.

This time I filled in the page, front and back, with an explanation of my crimes. Another full hour passed once I put the pencil down before Rian returned to the room. He didn't speak this time as he entered, just taking his seat and reading over my statement. "This is better. Not as good as your wife's, but you're getting better."

"Doing my best."

"Are you?"

"Yes."

"It seems like you're just trying to say what you think I want to hear, not how you really feel." I didn't answer. "That's okay, I know how you really feel. But that's why we're here, to work on that." He smiled as he stood up. "It's getting late. We'll work on this later." He nodded to the confessional.

"Okay."

Leading me out of the room, he opened the door to Sami's room and beckoned her out. "I'll take you two to tent ten. It's already past dark so it's time to be resting. Everyone else is already there." Sami nodded as she joined us in the hallway. She was looking a bit worn-down. Perhaps she hadn't handled the revelation of her sins as easily as Rian had suggested.

Outside, night had fallen and the camp was practically lifeless, no people moving about or lights guiding our way. Rian led us through a maze of tents before we finally reached the one marked "TEN" above the flap. He held the flap open for us. "Have a good night." Only darkness loomed ahead through the hole.

"Are there other people in there?" Sami whispered, in keeping with the stillness of the surroundings.

"Of course."

"Where are we supposed to sleep in there? Is there a bunk for us or something?"

"A bunk? Why would you want to be disconnected from the earth like that?" he questioned, enjoying our hesitance.

"So, on the ground, then?" I asked this time.

"Just as nature intended and provided."

"Did she provide the tent too?" Sami said dryly.

"Go inside." He had obviously tired of our questions.

Stepping past him, I led us into the darkness, two steps in, just enough for Sami to fit in behind me before Rian dropped the flap. It was truly dark now. We bumped into a few bodies on the floor. They stirred and mumbled at our intrusion as we reached the wall of the tent. Squatting down, we stretched out into enough space for us to lay down. The floor of the tent was a mix of grass and dirt. The grass probably didn't have much time left before it was completely worn away.

"At least it's warm," Sami whispered in my ear as we snuggled up.

"Yeah, lucky us," I answered, pushing my arm out to serve as a pillow.

* * *

"What are you still doing asleep!" The woman's voice jolted us both awake. I sat up suddenly. The surprise masked the pain I felt once I came to. My whole body ached from the uneven ground I had been laying on. A blond woman, mid-forties, stood over the both of us. She was wearing the same jumpsuit we were. "The sun has risen so that we might honor it. Yet you lie here disrespecting the natural order of life."

"Sorry, sorry. We didn't know when to get up," I mumbled, trying to get onto my feet. Sami hadn't spoken, but was struggling as much as I was with moving around.

"Let's go. I'm not going to let you drag down this tent's standing with your Polluter mentality," The woman screeched as Sami climbed to her feet. Following the woman outside, the sun was up, barely, little more than a half-circle on the horizon, burning through the early morning mist. She led us to the area outside of the tents where we had seen people sitting around in circles during our scouting trip. The area was full of people, probably the entire camp kneeling in the grass. They were arranged in groups, each one focused on its own leader.

The woman led us to the group with Rian in the center. He watched us approach with a slight smirk on his face. He didn't appear to have spent the night at one with nature in the dirt. "Now that we've all arrived, we can begin," he said. There was about fifty of us kneeling around him. He continued to speak, this time in a sing-song type of voice, as if singing a nursery rhyme. The rest of the group repeated after him as they worshiped, bowing forward to kiss the earth and praise the sky, a yoga session for people who took yoga way too serious. Sami and I tried to join in the best we could, like joining an exercise class already in progress.

After a few minutes of the activity, Rian called a stop. "Today's going to be a beautiful day. What do we call days like this?" he asked the question broadly to the group. Several hands shot up immediately. "Cassidy?" He pointed to a teenager near the front.

"Alyssa says days like today are grace days, because we don't deserve them, yet Gaia provides them anyways." The words tumbled out of her mouth, in memorized sureness.

"That's correct." Rian bent down and picked up a sack. Reaching into it, he produced a large carrot and handed it to Cassidy as a reward. "What else does *The Little Brown Book* say about days like this?" All the same hands shot up again. This time Rian picked a man to our left who hadn't raised his hand. "Victor?"

"Uh, it says that in the future, if Gaia forgives us, all days will be like this. No more storms, just peace."

"Very good, Victor," Rian encouraged, presenting him with a banana. He aimed back at the whole group. "Do we deserve such a thing?"

This time the group answered in unison, "No."

"Karen, do you deserve a world of only sunny days?" He directed this question at the woman who had roused us from the tent. She had taken a place a bit in front of us.

Before she answered, her body began to shake with terrific

sobs. "No, no I don't," she wailed.

Stepping between the bodies carefully, Rian approached her still-heaving body. "Why not?" he asked, standing in front of her now.

"Because. Because I'm a Polluter!" she cried out.

Pulling her head towards his leg, he patted it gently where it rested. "Yes. It's true, even the most dedicated among us have weakness inside us. We've all given offense to our dear Gaia." The group murmured its assent. "But we're trying to fix that, aren't we, Karen?" She nodded, the tears still streaming down her face. "We're doing our best, holding ourselves accountable, holding each other accountable, and sacrificing for our common home." He slipped an apple into Karen's hands.

"Yes, yes," the crowd agreed.

"Now, we have some newcomers here with us today." He pointed at us. "This is Kyle and Sami. They joined us yesterday. What are they?" He shouted the final words.

"Polluters!" the group chanted back.

"That's right, they are. But we're going to change that, aren't we?" He was standing in front of us now. "Do they deserve this beautiful day? This promise of a future free from fear?"

"NO!"

"Do they deserve this food that Gaia provided us?" He held up a cucumber for everyone to see.

"NO!"

"No, they don't! But remember what Alyssa says. These are grace days. We don't deserve them, but we get them anyways because Gaia is…"

"Gracious!" the group finished his sentence.

Holding the cucumber out to Sami, she took it. "Thank you," she said.

Rian looked at me and smiled before returning to the center of the circle. "Kyle and Sami are working on their confessions. They're having some trouble, but we'll help them see the path to the truth, won't we?" The group didn't chant this time, just muttered, their eyes glaring holes through us as they did. He continued, "Today we show our appreciation for Gaia through reclamation." The group clapped at this pronouncement, though it sounded slightly forced compared to some of the earlier enthusiasm. "Go forth and be better!"

That was the closing statement apparently, since everyone rose to their feet, moving back towards where we'd come from. "I guess we're following them," Sami whispered, clutching her cucumber tightly. Our group wound its way through the tents, ending up standing by the brown busses we'd seen so often. Everyone filed through the open doors. The driver was already waiting with the engine running. Sami and I ended up near the front of the bus, the seats having been taken farther back. "Should we eat this now?" she whispered again.

I shook my head in disagreement. I hadn't witnessed even a single positive vibe from our new friends, and the majority of them hadn't received any gifts of food at the morning meeting. Though they might've had food somewhere else, it made me feel like we were getting marked even more brightly as targets than our newness already had. Gnawing down on a juicy cucumber in front of everyone might be too provocative an action on our first day. "Put it in your pocket."

We idled in the bus for a while as the other groups filled it up. The ride was a bumpy twenty minutes. Even though it'd been a couple of months since either of us had ridden in a vehicle, it felt familiar. At the end of the drive, we tumbled out of the bus. We had pulled into the parking lot of a BP gas station. The other busses that had been in formation with us had splintered off. Each one parked in a different area around this intersection that featured several gas stations and other buildings. However, the scene was dominated by the mountain of rubble situated in the center of the intersection. It consisted of chunks of concrete, twisted rebar, and every other kind of construction material you could conceive, all piled up. Once off the bus, the source of the refuse was obvious—large areas of the gas station's concrete pad had been ripped up. The evidence of the destruction was evident all around, buildings partially torn apart and bare dirt basking in the sunlight after years spent confined under its concrete blanket.

Karen thrust a sledgehammer into my hands. It was different than the one I had used back at the Express, but the weight in my hands was familiar and disconcerting. She shoved a bucket into Sami's hands. "We're working over there today." She pointed to the rear corner of the lot. It looked like a dumpster used to live there. "Break the concrete up and carry it to the pile. Get to it." The rest of the group was already collecting their tools and moving towards it.

We followed, though slower than the rest. Our bare feet were touchy about walking around in the outdoors without shoes. Sami had made a run like that two days ago, but the terror had numbed the pain. Now there wasn't much terror, just annoyance, and annoyance doesn't help with pain. Since the parking lot was under construction, or rather deconstruction, it was littered with pebbles and other fragments, very unkind to bare feet. However, the rest of the group pushed forward without minding the pain, their feet apparently hardened into some kind of hobbit hoof.

Soon the air was filled with the sounds of metal on concrete. Our group was kicking up quite a racket, and the noise from the nearby groups joined in to disturb the natural silence that had laid over most of the land since the disappearance of a central electrical grid. I put my hammer to work. It wasn't easy. Concrete is naturally hard, hence the reason it's used so often. It took more concentrated blows to begin the cracking than it did when I was using it to burst through doors the other day. A system formed as we worked, the rest of the group having already refined the tactics. The hammer men busted through the slab, then people moved in with prybars or pickaxes, working the pieces apart and out of the dirt. Sami and the other girls or older men then collected the pieces, moving them to the ever-growing mountain of rubble.

Around noon, some food was brought out of the bus and we ate while sitting in the shade of the overhang around the pumps. The food was just some stale bread and a watery soup. It tasted like corn, but we were already used to that. Work continued for several hours after the meal. Karen's instructions at the start of the shift were the most words I heard spoken all day. Everyone kept their eyes down and focused on the work or making it through the day. Nothing about it was easy. The sun beat down on us and my hands blistered from the tool. The grime stuck to our bodies, which were coated in sweat. When the busses started back up in the late afternoon, I could barely walk. My feet were bloodied from several missteps. Sami looked slightly better, even though she walked with the stiffness of someone whose back had seized up. The tools were piled up around the building and the convoy started back to the camp.

Back in the parking lot of the school, we all filed out, Sami and I in the middle of the group, Rian standing astride our path, looking as fresh as ever. "Kyle and Sami, did you have a good first day?" The rest of the people around us pressed on.

"It was hard work," Sami said.

"But repairing the damage we've done to the world is worth the effort," he said matter-of-factly. "Now come with me."

We fell in behind him as he led us back to the school building. My legs were set in motion, even as my mind slipped away in a haze of exhaustion. Thoughts of a decent meal or at the very least being able to lay down and sleep all the rest of the day away had been what had kept me going for the last couple of hours, but our route had taken us back inside and straight to the confessional rooms.

Instead of sending us to separate rooms, he led us both in the room I had been in. Two chairs waited for us with our confessional pages laid out in front of them. We took our seats without instruction. Rian stayed standing in front of us. "We've been looking over your confessions. It's hard to believe what a perfect life you two led." It sounded sorta like a compliment, but more like an accusation.

"Uh, okay," I answered.

"Really, these are the only crimes against the environment you ever committed? You never did anything else wrong, in your entire lives?"

"These are the things you said we did, so we wrote about them. What else do you want?" I jabbed my finger against the papers.

"I think you misunderstand what your crimes are," he said slowly. "You think you made a couple of mistakes and got punished over them. What actually happened is that you've led sinful lives, abusive lives, taking from this planet with no qualms or regrets. It finally caught up with you last week and the only way forward is to bare your soul, atone for the damage you've done, and admit all of your failures."

"So you want a confession for our entire lives?" Sami asked.

"Isn't that what you should want too? Isn't that what's screaming in our lives to be set free? Wouldn't you be so much happier being free from all that guilt?" He was pacing in front of us, working up a pitch like a Southern pastor on Sunday.

"Perhaps," Sami answered again. I didn't know what to say, once again. By the ridiculous standards that were now in force, we had led a crime-ridden life. Driving cars since we were sixteen, running the AC, throwing food away. We even flew on airplanes multiple times without ever thinking about the damage it was doing to the world around us. Just looking at an airplane these days would probably get you shot on the spot, though I'm not up to date on current FAA regulations. Admitting to all of this would fill a book for each of us. Even worse, considering how seriously they had taken the fact that I had a car parked in the shed behind my house, I wasn't about to announce that I had once flown to Korea when I was a teenager.

"Perhaps?" Rian's voice raised, his face beginning to shade red. "Perhaps you contributed to murdering the planet? No big deal, it just slipped your mind, just an everyday kinda thing, right?" Neither of us answered again. The answer to me was obvious, but also unmentionable. "I'm starting to feel like you aren't actually committed to the cause. 'Come join the Dirts, get some free food and a place to sleep! They'll take care of us, even though we're felons!' Is that what you think? Are you just pretending to believe to take advantage of us, like you did to the planet? Because we're not as forgiving as Gaia, and our punishments are a lot harsher."

"No," Sami cut in. "We're sorry. We're here to make up for it. We just don't know how."

He considered his thoughts for a minute, looking at each of us. Sami was able to mask her opinions easier, fit in with people and make them comfortable. That wasn't something I could do very well, despite my job. At work I could pretend to get along with people well enough to sell them a car, even though I was really just acting, looking like I was having a good time listening to them ramble about whatever nonsense they wanted to talk about that day. I'd worked out a script of conversation topics, good comments or jokes. This worked since I only saw these people a couple of times in their entire lives, not long enough for them to see through the act. That ability isn't very useful in my current situation, though. I didn't know my lines and I was seeing too much of these people for them not to see through the act. Sitting there dumbly was about the best I could manage, trying to swallow the words I wanted to say.

"I want to hear you beg for forgiveness," Rian was continuing. "I want to see that you truly believe. I want you to devote yourselves to our cause."

"We *are* trying," I answered.

"I know." He laid his hand on my shoulder. "But you need to try harder."

"Alright. I will."

"Come on, let's go." He nodded his head to the door.

Outside the room was Kelly. She was holding two identical flimsy plastic binders. Our names were plastered in big Sharpie letters on the front of them. Handing them to us, we flipped them open. The first page was a copied version of our current confession, the rest of it filled with empty pages. "These are for you to work on in your tent. You can work on these in your free time and bare your soul. It's therapeutic for you to face your misdeeds honestly so we can all grow together."

"Okay, we will," I said, flipping it shut.

"Go on back to your tent. We'll meet every few days to look over the progress you're making with your work."

Once we were outside, we slowed our pace a bit. The pain of today's labor was taking its toll, and we weren't ready to see anyone else for a few minutes. "I hope this is some form of hazing and that things get better," Sami said softly as we wound our way through the tents.

"I thought there'd be more food," I said. My stomach had been cramping since our meager lunch.

"I still have that cucumber in my pocket. We can eat that

tonight too."

"I have a cucumber in my pocket too."

"I'm too tired to eat that one."

"Heard that before."

She squeezed my hand as we turned down the final approach to our tent. "It'll get better. They're just testing us at first. Let's write the confession like they want and we can fit into their gang."

"I hope you're right."

It was our first time in the tent during actual daylight. It was spartan to be generous, bare side walls and just the dead grass and dirt for a floor. Sitting around the edges of the tent was our apparent tentmates. They each seemed to have their own space marked out with a small bundle of possessions with them, mostly rags that could pass as bedding. There were six of them staring at us. Karen was the only one of them we had met, even though they'd all been with us all day on the bus and at the gas station. "Hi everyone." Sami put her friendly voice on.

Karen pointed to the space we had found open the night before. "That's your area. Respect it as you would your home, because it's what nature's given you."

"Okay, we will," I answered as we both sat down.

"Cassidy, you can start," Karen said, looking to the girl to her left, the one we had seen earn a carrot this morning. Now that she faced us across the tent, we got our first good look at the young girl, still a teenager. She was pretty, but also gave off the impression that she was no stranger to these types of settings. A person who gravitated to groups outside the mainstream even of the old world. Her face was peaceful, as was her speech, even if there was a specter of rage hiding behind it.

"With honor," she said, inclining her head to Karen before she turned to us. "You've brought this horror upon us. You've sinned against Gaia. You show no shame or humility. It disgusts me, and it disgusts the earth. If it were to open up and swallow us all down to our deaths just for sitting with you, it'd be justified. Your entire existence is a sin against nature." Her face had contorted with rage as she spoke, nearly trembling as she struggled to keep the words flowing.

"Very good," Karen praised. "Now Carter." She looked to the man next to Cassidy. Carter was a thin man, even in a world where no one had enough to eat, except for his head which was large and blocky. He was pushing middle-age, even if he carried himself like a twenty-year-old. It was hard for him to maintain the appearance of youth in these circumstances and the matching baggy sacks we were all wearing, but he tried his best.

"I remember my first time in front, having to hear about my issues from the group. It wasn't the funnest day. I put my mind to it, though, and got things turned around pretty. Just the other day I actually remembered a couple of times when I was a kid that we set a tire on fire just for fun. Can you believe that? Setting a tire on fire just for fun? What a problem I was. I did so much bad. It makes me sick to think of what those tires did to the air. I'm better now. I only set my guitar on fire." He paused his monologue, looking around the rest of group, hoping for some laughter.

"Carter," Karen cut in before he could start again. "We all know how good you are on the guitar. However, the exercise is about correcting Kyle and Sami."

"You're right, you're right. I was just trying to point out how even the worst of Polluters can make their way back like I did." He finally turned his attention to us. "You have to realize that everything you've been taught is wrong. The way you've lived your whole life is wrong. Or, it's not just wrong, it's a sin, a crime against the planet, against life itself. The sooner you admit that, the better off you'll be."

"Okay, how about Jenny? What do you have to say?" Karen cut Carter off again, directing the focus to the woman seated to our left. She was in her fifties and looked like she had spent most of her life as a housewife. Her face was too pinched to be considered pretty, large eyes and a dated hairstyle she must be going to great pains to maintain in the current situation.

"Yes, I think it's shameful how you lived your life." She spoke softly but earnestly, leaning into the words as she spoke. "I'm sure you drove big cars fast and recklessly, no worries about the future or the harm you were causing the people all around you. I've seen people like you my whole life, young and full of themselves, making messes for the rest of us to clean up. Shame on you!"

"Kyle was a car salesman," Karen said. The entire group recoiled in horror. Jenny actually clutched her chest.

"How many cars did you sell?" she demanded, an edge appearing in her voice.

"Uhhh, I don't know."

"Too busy to keep track. You might as well been selling meth. You should suffer the same punishment they get. Alyssa is right for the measures she's taken against the drug dealers in this country, and you're worse than them. You disgust me." She spat in the dirt in front of me, before turning to Sami. "And you, a woman. A woman should know better. She should always be thinking of her children and what kind of world we're leaving to them. But you were right there by him, destroying everything you touched like some kind of King Midas of filth." There wasn't much loose earth on the floor of the tent, but Jenny had a pocketful already loaded as she flung it at Sami. Dirt and small rocks bounced off us.

"That was excellent, Jenny. You're doing so well." Karen cooed like a mother whose child just figured out how to make pee-pee in the toilet. Jenny just smiled at the praise. "Alright, Ed, it's your turn."

Ed was seated to our right, the man version of Jenny. In his fifties, balding and with a gut, he looked extra-depressing even in this miserable setting. "I've been sitting here listening to this." He rocked as he spoke, staring at the ground. "And it makes me sick. These people don't deserve to be here. They don't deserve to sit here with us who are doing so much to better the planet. Everyone points out their flaws, yet they just sit there like it's no big deal. They don't care about any of this. They're scum!" His voice raised as he spoke, looking directly at us now. "Pond scum, that's right! They should be hung out there on the contemplation grounds for everyone to see, to remind everyone of what's at stake! This needs to be taken seriously and they're *laughing* at us." He leaned forward so he could get a better look at me around Sami, who was frozen staring straight ahead. "How big was your house?" he demanded.

"I don't know."

"Yes you do. It was the first thing you did when you moved in. Now, how big was it?"

"Like two thousand square feet."

"*Two thousand square feet??!!* That's disgusting. You're a pig! You think you deserved that much space? That the world owed it to you, huh? Putting in all that important work selling cars? Really helping out your fellow creatures? You filthy piece of shit." Ed was shaking, the spittle flying from his lips as he raged.

"Not so loud," Karen interjected, taking the wind out of Ed's sails. "When we get angry like that, we disrespect Gaia. What does Alyssa say about that?" She looked around the group.

Jenny raised her hand and spoke after Karen nodded to her. "Alyssa says that Gaia supplies all our energy and that using that energy for anger is a waste of it. It should be poured into our work and not our words."

"That's right, Jenny." Karen smiled at her again, "Our actions must always be focused on what is best for Gaia. Yelling keeps us out of balance with nature."

Ed looked to the ground, nodding his head in acceptance of the verdict. "I'm a failure. I confess."

"It's okay, Ed, we all get emotional when we see people who are abusing our precious earth. It's a sign that you care deeply about your fellow creatures."

"I do," he mumbled.

"All is forgiven, then. On that note, let's call an end to this session. I think…"

"Wait." The man sitting to her right cut in. It was the first time he had spoken. He was in his thirties, but very athletic-looking, probably more of a bodybuilder type than traditional athlete.

"Yes, Brock?"

"She still has the cucumber Rian gave her this morning." His eyes focused on the bulge along Sami's leg. All the eyes in the tent turned to us. This time they were tight with greed.

"I see it," Ed snapped, grabbing for Sami's pocket. She struggled against his hands. I grabbed for him, but he had it out quickly, waving in front of us triumphantly.

"Yes, I don't think you deserve that, not one bit," Karen said, shaking her head as she smiled. "Consider it a payment to your fellow tentmates for the trouble you've caused."

"Let's go find something to cut it up." Cassidy said eagerly. The whole group scrambled out in Karen's wake, like dogs following a full plate of food on the way to the dinner table. Once they were all gone, their yipping blending into the sounds of the camp, Sami collapsed her head into my lap, silently crying.

CHAPTER ELEVEN
BOOK

The next morning we were able to wake up as everyone else did, at the crack of dawn. Yesterday my body ached from sleeping on the ground, but today the pain from the ground wasn't noticeable because of the pain from yesterday's labors. My whole body hurt. The skin on my battered hands had tightened during the night, turning them practically into claws by morning. Sami had to help rub the flexibility back into them. We both trudged out of the tent with the rest of our group, heading to the open fields for this morning's wellness session. The entire episode played out about the exact same as it had the day before; Rian pontificated for a while, doling out food items to the lucky few, and Karen cried aggressively as penitence for her sins. In our favor, though, this time we weren't involved in the proceedings at all. We followed the prompts and played along, not attracting any attention today.

When he was finished tending his flock, he announced that today would be a day of introspection. The group clapped again at the news, the vigor being a bit more present than it was yesterday. We clapped a bit harder as well. Anything had to be better than busting up concrete. All of the groups began breaking up, some of them moving in the direction of the buses. Ours remained mostly in place, just some stretching of the legs or extra worshiping from Karen. Moving towards Carter, who was still just sitting in the grass, I asked, "What does that mean we're doing today?" I couldn't say that any of our group seemed friendly, but Carter seemed to be the least outright hostile. Disliking us appeared to be mandated, so he obeyed. The rest took the dislike to heart.

"We'll be engaging in an introspective discussion of our failures and how to better the world," he said mildly.

"Alright." The answer was only marginally more informative than what Rian had said, but it was something, I thought as I crawled back to Sami.

"Is that what we did last night?" she asked.

"I dunno, maybe."

"I don't want to do that again." That was for sure. Sitting in a circle and having people say terrible things about you is rather upsetting.

Once the groups that'd been tasked with other activities were gone, the remaining people spread even farther out. Karen led us to the far side of the field, where we sat in the grass, in a tight circle, about the size of the tent. "I'd like to admit something to start this session off," she said, speaking from her knees and looking around all of us. "I failed us all last night. I failed myself, I failed Alyssa, and I failed Gaia." She took a deep breath, letting the charges hang in the air. "I dreamed of eating a cheeseburger." She said the last words quietly, as if admitting a great crime. The rest of the group heard the admission with a stoic response, though Jenny put her head down. "I've been trying to be better, to rid my mind of thoughts that betray Gaia, the ideas the Polluters put in there. But I'm weak." Her eyes watered again.

"I admit, I've had dreams like that too," Carter added on. "I know it's wrong, but my stomach doesn't. It still wants it." The rest of the group nodded knowingly.

Sami stirred next to me. "You're probably just hungry. I know I am."

"Gaia provides us with what we need to survive, that's what *The Little Brown Book* says." Jenny spoke this time. "Desiring more is to be greedy, to rob Gaia and your fellow creatures of their share of it."

"That's absolutely right," Karen answered. "The book speaks the truth. I study it every night, trying to understand it better, to follow it more closely. But I can't live up to Alyssa. She's an inspiration to us all." The group muttered agreeably. "Kyle..." She was looking at me. "You haven't said much. What do you think?"

First I thought it was unfair. Several people hadn't said much yet—we had just started this round—so calling it out was premature. Though I didn't plan on really saying anything to begin with. "I think Sami was right. You're probably just hungry and your mind can't stop thinking about food."

"You think a cow is food?" Cassidy cut in for the first time.

"Well, she was dreaming about eating a cheeseburger. That seems like food to me," I answered.

"Cows have as much right to exist and be seen on this planet as we do. Eating them is a sin against Gaia," Cassidy spat back.

"Alright."

"You disagree, Kyle?" Karen prodded.

A lot of my opinions border on controversial even among polite company, so keeping them to myself was a habit, though Sami got to hear the brunt of them in private. "I've always just believed that people are more important than animals. We should try to make sure everyone has something to eat."

"That's wrong," Brock said sharply. "It's clearly against what the Book teaches us."

Karen held her hand up to hold him off. "I know what the Book says, Brock. People thinking they're more important than the natural cycles of the earth is what's gotten us in this mess. It's people like you who believe they're above the natural order of things, who have cheated the rest of us of our lives. Brock is right—humanity is *not* automatically more important than anything else. We're the creations of nature and must respect the rights of our fellow creatures."

"Do you understand now?" Cassidy asked, smirking.

"Yes," I said simply, holding a straight face.

"No he doesn't. He's lying!" Ed shouted this time, joining the conversation for the first time.

"Kyle, we see you're holding back. You must be open with us if you're to improve," Karen coxed me.

Gripping the grass tightly in my hands, I struggled to hold back. I've always naturally leaned a bit conservative—it's just in my DNA, I guess—and the pressure to conform to modern ways of thinking had been pressing on me my entire life. And yet I had pretty successfully resisted until now. I had treasured my beliefs since I had started forming my first political thoughts in my teenage years. Some say that if you're a conservative when you're young, you lack a heart. That might well be the case, but it's never personally felt like that to me. I just believe in making things better in a realistic manner instead of just endless empty talk about feelings.

"He understands. He's just new to this type of thinking," Sami said, trying to deflect the group.

"I want to hear him say it," taunted Brock.

I was now officially pissed off, and I could feel the truth starting to bubble out of me no matter how much I wanted to stuff it back in. "If Gaia created us in a way so that we can eat and digest animals without getting sick, than Gaia wants us to be meat-eaters. It's one of the fundamental building blocks behind why the human race has triumphed over the millennia, because we're omnivores and can adapt to our surroundings! Cows can only eat grass, lions can only eat gazelles, but we can eat it all!"

"You're mistaken," Brock shot back. "In fact, your whole existence is a mistake."

"If I'm a mistake, than Gaia made the mistake."

"YOU TAKE THAT BACK!" Ed screamed, his temper flaring once again.

"Calm down, calm down," Karen said sharply, bringing Ed to a hateful near-silence, continuing to mutter curses under his breath. "Kyle. We've all been in your shoes at some point, blaming others for our mistakes, our family, our friends, even Gaia herself. But Alyssa is clear, it's no one else's fault but our own. We are responsible for our failures. You'll come to see that soon."

"What's going on over here?" The voice was Rian's. He

joined our group, standing behind Jenny. "I heard voices being raised."

"I've failed," Ed said, bowing his head to the ground. "I used my energy wastefully."

"What caused the misplaced energy?" he asked, looking directly at me.

"Kyle believes people should continue to abuse Gaia to benefit the human race exclusively," Jenny said. "He won't accept that he's wrong, so he's trying to blame Gaia for his evil acts."

"Is that so, Kyle?" he asked.

"Apparently."

"People like you have been resisting admitting their faults for years now, haven't they?" The group agreed. "But they're being educated now. Alyssa has seen to that. Every day we see another former Polluter admitting their sins and accepting their punishment. They looked at us defiantly for so long while we breathed in their filth, but now things are being made right."

"That's right," the group said.

"Kyle, are you ready to admit that you're wrong and you need to change your ways?" He stood directly in front of me now.

"Yes." I answered as firmly as possible. I had promised Sami that I would do my best to fit in, to escape the microscope that had been on us since we'd arrived. It wasn't worth fighting over.

Rian bent down, looking deep into my eyes. "The eyes always tell the truth, honesty or defiance. Defiance lurks in the eyes like a dragon waiting to spit its fire. What do you think I see in your eyes, Kyle?"

"I don't know," I answered as evenly as possible.

He smiled slowly. "I *will* eventually see your conviction in your eyes. You're still fighting it, but I'll see it in your eyes soon." He smiled and looked back around the group. "*The Little Brown Book* teaches us that Gaia will eventually decide its own natural number of humans needed to maintain balance on the earth. How many of our species will remain afterward to enjoy the wondrous life provided us is yet to be decided, but Gaia is making her will known." The group was silent, contemplating the future world and their possible place in it. "Now I think it's time to do some reading. Learn the words of the Book and let Alyssa guide your thoughts." He left our circle.

The rest of the group fished into their pockets and pulled out the much talked-about book. It was smallish, almost like it was designed to fit in the floppy breast pocket of our jumpsuits. It had a brown cardstock cover, front and back. The title of the book and the President's name was embossed in block letters across the front, in the style of old hipster letterpress equipment. All the copies looked well-worn, the covers marked in creases and scuffs.

"Where should we start today?" Jenny asked.

"I think Rian wanted us to move to a happier note." Cassidy answered.

"That's a good point. Let's start on Chapter 8, 'Our Duties to Nature.'" Karen flipped her book open. "Who'd like to start?"

Sami held her hand up. "We don't have a copy," she said politely.

"We know," Brock muttered, loud enough for everyone to hear. "You haven't earned one yet."

"We'll let you read one of ours when it's your turn," Karen answered. "Brock, why don't you start us off."

Brock read for a while, until he reached a natural stopping point and Ed took up the narrative.

The thoughts that President Rodriguez had committed to the page of her political manifesto resulted in writing that was one-third political essay, one-third religious sermon and one-third Jane Fonda workout video energy. Her writings highlighted the flaws in the economic system she had so deftly built her career on pointing out to the public, but instead of building upon her points logically to find a better solution, she veered into a fever dream of mysticism, paranoia and panic about the impending doom of humanity if we didn't follow her instincts to the letter. Manifestos are by nature religious in the abstract meaning of the word, logical thoughts twisted by the emotions of the writer and enticing to the reader. Like a Stephen King book that begins in the familiar, luring the constant reader in, and before they know it they're battling an extra-dimensional evil being dressed as a clown.

We did a two full rounds of reading, almost half the book by the time Karen finished her second turn, setting her book aside. "That was invigorating, wasn't it?"

"I learn something new every time I hear her words," Cassidy said, caressing the book as she spoke. "They speak straight to the heart."

"It's time we break to enjoy the nourishment Gaia has provided today," Karen spoke as she stood up. "Let's meet down there." The group broke up quickly. Some moved off towards the tents while Cassidy laid face down on the grass, as if she was trying to see through to the planet's core. Jenny stood and walked in a circle, her nose deep in the book, muttering the words aloud to herself. My only thought was food; my mind, my heart and most of all my belly wanted it. Sami and I followed Carter and Ed as they headed back into the tent maze, hopefully towards some kind of eating area. Our only other meal since arriving here had been at the eroding gas station. We had missed about four meals so far.

We followed our tentmates to the far side of the school building, passing several SUVs that still ran on gas, as well as sleek European electric cars that actually worked well. They were hiding behind several layers of fencing, the gate locked securely in place. The SUVs were basic-looking, but the accompanying trucks were a Land Rover and a Mercedes G Class. All were painted our favorite shade of brown and shining in the sun. "Quite the fleet in there," Sami mentioned as we passed.

"Not the most eco-friendly assortment either."

"We probably just haven't got to that part of the book yet."

We finally made it to the cafeteria. Unsurprisingly, it was not an impressive sight. There was several large vats lined up, an attendant manning each of them. We trailed Carter and Ed in line. The first person handed us each a stiff slice of bread, the next a vegetable. I got a chunk of celery and Sami got a large carrot. At the final station, the attendant dipped a bowl into some watery soup for each of us and sent us on our way. Still, it was better than we'd been eating the past few days. We picked a spot on the grass near enough to Carter and Ed to not seem like we were hiding, but far enough to be sorta alone for a few minutes.

"I'm guessing we won't be seeing much protein around here."

"Probably not. You heard their feelings on cheeseburgers."

"I wonder how they feel about Chick-Fil-A," I mused.

"A company that used cows to encourage us to eat more chicken? You probably get shot on the spot for mentioning it" The conversation that had been lacking the past few days was a welcome relief. It even made the food taste a little bit better and last a little bit longer. Long enough for Karen to join us on our patch of grass. She took a seat across from both of us, setting her food on the ground in order to pray first. I've seen plenty of people pray before a meal, having done it myself on occasion, however Karen seemed to also be praying to her food as much as she was to nature in general. Once she finished that, she gave us a smile. "We're learning a lot today, I think."

"It's very interesting," Sami said in her most sincere voice.

"Oh yes. Every day there's something new to learn, a new path to be more connected to Gaia." She rambled as she ate her food.

"It's a lot to take in so quickly," I said.

"Very much. It doesn't get much easier, either. Always something new to learn."

"I was wondering if we could get a copy of the book? So we could read it ourselves," I asked. The entire foundation of the camp seemed to revolve around that book. When the Dirts first started appearing in society, they were always carrying flyers or brochures, like normal political parties. Then they started carrying these books. You would see them reading them all over town, at the coffeehouses or in line at the store. The rest of us paid it no mind. Whatever they wanted to read was their business. Better that than shoving another piece of paper about soil crimes in my hand.

"You want a copy of the book?" Karen asked, her face puzzled. "Already?"

"It would help us study. Everyone else is so far ahead of us, and we need to work on our confessions." Sami answered this one.

"Oh my goodness, this is a miracle. This is truly a miracle.

All because of my work this morning. It really worked." Karen was again rambling, to herself this time. "We need to go to the library right away," she exclaimed, jumping to her feet and leaving the food on the ground. "Come on, come on." We followed her motioning and trotted after her to the school buildings.

Karen led us straight to Kelly's office where we had signed up for all this two days ago. "Kelly, they want a copy of the book!" she announced as we entered. Kelly was sitting behind her computer eating a sandwich.

"Really? That's great news!" She flashed us a smile. "Go get Rian and I'll take them to the library." Karen dashed off before another word could be said, leaving us standing awkwardly in the doorway.

"Why is she so excited?" Sami asked.

"It's a big deal to ask for your own copy of the book. It's the last big step in joining the cause fully. It's like your new birthday. Look here." She pulled her own copy out of her pocket and flipped the cover open. On the first page was her neatly written name, a date from last December, and several signatures. "It's a cause for celebration to join our ranks and have a book bestowed upon you. Normally it takes weeks for someone to see that their errors are beyond their own abilities to heal."

"I guess we're fast learners," I said. The mythical status of this book was frightening. I just wanted to read it so I could learn my new lines and start saying the correct thoughts. Obviously recitals of verse had become a measure of one's standing here, like some kind of perverse Bible camp. I had volunteered us for their version of a baptism.

"Let's go to the library, before Rian gets there." Kelly led us down the hallways to the high school's gymnasium. The basketball court's hardwood was under our feet, but there was no other signs of what this room had been originally designed for. Instead, the entire space had been converted into a printing press operation. Kelly led us through the maze of book parts. First there were the stacks and stacks of paper around the walls, waiting to be cut down to size. In the middle of the room were several rows of hand-powered antique printing machines, all being operated by the brown-dressed workers. One station for cutting the pages, then another for pressing the ink of Alyssa's words upon them, and then finally one for stitching and gluing the entire book together.

"I've never seen books being made by hand," Sami commented.

"It's marvelous, isn't it?" Kelly squealed. "A group of Gaians up in Chicago had been running an art press in the city, and they just got done moving the last of the equipment here the other day. Just think of how many lives are going to be changed because of what's happening in this room."

She had finally led us to the far end of the room, where close to a thousand of the books were stacked against the walls. "Now, this is very important. You need to move through the books and feel them. Look for the one that speaks to you. Your connection to the book is important. It must speak straight to your heart." For emphasis she poked each of us in the chest.

"Okay," I answered, stepping forward into the stacks. I doubted a book was going to speak to me, but if it did, I sincerely hoped it would be near the top of the piles.

Sami and I drifted through the books, each as brown as the previous one. We felt our way through the first rows, still in sight of Kelly who was waiting excitedly at the door. Once we pushed deeper and out of sight of her, I stopped feeling the spines, just looking around at the silliness of it all. "Find one that *speeeaks…*" I began saying in a ghostly voice.

Sami shot daggers at me that stopped me mid-sentence. "Just pick one," she said through gritted teeth, picking up one of the random books from the floor.

I pulled one off the nearest pile and smiled. "I guess we found them."

"Let's get this over with."

While we'd been searching, Kelly had been joined by Rian and Karen, who was glowing with excitement. They led us back out to Kelly's office. "Let me see them!" Karen exclaimed, reaching for our books. Sami handed hers over so Karen could caress it and flip through the pages. "It's wonderful, it's wonderful," she cooed before handing it back and holding out her hands for mine. "Could I, please?"

"Uh, sure." I handed it over.

"Ohhh, powerful. I can feel the energy coming from this book. You did well." She said it as if she was judging thoroughbreds.

"Sami, could you please hand me your book?" Rian said, standing behind the desk. She did and he opened it to the first page, writing her full name across the top and the current date. Signing his own name below it, he handed the pen to Kelly and then Karen, all signing as witnesses, I assumed. "It's an honor to present you with your book, Samantha. I know you'll use it as intended, and that you together will better the world because of it. Congratulations." He shook her hand firmly as he gave the book back. "Now your turn, Kyle, if you're ready."

"I am," I said in my firmest voice, looking him straight in the eyes. He smiled a bit and began repeating the process of inscribing the page and even the same short monologue to seal the deal. Karen and Kelly clapped wholeheartedly once the book was back in my hands.

Now that the ceremony was over, Karen was gushing forth with earnestness. "I just can't believe it happened so soon. We had just started working through your issues and you already see the light. I think I may have worked a miracle, honestly." She laughed at her own pride. "Excuse the indulgence. I mean, we have to praise Gaia for such a transformation, but I hope I helped, even if in the slightest way."

"You did tremendous work, Karen. The other tent leaders will take note," Rian said.

"Thank you so much. I just take such pride in my work. I really think if the others could learn from me, the planet would be in much better shape."

"Everyone will hear of your stunning success, Karen, don't worry about that." Karen blushed fully. "However, the celebrating must come to an end, because there's still work to be done. The rest of the group is probably waiting for all of you by now."

"Of course. Let's go tell them the good news." Grabbing both of us, Karen pulled us out and back to our little piece of grass.

The rest of the group seemed a bit less than excited about our sudden conversion to the faith. They clapped and smiled, but as Rian said, the eyes don't lie, and their eyes were not impressed. We spent the rest of the day working through the book, Sami and I reading from our own copies this time. As darkness approached we broke for dinner, which was as meager as the lunch had been, no sign of the sandwiches Kelly had been munching on in the office. After dinner, Sami and I set to work on our next confessional draft, this time with *The Little Brown Book* to guide us. Before we were having to guess at what was being looked for in our writing; now we had the manifesto of the ideology that was judging us. Skimming through the book help us define our faults and the approved methods for repentance.

Once darkness arrived, we put our homework aside and curled up together. Our voices were hoarse and my knees and butt hurt from sitting on the ground all day, but we were in much better shape than we had been the night before.

* * *

The sun didn't come up the next morning. Well, it did, but it couldn't be seen. The clouds and rain blocked out the light. Only the dim gloom of a rainy day met us that morning when we were awaken by Karen screaming at the entryway to the tent. Sitting up with a bolt, I took in the bleary surroundings. Everyone else was waking up in a hurry as well, as Karen rocked back and forth in the doorway crying and chanting unintelligibly, the rain pelting her in the face. Everyone else in the tent started making their own sounds of mourning. Jenny was already weeping and Carter was muttering to himself as they crowded around Karen, staring into the rainy mess.

"What's going on?" Sami groaned, struggling up to a sitting position.

"It's raining outside," I whispered back.

"Good," she grunted, falling back to the ground.

"No." Grabbing her, I pulled her back up. "Rain is a bad thing, remember?" I whispered harshly in her ear. "We need to pray it away with them."

"Fine," she grumbled, accepting the necessity of this cosplay.

We crawled over to join the group. Each person was performing their own version of a plea for deliverance, some crying at the sky, others chanting the prayer we performed every morning. Ed was rubbing his face in the dirt. We chose the morning prayer as our method.

"EVERY CREATURE REPORT TO THE CONTEMPLATION GROUNDS." The amplified voice boomed across the space. Apparently the speaker system for the school still worked.

Dragging herself from the floor, Karen readied us. "Be brave, everyone. This is the will of Gaia." Stepping into the rain, she cowered under the hail of drops and led us towards the grassy fields. All of the tents were emptying in a similar manner, people running and ducking the raindrops. When we reached the field, the leaders were already standing there, soaking wet in the slick field. We filed in, massing even closer to our respective leaders than normal.

"FAILURE!" Rian screamed as we rushed in. "POLLUTION! FILTH!" Karen and Jenny were at the front of the group, throwing themselves at Rian's feet in despair. "WHY IS GAIA PUNISHING US? WHAT HAPPENED TO ANGER HER?" He paced back and forth in front of the people.

The majority of the group responded in unison, Sami as well, being a step ahead of me, "WE FAILED."

"WHO FAILED?" Rian screamed.

"I DID!" Karen had sprung to her feet, shoulders squared, head forward as if at attention.

"What did you do?" His voice had dropped to a threatening growl.

"I am weak! My mind dreams of things it shouldn't! It dreams of filth!"

"Where else have you failed?"

"Gaia told me to fast last night, to give my share back to the world, but I ate anyways. I was greedy."

Reaching down to the ground, Rian picked up something I

hadn't noticed, a stick about three feet long, its wooden texture gleaming in the rain. "GREED!" he screamed, loading up and whipping the stick against Karen's arm and back. The hiss as it slipped through the rain was as unnerving as the smack of it finding her bare skin. She cried out and staggered a step as Rian reared back again, "GLUTTONY!" He brought it home again. "FILTH!" The stick landed the third time, this one against her thighs above the knee. She stumbled fully this time, ending up in the muddy grass. Rian lunged forward, bringing the stick down again and again on her back. She screamed with each hit before collapsing fully into the earth.

Rian turned to face the rest of us, waving and jabbing at people with his stick. "You all think this is a *JOKE*?" he shouted. "You think this isn't *SERIOUS*? Just a fucking *CAMPING* trip?" This time the group had lost its collective tongue. "This is the real deal! This is the fate of the entire fucking planet we're dealing with, and everyone here's pissing and moaning about getting an extra piece of bread! *FUCK YOU!!!*" He brought the stick down several times on a person I didn't recognize. He shrieked, trying to shield himself from the strikes. "You think you don't deserve these, Josh? You think you're special shit? You think Gaia gives a fuck about you?!"

"No," Josh said, his voice faltering.

"*THEN TAKE YOUR PUNISHMEEENT!!!*" Rian unleashed another wave of attacks. Josh curled into a ball as he received them. Rian raised back up, red-faced and panting from the exertion. "Everyone on the goddamn buses. NOW!"

We had all been just about frozen in the field since the caning had started, but at that word the spell was broken. Everyone jumped to their feet, tripping and slipping as we rushed out of the field and through the tents towards the parking lot. Sami and I had been in the rear of the group in the field, so we led the charge back, pulling the doors open to the first bus we came to and hurrying all the way to the back. Normal days at the camp had only a group or two heading out on the busses, but today the entire camp was shipping out, so the seats were quickly filled up and people flopped down on the floor or squeezed in tighter on the seats.

Karen was the last person to climb aboard our bus. She was soaking wet, as we all were, but also streaked with blood and mud. She fell to the floor next to the driver and cried extravagantly the entire ride, her loud dry sobs echoing through the bus. She only paused once, so she could start coughing and spitting all over the floor. Despite the urgency of the impending worldwide meltdown while we were at the morning meeting, the buses traveled at their normal leisurely speed all the way out to the deconstruction zone. That just made the sounds from the front of the bus even more uncomfortable.

Our bus pulled into the same gas station parking lot we had been at before. Work had continued the day before while we were studying, so it looked slightly different, but it was still just a partially torn-apart gas station. I found a sledgehammer from the pile of tools and Sami picked up a bucket. "This is going to suck," Sami whispered while we were separated from the pack.

"That's what we get for making it rain."

"That should be on the back cover of the book."

"Heretic," I answered as we joined the group, already pounding away at the concrete.

* * *

By lunchtime it was raining even harder, which had the effect of raising tensions to an almost unbearable level. Three people had broken down completely in hysterics, having to be dragged back on the bus to keep a full-blown panic from breaking out.

Lunch arrived, even more depressing than the previous meals had been. A handful of rice and some beans. Probably a message about how we didn't deserve to eat at all. Once the food had been doled out, the lunch crew threw out some speakers the people huddled around. They were playing speeches from the President. Her shrill and earnest voice cutting through the air, I could see her beautiful but frightening face through the sounds. It was like our version of the Great and Powerful Oz, just a disembodied head endlessly scolding us. Several people in the group had obviously memorized the speech, since they could be heard speaking along with the lines. The rest just stared in rapt attention. Once the first speech finished we went back to work, but the recordings continued, urging us onward to great efforts on behalf of the planet.

"Are you doing okay?" I asked Sami when she returned with her bucket. I had been slowly working my way farther from the main group as I hammered out the concrete. It had taken an hour, but I was finally about fifteen feet from the rest of them. It didn't make my job any easier—hitting concrete with a hammer is the same no matter where you're standing—but it made it a bit easier for Sami, since she could kill an extra minute or so waiting on me to finish busting up pieces so they'd fit in the bucket.

"I'm fine. Are you?"

"Yeah. My back and hips are killing me, though."

"Sorry," she whispered, putting a chunk of rubble in her bucket. "We can switch if you want."

"That's alright." I swung the hammer down again. "Hammering is for the men."

I tried to listen to the speech for a while, something to take my mind of off the back-breaking labor, but it didn't help. It just got me distracted; having arguments with her in my head ended up slowing my swinging. So I shut the noise out and thought about Star Wars.

It had to be late afternoon when Rian's SUV arrived. Time is hard to track when you can't see the sun and you aren't wearing your 'Let. Even though time felt like it was moving at a snail's pace, I'm pretty sure it was towards the later side of the day. His SUV pulled in behind the bus and he climbed out of the passenger seat. He was dry-looking, his clothes obviously having been changed since this morning in the field, and he was wearing a brown rain jacket over his normal outfit. Everyone kept working as he approached. The memory of this morning's beatings was still fresh. "How's everybody doing?" he called out. His falsely pleasant voice was unsettling.

Nobody answered, keeping their eyes down on their tools, the bucket people stepping a little quicker than normal. "Everyone's working so hard. Such seriousness. But I have to ask myself, have you been working this hard all day? Or did you all just step it up when I showed up?" He continued roaming through the people as they tried to work and not attract his attention. "Look at me when I'm speaking!" he shouted, bringing all the work to a stop and the eyes finally on him. "That's better. It shows you can at least show some respect to something, because it sure as shit isn't the planet. All day you've been out here, but Gaia still isn't happy with your effort, is she? It's still raining, reminding us all with every drop what filthy failures you all are. Carter!"

Carted snapped up. "Yes?"

"Are you a failure?"

"I am," he answered meekly.

"Have you been slacking today, not giving your entire self to the needs of the planet?"

"Yes." He cast his eyes down.

"That's what I thought." He scanned the group again. "Kyle!"

My name caught me off-guard. My eyes had begun to wander, surveying the rest of the group. I looked back at Rian. He was staring at me in an odd way, Cassidy standing behind him, the same odd expression hinting of a smile on her lips.

"Yes?"

"What are you thinking? What does Alyssa's message mean to you?" He moved closer to me through the crowd.

"Oh, it makes sense to me."

"It makes sense, huh?" He was directly in front of me now.

"Yeah. We took up too much space, so we should give as much as we can back."

"That's a good view on the issue." He reached forward for my sledgehammer I had in front of me. The head was resting on the ground, the end of the handle in my clasped hands. "I can hold that for you. You've had a hard day." He slipped it from my hands, holding it just as I had. "But there's more, isn't there?"

"No, not really." I shook my head.

"Yes there is. I can see it in your eyes. Let's hear it. That's what we're all doing, learning from each other and educating each other, right?" Looking around the group, they nodded agreeably.

"Okay, well. I just think that busting concrete like this is kinda a waste of time. Wouldn't it be better to be cleaning out rivers or a forest or something? That's where the real pollution is. This is just dirt." I pointed around us. "Nothing's going to grow here anytime soon. And we aren't even really getting rid of it, we're just moving it into one big pile."

"So you think we should be rehabilitating more sensitive areas? So long as you don't have to swing a hammer anymore, right?" He chuckled, and then I saw a blur of motion.

I didn't realize what was transpiring as it was happening. No feeling or sense prepared me. The pain was the first thing I felt. First it was dull, a shocked reaction before the real sharp agonizing stuff hit me. Looking down, I could see the indention the sledgehammer had left on the top of my foot. It was already turning a blueish purple as blood leaked from the top of it. I swayed for a second. I didn't see the second blow coming until the head connected with my flesh, the cracking of bone echoing up my body. Rian had lifted the head of the sledge and driven it straight down into the top of my foot. Dropping to the ground in the aftershock of the second blow, I couldn't even scream. The breath was caught in my lungs as the pain seized my body. I rolled on the ground, looking for a place where I could escape the insane waves of pain radiating up my leg.

"EVERYBODY GET BACK TO WORK!" I heard Rian screaming over the pain. The crowd around us parted, people sprinting away from the scene. Grabbing me by my hair, Rian forced our faces together, inches apart at the nose. "Now I only see pain in your eyes," he said softly. "But that's the path to honesty. Soon we'll see truth." He dropped my head back to the wet concrete. He strode off as Sami grabbed me. Tears were streaming down her face as she hugged my head against her. With my face pressed against her, I let out the first scream. The pain was straining to escape. It was the only way.

CHAPTER TWELVE

PAIN

Exquisite pain. It was a phrase I had heard my whole life, but never really understood. Exquisite seemed like a weird word to use to describe pain. I imagined pain wearing a monocle and carrying a cane, like Mr. Peanut or the Monopoly man. I had now met exquisite pain. I've had my nose broken a few times in the past, my arm twice. All of those were from some childhood activity gone wrong, baseball to the face or falling on the playground. I know they must've hurt, since that's what broken bones do, but I don't remember the pain; it was more of the shock of being injured that's locked in my memory, the trips to the hospital and the casts being applied. All I know right now, though, is the pain. My entire foot is swollen and disfigured. Even before the second blow landed, the color had shifted, and now after a few hours it's practically black.

Sami had held me for a while, but that wasn't doing much for either of us. She half-carried half-dragged me to the remains of the gas station structure and found a decent place for me to lay down with my foot elevated. That was the best solution we could think of in the wilderness we were lost in. Everyone else had completely ignored us since the incident with Rian. Karen walked past Sami without looking when she approached her about a first aid kit. I sent Sami away after a while so I could suffer in peace. She went back to the bucket brigade, carrying the concrete to the giant mound. Everyone was carefully avoiding my former sledgehammer where Rian had dropped it to the ground. It laid there as a reminder for the rest of the day.

Once the word spread that we were heading home, Sami helped me make it to the bus. We were the last ones to climb aboard. Everyone continued their practice of leaving us alone, even as we struggled up the steps with the entire bus watching. The journey back to the tent was terrible. The wet and uneven ground was much harder to navigate. We had several missteps that put pressure on my right foot, which then caused me to crumple into a heap on the ground all over again. Now we were finally back in the tent. "Do you think there's a medical tent here?" Sami asked. We had been laying in our sleeping spot for a while, soaked to the bone and covered in mud.

"Dunno." The throbbing pain was echoing up my entire body.

"Are you hungry?"

"Dunno."

"I'll go get you some food. Better to have it here if you want it."

"Okay."

She slipped off, leaving me alone with my exquisite pain. For the first hours, I hadn't been able to think at all. The pain occupied every inch of my brain. Now with just the sound of the rain drumming on the tent to keep me company, the pain faded enough to make room for other thoughts in my head. Our situation here had been less than ideal even before this happened. This camp wasn't the answer we had been looking for, and in fact it had quickly become more threatening than what we'd faced previously. Then it got immeasurably worse with two blows of a sledgehammer. Even if they let us leave at this point, there wasn't much we could do. We weren't going to get very far with only three legs. And honestly, they were never going to let us leave. This place had the feel of a prison with no walls. We weren't in a position to stage a breakout, either. Sami isn't tiny, but she wasn't going to be able to handle carrying me. Carrying someone is a lot harder than it looks in the movies. We were stuck, which probably was Rian's actual goal when he smashed my foot; not punishment, but stranding us here with them, and no other option but to make peace with their way of life.

The mud at the flap squished as someone entered. Battling back to the visual world, I saw Karen had entered the tent. She gave me a quick glance before settling down in her spot and sticking her nose deep into the book. Sami returned after a few more minutes. She was soaking wet, but I could still see the tears in her eyes. "They won't give me any food to bring back here for you. They said you have to be there to get your own food." She sobbed, grabbing ahold of my hand.

"That's alright, I'm not hungry."

"No, you need to eat, you need your strength." Sami looked over at Karen, who was pointedly ignoring us. "Karen, what can we do?" She rushed over, grabbing ahold of Karen's arm.

"There's a wellness tent on the other side of camp," she said begrudgingly. "But I don't know if you'll do any better over there."

"Will he be able to eat over there?"

"Yes, they'll feed him."

Coming back to my side, Sami slid her hands under my shoulder. "Okay, let's get going."

* * *

The journey to the wellness tent took over an hour. Slipping in the mud, dodging people hurrying past, and winding through the tents made for a terrible time of it. Once we reached the edge of the parking lot, things got a bit easier. The asphalt was easier to walk on and we could see the large tent on the other side. We had passed through here a couple of times already but had never noticed it. The tent resembled an outcast from the rest of camp.

"What are you going to say once we get there?" Sami questioned.

"Nothing stupid."

"That's right, nothing stupid. Just play along, say what needs to be said, and lay low."

"I will."

"You better. Otherwise we might not get out of here."

Pushing the flap open, we stepped in. It was dim like our tent had been, but the smell was terrible. Once our eyes adjusted, we moved forward through the rows of people laid out on the ground. The sleeping arrangements seemed the same as our tent, dirt patches marking each person's space. At the back of the tent there was a desk with a couple of people watching us approach. "What do you want?" The speaker was an older lady who was seated at the desk, her hair pulled back tight and large glasses covering her pinched face.

"His foot is broken," Sami answered. "He needs some help."

"How did it happen?" the old lady inquired, glaring at me.

"It got smashed today while we were working."

"So I've heard." Her eyes searched us over again. "Put him over there. A space opened up today." She motioned us towards the right side of the tent. The two men standing behind her didn't move a muscle to help, despite their appearance of being orderlies. Once again we worked on our craft of walking as a team; this time, though, we were dodging the bodies laid out in front of us. Most everyone I had seen in this makeshift hospital looked in much worse condition than I was. The bare spot on the ground was damp and slightly muddy, but everything seemed to be that way around here.

The traditional old-man sigh hiding deep inside me found its way out as I finally laid down. "I need to go to sleep," I whispered to Sami, my eyes already closed.

"I'll stay here with you."

"You should go. Get some food and some rest. I'll be okay here." I squeezed her hand. "I love you."

"I love you," she said softly as I drifted off.

* * *

It was the next morning when I was awoken for my medical exam. Not many exams that start with being kicked awake end well, so my hopes weren't high.

"You sleep a lot," grunted the orderly who was standing on my left side as I woke up. The orderlies were on either side while the old woman was kneeling by my foot, inspecting every inch of it.

"Does this hurt?" she asked abruptly as she jammed a finger into the swollen flesh. *Arrhh* was my response, thrashing from the pain, but she held my foot in place. "How about here?" She probed it again to the same result. "Your foot looks broken in several places," she finally announced. She then fished her copy of the *Little Brown Book* out of her pouch, flipping through it aggressively until she found the page she was looking for and began reading. This was my first test. The old Kyle would've rolled his eyes furiously at this point. I instead focused my mind on Sami. She had carried me all the way over here. If she could do that, I could keep my mouth closed a little while longer.

The old lady finished reading and tucked the book back into her pocket. "Alyssa's words are very clear on this subject. Injuries heal themselves naturally unless the person is out of tune with Gaia. Go get a bucket," she instructed one of the men.

"I could really use some food as well," I said as the man trotted off.

"Food is reserved for creatures that have shown actual improvement," the old lady lectured me. "We mustn't attempt to command nature, but let it guide us."

"I understand," I said slowly, swallowing the desire to scream at her medical malpractice. "But I really need all the help I can get. Alyssa also tells us that nature cannot function properly unless given the resources it needs, and I really need something to eat." I recalled whatever random nonsense I could from the book that might get me a little food. It was the nature of the thing that its text that could be applied to literally anything. She nodded to the orderly, who produced an ear of corn from his bag and tossed to me. "Thank you so much." They continued on their way.

I had been savoring every nibble on the corncob for only a couple of minutes before the other orderly returned with my treatment. Without warning, he grabbed my enlarged, multicolored foot and jammed it into the bucket, full of mud. He then took several multicolored stones from his pocket, rubbing each one and muttering to himself as he pressed them into the mud around my now submerged leg. "Leave it in there. Let nature do its work," he said gruffly before walking off to join the old lady doctor.

Adrenaline shot through my body from the intense pain of my foot being manhandled. I battled the desire to scream at them for the insanity of it all. I could feel my copy of the Book floating around in my pocket. Reading has never to my knowledge been suggested as a cure for broken bones, but there wasn't much else that could distract me from my present situation. The chapter on medicine did stand out rather sharply now. Modern Western medicine is evil—pills, surgery, robots, and everything else coming out of those shady multinational corporations were acts against nature. If there was somebody around to listen, I would've made the argument that a splint on a broken extremity wasn't exactly modern; there's evidence even Neanderthals used them. However, as I now had been made aware, my thoughts on most matters were unwelcome to the Dirts, so I again kept them to myself. Sami would've been proud. I wonder what enlightened era had treated broken bones with buckets of mud and a crystal "energy ring." I doubt even the Neanderthals could've been that naive.

The book did help me shut myself off from what was happening around me, because the tent wasn't a happy place. It had very little ventilation so it was stuffy and hot, filled with the smells of sick sweaty people laying in the dirt and waiting to die. The care provided by the staff was minimal, but their midday rounds had brought them back to my foot. The old lady ignored my leg and instead checked the consistency of the mud. It had begun to dry out, though it was still to her liking as they moved on without a word. Several other patients didn't fare as well. At the opposite side of the tent there was an altercation. It looked like the patient started screaming when they approached. Maybe his mud had dried incorrectly. Either way, he flailed about for a bit before the orderlies dragged him out of his spot and all the way out of the tent. That was the last we saw of him. Twice during the day I saw them remove bodies from the rows of patients, wrapping the limp corpse up in a sheet and carrying it out. It was obvious from the silence that hung between the patients that talking was strongly discouraged; even if it hadn't been, the old man on my right and teenage girl on my left were practically comatose.

Dusk was upon us when Sami returned. I didn't notice her until she was right on top of me; my mind was mindlessly surfing the teachings of the Book. "Hi babe," she greeted me, kneeling down beside me.

"Hey." I took her hand. "How are you?"

"I'm fine. We just spent the day reading and talking again. A lot of focus on punishment for not letting go of old beliefs."

"I wonder what spurred that?" I said, the first joke I had told in quite a while.

"What is this?" she asked, sticking her finger into my mud bucket, which was now just a dirt bucket.

"It's my treatment."

"What?!" she said angrily, looking around like there might be a doctor making his rounds that she could tell off.

"Just go with it, that's what you told me to do." I pulled her back down towards me.

She looked at the bucket for a bit longer. "Did they at least feed you?"

"I got them to give me a corn cob." I pulled it out of my pocket. I'd been sucking on it during the day, like a dog with a bone.

"I brought you this." She handed over my confession folder. "Thought it might look good if you worked on it."

"Yeah, I was going to ask you to bring it. I've been reading this book all day long, though I don't know if anyone noticed."

"Are you learning anything?"

"I've decided to read it as if I'm an actor learning my script. That's what this is, a script for a character we're supposed to play."

"Ugh, you did always think you could act."

"At this point, I think our lives depend on staying in character, so maybe less crapping on my fantasies, my dear?"

"Alright, whatever you have to do to blend in."

I gave her hand another squeeze. "You should go, though. I don't think they keep visiting hours here."

"Okay. I'll stop by tomorrow."

"Love you."

"Love you."

* * *

Several indecipherable days passed. The old lady inspected my foot every morning. No change apparent, so more mud was ordered. Since no progress was visible on my foot, it meant that I was failing to connect with nature, which meant my food was nonexistent. I still had my corncob, though it had ceased to be the source of anything food-like, only one step away from chewing on bark at this point. My work on the confession had taken a hit. I had made progress on it the morning after Sami brought it to me, probably some of my best work. Once my stomach pains had eclipsed my foot pain, though, I wasn't able to focus on writing anymore. Even if I could find the clarity, physically writing the words was too much effort. My ability to read lasted a bit longer, though I don't know if I was actually reading or just staring at the pages for a while.

Sami made it back on the fourth day. I didn't realize she was there until she was leaning over my face. "Kyle, can you hear me?"

"Yeah."

"You look terrible. What's wrong?"

"No food."

"Here, I got this today." She pulled a banana out of her pocket and peeled it open. Many times previous in our lives she had offered me food, to which my response was just to open my mouth, like a little bird. Normally she didn't play that game, but today she didn't even hesitate. Pulling the banana apart, she fed the pieces to me. We were only missing the highchair.

We got halfway through before the old lady appeared, flanked by her henchmen. "What are you doing?" she demanded.

"I'm giving him some food. He's hungry," Sami shot back. My mouth was full of banana and even if it wasn't, arguing was too much of a strain on my mind.

"He's my patient, and eating isn't recommended until nature starts to heal him."

"That's insane. He's my husband and I'm going to feed him, and I don't care what you think of that."

The old lady nodded and the orderlies moved forward. "You need to come with us." She motioned for her to leave. They were halfway out of the tent when she broke free and ran back to my side, wrapping her arms around me. In between her exaggerated sobs she whispered into my ear, "I'm coming back for you tonight. Be ready at the edge of the tent at 10:00."

The orderlies seized her arms before she could say anything else and started dragging her out of the tent. The banana ended up on the ground next to me during the scuffle. The old lady noticed it and picked it up, tossing it into a bucket at the corner of the tent.

CHAPTER THIRTEEN

PIPES

People often describe things as "ugh, the worst day ever." It's normally applied to a movie that didn't live up to the hype or a rainy day at the park. The past few days, however, truly marked the worst days in my entire life, at least up until that point. In my previous life of comfort, I had always tried to find some optimism during the worst periods by suggesting that however dark things might get in the future, they probably couldn't get any worse than it was currently. Having your foot crushed, then treated with a bucket of mud while laying on dirt and being starved to death, had finally eclipsed that time the rental car got a flat tire in the muddy parking lot during our honeymoon.

Time had slowed down and the hunger pains kept me from being able to truly sleep. Everything had started to blur together into a very hungry haze. Nighttime was a disheartening time in the wellness tent. The lack of overseers meant that the threat of punishment was gone and pain that had been sequestered during the day was released. The cries and moans that had been stifled all day long arrived for all to hear. The first couple days in the tent I had been so exhausted that I slept through everything. Once the exhaustion wore off, I had seamlessly transitioned into the hazy fog of starvation, so the whole world was distorted by the bubble around my head. Tonight, I bore witness to the entire scene in my right mind. An hour into our unsupervised time, I had extracted my foot from the bucket of mud and dirt. It wasn't a pretty sight, still swollen and misshapen, but the color was at least a uniform brown from the dirt that was caked on from the days it had spent in the mud.

The absurdity of the entire situation hit me like the smell of my mud-covered foot. It was time to leave. Rolling over, I pulled myself the couple of feet to the edge of the tent. The bottom edge was tied down to keep it from flapping, but there was enough slack at my point that I could slide my body underneath. For the first time in days I felt the cool air on my face. It was hard to fathom that I had even been able to breathe inside the foul tent.

Sami was on me in an instant. I started to speak, but she signaled for silence. Grabbing me under my arms, she dragged me across the field. I don't think I've ever been literally dragged anywhere by my wife before. It was a humbling experience. Luckily there wasn't anyone around to witness it. "Wait here," she whispered, leaning me against a concrete housing. She climbed up on top of it and pulled a trap door open, disappearing into the hole. I understood where we were; it was an access point for the drainage system on the school property. Looks like we'd be escaping under the earth.

Sami was back quickly, carrying a backpack. "Here, take a drink." She held out a water bottle. The water felt ice cold in my dried-out mouth. "Now these." She held out a couple of pills in the palm of her hand.

"What are they?" I croaked.

"Just some Advil. You're gonna need them for your foot. I have a surprise for you if you take them." Just a hint of playfulness crept into her voice. I swallowed the pills with another sip of water. I don't think I could have managed to get them down without the extra liquid.

"Now, eat this while I put the cast on." She held out a Snickers bar. Part of me was willing to start eating it without unwrapping it, but I got ahold of myself. "Don't make any noise," she ordered as I started unwrapping my gift and she brushed my foot off. The foot was still very tender—every touch was painful

—but I focused hard on the chocolate on my lips. She pulled out a foot cast from the backpack, one of those kinds that's plastic and covered in Velcro so it's removable. It felt like she was feeding my foot into a wood chipper as she slid it over my foot and tightened it down. Those Advil had their work cut out for them.

"Okay." Sami was back up at my Snickers-eating face. "It's about a ten-foot climb down the ladder in there. You think you can do it?"

"Yeah, I think I can." The candy bar, Advil and adrenaline had me practically shaking as they powered my empty body.

"Let's go." She slipped the wrapper and water bottle back into her backpack, then helped lift me up onto the top of the structure. It was very tricky work, getting my weakened, broken body in position at the ladder. Once I got my good foot on the first rung, I felt comfortable. Not too comfortable. I hugged the ladder the whole way down with my whole body. Reaching the bottom of the pit, I crumpled down to the ground against the interior concrete wall. It was much cooler down here, and slightly wet.

Sami had watched the entire process from above. Once I was on the ground, she swung herself in, pulling the door closed as she came down. With the door open, the space was barely lit; once the door closed it was pitch black. Watching with my ears, Sami reached the ground and shuffled to the other side of the space, then back to me. Clicking on a flashlight, we had some light again. She had a wad of cloth covering the lens, so we only got a glow instead of a beam. "Hold this. Keep it covered." She handed the light and its filter to me.

"Is that a rollerskate?" I asked. Sami had another smaller bag now, from which she pulled out what looked like a child's skate, but the shoe part was cut away so it was really just the skate part.

"Yeah. Give me your foot." She pulled out a couple pieces of rope. "It's a long way through this pipe, and I think it'll be easier if your foot could just roll along." She attached the skate to the side of my new cast, so if I was crawling on my belly, it would ride on the wheels. "Alright, are you ready?" she asked as she stood up, shoving the smaller bag into the backpack.

"Yeah, I guess so."

"We have about an hour ahead of us in the pipes. I'm going to be in front. If you can't keep going, I'll go to an opening and turn around and come back and drag you out. If I'm behind you I won't be able to push you." Fumbling for one more thing out of the bag, she pulled out another piece of rope, this one about ten feet long. "I'm going to tie this around my foot so it trails behind. Tug on it if you need to rest or are getting too far back. It's hard to hear in here."

"Okay, let's do it."

Balling the backpack up, she shoved it into the pipe first, then went head-first after it. Once her feet were through, I followed. The pipe was just slightly wider than my shoulders. An inch of mud covered the bottom, but I had gotten used to mud over the past few days. Ahead of me Sami was pushing forward, the flashlight giving its faint glow through the interior of the pipe.

"Are you in?" Sami had paused, leaning on her side to direct her voice back as much as possible.

"Yeah, I'm in."

"Here we go."

It was hard going. The rollerskate on my foot did help allow my useless foot to just roll along with me, but lacking that extremity for the crawling threw the whole rhythm off. I had to shift to using my knees as the primary movers. It wasn't the easiest, but I kept pace with Sami until the first opening. This space seemed the same as the one we had started from, just that it had a storm grate at the top, meaning we were somewhere in the parking lot. Handing me the bottle of water, I took a long drink before handing it back, Sami stowed it and ducked in the next pipe. So it continued for what felt like several hours, but time kinda loses meaning down in the center of the earth. We passed through four more drain housings before we were finally birthed out of the pipe into the forest, covered in mud and aching head to toe.

"I hope that's the last time I ever have to crawl through sewer pipes," Sami groaned, rubbing her elbows.

"Why, how many times have you crawled through sewer pipes?" I asked, sitting on the concrete ledge of the spillway.

"I've done it twice the past two nights." Sami bent down and untied the skate from my cast, shoving it back into her backpack. "Alright, let's get going." She pulled me up to my feet. "It's not too much farther."

"Where are we going?" We were on our way now. Even though we were on our feet, we weren't moving that much faster than we had been in the pipes. The uneven ground kept us slowed down.

"First the road. We're almost there, just a little farther."

Once we stumbled onto the hardtop of the road, things got easier. Walking in tandem was still terrible, but the level and firm surface let us get in sync. Two miles we covered walking like that before we reached our prior home, the gym and bowling alley. The very first glow of the sun was starting to show in the sky as we passed through the bowling alley doors.

"Back this way." Sami led us towards the back of the building. The space was a large rectangle; the offices and party rooms were on your left side as you entered, the lanes to the right. In the back the row of rooms turned ninety degrees with the wall, and there were the bathrooms.

"This is the hard part," she said as she started grabbing chairs and tables. "I couldn't find a ladder."

"Are you saying everything we've done so far has been the *easy* part?"

"We just have to get on top of the rooms." She motioned up the wall. The ceiling in the building was high. The sprinkler system, electrical wiring and AC ducts were all exposed as they snaked around the open space. The rooms all had walls about ten feet high, and then just open space above them up to the ceiling.

"Help me lift this." She pulled a third table over. We put it on top of the table pressed against the wall. With the other table pushed against them, it made table-sized steps. "Now your turn." She pushed me up onto the first table. From there I eased myself onto the second table. It was more stable than I thought it would be, but I was still sitting on top of two tables.

"Here." Sami held up a chair for me to grab. "Use this to get the rest of the way up onto the roof." While she leaned her weight into the tables to keep them steady against the wall, I started working the final stage of the ascent. The chair went against the wall and, slithering my body onto it, I reached the summit. Pulling my body over the final lip, I was now on the roof of the bathrooms.

"Good, now wait there." Pulling two ropes out of her bag, she tossed the backpack up to me. From the first table she took the rope and ran it underneath and along the wall side of the center-mounted table leg of the second table, then did the same with the second rope but on the room side of the mount. Handing the ropes to me, she scampered the rest of the way up to the roof. "Watch out." Nodding for me to lean out of the way, she hooked the chair we had used and flung it into the middle of the room. Most everything was in disarray already, so one thrown chair wasn't even noticeable.

"Alright, you hold these two." She handed me the ends of each rope, with the opposite ends in her hand. "We're going to lift the table up and then swing it over to the ground."

"Okay."

Both of us were leaning over the wall and pulled the slack out of the lines. "On three, nice and easy." It was shaky, but we managed what we were aiming for. The table lifted up and swung over to the open space on the ground, where we set it down.

"Let go of your ropes," Sami said once it was fully landed. Mine hit the floor as Sami spooled them back from her side. "Now there's no evidence of us climbing up here."

"I hope you have a plan for getting down."

"It's easier to fall down than jump up." Having picked up the bags, she led us across the ceiling towards a large AC vent. "We're hiding in here." She pulled the vent grate open. There was another bag sitting inside the duct for us. The duct we were facing was about the same diameter as the pipe we had spent all night crawling through, about ten feet long from where it teed off the main run that ran the length of the building.

The new bag contained more food and water bottles, as well as two N95 masks. "We're going to have to wear these. It's really dusty in there."

"Alright."

"Let's eat real quick." This bag had a couple bags of chips

and two pieces of corn. It was the quickest meal we'd ever eaten.

"Mask on," she ordered. "Crawl all the way in and go to the left. Once you get turned, back up so you're on the right side."

I nodded from behind my mask and climbed in. This pipe was smoother than the drainage pipes, so it was easier on the knees and elbows. Reaching the end of the run, I twisted to go left and get my body reoriented. Down the left side of the run I could see several trash bags, the ones we had hidden all of our stuff in before we had gone into the camp. Sami had already stashed them here. Once I was in position, Sami made her entrance. She came in feet-first, kicking the backpacks in ahead of her. That way she could close the grate behind us. She was also moving very slowly, pausing after every push to do something I couldn't see, since she was blocking my view. Grabbing the backpacks from behind her, I pulled them to my side so she could make the turn easier. Once she had maneuvered out of the way, I could see what she had been doing on her way in. She had a couple of cardboard boxes that she had filled with dust, and she had been sprinkling it around with each push so it wasn't obvious that people had crawled through it.

After arranging the last little bit of dust, Sami pushed herself fully back into her side of the pipe and gave a thumbs-up. We were finally done, having reached our hideout and covered our tracks. Making the universal sleeping motion, Sami clicked off her flashlight and we were in the dark. All it took was closing my eyes and my body immediately shut down.

* * *

The voices and crashes in the bowling alley woke me up. Sami was already awake. Though I could hardly see her in the darkness, she was holding her finger over her invisible mouth, signaling silence. The voices were indistinct. The distance between us and them kept the noise at just dull mumble. From the movement of the crashes and chatter of voices, it was clear they were looking for something, which could only be us. I hadn't had a chance to really think about what measures the camp would take to search for us and return us to our tents. If they were willing to use dogs, we'd be found. If they were willing to use technology, we'd be found. Infrared, night vision and Predator drones; those things would eventually find us, just like they found Bin Laden. However, if the organization stuck to their nature-centric principles, we should stand a good chance of staying hidden. At this point, someone would have to deliberately climb up into the ceiling and crawl into the AC duct to find us. We were betting on the odds of that happening being pretty low, unless they were prepared to search every building that thoroughly. Our best bet would be for them to realize that we had used the drainage system to escape undetected. That would probably get them to focus on the area around the drainage pipe as a good hiding spot, maybe sending out dozens of creatures to crawl around in the muck looking for us.

Sami had chosen the best possible spot for our hiding place. With my mobility limitations, we could've only made it so far under the cover of darkness. If my foot had been whole, we could've set off at a nice jog once we popped out of the pipes, and been miles away by the time the sun came up. That far away, we could've picked any random place to catch some sleep and know that we were far enough away that the searchers wouldn't catch up to us. With the injury, that option wasn't available and our radius was limited, so it was better to dig in and wait it out. Hopefully the searchers would assume we had pushed farther on in our desperation, hopefully pushing the main search area out past our hole.

For about thirty minutes we listened to the thumping around in the room below us, but the voices never got closer. They seemingly were confining themselves to searching only the obvious places they could find on the ground. Finally it was quiet again as the voices drifted off, probably to start ransacking the gym next door.

Sami suggested sleeping again with her hands and we were out once again.

* * *

It was dark by the time we woke back up. Of course, it

was pretty much dark all the time in our pipe home, but the glow of light from the other side of the grate had disappeared completely. Crawling forward, Sami came to my side of the tee junction. "I think we should stay in here for the rest of the night. They might've left someone behind to watch for us," she whispered, pulling her mask away from her face.

"I was hoping to go for a run, stretch the legs out."

"I'll bring back an exercise bike later."

Pushing back to her side, she pulled out some of the bags that were behind her and fished out more food for us. We were running low on anything that could be described as real food. Most of it was candy bars, chips and other junk food, but it was better than the literal nothing I'd been eating for the past week. The rest of the night was spent staring into the blackness of the pipe or sleeping.

Sami shook me gently awake the next morning. The dimness of the sun was just seeping into our world. "I'm going out to look around. You wait here." She crawled towards the exit. She was moving very carefully, trying to keep as silent as possible, hard to do in a metal pipe while dragging a bag with you, but she was managing.

After slipping through the grate, I lost sight of her. She stayed quiet enough out there that I couldn't tell if she was moving around, so I was back to being alone.

"Okay, I think we're clear." She startled me, sticking her head back through the grate. "Can you bring the bags or should I come back in?"

"I'll bring them." Pushing myself forward to her side, I snagged the bags and made for the exit.

Sami had been using the rope to climb to the ground and back, but she rebuilt the table and chair ramp for me to use. Quite the red carpet treatment. "What's the plan now?" I asked, once we were both safely on the ground.

"Remember I told you about the medical clinic we passed when we came here the first time?"

"I do."

"That's where I found your cast and the Advil. Lucky it was there, because that was about as far as I could search and still make it back to Camp Meadow before anyone noticed my absence. That's our next stop."

"Are we camping there tonight?"

"I don't know. That's as far as my plan goes—escape through the pipes, hide in the ducts, get back to the clinic."

"A crutch might be useful, if we can find a nice stick."

"Let's get going, then." She pulled me up.

Our tandem walk was slow and as frustrating as ever. Creeping through the woods slowly, we finally reached the opposite edge, overlooking another small strip of buildings, this time from the backside. "What's in there?" I asked. We were still hunkered down in the tree line, surveying the area.

"The clinic is the bigger one on the right, then a cellphone store and a dry cleaners, and the last one is a rehab-type gym."

"Had they already been searched?"

"I don't think so. I had to break a window to get into the clinic. There aren't many homes over this way, so I don't think anyone's wandered all the way over here yet. Even if they have, they probably aren't going to find much. The clinic doesn't have any serious medical supplies. Advil was the strongest medicine I could find."

"Well, hopefully we can find something useful," I answered. There must be some kind of break room or office space where we could find some stashed food.

"I don't think there's anyone here," Sami said, "but we should carry these again anyways." She pulled our two guns out of the backpacks. She tucked hers into her pocket and hooked the gun belt around me.

"Maybe we'll find a wheelchair," I said as we started towards the building.

"You think I'm going to push you around town in a wheelchair during the apocalypse?"

"Wouldn't it be better than carrying me?"

She sighed. "I'm already regretting this."

Sami had been right about the clinic; the majority of the medical supplies were unimpressive. Rubber gloves, gauze, wraps, ointments and tongue depressors. There were a few casts like mine left, but we only really needed the one. We combed through the place carefully and put together some stuff to keep. The medical items were small-time, but it wouldn't hurt to have some with us.

Next was the cell phone store. The phones were of no use, but we did find some weed stashed in the employee area, along with a bag of pistachios.

"You should eat those," Sami said when I pulled them out. "That's some actual food."

"Let's finish first."

Next we cracked the window of the dry cleaners. Zero edible items were found, but we did help ourselves to some new clothes, which were very clean. Ideally we would be wearing some tougher clothing, made for the outdoors, but that isn't the type of stuff that ends up at the dry cleaners. But beggars can't be choosers, so we went with what was available. We both ended up with a pair of slacks, more on the dressier side, but they would do. I found a couple of t-shirts and a lightweight sweater. Not sure who's getting t-shirts dry-cleaned, but either way they were mine now. Sami went with a man's sweater and we cut back the sleeves. All of the women's tops were going-out type of clothes—wearable, but kinda ridiculous for wandering the streets or hiding in the woods.

Our expectations were low when we started into the gym. Even though the last gym we had visited had worked well for us, this one was much smaller, and kettle bells weren't going to be of any use. The front half of the building was completely open with an astroturf type of floor. The walls were covered in different workout equipment, light weights, yoga mats, resistance bands and weighted balls. After that were a couple computer desks and chairs, obviously the check-in area. That led into the hallway. First room back there was a water massager, across from that was a bathroom, and then a small locker room with a changing space blocked off by a curtain. The lockers were really just cubbies where you could stuff your gym bag or shoes. My eyes fell on the bench and so did I. "I just need to sit down for a minute," I said.

"Good idea." She dropped down to the floor in front of me. "I feel like I'm dressed too fancy to be sitting on the floor," she said, picking at the new slacks she was wearing.

"You also spent the night in an AC duct, honey."

Sami snorted and started pulling the gym bags out of the cubbies. "Look through this one," she ordered, tossing it to me as she unzipped hers.

"Nothing but gym clothes," I answered, emptying it out next to me.

"I got some deodorant." She sniffed the end of it.

She pulled the next one off the shelf and the bag emitted a rattling sound. I've heard it described as the West Virginia mating call. Pulling the bag apart quickly, she found a pill bottle in the side pocket, the orange plastic glowing in the artificial light. She just stared at it for a minute before handing it over. It used to belong to Derrek Howzer, and that man had a prescription for Vicodin which he had conveniently forgotten in his gym bag.

"Everything's coming up Kyle today," Sami said, rifling through the rest of the bags but to no avail.

I popped the lid off the bottle and shook out one of the pills into my hand. "I've never taken Vicodin."

"If you don't take them, I will," she answered. I laughed and choked the pill down. "Come on, let's check the rest of the place before you pass out."

Across the hall was the standard supply room, toilet paper, mop and so on. "Nothing good over here," I announced, looking back at Sami who was still staring into the next room. "Something good?"

"You'll want to see it for yourself." She stepped out of the way for me. It was another supply room, but for workout gear. Some deflated balls and a large tractor tire was squeezed into the space. Hanging against the back wall was several pairs of crutches. "Of course," she said excitedly. "They'd have people on crutches here all the time. I should've checked here the other night."

Pulling all of them out, I started testing them, trying out various pairs like I was picking a new pair of shoes. "I like these ones." I grabbed the second pair, the right length and a bit more cushioned than the others.

"Think how fast we can move now," Sami said.

"I still think a wheelchair would work too." I sprinted out to the open area and back, grateful to be something close to mobile again.

"Maybe after I break your other foot," she said over her shoulder, leading us to the final room in the back. This room spanned the width of the building. With its glass door centered at the end of the hallway, the darkness kept us from really seeing what it looked like until the door opened. It was part kitchen, part smoothie bar, a nice place to cool down and refresh after a workout. My first thought was that it would be disappointing, since surely all of the food items would be spoiled by now, until Sami's beam curved left and found an entire wall of undisturbed protein powders, drinks, cookies and various other supplements. All pristine in their packaging.

"Wow," was all Sami managed to say.

Stepping past the smoothie counter and turning the lock on the exterior back door, I pushed it open. Sunlight and the breeze swept in, giving our little oasis an even more beautiful setting. "Let's get sorting," I said.

We started on the fridges, Sami going through the cooler and me the mini-fridges. Hers contained a few things gone bad, but also Gatorade and water bottles that were fine, just warm. The mini-fridges were all bad—ice cream, milk, yogurt and fruits that had all started melting away once the electricity failed. After that, things were better; nuts still in sealed jars, a couple of different cereals, and wrapped chocolate bars were all part of the smoothie station. Before long we had transferred all the expired goop into a pile in the grass behind the building, and all our still good food piled up on the countertop.

"I think it's time for breakfast," Sami said.

"And then a nap," I answered. The effects of the pill had my head swimming already.

* * *

"I never liked the way protein tastes with water," I said as Sami mixed up a second cup of the chocolate-flavored powder.

"Well, maybe we can find a cow so you can mix it with some milk."

"I don't think I'd be able to restrain myself from butchering that poor cow."

"Rather have a hamburger than a glass of milk?"

"Yes. I am still an American, after all."

We had spent the last hour casually enjoying our newfound bounty. We rationed out the actual food items to prolong their existence; however, the couple dozen large jugs of protein were a luxury we could indulge in.

"So I guess we're living in this gym now?" I asked after my first sip of my new drink.

"I'm not in charge anymore," Sami answered. "That's up to you."

"You got us out of there safely. Seems like you know what you're doing."

"Yes, and I also suggested we go in there in the first place, and they almost killed you."

"Not the first time we've seen that."

"This does seem like a decent place to hole up until your foot heals a bit."

"True. We finally have some food, and the mats will make a better bed than the dirt we've been sleeping on." I could still feel the sores on my body from having laid motionless on the ground during my stay in the wellness tent.

"So we live here for the rest of our lives?"

"No, just until the food runs out or I can start to walk better."

"And then?"

"If I had my way, we'd get to Alaska." My younger sister, Lindsay, lived in a small town in Alaska with her husband Josh. He had just finished pilot school and was working as a bush pilot out there. Sami and I had visited once for the wedding. If you thought Alaska itself was remote, this town was only accessible by a two-hour plane ride out into the wilderness. It was interesting, but not where I wanted to live. Of course, that was when life was functioning normally here in the lower forty-eight. I had talked to

Lindsay once things had started to take a turn for the worse down here. She had said things were pretty much normal up there still and maybe we should think about coming up. By the time I realized we should have, it was too late.

"Alaska's a long walk."

"True, but your parents' house is on the way."

"You mean my dad's." Sami always corrected me on this point.

"Either way, that's really our only option outside of Joliet." Going to Dakota had barely even qualified as an option at every other point in our life. I actually thought I might live through the rest of my life without ever seeing Daniel or Carla ever again. Now we were left with no other options for surviving than trying to seek out a familiar face. Even if it was unfriendly, it was better than another stranger.

"I guess we're going to Dakota," Sami said with a sigh.

Dakota, Illinois was up in the northwestern corner of the state, where Iowa and Wisconsin come together as well. "We need to get a map," I said.

"I remember how to get there."

"I do too, via the highway. But we need to travel by the back roads. Avoid as many people as possible."

"How long do you think it'd take to get there?"

I started doing the math. At an average of 60 mph, a two-hour drive like it usually took us would mean we were roughly 120 miles away. The history books I'm always reading seem to agree that an army can march about 20 miles per day, which sounded like a good estimate for us too, if we were healthy. Which would mean at least six days of walking. With the current state of my foot, I had no idea how much longer it would take.

"A week minimum, but probably longer in my condition."

"What if we had bikes?"

None of my history books had armies marching on bikes. "I don't know, but less than walking."

"I'll find us some," Sami said firmly.

* * *

The rest of the day we spent our time feathering our new nest. We emptied out the storeroom we found the crutches in and filled it with our new bedding. Now that we had some mattress material, we went back and found some blankets at the dry cleaners to round out our new bedroom. By the end of the day we were pretty happy with our new home. "This is probably the best we've had since the fire," I said, dropping from the crutches into our bed.

"I dunno, it was pretty nice at the hotel until the raping and murdering started," Sami said, laying down next to me.

"I agree, that was definitely when things took a turn for the worse."

"Any ideas where I should start looking for bikes?" she asked, leaning over.

"We haven't seen many people around since we left, so there could be some left in the stores. There's that sporting goods store on Jefferson."

"Yeah, I just worry about venturing into that area. There's got to be some people already laying claim to that space."

"Then private homes are probably the best bet. Check the garages. It seems like everyone has a bike hanging up in there."

"And maps?"

"Do gas stations still sell maps?"

"I don't know, I've never looked."

"That might be trickier. Maybe a bookstore. I know they'll have an atlas at least, and maybe actual maps."

"Okay."

"Speaking of books, do you think you could find me some?"

"Think you're going to get bored in here?"

"Well, I'd prefer an Xbox if you see any electricity. Otherwise books will be acceptable."

"If I brought an Xbox in here you'd never leave. Any special requests?"

"Not really. I'll take anything you can find, though I reserve the right to complain about it if I don't like them."

"As to be expected from you."

We paused, our back and forth having reached a natural end. Sami raised up and stared at my shoulder, her sign that she wanted me to move my arm so she could snuggle into me. I obliged and she curled up against me. "I missed you," she whispered.

"I missed you too, my dear."

CHAPTER FOURTEEN
DOGS

Our next two weeks were spent in relative comfort in our new home. My convalescence kept me tied to our building complex. When I got bored I'd roam around the cellphone store, the dry cleaners and the clinic, always looking for something new, but there wasn't much to be found. But most of my time was spent sleeping as I worked my way through the remaining pills. The exhaustion of the past weeks had caught up with me, and the long-delayed dulling of the pain let me slip into a deep and uninterrupted sleep as if I was a newborn baby. Sami had kept busy picking the surrounding area, but with little to show for her efforts. The immediate area around us was mostly industrial-type buildings. These contained small amounts of food, mostly out of breakroom vending machines or office desks, but nothing serious, just supplemental to our main diet of watery protein shakes. She had also found a couple short paperback books, which each lasted me less than a day.

"This is as far as I've made it." Sami was pointing to the wall, where she had drawn a crude map of the local area based on her exploration. "Once I cross this road, it starts to become residential. However, that's starting to get close to the Express again, and things sound bad in that direction."

"What do you mean?" I asked. We knew of course that we had to avoid wandering into the reach of anyone from the Express. The odds of us being tortured to death were pretty high after I killed off three of their leaders.

"Lots of gunfire coming out of that space, and I've dodged several government convoys moving through there. Reminds me of watching the news as a kid when we invaded Iraq."

"That makes sense. They aren't going to let this anarchy situation go on forever."

"Yeah, which means they're working their way here. The closest I've seen them is still several miles away, but we can't be here when they finally get to this section." She continued with her briefing. "Straight ahead I've made it to here, a Jiffy Lube on Baker. Across the street it starts to become poorer neighborhoods. I spent some time watching from that area. It looks like there's still a lot of people living in there, and I've seen a lot of guns but no fighting. I think they're arming up for when the Dirts arrive."

"So farther into town isn't an option."

"Yeah, we seem to have luckily landed in kind of a no-man's-land here. No one lives over here and there isn't much to appropriate anyway. Mechanic shops, small industrial and warehouses don't mean much nowadays."

"And to the right?" A right turn out of our home would take us west, in the general direction of Dakota.

"It's more of the same so far, warehouses and other businesses. There does seem to be a group operating out of a UPS shipping facility. I watched it for a bit but that's as far as I went."

"Depending on what was being shipped when operations stopped, they could've found some good supplies there." Then again, there'd be a lot of boxes to go through in a place like that.

"That and it's pretty secure, a tall fence with barbed wire all the way around, and gates at the entrance."

"Well that's the direction we need to go, farther west. Have you seen any way to slip around?"

"Yeah, there's a couple roads around it. I assume they stay behind the fence during the night."

"So we get close enough to watch during the day and see if we notice any lookouts, then slip by during the night."

"How much more food do we have?" she asked, taking a seat next to me on a large rubber workout ball.

"We still have plenty of powder, but we're running low on everything else, including water to mix with the powder."

"It's not like we can carry much water anyways."

"Yeah, we're going to have to find it on our way." This was something I had given a lot of thought to. We'd need to be able to boil water on our march to drink and use for the powder. Eating it unmixed was practically impossible. I had once tried swallowing some without any extra liquid, but it wouldn't go down my throat, leading to a lot coughing and gagging.

"We need a map," Sami said. It was true; a map and bikes were at the top of the list of our needs. My estimate of a week of walking was based on making about 20 miles a day, something impossible to do with me on crutches. With bikes we figured we'd be able to power through and get to Dakota before we exhausted our supplies. On foot and without a map to keep us going in the right direction, and guide us to water when needed, this trip might stretch into several weeks. "I just don't know where to look," she said glumly.

"I know. Paper maps might not even exist anymore, as far as I know." We were quiet again as we remembered the life we had once lived. Everything we could ever need was either on our 'Let already, or only free two-day shipping away.

"What about a phone book?" Sami said abruptly. "That might have a list of places that might have bikes or maps."

"I don't know if there are any map stores..." I stopped myself before my mind could catch up. "But there are bike stores. That's it, the bike store!" Sami was just watching me. My thinking face had arrived. "I was looking for something, I was looking for..." I closed my eyes, trying to bring the memories forward. "I was looking for the window place. We had that window with the water in it and it took forever to find a place that could fix it."

"I remember that place," Sami said. "It was out in Oswego."

"I ended up on the wrong street and there was an

outdoorsy kinda place. Camping gear, hiking gear, stuff like that. There were a bunch of trail bikes outside, I remember because it was interesting-looking from the street." I opened my eyes. "We need to get there."

"And bikes and trails probably means maps," Sami added.

"Yes, it probably does."

* * *

The next two days were spent preparing to move out. Sami was working on our route to the west side, keeping an eye on the UPS group and figuring out how to get around them. It was too far for her to get to the other side and scout it out, so we would be moving in blind once we got past the actual building. She had picked out an advantage point for us to watch once we got there while we waited for dark, and had already hid some of our food and supplies there.

My job was less interesting; it was resting and packing the backpacks. Sami had found a couple of decent hiking packs over the past two weeks, so I emptied everything out and went to work making the most efficiently packed bags we could have. We'd been bringing along now a lot of random things with us that we'd collected while on our own—multiple knives, flashlights, batteries that didn't fit any of the flashlights, things like that. Our first priority was to carry as much protein powder as possible. I shifted it out of the normal jugs and into plastic bags so it was more space-efficient. I even created a sling for the yoga mats we had been using for beds, so we could roll them up and strap them to our bags. We were short on blankets; all of the ones from the dry cleaners were large and too bulky to carry with us. Instead we'd be carrying a couple of towels for general purposes and makeshift blankets.

We had both spent some time drawing on the wall, trying to recreate a map from memory of the area where the bike store was located. By the end of the second day we were about ready to move out. Sami had finished her recon for the day and was back. "It takes me about three hours to get to the lookout building," she said once she'd shaken off her scouting gear and joined me in the front room with the crude map.

"Maybe double with the crutches?" I ventured. My foot wasn't in pain anymore, but it wasn't ready yet to support my full weight.

"Probably," she agreed, plopping down on her usual rubber ball seat next to me.

"No matter what, it should work. Get there with enough time that we can eat and each get some sleep while we wait."

"I also looked for other ways around the building. To the south side, it gets deeper into the city, and it looks like a pretty active area in there. It seems like the UPS gang is right on the edge of contested territory. So we're going to have to go along the north side. There are several streets and buildings there." She motioned to what had been drawn in on the wall map. "Then it's that runoff pond marshy area. It's fenced in pretty deep into the woods. So to go that way we'd have to get through the fence and the marsh, or detour all the way around through the woods."

"Well, we'll just have to get through those streets," I answered. Our short foray through the woods escaping the camp had been difficult. Going back into them would slow us down significantly.

"You got the bags packed?"

"Yep, I got us slimmed down to the essentials and as much powder as I could fit. I think it's about three weeks' supply if we're careful with it."

"And water?"

"That's the hard part. Water's heavy and doesn't compress very well. I got us each twenty bottles, maybe enough to last us five days. I have these small backpacks we can wear on the front that we can load down with water, but we're really increasing the weight."

"Well, let's take them tomorrow and see how it works on our way to the lookout position."

"Other than the rations side, I think we're well-equipped. We each have a headlamp with fresh batteries that gives off red filtered light. That'll help for moving in the dark."

"Oh, I forgot, I found us dessert for tonight," Sami said,

cutting me off as she grabbed her bag, pulling out two packages of Twinkies. "Found them in the lookout building today."

"Nice. That'll be a nice touch to our final meal here."

Our meal was as good as it could possibly be. We chowed down on everything we'd be leaving behind—assorted chips, candies, and of course plenty of protein powder, topped off with Sami's newfound Twinkies. Then we curled up into our luxurious bed of blankets and foam pads for one last good night of sleep.

* * *

The faintness of the sun creeping through the building woke us up the next morning. "I'll get breakfast," Sami muttered, crawling out of bed first. Within twenty minutes we were fed, dressed and loaded down with our gear. "How's it feel with the bags?" she asked as she followed me out of the building. I had been working on my crutch technique since we had first found them, and had gotten pretty quick with the artificial legs. Carrying the two fully packed bags made the process a lot harder, however, and even though I'd been practicing under load for the past few days, it didn't make it any easier.

"I wish we had found one of those scooter things for broken feet," I answered.

"Maybe a golf cart too?"

"Well, now you're just being silly."

We kept marching on. One aspect in our favor was the overcast sky, meaning we didn't have the sun bearing down full power.

"Let me take your water bag," Sami said, pulling me to a stop.

"No, You have your own. I can carry mine."

"Yes, but walking at your speed, I can carry more than normal." She was right—we were each loaded down about the same amount, even though I was chained to the crutches and she'd been walking miles and miles every day for the past few weeks.

"Fine." I slipped the front pack off my shoulders. Sami

looped it around her shoulders, still on the front side, riding next to her own water bag.

"All good," she said, and we went back to marching pace.

We reached the lookout building by mid-afternoon. About the latest we had planned on being there, but we made it. Sami had picked out a third-floor window from an office building that gave us a good view of the UPS facility and the roads running on the north side that we'd follow this evening.

"Its two p.m. now. We probably don't want to start moving until about ten o'clock," Sami said, checking her new analog watch she'd found last week. "We've got eight hours."

"I can take first watch," I offered.

"No, I won't be able to sleep right now. You go first."

"Alright, boss."

Even though Sami had spent some time here watching the compound, there was no sign she had, in case anyone wandered in while she was gone. However, she dragged back her office chair and the food stash she had left here the other day. A quick shake later and we were both in our spots, Sami in her chair watching through the window and me on the foam pad in the corner.

Four hours later we traded posts. I could've really used some ice for my foot, but we hadn't seen ice since we last had the generator running at our house. The daylight portion of the surveilling was boring. There were some people on the roof of the shipping facility. They seemed to be lookouts in their own right. Several people were moving around outside. Behind the fence they'd constructed several long wooden planter boxes that they were tending to. Urban farming had quickly become the go-to activity for just about every community around. Several other groups came and went from the south side of the compound. That direction led deeper into the metropolis, meaning other people. Perhaps some of these communities had already created trading or cooperative relationships. It'd be better than the militant nature of the Express.

The area had returned to a working tribal system in response to the crisis. The better organized were probably able to guard their boundaries to keep the government influence out. Dirts didn't have enough muscle yet to bring everyone physically under their thumb, so they were currently working their way through the low-resistance areas like our former neighborhood. Once areas like that were completely controlled and they could start leveraging those people into the Dirts en masse, they could enlarge their forces and extend their control into the currently independent spaces. Before long, everyone would be answering to an Arborist and carrying around their own copy of *The Little Brown Book*. Camps like the one at the school were really the training ground for the next wave of instructors. Once people from the Express or UPS were brought under control, they would be sent to be reeducated by people like Cassidy, Jenny and Carter, leading their own groups towards atonement to the Earth.

Watching the small groups that were outside the fence begin to wander back, I noticed them concentrating around the corner of the building. Our viewing position only gave a view of the north and east sides of the building. The south side was the farthest away, and that's where the people were gathering. Maybe it was some kind of check-in process—make sure everyone who had gone out had made their way back—however, it wasn't anywhere near the main entrance. Everyone I'd seen going in and out had used the same door. The group reached about twenty people in number, standing around idly, then they turned and marched around the south side of the building, out of my sight. Even though Sami had watched this building several times, she hadn't been here this late. If she had, she would've spent about three hours walking home in the dark, which would've been too dangerous. So if this was a routine activity, she hadn't seen it. Checking the watch she had left out, we saw that it was about 7:30 p.m. We still had about an hour of the fading sun left.

The noise started faintly at first, something I didn't even notice when it started, then suddenly I realized what I was hearing. Dogs. The general commotion that a large group of dogs make when they're excited. It was coming from the south side of the building, but was getting louder. The group returned to my line of sight as they passed around the edge of the building. The twenty people were now wrangling about forty dogs or so, my math based on the fact that most of them seemed to have a leash in each hand.

"Sami!" I whispered harshly as I tossed an empty water bottle at her in the corner. She responded by rolling over. "Sami!" I hissed louder this time, following it with a coffee mug that had been sitting by the window.

It hit her in the hip, causing her to jump awake. "What!"

"Get over here."

She stumbled to the window, which we were both easing away from now. During the rest of the watch we had been casual about watching through it, but now we were peeping around the edges. "That's a lot of dogs," she whispered. The group had exited the entrance gate and began splitting up, some of them turning left and towards the south side of the building, leading their dogs out of sight. The majority kept to the right, heading along the east side, bringing them towards us.

"Are they hunting us?" Sami asked, her hand drifting down to the pistol on her hip.

"I don't know, but we aren't outrunning dogs at this point," I answered, my mind racing through the situation. Armed people with dogs on leashes give the appearance of a hunting party in general, but it didn't really fit with the circumstances either. Why go hunting at night? If they had gotten wind of us somehow, why wouldn't they make a beeline for our hideout?

As the group moved along, their intentions become more apparent. More and more people split from the group, going their separate ways, bringing several onto the street we were on, just farther south. The first person who'd separated revealed their purpose when he reached the cross street, picked up a chain that was coiled up at the bottom of a stop sign, and fastened it to one of his dogs' collars while unclipping the leash he'd been using. That dog continued to try following the man and the remaining dog, whining and yipping at them both as they moved north along our street towards us; but after what had to be at least a hundred feet, the new leash finally tightened and the dog came to a whimpering stop.

"They're using them as guard dogs around the whole perimeter." I voiced the realization. The group was fully dispersed by now, the men tethering their dogs to new leashes, forming a living fence.

"Shit, there's a chain right there," Sami groaned. This time she was looking in the other direction at the streetcorner to our right. Previously unnoticed, there was a pile of chain at the base of a traffic light pole.

"Move back," I ordered as I stood up. We crept back into the shadows of the room as one of the dog handlers approached under our window, hooking up a large Doberman to the chain at our corner. Ducking down, Sami grabbed a marker from the desk in the room and started sketching a map on the wall of what we could see. It was a good idea. If our plan was going to work, we'd need to know where the dogs were.

"There's one at the next intersection too," I said. That was the last road to the north of us. It faced the runoff pond and woods on that side. Sami marked it on the new map. "Two more somewhere on that street facing the pond. I can't see it but the guy left them over there."

The light was fading now. Seeing down the streets became nearly impossible as the last few dogs were placed and the men headed back towards the gate. Finally the rattling of the gate echoed out as it was shut, and a few glimpses of light were seen as the last people entered the UPS building. Our new guard was roaming around under our building. The sound of his chain dragging and claws clicking on the pavement echoed through our hideout.

"Now what do we do?" Sami sank down to the floor.

"I wonder if he likes protein powder?" Sami didn't answer and despite the darkness, I could see the glare. *No jokes now* was the message. So of course I continued with them. "We both can't outrun him. Of course, this is the classic 'I just have to run faster than you' situation."

"Kyle!"

"Okay, let's think." I closed my eyes and leaned back, traditional thinking pose. I always felt like Professor Xavier when I focused like this. We couldn't shoot the dog; Sami wouldn't be on board with that plan, since she loved dogs. More importantly, the sound of the gunshot would surely bring out the people, and all the other dogs would start going crazy, drastically reducing the odds of us getting through. If we were able to silence the gun, we might be able to sneak past, but the dead dog would be found and we would probably have the same issue on the other side of the perimeter. That might lead to a search party being sent after us in the morning and, since our mobility was limited, we wouldn't get far enough away during the night. We could detour around through the woods, but it would be a hard trek and add probably a full day to our walking. That was the last resort.

"What would they do in the movies?" I finally asked.

"What do you mean?"

"What do they do in movies when they need to get past some dogs?"

"In Harry Potter they played a flute to put the dog to sleep." Sami answered with a joke this time.

"Do you have a flute?" I countered.

"No."

"The most common movie trick is to distract the dog with a treat, or food with sleeping pills in it. But we don't have any pills or food that a dog would want." I continued my thinking out loud. "If we can't feed him or put him to sleep, we need to outsmart him. We need to…trap him. Yeah, let's trap him in the building. We lure him in and close the door behind him." I opened my eyes. We had the strategy, and now we needed tactics.

"Let's move our stuff downstairs and figure out how to get him." Sami started to stand up.

"Wait, let's eat first."

Twenty minutes later we were fed and downstairs with a plan developing. The dog could be lured in through the front door, but the problem would be getting it closed behind him, and then whoever was baiting him getting out the back before the dog caught up. We couldn't have the dog actually start chasing us; that would result in barking and probably attracting attention.

"How about the stairwell?" Sami suggested. There were two sets of stairs in the building, one in the front and one in the back. We had used the rear set to get here, but the front stairwell was close to where the dog was.

"That'll work. Easy to avoid him in there, and the thicker walls will muffle any barking once he's inside."

So we set up the trap. Across from the door for the stairs was an office. That was my hiding spot. I found a door stopper and then cut some string from the blinds . That way we could hold the stairwell door open with the stopper and I could pull the string from the office, closing the door once the dog had passed through. Sami checked the second-floor door and made sure it was open so she wouldn't end up getting trapped in with the dog.

"Okay, that works." I pulled the string from my hiding spot and the stairwell door swung close.

"Make sure he goes in a bit before you pull it. You don't want him blocking it," Sami suggested.

"Yeah, I'll watch the chain so I know how far in he is." Sami reset the stopper on the door and we were ready. "Be careful. Don't let him see you," I said. I had my gun ready. If things went bad, we were shooting our way out and fleeing back as fast as we could.

Sami nodded as she crept forward to the front door. It would've been easier and safer if we both could've been up there for this part, one person watching the dog through the windows and the other doing the whistling, but we decided it was too risky with my foot. If the dog started running, I probably wouldn't be able to get back to my position in time, and the whole operation would fail.

Up front Sami was adjusting the window blinds so she had a better view of the dog. He'd been down the street for a while, just doing dog stuff. "Here we go," Sami called back, before she pushed open the front door and slid another door stopper under it, locking it open. Then she started with the whistling. Soft at first, finding the right volume for the dog to hear and locate. I could only see her back as she leaned through the doorway, but her body was still telling me the story of what was happening. Once she had its attention, she worked her way back through the room towards me, keeping her eyes focused through the windows and the approaching guard.

Reaching the stairwell door, she slipped through, carefully avoiding the string and door stopper. From just inside the darkness she changed her tune, stopping with the whistling and starting with the traditional dog sounds. "Here, doggy doggy, come here, boy." The snout of the Doberman appeared in the open doorway, followed by his entire body. The dogs were well trained and cautious. He seemed to be searching the interior before he ventured in, as if he expected a trap. Slowly he crossed through the doorway. Instead of the normal brash barking guard dog you usually expect, he walked like a predator stalking his prey, small deliberate steps followed by the sounds of Sami receding farther into the stairs.

Holding my breath, I watched him reach the stairwell doorway. Sniffing the ground for our scent and checking his surroundings again, he entered the stairwell slowly, his chain dragging behind him. Once his tail disappeared, I counted the links of the chain as they slithered through. Several feet of chain vanished into the darkness before I yanked the string. It tightened and the doorstop popped free, the heavy door swinging shut right over the chain. If he was smart enough to free himself from that trap, he deserved to catch us.

Climbing back to my feet, I crutched up and crept to the front door, peeking out. Nothing was unusual out there, and the missing guard hadn't been noticed. We had succeeded, but it was still going to be a very long night. Now we were facing a trek into unfamiliar territory with guard dogs actively patrolling the area.. Heading towards the back stairwell now, I was careful to step over the dog's chain as I passed. The dog, sensing my presence anyway, lunged into the door. His muffled barks were still loud enough that I fell against the opposite wall in surprise.

"You alright?" Sami called from the end of the hallway.

"Yeah, just startled."

"Wait there. I'll bring your stuff to you."

"How'd it go up there?" I asked as she lugged our backpacks into the front room.

"It was easy. I went up to the door and just leaned over the railing."

"Let's hope the next one is as easy," I said as she lifted my front pack up for me to slip into.

"I hope he's okay in there," Sami worried, looking at the stairwell door that was still shaking from the Doberman trying to scratch his way through it.

"He'll be fine. He'll take a nap and they'll let him out in the morning." I turned towards the door. "But we need to get moving."

Out front everything was still peaceful. From this vantage point we couldn't see the other guard dogs that were stationed farther down the street, but we knew they were there. "Grab that, we might need it," I said, pointing to the door stop that was keeping the front door open. Sami scooped it up and let the door close gently behind us.

Moving forward was slower than we had expected. The darkness seemed darker down on the street than it had before, and we were watching intently for any signs from the rest of the guard dogs. Move a few feet and listen, duck behind a car and scan the area ahead. It felt like we had moved at a faster pace when we were crawling through the drainage pipes underground.

"I think I see something," Sami whispered as I joined her behind a car still parked on the street. "Over there by the gas pumps." Sure enough, with help of the moon I could make out the low-slung body of a German Shepherd prowling around the gas pumps at the corner ahead of us.

"I was kinda hoping we might run into a goldendoodle or something like that," I whispered. German Shepherds have a violent look to them. It might have something to do with the Nazis, which isn't really fair—I don't think a dog breed really has any political opinions—but no matter what the case, it makes you feel like you're fleeing the Gestapo when you come face-to-face with one of them.

"This is a bad spot," Sami said. She was right—this intersection was empty on three sides, the gas station the only building in the immediate area. Which left us with few places to trap this guard.

"How about that car?" I answered. There was a Jeep sitting on the edge of the gas station parking lot.

"What about it?"

"Maybe we can lure him into the Jeep and get the doors closed."

"That's going to be hard," she said, visibly exhaling. "We're gonna be a lot closer to him than we want to be."

"I know, but I don't know what else to try. He's right in front of the gas station, so we can't get into it, and even if we did, we don't know if there's anywhere to trap him in there. He'll see us if we try to slip past him."

Sami was quiet, weighing our options. We couldn't tell what the dog was tethered to, so there was no way of telling how long his leash was, though you could expect it to be long enough to reach his whole patrolling area.

"How do we do it?" she finally asked.

"You get in the back driver seat and open the front passenger door. I'll be on the roof. When he jumps in, I lean out and slam the door closed, and you jump out your door."

"Alright," she answered softly. It wasn't a great plan, but it was the best we had, and we needed to keep moving. Our dog traps would be noticed in the morning and, if we were still nearby, they had a good shot of tracking us down. We had to get through the perimeter and put some distance between us and them. The more time we lost inside, the more at risk we'd be on the other side.

Approaching the Jeep, we moved even slower than before, this time at an angle, trying to keep it between us and the dog to exploit the blind spot. We were also lucky that there didn't seem to be any wind to worry about; our sneaking abilities weren't on that level yet. The driver's door was ajar, some good fortune since our plan could've fallen apart if the doors had been locked. Breaking a window to get in would have gotten the dog on us a lot faster than we wanted. Slipping our bags off and leaving them in the grass, we slithered the last few feet until we were pressed up against the car. Sami popped the rear door open and I used it as a foothold to get my body onto the roof. It wasn't a pretty process, but I managed with minimal noise, though once I got my eyes on the dog I saw that he was already looking in our direction, starting to sense our presence.

Underneath me I could feel Sami moving around in the car. She pulled the rear door shut but not latched so she could jump out quickly. I felt the front passenger door pop and then swing open. The German Shepherd immediately sank down into his hunting pose, his legs bent and head lowered, ready to strike.

German Shepherds are better attack dogs than guard dogs. If he'd been thinking logically, he would've started calling for help by barking. Instead he decided to pursue us on his own, thinking his quiet approach was helping him when it was actually playing to our favor. If we could lock him up in the car, his barks would be muffled like the Doberman, and it'd be hard to hear it back at the UPS compound.

Creeping forward slowly, he reached the open car door and sniffed around. We both could hear Sami calling softly from inside, her patented dog-calling sounds. This time, though, the dog was more wary. After an inspection, he backed off and started circling the vehicle. Keeping as flat and still as humanly possible, I kept my eye on him as he moved around the front. On the other side he spotted our bags and inspected those, sniffing and nosing them about. If there'd been anything in there that a dog would be interested in, we would've already used it as bait, so he moved on. Next he went up against Sami's door. He knew she was in there and scratched at it, but he wasn't getting through the solid metal. Finally he gave up. Completing his circle around the car, he was back at the open door, listening to Sami try and bait him in. His nervous energy was building, pacing and whining as he fought the mental battle between the desire to jump in the car and the reasoning that he shouldn't.

Playing her last card, Sami popped open her door loudly. The sudden motion and thought that she might escape out the other side spurred the German Shepherd forward. He leapt into the passenger seat as Sami tumbled out of the rear door and I lunged over the side of the car, grabbing the top edge of the passenger door and slamming it shut. By putting my full force into the door, it slammed shut over the chain, catching it fast between the door and vehicle frame. The dog was now stuck in the passenger seat, keeping him from continuing after Sami.

"You alright?" I asked, leaning over the other side of the car. Sami was still in a heap on the ground, but she had managed to kick her door shut, muffling the barks that were starting now.

"Yeah."

I slithered down the front of the Jeep as the German Shephard just glared at me through the window. He had a look of pure hatred in his eyes. It seemed like he took being tricked very personally. "Let's get going before Adolf here figures out how to open the door."

Fishing our bags out of the grass, we loaded back down. "You sure you're okay?" I asked. Sami still looked like she was in shock.

"Yeah. It was just scary when he jumped in."

Wrapping my arms around her, I pulled her in. "It's alright, babe. We're going to be okay." We stood there for a few minutes. The never-ending stress of this world is probably the hardest adjustment. Before there were stresses, to be sure, but they were contained in situations that we already knew would be stressful. Now, every action, every decision is potentially fatal. Just trying to feed ourselves is a constant struggle, something we have to focus on every day. We thought feeding ourselves in the previous world was difficult, even though we were constantly in a state of being a few minutes away from a fully prepared meal. Now there were no fallbacks. Find food or starve. Move or get caught. Trap a dog or get your face chewed off.

"We need to get going, honey," I said, finally breaking our moment.

Nodding, Sami picked up my second backpack and led us forward, as the Shepherd continued to watch us through the glass.

We trudged forward until the sun peeked over the horizon behind us. The journey had been conducted in nearly complete silence, just the sounds of Sami's shoes and my crutches. We moved carefully, but quicker than we had been earlier. Our assumption was that the west side of the compound would be deserted like the east had been. So it had been—just more industrial buildings, empty lots and small abandoned homes. By the time the sun arrived, we had traveled several miles in a zig-zag pattern, making it harder for anyone to follow us. At one intersection we found some blankets laying around, so we laid them down to walk across the street on, attempting to hide our scent in case the dogs were used to trail us.

"How about McDonald's?" I asked as I saw the golden arches glowing ahead of us in the dawn light.

"Good enough."

The McDonald's had already been cleaned out; all food service places got hit early on. So the windows were all broken and it looked like a tornado had gone through the interior. But it was otherwise empty, our kind of place. In the back we found the cramped office and threw enough of the garbage out until we had space for our mats and collapsed onto them.

* * *

I woke up first. Sami's watch said it was 6:12 p.m., which meant we had been sleeping for about twelve hours. I prepared us some breakfast, or dinner depending on how you view it. Waking Sami up gently, we chugged down our meal and got ready to move out. We only had a few hours of daylight left and we were close to our target, the bike store. The McDonald's lived on the main road through this area, but the bike shop was tucked away a bit. If we hurried we might be able to find it before dark. It might've been safer to move through the night, but navigating the streets and looking for a specific building in the darkness was really a waste of energy.

"I think that's it," Sami finally exclaimed, tugging me to my right. Even though the light was fading, we could make out the outline of a bike wheel plastered on the front window. The sign had been knocked down at some point and was getting suffocated by the weeds, and the bikes I remembered being out front weren't there anymore, but Sami had spotted it and we had finally made it.

The glass on the front door had been punched through, so we wouldn't be the first people to visit the shop, but hopefully they still had some bikes. "Where's your flashlight?" I asked Sami as we reached the front door. The fading sunlight had reduced the inside of the building to darkness. "We need to be careful here." Unlike the other places we had hidden recently, a store filled with bikes might attract people and result in them holing up here.

Dropping our bags off to the side and drawing our guns, we stepped through the doorway. We both almost dropped our guns when our lights hit the rows of bikes still lined up in their rows waiting to be sold. "Looks like we get our pick," said Sami, shining her light across all of them.

We moved through the rest of the building. It was bigger than you would expect for a bike shop. There were signs of people having been in here, but nothing that looked recent. Apparently most everyone had forgotten about this store, or decided they didn't really need bikes.

"Which one do you want?" I asked once we returned to marvel at our find.

"I'll take any of them at this point, even that one." She pointed to a child's bike with streamers coming out of the handlebars and a pink seat.

"Eight-year-old Sami would've really enjoyed that one."

"Not as much as twenty-eight-year-old Sami is going to enjoy it," she said with a laugh. "We might actually get to Dakota in just a couple of days now."

"Speaking of that, let's find a map."

Sure enough, there was a stack of paper foldout maps of the region with roads and bike trails on them, extending all the way to the Iowa boarder. "Thank God for these bike nerds," I said, tracing my finger along the map. There wasn't really a direct route to Dakota, and the shortest routes would've led us back through towns along the densely populated suburban areas of Chicago. We were going to go the other way, straight west into the cornfields and then feel our way north, avoiding as many settlements as possible. It would add mileage, but there'd be better odds of not running into people who would derail our plans.

"I think I like this one," Sami announced from her new seat after having sat on just about every bike in the store.

The sound of the front door opening caused us both to jump. Sami had put her gun back in her pocket, but mine was still sitting heavy in my hand. "What did I say…" the man was saying as he stepped through the door, his voice trailing off when he saw us.

"Get down!" I ordered, the gun and flashlight trained directly on him. Sami had hopped off the bike in a flash and was aiming on him as well.

"I don't want any trouble," the man stammered, holding his hands out.

"I said get down, on your knees!" I screamed.

"Okay, okay." He dropped down, instinctively holding his hands above his head.

"Get something to tie him up," I said to Sami.

"You don't have to do that. I don't want any trouble."

"Shut the hell up. You're lucky I don't shoot you right here."

"Daddy!" The second voice behind us in the dark caused everyone to jump. Sami spun around, her light flashing through the air.

"PLEASE, NO! KATIE, GO BACK IN THE BACK!" the man shouted, his face twisted in panic as he started forward.

"Don't move!" I screamed again. "Don't fucking move!" The man caught himself and remained kneeling, though visibly shaking now. "Sami?"

"It's just a kid," she answered, her voice low. The silence in the room was only broken by the child's wheezing.

"Okay, everyone stay calm for a minute," I instructed, lowering my voice and inching my way out of the center of the room and to the opposite side from Sami. The new vantage point let me see both of the intruders without having to fully turn away from the man. Sami was right, it was just a little girl, probably five or so, dressed in dirty clothes, tear streaks lining her face.

"I did what you said, Daddy," she choked out between sobs. "I hid under the trashcan, but they wouldn't leave."

"It's okay, Katie, it's okay. Everything is going to be okay." The man struggled to keep his voice steady.

"Katie." Sami addressed her, taking the lead from me. I doubted the girl would respond to anything I said. "Katie, do you see that spot on the ground where I'm pointing?" The little girl nodded. "I need you to walk over there and sit down and everything will be okay. Do you understand?" Katie nodded again and followed the instructions, taking a seat in front of the display case full of custom bike pedals.

Once she was seated, I focused all my attention back on the man. "Do you have a gun on you?"

He nodded. "In the back of my pants."

"Alright, I'm going to come over there and take it out," I said. "Just remember that she has a gun on your daughter. So don't do anything stupid."

He nodded again. I crept forward until I was even with him. Pressing the muzzle of my gun against his side, I reached under his shirt until I felt the rubber of the grip. Pulling it out, I saw it was a revolver, like the kind an old-school cop would carry.

"Now take off your backpack." I ordered. The man complied, taking great pains to move slowly as he did until it dropped to the floor behind him. "Now crawl over to your daughter." He stumbled forward on his knees until he joined Katie in front of the counter. She whimpered as he reached her, pulling her into his arms. "Get what we need and get it outside," I ordered Sami, keeping my gun trained on him.

Sami instantly sprang into action, wheeling the bike she had chosen outside and shoving a fistful of the maps into her pockets. She was only gone a moment before I felt her coming back through the front door.

"Check his bag," I said.

"No weapons. Just some food, a flashlight and some other crap," she answered, spilling the contents out on the floor.

"Okay," I answered. "Pick a bike out for me." Sami skimmed through the lineup and found a bright yellow one. The back end of it was elongated with extra framework around the rear tire. "I think this will work better for you," she said, pointing to the extra space. I nodded and she wheeled it out.

"Listen," I said, addressing the man. "We just need the bikes. We don't want anything else. You can keep your food. I'll even leave you the gun outside. I'm gonna take the bullets out and scatter them all around out there. You can find them in the morning. Do you understand?"

"I do."

"We're going to go out there and do our thing. You're going to stay in here for the rest of the night. If I even think you're coming out after us, all bets are off. Do you understand that?"

He nodded, pulling his daughter closer.

"I want to hear you say it."

"We won't do anything. We'll be here all night. We don't want any trouble."

Sami came back in with my bag and helped me loop it around my shoulders. "Watch them while I get mounted up," I said, trading places with her. Outside I popped the chamber of his gun open and sent the bullets flying into the grass. The gun went farther, out into the darkness. It might take them awhile, but they'd find it all pretty easily in the sunshine. Pulling my bike up, I took the seat and shoved my crutches along my back, under the backpack. It wasn't comfortable, but it would work until we were far enough away from here to take a break.

"I'm ready," I called back to Sami. She came running out and jumped on hers like a natural, and we rolled off down the street.

CHAPTER FIFTEEN
BIKES

Three days later we were within a few miles of Dakota. Even though it was barely big enough to register as a town, there were plenty of road signs letting us know as we approached. Sami's parents lived on the west side, so we would be looping around the town anyway on our path to the Rogers property. "How about over there?" Sami pointed to a copse of trees.

The terrain out here was mostly flat farmland. Houses or long driveways to houses were scattered around, sometimes more than a mile between them. But there were small streams and creeks crisscrossing the landscape, and with them were trees. It was under these canopies we had made camp the past few nights. The streams provided the water for boiling, but more importantly for our mental health, it let us bathe each day, a luxury we had been sorely missing.

"Looks good to me!" I shouted back, even though we were probably close enough to reach the Rogers today, although it would have kept us riding after sunset, which we hadn't done yet. Approaching in the dark might be accidentally dangerous; the farmlands we had traversed were definitely not tourist-friendly. Several times we had to backtrack or detour to avoid roadblocks or guard posts that refused to allow us to travel past them. After a few awkward encounters, we now just avoided all signs of people as a rule. The night before we had found a comfortable place to camp outside of the decent sized city of Rockford. The distant sounds of gunfire had drifted to us during our meal of corn and protein powder, the dull glow of fire and smoke visible on the horizon. Everywhere we traveled, the world had been reduced to anarchy, tribalism or totalitarianism. The farmers were circling the wagons against the outsiders, the urban areas were being turned into battlefields between rival factions, and the dull roar of brown-painted vehicles slowly expanded the reach of the regulatory climate state that was the new government.

Once we reached the tree line, we headed deeper into the depths away from the road. The farther from the road, the better. The benefit of the flat land was that we could spot the tops of the trucks well before they could see us on our bikes. Either way, we were now fairly safely hidden under the trees once again. "How far do you think we are now?" Sami asked once we had dismounted. Both of us were pulling our shoes off. Of course I only had one shoe; the other foot was still in the walking boot, but that needed to come off as well.

"Probably about two hours." I slipped my feet into the cool water of the creek.

"That'll make tomorrow an easy ride. Hopefully everything's alright when we get there."

"I think this is the exact situation they've been preparing for since they bought that farm." The Rogers lived an odd life. They owned a large lot, with the house located at the intersection of two barely paved country roads. There were three nearly identical homes on the other three corners, which created the farmland version of a little subdivision. On those four original plots there had eventually been built several other buildings clustered around the intersection, and a collection of farm hands occupied most of them. It'd turned into a sort of plantation commune centered around the intersection, with multiple families working the fields and living seemingly as one community. This had appealed to Carla, Sami's stepmother, far more than her father Daniel. Carla saw herself as a Laura Ingalls frontier woman type, but with a healthy dose of Marxism mixed in. Daniel was more of a head-down working type. He had worked at a factory before he met Carla, and now worked the farm without complaint under the direction of his wife. The recent developments with the Dirts probably didn't bother Daniel one bit. What did he care about politics or modern life? He'd never been on an airplane, or owned any tech fancier than a flip phone. His only real hobby was old cars, which he worked on in his shed and could ramble on about for hours if allowed. Carla was pretty overjoyed with the collapsing society, the final throes of the modern capitalistic system she seemed to hate, and a return to strong pre-tech pastoral living she believed she was born to live.

"How's your foot feeling?" Sami interrupted my thoughts about our destination.

"Better. I've been pedaling with my heel mostly, so it keeps the pressure off the broken part." It'd been roughly a month since it'd been crushed, and it was finally beginning to look normal. The swelling and discoloration had subsided, even though it was still very sensitive. Letting it float in the cold water was the highlight of my day, but it wasn't actually helping the healing process.

"You ready for some dinner?"

"Sure. What are you making tonight?"

"I was thinking just leftovers. I'm kinda tired from all the bike riding."

"Let me guess. We still have some corn and protein powder left?"

"If you don't like it, you're welcome to make dinner yourself," she teased back. Of course, my cooking skills had barely been developed even when we had food to cook with. My time as a single man had resulted in a lot of BLTs, spaghetti and takeout. Sami had set me straight when we got married and she started handling the cooking. She actually knew what she was doing. Currently, though, she had gotten in a bit of a rut, even if the corn was a nice addition to our meals. It was something we could actually fill up on, since there was more corn within sight than we could ever consume.

"Do you think they're eating better at your parents?" I asked, splashing down to fully sit in the water.

"Well, they do have some animals, so they should at least have more options."

"And hunting. There's plenty of deer and rabbits out here. Better than the rats and squirrels in the city." We'd had our own wildlife encounters a few times since we'd started riding, but it wasn't even worth trying to hunt with pistols.

"I really want a burger, and at this point I don't even care what kind of animal it comes from," Sami said as she started mixing our protein. "I'm just ready to stop moving for a while. I need a break from the constant battle." She took a seat on the ground with our cornshakes.

"Agreed," I said, crawling out of the water to join her at our improvised dinner table. There isn't much to say as a response to a statement like Sami's. Most husbands know that sometimes the only answer they're looking for is a nod of understanding. Especially in this situation, where there isn't anything positive to say anyway. The world wasn't going to magically get easier just because we made it to Dakota. Best case scenario, it's just a rest stop on our declining road towards the new normal. The old-world stress of having to wake up extra early so you can get to the gym before work, or your favorite team's ace blowing out his Achilles in the midst of a divisional race, is all gone. It's not a comfortable reality and not something Sami needs to hear. Holding on to hope of a return to normal might be what keeps her going every day.

"It's only a couple of hours tomorrow morning, and then we'll finally get our break, babe," I answered, one small hope each day to keep us moving.

* * *

The sun woke us up in the morning. I used to say that no day was ever a good day when it began before sunrise, and now our days always started with the sunrise. This day at least started with being able to wash our faces, a convenience we had been missing since we lost our home. The river water was shockingly cold in the morning, which got us started right.

"Walk to the road?" Sami asked once our bikes were loaded back down. Riding the bikes through the trees usually ended up being more frustrating than just pushing them out. On the ride in we had our momentum and hours of riding pushing us through the rough ground. On the way out, we were still stiff and starting from zero.

"Sure." I hooked my knee on the side of the bike and used it as a rolling crutch. We rolled through the brush and trees quickly. There was less brush than if we'd been in a full-fledged forest. The large tree canopies blocked out most of the direct sunlight, and the war against weeds and undergrowth that was waged aggressively in the cornfield had spread to even the unplanted areas, so it was rocks and roots that gave us the most resistance.

"Do you hear that?" Sami asked. If she had been capable of moving her ears, they would've perked up at the moment.

"I do now." The sounds of us pushing through was all I'd been hearing until I stopped moving. Now I could hear the sound of an engine cutting through the still morning background noise of birds and bugs moving around. Neither of us spoke. We'd been ducking into cornfields enough in the past week that it was second nature now anytime we heard a sound we didn't like. We were just in view of the road ahead of us and a small bridge spanning the water. We each pushed our bikes through the leafy barrier and followed in. Kickstanding them behind us, we dropped down to the ground. We were just deep enough into the stalks that we could still see the road through the vegetation.

Two brown SUVs came to a stop on the little bridge. Sami squeezed my hand as the doors started opening. I reached for the gun at my hip. Out of the rear passenger doors, uniformed Dirts climbed out, each carrying a stubby submachine gun. If they were looking for us, we were going to be outgunned. Their eyes only flicked around their surroundings in a casual manner, though. They weren't interested in what was happening out here.

The rear doors on both vehicles swung upwards automatically and four people were pulled out of the back of each of the vehicles. Five of them were wearing the brown jumpsuits of the camps; two of them were even clutching their copies of *The Little Brown Book*, despite their hands being bound. The other three people were dressed normally, though they looked rough themselves. The guards forced the people to kneel along the edge of the bridge. The two people with their books locked helplessly in their hands resisted, pleading to be heard and forgiven. From this distance it was just jibberish, and probably up close it sounded like jibberish as well. The rest of them obeyed meekly, resigned to their fate or in a state of shock.

The passenger door of the rear vehicle opened and a well-dressed Dirt officer stepped out, looking like a city dandy among the field hands in his crisp, tight-fitting uniform. Even the Dirt soldiers looked worn down. Their outfits were clearly made with the environment in mind, only a couple of steps above the burlap jumpsuits the camp convicts wore.

"Your decisions have brought you here!" the officer yelled, his voice carrying all the way out to us. "Your sins against Nature and your defilements of our shared Gaia. It is our sacred duty to purify this planet, and we bear that burden gladly." He paused for effect, but the rest of his band didn't seem too inspired by his speech. "And thus in death you are returned to Gaia, to be remade!" Stepping back, he cleared the way for the soldiers who had lined up behind the sacrifices.

"Fuck you!" one of the book holders screamed, throwing his book at him. *Crack.* The officer's drawn sidearm was smoking, as the formerly outspoken body slumped backward and into the water below. The remaining seven people were shaken. The serenity that had overtaken them in the lead-up had been broken by the summary execution. They started moving around, trying to flee, but it was too late. The officer had stepped aside quickly and the firing lane was clear. *BUUURRRPPPPPP.* The guards' guns belched flames and the mass of bodies tumbled, their previous movements interrupted by the impacting lead. All seven collapsed into the waiting stream. It only took seconds for the quiet to return, though it was hard to tell with the ringing in our ears.

Two of the guards moved forward to the edge, careful to avoid stepping in the blood spatters, and sent several more bullets into each floating body, just to make sure none of them were faking their execution. Finishing that assignment, they joined their comrades in the SUVs, which roared off. The entire exchange took three minutes at most.

Sami's face was pressed into the dirt, her free arm curled around her head, trying vainly to block all of her senses. The sound of the engines had long faded into the distance when I pulled her up. Dirt on her face had turned to mud while she'd been down there. "Let's wash your face," I said. Shaking her, she mumbled at me; I couldn't hear the words, but it was something about not wanting to go back to the stream. Fumbling with our bags, I pulled out my towel and a bottle of water. Once she was cleaned off, she pushed forward and into my arms again. I held her there until my legs went numb.

A few minutes later, Sami still hadn't come fully around, but we had to get moving. So after a while I pushed us forward to the road, crossing the bridge respectfully, keeping her from looking directly at the aftermath. Once we cleared that space, she began to return as we pedaled out the final couple of hours.

"I think this is the edge of their field," Sami called back, bringing her bike to a stop. We had wound our way through the last few miles and now were sitting at what looked like a property divider running through the field to our left. A couple of trees and a wire fence kept the corn rows on either side from meeting.

"Looks like the road's blocked." I came to a stop next to her. In the distance ahead there was clearly obstructions in the road.

"You were right. You figured they'd barricade themselves in." She rolled herself forward again.

"Careful," I called out. A person who was visibly holding a rifle had stepped out of the cornfields and taken a place behind the obstructions. Sami slowed her approach down, both of our bikes moving barely above tipping-over speed. Getting within shouting distance, I braked and brought the bike to a stop. Sami followed suit. "Let's see if he wants to talk before we get much closer. Hello!" I called out. "Can you hear me?"

A pause followed as the guard thought about how to respond. "The road is closed," the feminine voice called back.

"Tell them we're here to see my dad," Sami said. "We're looking for Daniel and Carla Rogers."

"What do you want with them?"

"This is Daniel's daughter, Samantha!" I yelled. "We're

here to see them!" The woman's head bobbed back and forth. "I think she has a radio," I said to Sami. "Must be calling headquarters."

"Alright, Miss Carla says you can enter!" the voice shouted back.

"Miss Carla," Sami muttered as we started riding forward.

"Just keep on up to the houses," the guard instructed as we passed by the barricade. She looked to be about eighteen years old and carrying a deer rifle. I doubt she could've managed to fire more than one shot with that thing. The recoil would probably dislocate her shoulder.

Continuing on, the houses came into view at the intersection ahead of us. The scene had changed dramatically since last time we had visited. Previously the community had been contained in their respective properties and the road remained clear. Now it'd been incorporated into the common space as a sorta village square for the residents. The side we approached from looked like it'd been appropriated as a communal eating space, with long tables and chairs spread out across the space. Once we were safely in the middle of the stretch of road, the houses still a ways ahead and the guard far enough behind us, I stopped. "What is it?" Sami asked, braking her bike as well.

"Let's put the guns in our bags, just in case."

Sami shrugged. Following my lead, we unhooked our belts and slipped them into our backpacks. "Think they'll take them?" she asked, once we were rolling forward again.

"I don't know, but let's keep them between us for now, shall we?"

"Okay, it's a secret."

Up ahead of us, a small welcoming committee had formed at the edge of the tables, watching our final approach. First in line was obviously Carla, standing at the head of the group as if welcoming us to her realm. Behind her was her son and Sami's half-brother Lincoln. He had shot up significantly since we had last seen him, now in those awkward teenage years of having an adult-sized body but still looking like a shy child. Next to Carla was another woman, younger than us, maybe twenty-five. Both she and Carla were wearing calico dresses that looked like they were cosplaying *Little House on the Prairie.*

"Samantha, welcome to our home," Carla welcomed us stiffly as we dismounted.

"Hello, Carla. It's good to see you," Sami answered. It sounded sweet, but the stiffness was still in her voice.

"Lincoln, say hello to your sister." Reaching behind her, Carla dragged Lincoln to the forefront.

"Hi, Sami."

"Hey, Linc. You're so big now!" This time the stiffness dropped from Sami's voice. She loved her half-brother despite how she felt about Carla.

"What happened to your foot?" Carla directed her gaze on me. Our relationship was even more awkward than Lincoln's had ever been.

"Uh, it got smashed pretty bad. It's a long story." It was actually the first time anyone had inquired about what had happened since the event.

"I see." Carla returned her eyes to Sami. "I guess you're looking for a place to stay?"

"Yeah. Things got pretty bad in town, so we thought we'd come see Daddy."

"Your father is no longer with us," Carla answered coolly.

Sami looked at me, then back to the trio in front of us. Lincoln had returned to staring at the ground. "Where is he?" They just continued staring. "Did he go somewhere?" she continued, her voice faltering.

"He passed on a couple of weeks ago," Carla finally answered. "But you're still family, so we'll find space for you, though heaven knows we're already bursting at the seams."

Starting to turn to the silent woman at her side, Sami cut back in. "My dad is dead?"

"Yes," Carla answered firmly, turning to the woman again. "Cindy, would you please find a bed for them and get them situated?"

"Yes, ma'am," Cindy answered. Lincoln was already wandering away from the conversation. Reaching out, I found Sami's hand. Looking at me, she was blank-faced. The shock of the information was still working through her.

"We'll see you at dinner," Carla said curtly before striding away.

"Follow me," Cindy directed. Once Carla was far enough away, the deference that'd been in Cindy's voice dropped. There was an icy edge to it now. We followed Cindy quietly, weaving our bikes through the maze of objects in the road until we reached a small cabin located on the backside of the Rogers house. "There's one room open on the right. The rest of the rooms are occupied. Please remain in your own space." She swung the door open. Leaning our bikes against the wall, we trooped in. Our new room was a ten-by-ten square, with a mattress on the ground and a couple blankets. "Dinner is served at 7 p.m." Turning on her heel, she started marching off.

"Wait." Calling out, Sami stopped her. "How did my dad die?"

"His heart gave out," Cindy answered stiffly, looking us up and down before continuing out as the door swung close behind her.

"I thought we'd be staying in the guest room," Sami murmured as she curled up next to me in the bed once we were alone. She may have spoken out loud, but it was a rhetorical statement. She was already shutting down as she was speaking. Sami had never been that close to her dad; she had always been more connected with her mother, and after her death, her relationship with Daniel faded even more. They were really just held together by the shared memory of her mother. Even so, the death of your father is something that affects you, regardless of the closeness. Complicating the situation was the sudden shock of the information. We'd been expecting to see Daniel for a while now, and Carla's completely indifferent attitude in announcing his death had thrown both of us for a loop. Our hopes for a pleasant stay at the Rogers house were pretty much dashed at this point, and we hadn't even been here for an hour yet.

I stayed in the bed, comforting Sami the best I could, until she fell asleep and rolled over. After that I went to the window. From our room we had a view of the intersection's center and all the main houses around it. There were the four main homes that first constituted the small community. Around them had sprung up a collection of small farmhand cabins like the one we were in. The circumstances suggested basically a mix of plantation servitude and cult. The number of residents seemed to have grown exceptionally since we'd last visited, judging by the amount of people moving around. The long tables we'd passed on our way in could fit about a hundred people. Previously there'd been maybe twenty to thirty people out here total, including the families who actually lived in the four homes. That increase would explain why we'd been shoved into a tiny bedroom in a makeshift cabin; they had ran out of space to fit everyone.

The clothes people were wearing also made the place look like an Amish settlement. The people out here had always dressed in a more practical manner—it was a working farm after all—but now there was a decided shift towards clothing that looked like it would've fit in at an antebellum plantation. The women, who were the decided majority of those I could see, were all wearing ankle-length dresses out of materials like denim and gingham, and some were even wearing bonnets. The few men that passed by were wearing loose-fitting white pullover shirts, not t-shirts but cut in an old style that looked more like a baggy sweater. They were all wearing jeans, though; that at least had a touch of modernity to it. Most of the activity in my view seemed to be centered around the field kitchen. Light smoke drifted out of the tent top, and people came in carrying baskets of produce and left with them emptied. Cooking three meals a day for a hundred people would keep you busy; by the time you finished with one, it'd already be time to start on the next.

The next few hours I kept watch as Sami slept fitfully behind me. Slowly the space began to fill with people, as more arrived and fewer left my sight. It appeared that the day's work was finishing up and people were preparing for dinner. "What are you doing?" Sami's soft voice came from the bed.

"Just watching," I answered as I lowered back down to her. "How are you?"

"I'm fine."

"Get some good sleep?"

"Yeah, I feel better."

"Do you want to talk about anything?" I asked, taking her hand in mine.

"No, not right now."

The door opened and Cindy was back. "Dinner," she announced sternly, like we were children who had been banished to our room. Following behind her, we trudged out of the cabin and across the lawn to the rows of tables where everyone was already finding their seats. Cindy left us at a couple of open seats in the middle of the dining space. The eyes of our tablemates, all women, darted across us a few times. Our twenty-first-century clothing stuck out among the homespun-looking dresses. From the other tables, the chatter of conversations echoed, though our table remained painfully silent, our neighbors carefully avoiding eye contact and focusing their attention on random objects near and far.

In front of us, Carla returned, stepping up on a low platform I hadn't noticed before, giving her an elevated position over the tables. Immediately the crowd lapsed into silence. "Good evening," she began, her voice quiet but discernible across the space. "This evening we gather once again to enjoy the fruits of our Earth Mother. Her children wanted and She provided."

"SHE PROVIDED!" chanted the observers in unison, Sami and I were caught unprepared for the chorus.

"The nourishment we receive is a grace and blessing bestowed upon us by our Earth Mother. Her children wanted and She provided."

"SHE PROVIDED!" the chant rang out again. This time we managed to keep up with them.

"May we strive to continue to remain in Her favor. Clear skies are a gift and darkness is punishment. She provided."

"SHE PROVIDED!" the group spoke with one voice yet again.

"Now let us consume our gifts," Carla finished, stepping down from the platform and heading towards a table set some ways apart from the rest of us. Several other older woman, two of whom I recognized as the owners of the other houses, and a couple of younger women, Cindy included, sat there with her. Once Carla had finished her speech, the mood around the tables returned to the jovial end-of-day energy that had existed before the sermon, as everyone stood up and began making their way towards the tent kitchen.

"We probably need these," I whispered to Sami, grabbing our plates from the table.

"Can you remember where we were sitting?" she asked as we stumbled into the line snaking its way forward.

"Yeah, I think so."

The line moved quickly. The process was clearly a familiar routine for the residents. At the front we each received an ear of corn, a tomato, a bread roll and a bowl of soup to carry back.

"The soup smells good," Sami said once we had found our way back to our table.

"Looks like potato?" I guessed. Potato soup was my favorite.

"It is."

"I haven't seen a potato in months."

It was the first meal we'd had in weeks that didn't center around warm protein water, and it was glorious. The corn out here had reached full ripeness and tasted perfect. As everyone finished up their meals, they began to disperse back out around the community. The girls at our table were the first to leave, having eaten very quickly. Soon, Sami and I were some of the last people remaining in our seats. We choose to enjoy our food to the fullest; after all, that's what our Earth Mother would've wanted.

"Should we go back to our room?" Sami asked, now that we were finished and the place was nearly cleared out.

"I dunno. Shouldn't we talk to Carla?"

"She seems kinda busy with her group." The table Carla was at remained full, the conversation continuing between all of the guests.

"Let's put our dishes away, then." Underneath the tent where we'd collected our food were several large bins where everyone had been returning their dinnerware before they left. Scooping ours up, we both wound through the tables towards the tent. I was watching Carla's still full table out of the corner of my eye. They seemed to be tracking our movements in return. After we had deposited our dishes, Cindy came up and announced, "The elders would like a word with you both."

"Cool," I answered, turning around. It was evidently the wrong answer, since Cindy was glaring at me, but we followed her back to the main table anyway.

"Everyone, this is Daniel's daughter, Samantha, and her husband Kyle," Carla still in her seat introduced us once we arrived. Addressing us now, she continued, "I'm sure you remember Miss Debra, Miss Lori and Miss Abigail from your previous visits."

"I do. How nice to see you all again," Sami answered politely. It was doubtful she remembered them at all. Their faces stuck out slightly to me from memory, but I don't think I'd known their names then either.

"How long will you be staying with us?" the one introduced as Miss Debra asked.

Sami shook her head, so I cut in. "We aren't really sure. We don't really have a plan."

"Typical," the woman who'd been called Miss Lori shot back. "You thought you could just run away from the city and move in here."

Carla interceded before I could answer. "It's only natural for them to come back to their family when things go bad in the city. They need help, and we are helping people." The other woman nodded begrudgingly.

"Are you willing to work?" the third woman, Miss Abigail, spoke to me again.

"Of course. We'll do anything we can, though I'm a bit handicapped at the moment."

"Ugh, *and* he's injured," Miss Debra scoffed, looking away from us.

"We'll find something you can handle," Carla spoke again. "Someone will come get you in the morning and get you set doing some chores."

"Okay, sounds great," I answered.

"Can't wait," Sami added.

Carla smiled and turned away from us, back to Miss

Debra. "I was thinking that the west side could be used for..." The rest of the table turned away from us as well, pointedly focusing on Carla. Tugging my hand, Sami pulled us away.

"Well, that was weird," I whispered once we were far enough away from the table.

"Of course. My stepmom's running a Luddite cult out here, what did you expect?"

"I don't think they like me." I glanced back at the table. "Weren't they all married last time we met them?"

"I dunno."

We pulled the front door of the cabin open. Previously we'd been the only people in there for most of the day, but now there were several others. Their faces turned to us as we entered. They had clearly been engaged in a loud discussion, but now they quieted and watched us. They were all late teen boys, about ten altogether.

"Hi," Sami greeted them politely. Several voices responded meekly, as well as a couple waves and head nods. "Is this the guys' cabin?"

"Yeah, pretty much," one of them answered.

"I hope me being here won't bother any of you. We just arrived today." None of them answered, just peering intently at us.

"Okay, well, we're going to go to bed," I said, steering Sami towards our room. "Nice to meet everyone." Once the door was closed and the voices had started back up in the hallway, I whispered to her, "No one here seems very chatty."

"They're probably just not used to meeting new people, or having a woman share their cabin."

"Yeah, that's kinda weird. I wonder why they put us in this one." At this point I still hadn't seen any males past their teenage years yet.

"Carla probably doesn't want us in the house. 'Just for the elders,'" she said with derision, rolling her eyes and making air-quote gestures with her fingers. "Now, let's go to bed, Nellie Oleson."

CHAPTER SIXTEEN

DISHES

The next morning we woke up as the sounds of our housemates started echoing through the thin walls. The building was too poorly insulated to block out the noise of everyone moving around. The sun was up already, though not by much. "You think they serve breakfast here?" Sami asked, sitting up suddenly.

"Probably."

"I could really use some real food for breakfast, not just gritty water."

"I can't argue with that." I pushed myself out of bed. Not having to climb on a bicycle seat was what I was most grateful about. The space between my legs was unspeakably bruised at this point.

"What about a bathroom?"

"What about a bathroom?" I answered back.

She stared at me impatiently. "Do you think there's one here?"

I had obviously picked the wrong morning to be jokey. "Probably."

Pulling her shoes on, she went hunting, leaving me alone in our room. The space was as bare as possible, barely big enough for a mattress. It had no other features except for the light switch on the wall and the light fixture on the ceiling. The lamp was larger than you would expect for a room of this size; maybe they had cut too big of a hole in the ceiling and had to cover it up, or maybe it was just the only random fixture they'd had available at the moment. The housing was wide with a frosted glass cover screwed to the bottom of it to conceal the lightbulbs. It was the only hiding spot in the room, a silly statement since it was pretty much in the center of the room and noticeable to anyone who entered. But who looked at a light fixture, much less in a world without electricity?

Hopping up on the bed, I unscrewed the glass cover to reveal the two bulbs inside. Retrieving our guns from the bags, I removed the holsters from the belts. Those could stay; they were just belts, after all. The guns, holsters and spare magazines were what needed to be hidden, though for good measure I added my 'Let to the pile. Although just a useless hunk of plastic and metal at this point, it had basically become my lucky charm, but out here I imagined they took a dim view on electronics regardless if they worked or not. I packed them into the removed light cover but it was too much to fit back into place over the bulbs, so I carefully crushed the bulbs and left the remains in the cover too. That let me get the screw threaded back on and the light fixture put back together. Without the glow of the lightbulbs, you didn't really notice the weird shapes behind the frosted glass. At least I hoped no one would.

Sami bounded back in. Sure enough, there was a modern bathroom in the back of the building that had been redesigned using "new" features from the past; buckets of water to pour into the toilets to make them flush, and a bucket with a valve on it hanging above the sink for washing up. It was more sophisticated than what we'd been doing in the stream the past few days, but it also reminded us of the simplicity with which we'd lived our lives less than a few months ago. We followed the gang of boys out towards the tables. This meal was being served buffet-style in an eat-as-you-arrive process. A biscuit and some ever-present corn were the only options. We'd kinda gone numb to the corn taste at this point, but the biscuits were heavenly, the first real freshly-made food we'd seen in months.

"Are you Kyle?" A middle-aged woman approached our table as we finished.

"Yes, that's me."

"I'm supposed to set you to work today," she explained. Her voice was flat and her face suggested that she wasn't very interested in her responsibilities.

"Okay. Is it time to start?"

"Yes. Follow me." Turning back towards the kitchen, she started walking away.

"Okay, I'll see you tonight." I gave Sami a kiss on the cheek.

"Have fun. Love you."

"You too, dear."

The woman didn't walk at a fast pace, so I was able to keep up with her even with my gimpy gait. She led me around the back of the cooking tent. "These need to be washed." She pointed at a large pile of dishes stacked up at the back of the tent.

"Where's the sink?" I looked around. The only thing around the dishes was a wheelbarrow.

"We don't use the good well water for the dishes," she snapped back. "We clean them in the creek."

"Actually, I didn't get your name. Mine's Kyle Harrison." I held my hand out. Maybe some friendliness would smooth out the rough spots of this interaction.

Ignoring my hand, she continued, "My name is Susan and I run the kitchen. I take that responsibility very seriously, and I don't like people who throw hitches into my routine. Use the wheelbarrow to take the dishes out to the creek. Scrub them clean, then bring them back and stack them on that table." She pointed to an empty table next to the table of dirty dishes. "The brushes are already out there." She nodded towards a distant collection of trees that usually marked water sources in the area.

"Okay, I'll get started." She was already leaving before I finished speaking, leaving just me, the wheelbarrow and a table full of dishes now. Handling the wheelbarrow was going to be tricky with a bad foot; just walking with an empty load would've been hard, much less crammed with dishes. They were an odd collection of flatware: ceramic plates, the standard form of dinnerware in the previous world, plastic plates like children would use, and then metal plates that looked home-forged, or maybe scavenged from a Civil War reenactment troupe. Along with the plates were bowls and cutlery all of the same diverse collection.

Filling up the wheelbarrow to the brim, I started the first journey. Working my way towards the road was difficult. The uneven ground interfered with my hop-stepping and threatened to overturn the cargo, perhaps the ultimate humiliation I could conceive. Once I reached the road, the trek smoothed out. The rubber wheel rolled smoothly across the packed dirt and I was able to create a working rhythm of movement.

Moving out of the tiny town in the opposite direction from where we had entered the day before, I made it to the creek in decent time. The small bridge spanning the water also served as the barricade location in that direction, an attempt to block anyone trying to enter the area. There was another girl manning the watchpost there as well. She looked to be in her late teens and again carried an oversized firearm, this one a shotgun. Just like with the previous guard, I figured she'd only manage one inaccurate shot if she was forced to fire the weapon. Ejecting a spent shell and chambering a new one looked like an action she would struggle to perform in the simplest settings, alone out here on the road facing some advancing menace. At very best, her single shot would serve as a warning to the community that trouble was approaching.

"How's it going?" she asked once I reached her station. A well-worn path led down from the road to the water's edge, where there were several dishwashing implements awaiting me.

"Alright. At least it's not too hot yet," I answered, setting the handles of the wheelbarrow down.

"Yeah, it's not bad yet, but it will be," she answered glumly.

Holding my hand out, I tried some charm again. "My name's Kyle Harrison."

"I'm Bethany, but everyone just calls me Beth." She

returned my handshake with a feminine grip. "What happened to your foot?" she asked, eying my cast.

"It uh, got crushed with a sledgehammer a few weeks ago."

"Somebody did that to you?" she asked, looking horrified.

"Yeah. There was a bit of a disagreement."

"Lady Abigail is always warning us about disagreements. That's why I like being out here at the guard post. No one to disagree with out here."

"That's true. Are there many disagreements back at the camp?" I probed for a peak behind the curtain.

"Not really, not anymore."

"But there was?"

"Just the normal stuff, I guess. Getting used to our new situation."

"I'm sure it was a big adjustment. So many people forced together all of a sudden. It's naturally going to be stressful."

"Oh yes, it was, but things are better now. We just have to trust the elders to look after us." She said it with a kind of finality that indicated she was done talking about the past.

"I guess I better start getting these dishes washed. There's several more loads still back there, so you'll be seeing me all day." I threw some extra cheer in my voice.

"Good luck," she answered, slipping back into the shaded spot on the side of the road from which she had come.

* * *

The dish washing took all day. After getting the wheelbarrow down to the water's edge and unloading the dishes, I would just splash into the river with the sponge and go to work on them. It was like washing dishes while in a bathtub. One benefit of our limited diet was that it didn't leave much residue on the dishes themselves, no congealed ketchup or melted cheese that had to be scoured from the surface. Once a load was clean, I'd hoof them back to the kitchen and load up the next batch. With a fully functioning leg, the chore would've been much shorter in duration, but hopping along slowed me down.

Lunch was another informal affair, as people drifted into the open air cafeteria in small groups, grabbing their helping and then moving on. My nominal supervisor Susan was nowhere to be found, so I took matters into my own hands and ate in between my trips out to the creek. My last trip back brought me to the kitchen as the dinner hour was beginning. The guests were already taking their seats and awaiting the start of the meal.

"That took long enough," Susan barked once I started unloading the clean dishes onto the table. The stacks of clean dinnerware had already been deployed in preparation for the meal.

"Sorry, it's a long walk out there." I answered.

She turned to some members of the kitchen staff. "Get the last of these out there before he runs off with them again." The kitchen girls grabbed them from me and hurried them out into action. She glared at me and the empty wheelbarrow again before stomping off.

I slipped out of the kitchen and towards the tables. Sami was already there, seated at a table with about five other girls who were all chatting together. She was wearing new clothes, the same kind of dress as the others wore around here, but in a pink color unique to Sami and the other five girls. Waving me over, I joined her on the bench. "Went shopping?" I asked, sliding into the seat.

"Oh yeah, they gave me something better to wear for the job..." She left the job description dangling.

"And what's your job?"

"Babysitting!" she whispered gleefully. "Ha, can you believe it? There's a bunch of little kids here and even some babies, and we watch and take care of them all day." She gestured to the rest of the girls at the table who were all looking at me.

"Oh, that's fun. How did it go?"

"It was great. The kids are all so sweet." Sami's face was practically glowing after a day of mothering. "What did you do?" She looked at my prune-hands.

"I washed dishes in the creek all day."

"Oh boy. I know how you hate doing the dishes."

"I don't hate doing the dishes," I answered, self-conscious of the fact that the girls had remained silent and were watching our interaction with fascination. "It was just a long walk out to the creek with my leg and all."

"I'm sorry, babe." She squeezed my knee. "Oh, I'm sorry." She finally noticed that the table's full attention was on us. "This is my husband, Kyle. Kyle, this is the babysitters club—Erin, Chelsea, Lilly, Jenny and Sophie." She pointed to each girl in turn. We all gave a polite nod to each other, but they didn't seem very interested in trading stories about the day.

Before the awkwardness became too much to bear, Carla climbed up on her podium and began the proceedings for dinner. The speech was slightly different than the night before, but the chanting remained, which we were ready for this time so that we didn't make complete fools of ourselves. Once we were done with our meal, the pink-gowned girl Sami had called Lilly said, "Sami, you should come with us. We're going to go pick some flowers to surprise the kids with tomorrow."

"Oh, that sounds fun," Sami answered before looking back at me. "But I should stay here with Kyle. He looks pretty beat."

"You can go," I responded. "I was just going to go lie down."

"Oh. Well." She paused. "Well, if you were just going to go to sleep anyway."

"Yeah, it's fine. I'll see you back at the room."

All the girls jumped up, squealing and ready to go frolic. "I love you," Sami whispered, giving me a parting kiss.

"Love you too. Have fun with the flowers."

I was asleep by the time Sami returned to our room that night. The next morning started the same way the last one did, with the noise of our roommates waking us up. In fact, the entire day felt like a repeat of the one before it, though that was becoming more of the norm in our reimagined world. After breakfast I shuffled off to the dishes and the trusty wheelbarrow, talked with Beth a bit at the bridge and trudged back and forth until I cleared the pile completely. True to my word, I went a little faster than the day before and had everything clean about twenty minutes before dinner. That meant I was one of the first ones to find a seat on the benches, waiting at the same one Sami and her babysitters had chosen previously. We had another awkward dinner with the gaggle of girls staring at me before they ran off again for another frolic or whatever they did when they were off duty.

The third day blurred into the previous two the same way —wheelbarrow, bridge, dishes, dinner, bed. At breakfast on the fourth, Sami was telling me about what the kids were doing; Sasha was trying to talk and Lexie kept trying to walk, and it was all just the cutest thing. "Kyle?" a voice interrupted. It was one of the boys from our cabin. I recognized him, though we hadn't been introduced.

"Yes?"

"You're with us in the fields today. Meetup is over there in ten minutes." He pointed behind us at the beginning of the cornfields.

"Okay, I'll be there," I answered as he walked away.

"Oooh, a promotion," Sami cooed.

"Yes, I'll soon be running this place," I joked back, though I wondered who was going to wash the dishes today and if they'd get it done faster than I did. Probably; odds would suggest they don't have a gimpy leg. "Have you seen much of Carla or Lincoln?" I asked, shifting the subject. I had only so far seen Carla at dinner as she gave her sermons, and I hadn't seen Lincoln even at the meals.

"Oh yeah, Carla's always coming in to see the kids. They love her."

"Really? She doesn't seem like the kid type."

"She is now, I guess. We've been talking a bit during nap time. She seems less weird now than before."

"Maybe it's just that the rest of the world has caught up to her level of weirdness," I countered.

"That could be. I've only seen Lincoln a couple of times. Everyone says he just does his own thing and avoids everyone. They call him the cat, because he acts like one of those jerk cats who won't come near anyone or do anything."

"I guess he hasn't changed, then."

"We should get going, though," she announced, standing up and grabbing both of our plates.

"Alright, I'll see you tonight." I followed suit and climbed up.

At the edge of the cornfield our entire cabin was assembled, all ten boys plus about ten girls. These girls were on the stouter side than the babysitting clique. "Everybody here?" asked the guy who had talked to me at breakfast. The group nodded before turning into the stalks and trudging forward. The pace wasn't too pressing, so I was able to keep up with the group as we worked our way deeper into the fields. Ten minutes later the group had formed up again. This time we were deep in the cornfield, but there were several wheelbarrows and sling bags surrounding us. The group was well-rehearsed in their movements, each person scooping up a bag and marching off in small groups around a wheelbarrow. A minute later it was just me, the guy who seemed to be in charge, and one other girl.

"Let's finish up this row," the boss man said. The girl went to work quickly, moving straight down the corn row with her bag.

"What was your name?" I asked, forgoing the attempted handshake this time.

"I'm Jacob."

"Okay, so I guess we're picking corn out here?"

"Yes. Pick the ear, put it in your bag. When the bag is full, empty it into the wheelbarrow." He answered briskly.

"Is there any trick to it? I haven't picked much corn." That was the truth. Sami had picked all the corn we'd eaten during our bicycle trip, and now I remembered her struggling with it a couple of times.

"Yes. Grab the ear with one hand, grab the stalk with the other, twist the ear, and then yank it down off the stalk." His instructions included synchronized miming.

"Okay, I think I got it."

"Head that way and work until you reach the end of the row." He nodded me in the direction the girl had already went.

She was already working full tilt by the time I caught up to her. "Hey." She nodded. "I'm supposed to work with you, I guess."

"Find an ear and start pulling." She ripped the one in her hands off the stalk as she spoke.

"Alright." I followed her lead. The first few ears fought back when I attempted to pick them, but after a few tries I found the touch; they needed a quick jerk and then would pop free pretty easily. Once the girl's bag was full, she went for the wheelbarrow. I still hadn't gotten her name, since she seemed to not have any interest in talking during working hours. My bag was nearly full by the time she returned.

"My name's Kyle. What's yours?" I asked as we dumped our picked ears into the transport. I almost laughed to myself. My attempt to socialize sounded like the language of a four-year-old who was just learning how to talk to other people.

"Mine's Jane," she answered stiffly.

"How long have you been here at the farms?"

"A couple of months." She was already back to picking the corn. That's all I managed to get out of her the rest of the morning.

The sun was directly overhead when all of the harvesting groups reconvened on the edge of the field. Lunch had been ferried out to us by some of the kitchen staff in yet another wheelbarrow. Everyone fetched their helpings, a veggie sandwich and a cooked potato per person. Jane moved purposely away from me, choosing to sit by herself. I took a seat next to two guys I knew from the cabin. One of them had helped Sami figure out the bathroom on the first morning.

"I'm Austin." He greeted me as I sat down, the first person who had actually offered their name to me since I'd arrived. "This is Ozzie." He pointed to his partner, who nodded back.

"I'm Kyle." I gave them each a smile.

"What happened to your foot?" Austin asked.

"Got smashed with a sledgehammer."

"Ouch," Ozzie groaned. "I broke mine once BMXing. That sounds worse, though."

"Yeah, I wouldn't recommend it."

"How is walking in that cast?"

"It's not great, but I manage. It's been worse the past couple days, because I've been washing dishes in the river, so it was always wet." My ankle had started to chaff under the wet fabric rubbing on my skin.

"Oh yeah, and that freaking wheelbarrow," Austin muttered.

"You guys washed dishes before?" I asked, since their reactions showed they were familiar with the routine.

"Yeah, that's the process out here. New guys go to dishwashing and new girls go to babysitting."

"Oh, my wife's doing babysitting now."

"The babysitting helps make the new girls part of the community, playing with their maternal instincts and such," Ozzie said a bit begrudgingly. "Dishwashing gets the new guys alone and teaches them their places out here."

"What is our place out here?"

"You're looking at it."

"Are there any animals out here?" I asked, changing the subject to another lurking question.

"Oh yeah." Austin perked up a bit. "Plenty of deer. We're always having to chase them away from the corn. Rabbits in the fields, all kinds of birds, and then the mice or rats are always running around."

"I meant like cows or chickens? Maybe a horse or even a dog?"

Austin immediately looked back down. "Nope, not here."

We continued in silence. I remember there being chickens out here vividly, because one morning Carla gave us a detailed description about where our morning eggs had come from, which was apparently a chicken's butt about an hour before I had sat down to eat. However, the space where the chicken coop had once been behind Carla's house was now cleared out. Even though these were corn farms, they always seemed to have a collection of farm animals, a pig or a couple of cows that lived in the barn down the road. Daniel seemed to like the animals because they didn't talk back, and Carla because it was part of this glorified pastoral homesteading lifestyle she dreamed of. However, so far on our stay out here I hadn't seen a single tame animal. Even the ever-present farm dogs that usually roamed around the small community had disappeared.

Jacob was prodding us back into the fields soon after we finished eating, so I was soon back to working the stalks again. Once we finished the row Jane and I had been working on, we skipped over a few rows that were already taken and started the process over again. When the wheelbarrow was full, she marched off with it and left me to keep picking alone. Manual labor had never been my strong suit; stuff like having your foot crushed doesn't happen in an office. Yet here I was, wishing for the dishwashing gig again. Splashing around in the water and under the shade of the trees was a nice place to be, compared to this. Out here in the field it was hot, the corn stalks were constantly cutting at you, the flies buzzed around and the dust kicked up, settling into the very pores of my skin. So it was a sweet relief when the word spread that it was quitting time, and our little troop set course back to the houses and a sit-down meal.

"How was it?" Sami asked as I sat down next to her. She was so fresh looking in her pink dress, contrasted with my dusty, sweaty well-worn clothes.

"It's…whatever." I finally said with a sigh. "I feel like there's some kind of joke in there about being a wage slave in the post-apocalyptic economy, but I'm too tired to find it."

She laughed. "I consider that a successful day, then."

"I guess I've just been too well-rested my whole life before this. You'll just have to come up with ways to exhaust me in the future to keep me well-trained."

"Suddenly feeling better now?" Sami rolled her eyes.

"No, I'm still too tired."

"In the nursery we make the kids take a nap when they act like you."

"Well, then sign me up for the nursery."

The babysitters club didn't have any fun events planned for the evening this time, so Sami and I settled into a shady spot on the edge of the field to watch the post-dinner playtime before bed, kids kicking a ball around while some of the guys exercised. With only one ball the sport playing was limited, so our cabinmates had taken to pushups and other exercises to express their manhood. It pushed their physical limits, but wasn't very entertaining to watch.

"Have you been able to talk to the girls in your group much?" I asked.

"Oh yeah, we talk all the time. About the kids, and what we're going to do tomorrow."

"Do you talk about each other at all, or just your jobs?"

"Just the job, I guess. Why do you ask?"

"I dunno, it just seems like no one wants to talk about themselves out here. Everyone's guarded."

"It's like we have mass PTSD," she answered.

"That's true, I guess. No one's here because things were great wherever they came from."

"Exactly. Besides, what do you care? You don't like hearing about other people anyways."

She was right. Most of my daily life was spent avoiding personal conversations with people I didn't know, precisely because I didn't want to know them. Now things were different. Keeping to yourself seemed like a defense mechanism. But what were they defending themselves against?

* * *

The next morning it wasn't the sound of our cabinmates moving around that woke me up, just me. My internal clock had readjusted and now I was waking up at the proper time on my own. It didn't take much to wake Sami up; my movements normally woke her up regardless of the situation. "Where is everyone?" she asked once we were outside on our way to breakfast. She was right. The past morning we'd been one of many working their way to the breakfast tables, spilling out of the several bunkhouses and homes on the properties. This time there were only a couple of people in sight and most of them were kitchen workers.

"I don't know. Maybe we're early?"

"It seems like the right time of day." She squinted at the sun. Her watch was staying in her backpack in our room for the time being.

We scooped up our breakfast helpings and found a spot to

sit, not that there was much competition. Susan the kitchen boss was on us before I even got the first bite into my mouth. "Start the dishes as soon as you finish eating," she ordered.

"I thought I was with the harvesting team now," I answered back, surprised by the sudden change of plans.

"There's no harvesting today, it's Earth Day. Only essential work, and washing dishes is essential work."

"Okay, I didn't know that," I answered, but she was already storming off.

"Is Earth Day a holiday or like the weekend?" Sami asked me once we were alone again.

"I don't know. No one talks to me about anything out here." I bit into my cucumber. "Did they say anything about today being special in the babysitters club?"

"Well, we'd been getting some of the kids ready for a kinda play that they're performing today. But I didn't know it was something special. I just thought it was an activity to keep them busy."

"A play?"

"A recital, whatever you want to call it. It's just the kids being silly in costumes and trying to dance. I think it's as much for the babysitters as it is for the kids. They're really excited about it."

"Yeah, a bunch of pageant moms in training."

"Don't say that," she said in a sharper tone than usual. "They're all very sweet and mean well."

"I'll take your word for it. They just stare at me."

"I think they're just nervous around a boy. They keep them mostly separated."

"So you're the special one. You're married so you get to see a boy all the time."

"Yes, they're *very jealous* of my access to you." Mocking me again. "Here they come." She nodded to our left as the pink-clad girls zoomed across the open space, heading for breakfast. They had a nervous energy about them as if they were the ones who'd be taking the stage today.

"I should get going if I'm going to finish the dishes before dinner," I said, not wanting to be around when the gaggle finally descended upon Sami.

"Alright, have a good day. Hope to see you at our show." She gave me a kiss before I hobbled off towards the dish pile and the trusty wheelbarrow. It seemed like I'd been demoted back to dishwasher, though maybe I was just the first person to breakfast and got recruited by chance. Everyone else seemed to be sleeping in. Maybe they were avoiding getting sentenced to spending the day at the creek when it seemed like it was a collective day off. Trekking between the creek and kitchen all day didn't feel much like a weekend, though it was better than harvesting corn all day. I hadn't been too excited about getting back out there in the dust and sliced up by the leaves. It was looking to be a pretty hot day already, so better to be spending it sloshing around in a shaded creek than sweating in the fields.

Beth was waiting for me when I reached the bridge with my first load. "Happy Earth Day," she greeted me brightly.

"Hey, Beth. Happy Earth Day."

"Back to washing again, huh?"

"I guess so. I was in the field picking corn yesterday."

"How was that? I've never been assigned to that."

"It was hot and dirty, but whatever."

"Most of the jobs are, unless you're babysitting," she mused, drifting back towards the shade of the trees that were between the sun and road at this hour.

"That seems like the life, huh?"

"Yeah, it was."

Setting the wheelbarrow down, she had my attention. "You were a babysitter?"

"Yeah, for a little while, when I first got here."

"That's what my wife's doing now."

"I heard. Is she having fun?"

"Yeah. Babies are better than washing dishes or picking corn."

"Or lugging this around." She gave the shotgun a shrug.

"Do all the girls spend time as a babysitter?"

"Most do. I guess some of the harvesters didn't, but they showed up alone," Beth answered, clearly trying hard to remember all of the guests at this commune.

"What do you mean, they showed up alone?"

"Without boyfriends or anything, just single girls," she said matter-of-factly.

"So the girls who arrive with a guy, they get assigned to babysitting?"

"Pretty much." Beth was drawing further away from me in the center of the road. She seemed to have a limit on how much conversation she could handle.

"So then you came out here with someone?"

"Yes, I came here with Austin. You probably met him yesterday. He's one of the harvesters." By the end of her statement she was back in the little shaded spot in the corn stalks, sitting on her stool. "Have fun with the dishes."

"Thanks. Have fun with the road." I answered with a bit more cheer than would be expected, giving the conversation a very light feeling at its end. Better for Beth to not think anything of my questions. She was the only one who would answer them forthrightly, though, like a genie, there was a limit on how many you could ask. Hopefully she would keep our chats between us.

* * *

On my third trip back it was hotter than ever. Still, it sounded like the entire little town had now woken up and was enjoying the downtime. The sounds of a guitar drifted through the air from the common area, where it looked like the kids' performance was going full-tilt, complete with costumes and a soundtrack produced by an impromptu small band. Even in this entertainment-starved environment, though, I had zero interest in attending the spectacle. Perhaps it was better that I was working, since faking enjoyment would've required a lot more effort. Mostly I was just wanting to stop for lunch on this trip. Normally the heat killed my appetite, but the permanently small portions of food nowadays cured that problem. I could eat no matter the temperature.

Glancing towards the showgrounds, I noticed an

unfamiliar but recognizable form watching the performance. Lincoln had finally revealed himself to the open air. It was the first time I'd seen him since our arrival, and he still didn't show any signs of wanting to be seen. He was pressed up against the side of the house, peering around the corner to watch the show from a distance, clearly trying to avoid being witnessed by the community. He didn't factor in that I'd be stumbling around behind him doing my chores, which gave me a perfect view of him. Detouring off the road, I left the wheelbarrow and slunk my way towards him. It was only about fifty feet away, and with the music playing ahead of us, he never heard me until I was right behind him. "Hello, Lincoln," I greeted him cheerily.

Giving a slight yelp, he spun around, and then eyed me like I'd caught him skimming through a Victoria's Secret catalog.

"I haven't seen you at all since we got here." I hoped I could brush through his extra-awkward teenager behaviors and quickly get into a real conversation.

"I stay in my room," he muttered. He said more, but that was all I could make out. That much was apparent just from his skin tone. Everyone else had developed a nice tan during this summer, as indoor work didn't exist anymore. However, Lincoln was still pale white, looking like this was his first encounter with the sun in days.

"Do you know what they're celebrating today? I think they said it's Earth Day?" I probed him further. He might be one of the only people in this community that'd be willing to talk about what was going on, if you could get him to actually speak at an audible level.

"It's Sunday," he mumbled again, pushing away from the house and trying to find a way past me.

Moving with him, we retreated towards his mother's house. He clearly wasn't up for conversations, but I wasn't going to let him off that easy. "What happened to all the husbands? What happened to Daniel?" I asked hurriedly, nearing the door.

Reaching for the handle, he gave me his last answer. "They died," he simply said as he slipped through the doorway.

"All of them?" My question floated unanswered and unheard as the door swung closed behind him, leaving me alone in front of Carla's porch.

I continued working the math as I retrieved the wheelbarrow. There were four homes here originally. The couples were all older to be sure, sixties and seventies, but all four of them dying in such a short span was highly unlikely. Of course, logic dictated that the other three could've died before this mess, because Daniel wouldn't have bothered to call Sami to tell her that his neighbors were dying. It was possible that it was just coincidence that they were all widows out here, and that Daniel died after the shutdown from natural causes. He was old, and without electricity the workload would've been suddenly much harder.

Dishes were done before dinnertime today. I was finally getting into the groove of my new profession, and each day my foot felt better too, smoothing my movement until I could nearly walk normally with the wheelbarrow in my hands. Even though only the kitchen staff was working through the afternoon, the common was nearly empty after the frolicking that had taken place in the grass for most of the day. It appeared that the entire town had retired for an afternoon nap, leaving the space with an odd stillness in the daylight.

Sami wasn't in our room when I finished working, but it was too late for me to take a nap before dinner. At this point I was most likely to sleep through the whole thing. So setting up position at the dinner tables, I waited for the town to come back to life. The time crept by slowly, even though I wasn't exceptionally tired when I sat down. Once my body stopped moving and I allowed myself to relax, I realized how tired I was. Focusing my mind was no use; my thoughts sank down in a pit of exhaustion as I spent the next hour drifting off, snapping back awake and then starting over as my head lolled forward towards the table. After a while, my neck couldn't take the load anymore, and I forced myself back to full consciousness. Oddly, I was still alone at the dinner tables, even though it was nearly time to eat, judging from the gnawing in the pit of my stomach. My attention was drawn to the field. That was where the crowd was gathering again, as if there was another show about to happen, everyone arranged out on the grass like it was a group picnic.

Heading that way, I discovered the food had also been prepared for the picnic meal concept. Everyone who had food was eating out of various containers, cardboard and plastic boxes being the most common. There was still a row of them waiting to be consumed on some tables at the edge of the field. Grabbing one and moving into the field, I searched for Sami. It wasn't hard; the pink dresses stood out among the green of nature and the blandness of humanity. The babysitters club was arranged on the grass in the middle of everyone, the children clustered around them like puppies. Sami caught my eye and gave me a wave. She was practically in the dead center of the population with the kids pressing even tighter around her. Getting through to her would be more trouble than it was worth, so I just waved back, motioning that I was going to enjoy my dinner on the perimeter of the gathering.

Finding a patch of the softest looking grass, I made a seat for myself and dug into dinner. There was more than normal. Even if my heart had been let down by the lack of meat, it was partially healed by the quantity revealed. More than two of our normal meals were contained in my plastic tub, my own portable feast for my first Earth Day. As the group chewing subsided, the noise increased from the community. Several songs broke out among the people, being chanted out loud as a group effort. My contributions could be described as minimal at best. Even so, there was a lightheartedness that accompanied this meal and the people who enjoyed it in the field.

As the mood settled, Abigail went to the front of the group and started her remarks with another prayer to Mother Earth. She touted several people for their accomplishments this week—most corn picked, most garden tended, most love given. Some of the achievements seemed concrete, others were rather vague. Once she finished, Lori spoke. This message was all about community and how it was our strength that would see us through this crisis of humanity. It was a moving message if you believe in such things; clearly the other residents did, and were quite moved. To me it seemed a tad overdone.

Then it was Carla's turn. Obviously Abigail and Lori were just the opening acts for the headliner. As Carla moved forward, the crowd became instantly silent, showing a deference for her that it hadn't been as strict about for the previous speakers. "Good evening, everyone," she began. "Every Earth Day is a reminder of how far we have come. We gather here to give thanks to the planet for blessing us with what we need to survive, and we honor our Earth Mother by not taking more than we need. Humans have long separated themselves from nature by allowing greed and selfishness to guide their behavior, instead of listening to the guidance the earth provides. Now we pay that cost." She paused, surveying the crowd that was hanging on her every word.

"This community has been a light in that storm, and Mother Earth has blessed us with fair weather and bountiful crops. This means we obey Her commands and we hold each other accountable for the sins that are committed against Her. Sins against the earth must be punished, for the good of the community and the salvation of the planet." Carla finished her statement strongly, turning to face the far right corner of the field, behind all of our backs. The crowd spun with her, focusing their eyes on the barn that sat on the edge of field. My eyes searched it over. At the door stood Carla's assistant, Cindy. The barn had been there the entire time without me ever noticing it; it probably existed before any of us were born, judging from its dilapidated state and intense undergrowth surrounding it.

Once Cindy saw that all of our eyes were turned to her, she pulled the barn door open, revealing four disheveled figures who stumbled forward into the waning daylight. They were all wearing the same dirty brown burlap sacks, like literal potato sacks with holes for their arms and heads, their hair matted and stiff, their faces streaked with dirt and sweat streaks that had left clean lines down their face.

Marching forward, Cindy led them to the front of the group, next to Carla who hadn't moved. Reaching her, all four of the barn people fell to her feet, their hands clutching at the hem of her dress. "Have you admitted your sins?" she asked harshly. The four muttered their replies. Only Cindy and Carla were close enough to hear their exhausted voices. "Have you atoned?" she continued. The group spoke again.

Turning back to the rest of us, Carla spoke for all to hear

again. "These four have received their punishment, and the clear skies are Mother Earth's blessing, smiling back at her repentant children. Their debt is paid!" The rest of the community broke into applause as the four climbed back to their feet. "Remove your sacks and enjoy what the earth has provided." The three young men and one girl shed their burlap bags in front of us, revealing naked bodies that were as equally filthy as their faces. They stumbled towards the tables that still held the unused boxes of food we had picked from. They attacked them like they hadn't eaten in a week. I suddenly realized that they probably hadn't.

The nervousness of the moment was creeping through the crowd. The noise of the newly freed prisoners eating their food was the only sounds to be heard as Carla's glare seared across the people in front of her. "This week, there have been four more sinners in our midst who require penitence." Her voice was level and sharp, the entire crowd hanging on her every word. "Erin!" she yelled the name in rage.

Erin climbed to her feet. She was already sobbing into her pink dress. Despite having had the children crawling all over her just minutes before, the space around her had emptied like she had the plague.

"You have been caught gossiping and neglecting your charges." Carla announced her crimes to the public. "Humble yourself."

Still sobbing nearly uncontrollably, Erin undid the clasps of her dress and it fell to the ground. Contorting her nude body to try and shield parts of herself from our gaze, she swayed in the wind like a weird scarecrow.

"Bethany!" Carla's voice rang out, snapping our attention back from Erin's plight. My border guard friend from the dishwashing spot stood up. She wasn't crying yet, just white shock etched into her face. "You have been accused of laziness and dereliction of duty," Carla screeched again. "Bare yourself." Bethany followed Erin's example and dropped her dress to the ground, but chose instead to stare aggressively at the ground to avoid the community's eyes.

"Ozzie!" Carla's voice rang out again. Ozzie from the harvesting team rose up. He held himself a bit more confidently than the girls had done so far.

"You are accused of gossip and rumor-mongering. Bare yourself." Malice had slipped into Carla's voice for this pronouncement. Doing as he was ordered, Ozzie pulled his shirt off and let his pants fall to the ground, making him the third person standing in the nude in the field.

I hadn't spoken to Erin since we arrived, though I knew Sami had. Bethany and Ozzie had both talked to me, though, Bethany probably more than anyone when we were alone out at the riverbank. The darkness of the thought was creeping through my mind as Carla spoke again. "Kyle." With my name ringing through the air, the entire crowd turning to face me, I got to my feet numbly. "You are accused of disruption, laziness and threats against nature." The clothes were next, I told myself. That's how the process had worked with the other accused criminals.

Instead, Carla continued her assault. "Even though we allowed you into our community, you have spent your time here disrupting and corrupting our residents. You lured Ozzie and Bethany into disobedience with your evil tendencies, and then you started attacking the very structure of our life and faith, which is nearly unforgivable. Beseech Mother Earth to rectify your ways and cure your heart before it's too late to be redeemed." The malice that had been in her voice when addressing Ozzie had doubled as she laid out my crimes. My sins were unique enough to warrant an explanation of them. Seemingly I had baited Ozzie and Bethany into their failures, so as the root problem I got made a public example of to warn people about associating with me.

"Bare yourself!" the order finally cut through the air and I obeyed, my clothes in a pile at my feet. Once I was undressed, the focus of the crowd shifted back to Carla. "To the barn!" she screamed. The commotion followed immediately. Rising up as one mass, the residents pushed into me, forcing me back towards the barn on the wave of humanity. It wasn't as traumatic for me, since I was already on the edge of the gathering, and giving ground easily let me stay ahead of the pushers as they herded me into the barn. Ozzie, Erin and Bethany had a worse time, since they started in the middle of the crowd. The battering they'd taken was evident as soon as they fell out of the wall of people and into the barn with me—split lips, dirt on their knees from having fallen during the pursuit, and bruises welling across their bodies. They burst into the barn and out of the tornado of their enraged neighbors.

Once we were all inside, Cindy threw in four new burlap sacks, then slammed the door shut. The crowd didn't dissipate, though, but remained encircling the barn and shouting curses at us, slamming their fists against the weakened wood and screaming threats against us for our sins against Mother Earth.

"This thing might collapse!" Scanning the already buckled framework and drooping boards, I saw that the entire barn was already leaning to one side. If the angry mob put their mind to it, they could've brought it down on our heads.

Erin hadn't moved from where she'd landed when the crowd spit her out, sobbing on the dirt floor, turning it to mud. Bethany had stumbled a bit farther in, landing against an upright beam before dropping to the ground. Her shocked reaction was still locked in place, blank eyes staring at the ground.

"Get down!" Ozzie hissed, yanking my hand, pulling me down against one of the stalls. "If they can't see you they'll relax." At this level we were partially shielded from sight. He was right—once my body wasn't easily visible through the gaps in the walls, the crowd began to calm down. The fury of the mob is easily stirred and easily dampened. After a while, the only sound was Erin still dry-sobbing from the ground. As the sun faded, the people receded back to their regular routines and their beds, leaving the four of us locked in the barn.

"Now what do we do?" I asked Ozzie once I was sure we were truly alone.

"Get some sleep. It's going to be a long day tomorrow," he answered, moving away from our hiding spot and into the stall opposite of me, where he started arranging a space as a bed.

CHAPTER SEVENTEEN

SICKLE

It was not a comfortable night of sleep in the barn, a surprise to be sure. Following Ozzie's lead I had picked one of the stalls for my bed. It was obvious that someone from the previously freed occupants had spent his nights here. What hay there was had been laid out in a mock mattress and a bundle of rags for a pillow; not much for a blanket, though it was still hot enough that a blanket wasn't needed. Bethany had stayed huddled by herself until after dark, finally summoning her strength to wander into a corner and curl up. Erin spent the entire night exactly where she had landed when the crowd expelled her, prostate on the packed ground of the entrance.

Normally it's hard to find sleep after such an eventful evening. In the old world I probably would've spent a couple hours tossing and turning in bed, playing on my phone or mindlessly watching TV. Here in this barn, sleep came quickly. The stress of public shaming and imprisonment should've kept my mind busy throughout the night, but it didn't this time. My mind shut down completely and easily once I decided it was time to go to sleep. A survival mechanism for this world where my mental state was stressed all the time. If the anxiousness kept me awake, I would've never been able to sleep in the months that had passed.

The wake-up call came at the crack of dawn, the front door sliding open and some angry voices rousing us all from our fitful slumber. Two large gruff-looking women were standing at the door. They were unfamiliar to me, having escaped my notice if I had seen them during my week here.

We were issued cheap sandals to go with the dirty sacks we'd been given the night before. Once we were dressed, the march started. The chill of the predawn air was still around, the nighttime dew soaking our feet as we trudged through the grass. Entering the cornfields, we continued to march for what felt like a mile until we finally popped out of the corn stalks and into an open space. It was still the corn fields except here the stalks had been cut off about a foot above the ground, leaving a gaping hole in the unending rows of corn.

The two woman led us into the opening. There was a pile of tools and several of the ever-present wheelbarrows. In a world without engines or animals, wheelbarrows were the go-to for just about everything that needed to be moved. The tools were handed out, machetes and sickles. Considering the situation, I wouldn't have been surprised if this was a gladiator-type experience and we were being handed our weapons for some kind of fight to the death.

"Start working that line," one of the ladies instructed, pointing behind us to the row of still standing corn stalks. Apparently the tools were to be used against their intended targets, plant life, and not the more amusing human lives. Ozzie led us forward. It was obvious it wasn't the first time he'd been out here, so I followed his lead. Bethany seemed prepared as well, though resentful of being cast back here. Erin remained a complete wreck. It was obviously her first time as field hand.

And so we started chopping. It was demanding, though it was better than breaking apart the concrete of a gas station just to prove some kind of abstract point. Here in the field there was at least a purpose being served other than just making us perform mindless backbreaking work. The corn stalks needed to come down; they'd already been harvested, and now they were just taking up space. Cutting them down meant they'd start decomposing back into the soil, preparing it for next year's planting. A machine could've probably cut down the entire field in a couple of hours, but instead it took us all day to clear about an acre of space. Lunch was served from a bucket, watery soup and half an ear of corn each, then it was back to work. Our minders, the two women who had led us out here, remained all day. Their primary objective seemed to be finding the best shade, though they'd occasionally harass us about our work—not going fast enough, too much resting, or something along that nature. I considered ourselves lucky that the overseers weren't carrying whips as previous generations of their profession had done. Still, we kept working until the sun was nearly down. Back in town, dinner would've been about done by the time we began heading back. That explains why I hadn't noticed the condemned before; they left in the dark and returned in the dark, all daylight hours spent in the fields.

Staggering back into the barn, the door slid closed behind us, sealing us in for another night of detention. Dinner was the same as lunch, this time waiting for us in the middle of the barn, cold and watery. But it was edible; that's what mattered. "Don't stay there." Bethany spoke. It was the first words any of us had said all day. It echoed through the darkening space like a gunshot. She was looking at Erin, who was preparing to curl up in the same patch of dirt she had spent last night in. "Come over by me. It's more comfortable." She motioned Erin towards the far corner where there was some hay that hadn't been used yet. Meekly Erin followed, though her soft sobs could be heard as we all drifted off to sleep. The improved bedding hadn't helped her mental state.

The next morning began the same way, a dawn awakening and a march to the field. Our pace of work had begun slowing from the day before as the sore muscles and blistered hands wore on us. By the end of the day, Erin couldn't swing her machete hard enough to even dent the stalk. It might have well been grown out of steel.

The third day passed exactly has the previous two had, our cleared space decreasing and the yelling from the overseers increasing. Back in the barn, Erin didn't even stop to eat at our communal dinner; she stumbled past and collapsed into a heap on the little hay bed.

"She needs to eat," I said, my voice coming out cracked and rough from disuse. It was the first words I had spoken out loud in several days.

"I'll feed her when I finish," Bethany answered without looking up.

The silence returned as we continued to lick every drop out of our bowls and gnaw the cob down to nothing. "She's taking this really hard," I finally said. "It's just a week, right?" Ozzie and Bethany had clearly resigned themselves to their fate; having already weathered this storm before, they were mentally prepared to get through the sentence.

"A week out here, yes," Bethany answered. "But she won't be a babysitter anymore, favored status gone. When she gets out she'll get a bland dress and just be another girl in the kitchen or garden."

"That's part of the punishment? Losing your job? Will you not be a guard anymore?"

"Heh," Ozzie interrupted. "Guard isn't special. We'll all go back to our usual positions. But the babysitters get rotated out. Each time a new girl comes in, an old girl has to go."

"Sami's the new girl?"

"Yep. As soon as she put on the pink dress, it was fated that one of the others was going to lose theirs. That's why they were so gung-ho this week. Each of them was trying to prove worthy of hanging around longer."

"Our punishment is a week of this, then it's back to normal," Bethany added. "But she loses her friends, the kids and her fancy room in the big house."

"Were you a babysitter before?" I asked of her.

"I was, until Ozzie and Jenny showed up. Then the gossiping crime and now I'm out at the frontier all day, unless I get caught talking to you."

"Is Jenny your wife?" I turned to Ozzie.

"No, she was just my girlfriend."

"And now?"

"Now she's a babysitter and I'm in the fields." He tossed his bowl and cob back into the bucket. "I'm full," he announced as he crawled off to his stall.

"I'll get her to eat something." Bethany whispered, picking up Erin's rations and moving off as well.

Day four was *Groundhog's Day* yet again. Erin was barely functioning, even though Bethany had gotten her to eat dinner last night. I was beginning to feel better. My body had started adjusting to the change in activity, and my chopping improved from the day before. Finding a rhythm and locking into it was the best way to get through the day. Back in the barn for dinner, the group separated instead of eating together, Ozzie in his stall, Erin and Bethany in their corner. Talking was avoided completely once again.

The fifth continued as the past few had—wake up, cut down corn stalks, walk back to the barn at dark. "I think we're getting better at this," I said once the door was closed behind us and we went for our dinner. No one answered, instead grabbing for their food and starting to disperse again. "Eating alone again?" I pressed the issue while we were all still together.

"Haven't you done enough?" Erin hissed, the first words she had spoken since we'd arrived.

"What?" I responded in surprise. Her speaking had caught me off-guard.

"What more do you want from us? You got us all sent here, and now you want to be friends." Her voice was raising in anger.

"What do you mean I got you sent here? We've never spoken." I looked at her enraged face. Bethany and Ozzie remained blank.

"You and your wife showed up and everything went to shit because of you two. You men are all the same, getting everyone else in trouble and acting like it's not your fault."

"What are you talking about?" I looked around the three faces. Erin was raging, and Ozzie and Bethany had become drawn, glaring at me. "I didn't get you in trouble."

"Yes you did, talking to Bethany out on the road, prying into Ozzie in the fields. The elders heard about all of that. They gave you a chance because of Sami but they know what you men do, they saw as soon as you got here how you started poisoning everyone around you just like you did with this planet."

"Is that what this is about? Blaming me for the storms or the hurricanes? Everything in the world is my fault? Because I had a nice car or a big house?"

"No, because you're a *man* and men *destroy* things."

"Ozzie's a man. Is he destroying everything?"

"You're too old to be here," Ozzie cut in sharply, shaking his head. "Things are different now, and you have to make peace with that the way the other men couldn't."

"I don't know what that means!" I shouted back at them, even though they'd ended the conversation by walking away as Ozzie finished. He went to his stall and the girls back to their corner, leaving me alone with my bowl of soup and piece of corn.

Day six started the same, but it felt different. Previously I had felt a sense of camaraderie with the other three. Accused of flimsy crimes publicly and sent to suffer to fuel the policies of a police state, we should have bonded. Instead we succumbed to the desires of the regime and turned on each other. A ruled class divided cannot stand up to the elites. It didn't matter if they were burning our home down, executing strangers, forcing sex, smashing concrete or cutting down corn—the system was the same, acts of subordination to an authority figure to display your subservience, and turning on your fellow man to prove your loyalty. All regimes function on the same theory—Soviet Russia, modern Russia, ISIS, Scientology, the Sith or Ancient Egypt— impossible-to-follow rules that result in everyone being a criminal and begging forgiveness from the regime that created the arbitrary restrictions.

My head spun as we spent our day cutting down corn stalks. The air was different, even our two angry woman guards could tell. The group had found its outcast, the nonbeliever, the lesson they were really sent out here to learn, that I was someone who didn't believe what they believed, which makes me the enemy. Being the enemy is hard; I'm sure that shouldn't be a revelation, but it was to me. I'd been the bad guy before, the selfish boyfriend, inattentive husband, angry brother, disrespectful son, difficult co-worker, and even the bad dinner guest. In those moments you might feel like the enemy to someone, the lines drawn; and even if you're right, you still know the opposing party views you poorly. However, that stigma doesn't follow you out the door. Fight with a co-worker, the waitress doesn't care, she just sees you as another person. That's not how it works here at the Rogers farm in Dakota, Illinois. Here, if you are one person's enemy, you have the entire population arrayed against you. There is no reprieve from the judgment, no friendly face to look at or even a neutral face. They are all angry.

We continued as we had the previous days and cleared more space, though my heart wasn't in the menial labor today and it showed as my stalks-per-minute ratio fell, resulting in increasing scorn from the supervisors. Sensing that the breakdown in the group's collective spirit had occurred, they exploited the opening by riding my back all day long. It took everything I had to remain quiet, focusing my rage on the innocent corn stalks. The break actually helped Erin; for the first time since we'd been banished, she was managing to keep her head up and actually look alive. Venting her spleen on me the night before had finally given her some peace. She had her enemy now. From her perspective it wasn't her fault or Sami's fault or the elders who setup this oppressive system's fault. It was mine; I was the disruptor, the snake in the garden who had led her astray, even if it was far-fetched since we'd never spoken to each other prior to last night. That's what she'd chosen to believe.

Our evening was spent awkwardly in the barn once again, this time the three of them huddled in the girls' corner, leaving me alone at the slop bucket. The whispers of their voices carried over enough to tell me they were furiously laying their souls bare about my transgressions. The realization hit me that they were probably getting their story straight. Tomorrow was our scheduled release, so they had to get their story straight about how I had tried to corrupt them and they had lived to tell the tale.

Day seven began even earlier than the others, obviously since our release was going to happen at the community dinner before dark, which meant we had to be back from work earlier than we were normally, hence we had to start earlier too. The predawn glow gave us just enough light to see what we were cutting, though I was afraid that in the dark, I might end up being the thing that got chopped. Finishing me off might've been their ticket to redemption, so I worked with an eye on everyone until the sun was bright enough that there wasn't any sneaking around possible.

Early evening we were told to pack it up. Our tools were stacked in the center so our guards could tally them up, as if we were going to steal a machete or sickle. Not much on the black market, though I guess it'd be useful for a murder-suicide, which wasn't beyond the realm of possibilities out here. Our guards marched us on a different route home tonight than we'd used the rest of the week. This one brought us to the road and then back to the houses. The reasoning was obvious; we entered the barn from the backside, out of view of the community gathered in the field, enjoying their Earth Day meals and rousing speeches. They shouldn't have to see us prisoners until the official reveal.

Locking the door behind us, we were back inside the barn. Running immediately to the other side, Ozzie and Erin pressed their faces to the gaps of the exterior paneling, attempting to join mentally with the people that were in the field. "You won't last much longer here. None of the men do," Bethany whispered into my ear as soon as the other two reached the wall. The monotone delivery made it sound like a threat, a promise that she wouldn't be coming back here, but I would. Her eyes told a different story for the second I locked onto them, before she ran to join the others. It was a warning, the fact that's noticed and accepted in this town but never discussed. What happened to Mr. Rogers and the other husbands?

I didn't care about trying to hear whatever nonsense was being spilled out in front of the crowd, so I hung around the middle of the barn, where our dinner was normally waiting. Thankfully, there was something to distract the others. The awkwardness of waiting in the barn with no food to busy ourselves would've been all-consuming. They strained to hear a blown-over word from the ladies, and I heard Bethany's words replying over and over in my head. We had to leave again—it obviously wasn't safe here—but we were out of options. This had been our last choice; it was here or roaming the countryside on our bikes, dodging the firing squads and stealing corn for as long as we could.

Finally Cindy appeared at the front of the barn. "Is everyone ready?" she asked through the gaps.

"Yes!" the eager voice of Erin rang out. She had moved past her grief and was just ready to get back out there. Maybe she could charm her way back into the good graces of the babysitters club. Anything was better than being here. Moving forward, I joined the row of inmates at the door so when it slid open we were all revealed. I thought it would be more humiliating than it was, thinking of how disheveled and pathetic the previous prisoners were. I knew what we looked like, battered, filthy and gaunt. All I could think of was food. The same thought occupied my stomach on our march. I had given into the frustration of our diet for the past seven days. It wasn't the first time I'd been nearly starved recently, so my belly had made peace with it while it'd been happening. Now the meal was within reach and it was ready for it.

Reaching the front of the group, we fell at Carla's feet. I followed the lead of Ozzie and Bethany, who again proved it wasn't the first time they had been here. The hem of Carla's dress was in my fingers, mashing the dirt of my hands into the soft fabric as gently as I could. Dirtying the hem of her dress wasn't much or really anything at all, but it was all I had at the moment. We spoke our atonement and then shed the rags that we wore. The bright whiteness of my body shocked even me. My exposed arms, legs and face had become practically black during the last week as the dirt soaked into my skin. Across the rest of my body the white skin gleamed through the dust that had been collected.

Ozzie led the charge to the food tables once we were dismissed. The entire episode was like a dream I was witnessing. All my body could think about was eating something. Last week I had been surprised by the generous portions of food that each basket contained; this time I could never have been satisfied no matter how much was there, even though I paced myself as my stomach cramped and rebelled against the food it had demanded.

The party was breaking up by the time my mind cleared. If more people had been sent to the barn I had missed it completely. My other three inmates had also disappeared. They didn't want to be seen with me any more than they already had been, and probably not by the other people they were friendly with either. It wasn't a flattering portrait to be naked, covered in dirt, gorging yourself on the first real meal you've had in a week, food smeared all over your face. Being to a point past humiliation had arrived for me, though. I held my spot and let the crowd see me as it drifted apart, fading back into the buildings. I even missed the departure of Sami and the other pink dresses; they had slipped off while I'd been focused on my food. Probably for the best. Even though she was my wife, Sami would be better served if she didn't make a public scene welcoming back her banished filthy husband. That could wait.

There was one thing I wanted nearly as much as food, and that was a shower. However, that was unattainable, so a soak in the creek would be the best option. Pulling myself up, I set out on the familiar path to the dishwashing spot in the fading light. There was a different girl standing guard at the barricade this time. She refused to even look in my direction, purposely ignoring my approach and venture into the water. It was cold, but my mind was still a bit fuzzy, so I just powered through regardless of the temperature. Even in the dim light of dusk, I could see the darkening of the water as it washed away the grime from my body. It looked like someone had thrown a shovel full of dirt into the stream. Scrubbing every inch of my body, I emerged from the water feeling a bit reborn. Only my fingernails still bore the mark of the fields, the dirt having been jammed deeper than I could get at the moment, but it was good enough. I hadn't brought my towel, so drip-drying was the only solution as I trekked back to our cabin. The guard continued to ignore me as I sloshed past her in the darkness.

The cabin was silent when I got back. The party died down pretty quickly out here. In the bedroom there was a new pair of clothes folded on the bed for me. Gone were the clothes I had worn since leaving Joliet; now I had the uniform of Dakota. It worked for me; these were newer, and looking fashionable hadn't been a worry of mine in a while. There was one other surprise waiting for me; Sami's stuff was gone, her bag as well as the second pillow on the bed. They hadn't left her here alone in the boys' dormitory while I was gone; she probably got moved to

Erin's vacated bunk in the Rogers house where the rest of the babysitters lived. It was another night alone, though at least I had a real bed this time.

285

CHAPTER EIGHTEEN

BARN

I was the last one awake in the cabin today, striving for every second of sleep I could manage. The only thing that propelled me out of bed was the idea of missing out on breakfast. My stomach had struggled with the food last night, but it definitely wanted some more by now.

Pulling on my new clothes felt good. Even though they looked roughly hewn, they were comfortable and had a new feeling to them. The scraps I'd collected from the dry cleaners and the bike shop had worn down quickly during the constant use; these felt like they would stick around for the long haul. The only other item in the room was my backpack, now that Sami's stuff had been moved. My eye caught it because it was deflated-looking. Pulling it open revealed it'd been emptied out while I'd been away. All of our supplies were gone, and it was just a completely empty bag now, uselessly sitting on my floor. I dropped it and cast my eyes upwards to the ceiling light. The small outlines of the broken glass from the bulbs were visible through the frosted glass, and the larger black outlines of what I had stashed in there were still visible. I didn't have time to check; being late for breakfast might result in someone being sent to get me, and finding me standing on the bed with a lamp cover full of guns might cause some issues I wasn't ready for this morning. Still, I was sure they were up there; the shadows through the glass looked unchanged. Even Sami didn't know I had hidden them there, and if they were working her over, she wouldn't mention that we'd brought two guns with us.

The babysitters club was already leaving by the time I got out for breakfast. In fact, most of the people had already left. Talking to Sami would have to wait until dinner, it looked like. "You're late," Susan growled as I collected my breakfast.

"Sorry, I overslept," I replied evenly. Considering how the past week had gone, I was surprised I was out of bed at all.

"That's not a good look after what you've done." She glared at me. "Get to work." She stomped off.

She was right—I wasn't making any new friends here by being late on my first day back from prison. But then, I wasn't too concerned about making friends anymore. My time at this town was dwindling fast one way or another. Bethany's warning last night in the barn was still ringing in my ears. Odds were I'd be condemned again this next Earth Day and sent back out to the fields, probably being forced to work until I died or the issue was forced. A product of the old world, I wasn't going to be able to adapt to the new reality. I had failed in the Dirt camp and I was failing here. The thoughts of how unfit I was for this world continued as I scarfed down my breakfast and loaded up the wheelbarrow for my first run of the morning.

At the washing spot, Bethany was back at her guard post, the shotgun looking even more oversized in her depleted hands. At this point it would've been surprising if she could even rack a round into the chamber if she was forced to. The starvation rations and work of the past week had shrunk all of us noticeably. Remaining pointedly in her sheltered space out of the sun as I approached, she refused to look in my direction as I headed down to the stream. I couldn't blame her; getting caught talking to me last week had been enough to get her punished, so talking to me now seemed like an even worse idea, and probably carried stiffer penalties, if such a thing even existed.

Burying my head into the dishwashing for the rest of the day was easy. The work was much easier than what I'd been doing, and the cold slosh of the water was a reminder of how much worse it could be. Even so, my strength was mostly sapped, so the trips got longer and the washing dragged, putting me right up against the dinner deadline with my last load, which greatly upset my boss.

The last run was my quickest. This was because my stomach had gotten involved and insisted that I eat again; it was still running at a deficit and needed more. Getting back with the dishes just as the food started being served resulted in more reprimands and scowls from the rest of the kitchen staff as they hurried to put the freshly cleaned dishware to use. As usual, the babysitters were clumped up in the middle of the space. Sami was with them, enjoying herself, while I stumbled out to a table that was empty on the edge of the dining space. Eating alone wasn't a bother; I wasn't ready to talk to anyone anyway, and there wasn't much to talk about one way or another. Catching Sami before she got washed away with the rest of the pink dresses was my only concern. I didn't know at this point if she was avoiding me or if the group was keeping her trapped and unable to get away without attracting too much attention.

Finally, a while after they'd finished their food and worn out their bubbly conversation, the babysitters started preparing to leave. This was my chance. Moving quickly and getting around the tables, I went in on an interception course, heading them off before they could get back to the Rogers house. Sami was in the rear of the group. Grabbing for her hand, I stalled her. Only the two girls next to her even noticed I was there; the rest of the group kept marching forward, only their girlish chatter concerning them. Her eyes were big, having been surprised when I grabbed her, though the look in her eyes changed quickly to worry once she realized what was happening. "Are you okay?" I said, my voice soft.

"Yeah, I'm okay. Are you?" She fumbled for her words.

"I made it through. It was hard, but I'm here."

Searching me over, her eyes lingered on my arms and hands, still showing the effects of increasing malnutrition. Behind her, all the babysitters had stopped and were watching from the edge of earshot. "They don't want us talking to each other," she whispered. "They've been warning me about it the entire week." One of the babysitters gave a theatrical cough to get Sami's attention, and looking back at me quickly, she gave me a silent "sorry" look before rejoining the group on their walk back to the house.

It was official now; something had to be done. Sami had devised a plan to smuggle me out of the Dirt camp and got us both to freedom, so now it was my turn to pay her back. It would be easier to sneak out of this place—disappear into the corn fields and in minutes they wouldn't be able to track us anywhere. The problem here is that we'd be stuck right back in the place we were before arriving, with nowhere else to go and no idea what to do about it.

Trudging over against the wall of the bunkhouse I sank down and worked on the problem. The mental exercise carried me late into the night. By the time my awareness of the present returned, it was completely dark and the moon high in the sky. Only the sound of the bugs and owls could be heard, the entire encampment fast asleep. Climbing back to my feet, I went and prowled through the night around Carla's fiefdom. Behind me was the prison barn, the door securely locked from the outside, though the walls were so fragile it wouldn't have taken much to bust yourself out if you wanted to. Like most situations now, the prison is mostly in your mind. Around the corner of the house was the window to what'd been the guest room when we'd last stayed there. Maybe that's where Sami was now, but it could be anything at this point. Next to it was another barn. This one was in good shape, Daniel having built it only a couple of years before. It was his tinkering shed, a place for his hand tools, and probably for him to hide from Carla when he needed a break. I'd passed it a couple of times since we'd been here. No one ever seemed to use it, yet the door had a large lock on it. Or it normally had a large lock on it, but this time the latch was open and the lock was sitting on the ground.

Moving closer and pressing my ear against the crack in the door, I listened. There was a sound coming from inside the darkened space. Small clicks, punctuated by the sound of vibrations. Then the faint sound of a voice. It was too muffled to discern what it was saying, but I knew I had heard it. There was a person in there somewhere.

Pressing against the door, it slid open easily on its rollers just wide enough for me to slip through. Inside it was dark, obviously. With the door closed again, the only light was the moonlight shining through the small windows. Once my eyes adjusted, I could see enough to get a lay of the room. Typical barn layout, with stuff piled along the walls on the shelves. The reflective strips from our bikes shone from the other side of the room. This was apparently where the contraband was taken when it was seized. Good to know if I ended up needing them again.

The noise I'd followed in here had started up again, still muffled. My ears drew me towards the rear of the barn. Walking in the dark wasn't easy, so I dropped to my hands and knees, feeling ahead to keep from running into something that'd give me away. Getting caught in here wouldn't look too good. Reaching the back wall, I could hear the sounds clearly now. It was familiar but I couldn't put my finger on it. Running my fingers along the seams of the boards didn't give any answers. This should be the exterior wall of the building, so how could the sound be coming from inside a thin wall? I knew there wasn't anyone on the outside of the building. That's when I noticed that, up close against the wall, there was minute flickers of light seeping through the gaps between the planks. From across the room you wouldn't have been able to tell, but this close I could see it. I suddenly realized that I wasn't looking at the exterior wall at all, but rather a fake exterior wall, with some sort of hidden space between it and the real outer wall.

Feeling my way gently, I eventually reached a recessed hidden door that you push once to have spring open. Stepping through, I found a room that was three feet wide and as tall and long as the barn itself. At the far end was a TV. Its glowing screen was showing a video game battle between Star Wars characters. On the chair in front of the TV was Lincoln, his shocked white face distorted by the shadows of the confined space. He was half-turned in his chair, staring at the intruder, still wearing his gaming headset with a microphone pointed crazily into the air. There were posters on the walls of anime characters, and smaller gaming devices were strewn about on the plush rug that was laid out to cover the concrete floor.

Lincoln didn't move as I approached, just his eyes following me until I was standing directly behind his small lounger chair that served as his gaming seat. The only thing missing from the scene was the trash pile of junk food and soda cans piled up on the floor. Apparently, even in a world where he could pull off this secret gamer cave, such commodities were hard to find. "How do you have power?" I finally whispered.

"Solar panels," he whispered back. Squinting past the glare, I saw that the TV was sitting on a board, laid across what looked like a generator of some kind, connected to thick cords that snaked into the wall.

"Where did you get all of this?"

"Dad built this place for me when he built the barn."

"So you've been sleeping all day so you can play during the night? That's why we never see you?"

"Yeah." Lincoln pulled his headset off and set it down. "Please don't tell my mom." His voice trembled.

"Are you playing *online*?" I blurted out once my eyes made sense of what I was seeing on the screen.

"Yeah. Do you want to play?" He held the Xbox controller out to me.

"How do you have internet access?" I ignored the controller.

"We had a satellite receiver for WiFi before. I just moved it out here."

"Who are you playing against? No one else has electricity."

"It's not like that everywhere. A lot of places are still pretty normal."

"You mean like other countries?"

"There too, but a bunch of the states have started doing their own thing. It's like a civil war in some places?"

"Where? What states? There's a war going on?"

"I think it's down south, a bunch of the states fighting the government. And out west. And I think Alaska is too." He answered impatiently, turning back to his game.

*"Wait!" grabbing his shoulder. "Alaska is still kind of normal?"

"Yeah I think so."

"Do you have a cable I can charge a 'Let with?" My thoughts were suddenly frantic, my sister was in Alaska, normally thousands of miles away, but suddenly now just a phone call away.

"Yeah, but I'm charging mine now." He motioned to his 'Let laying unnoticed on the ground. The green pulsating ring around the edges showed it was fully charged.

"I'm going to get mine so I can call my sister."

"Okay, but you can't wake anyone up. We'll get in trouble if they even see us out at night."

"I know. Just wait here, I'll be right back." Turning around, I nearly dove back through the opening and into the darkened barn. The darkness hit hard. My eyes had become adjusted to the brightness of the TV screen and left me practically blind out here. It was good because it slowed my mind down. The sudden rush of possibility had me ready to run through the wall, but what was needed here was patience.

Crouching on the ground until my night vision returned, I moved to the doorway. It was silent out there, just the noise of the bugs doing whatever they do during the night. I slipped through the sliding door and across the yard like a cat burglar and back to the cabin my room was in. Opening the door quietly, I crawled my way through into my room, on my hands and knees. My weight was dispersed and lessened any squeaking of the floorboards or thumps of my feet. Pressing the door closed behind me, I climbed on top of the bed. Unscrewing the light cover in the dark was difficult, but I managed without dropping anything and got the whole container spread out onto the mattress. Everything I had left was there—two loaded guns, the holsters, the spare mags and now the jewel, my powerless 'Let.

Hiding the rest of it under the mattress for the time being and returning the cover, I was back in the grass without a sound. The barn was still pitch-black, but I powered through to the hidden door like I'd been there a million times. Lincoln had returned to gaming while I had been away, and was already in the midst of an epic battle against Imperial stormtroopers, ignoring my return. I unplugged his device and gingerly slipped the power connector into mine. The 'Let gave a slight shudder and lit up when it felt the charge. Its face showed an empty battery symbol with the charging symbol plastered over it. For the first time since I'd dared to use the generator at my house months ago, it was getting charged.

Every electronics owner knows of that infuriating delay between when you start charging your device from zero and when it finally has enough power to actually turn on. Impatience is always a factor during that waiting period. This time wasn't like that. Instead it was a period to collect my thoughts and marvel at what we'd been missing. So many of our recent problems could've been solved with a little electricity for our devices and a network to connect them. And here it was, hidden in the back of a barn, so a teenager could keep playing his video games while everyone around him lived like it was the 1800s.

Finally the moment arrived and my 'Let started powering up, bringing the background photo of our wedding ceremony onto the screen. How clean and well-fed we looked in that picture. That day had been stressful and nerve-wracking, but those people didn't know anything of actual stress. Life for them had been one long ride of easy decisions and coasting through life. Clicking through the menus, I came to the WiFi tab. Having not used my fingers in such delicate ways in a long time, navigating the touchscreen took longer than it used to.

Lincoln's signal showed up immediately: "Rogers Home." Full bars and password-protected. "What's the password?"

"lincolnssecretlair, all lowercase," he said, eyes still focused on the game.

Typing the code in worked on the first try, and my 'Let started shaking as it became flooded with weeks of updates, messages and notifications pouring in. Clicking into the phone page showed multiple missed calls from my sister Lindsay. It looked like she'd been calling and texting a couple times a day for weeks. Lincoln finally stopped playing the game as I was pressing "call back." Even he was interested in hearing from someone outside town.

It rang once before she answered. "Kyle?" her voice joined

us in the room, sounding confused as if she was receiving a call from a dead man.

"Hey, Linds," I answered back with a choked voice.

"Oh my God," she whispered before the sobbing began. It took a minute or two before she calmed down, which gave me the chance to compose myself too. "Where are you?" she finally managed to ask after recovering her voice.

"We're at Sami's parents in Dakota."

"Are you okay? How are things there? All we hear is about how bad it's gotten there."

"I'm doing alright. It's been rough but we're still in one piece."

"That's good. How is it there? Are you making it?"

I paused and then exhaled. How could you describe what we'd been fighting through since even before our house got lit up? "It's not great, Linds. Not good at all. Even here at the farm it's gotten pretty weird."

"You need to get out of there. Come up here!"

"Believe me, we want to. But we can't walk that far."

"Kyle, there are flights. There are evac flights that the new government is running. Josh is flying for them. You need to get on the next one." Josh was Lindsay's husband who had been a pilot for a local airline based out of Anchorage.

"What?" I hadn't seen a plane in the air in months, and even then it was just military flights. "Where do we go? When?"

"Hang on, let me get the maps." The sound of her moving around and shuffling papers echoed through the speakers as Lincoln scooped up his 'Let, bringing his own maps app up to the front of the screen. "Okay, okay, I got it," Lindsay panted into the phone. "The closest flight to you is leaving from Gogebic County Airport, Thursday at midnight. It's in the upper peninsula of Michigan, right on the lake."

"How do you spell it?" Lincoln chimed in.

"G-O-G-E-B-I-C," Lindsay answered slowly.

"Okay, here it is." Lincoln showed me the map, the tiny town and airfield highlighted and our route from the Rogers Farm to there shown. It said we were 330 miles away.

"Can you make it there in time?" Worry creeping back into Linds' voice. "You have about forty-eight hours." Doing the time math in her head.

"150 miles a day on bicycles is stretching it pretty badly," I muttered out loud.

"We can drive my dad's car," Lincoln said suddenly.

"What?!" I said turning my full attention to Lincoln. "There is a working car here?"

"Yeah." Lincoln answered with a tone that suggested I was crazy for not believing him.

"Lindsay, we will be at that airport in forty-eight hours. Tell Josh we'll be waiting on him. But I need to go figure this out right now."

"Okay. I love you, Kyle."

"I love you too, Lindsay."

Disconnecting my call, I grabbed Lincoln's 'Let. It showed five-plus hours of driving to get there, though the map was kind enough to mention that there might be unknown obstacles, considering the current situation. "Okay," I said, turning my attention to him. "Now what's this about a car?"

"First you have to promise me something." His voice got a little stiffer. "You have to take me with you."

"Lincoln, no. This is your home. Your mother is here."

"I'm not staying here. She killed my dad."

I sighed. The question had been nagging at me for days. "Tell me what happened," I said.

Taking a deep breath, he began, "When this all started, the men didn't take it seriously. Dad, Mr. Owens, Mr. Hawkins and Mr. Dumont just kept doing their work like normal, using the tractors and everything. Mom started fighting them about it around the home at first, refusing to use electricity in the house. Then one day when things had started to get pretty bad in town, Mom took the car and drove in. When she came back she had like ten extra people with her. She put them in the cabins, and suddenly it was like she had her own little army. People kept coming in too, people from town who'd heard about how it was out here. They started blocking Dad whenever he wanted to use his tractor or drive his truck. After a while Dad and the other guys realized they were outnumbered and that Mom was in charge now. That's when all of this got set up, the chores and the babysitters and their own special clothes. Only Dad and the other men refused to participate. Then one day at breakfast Mom started screaming at them for making it cloudy or something, and they got carried off and locked in the barn. They were the first ones.

"After things calmed down, Mr. Dumont kicked a hole in the wall and came out, but Cindy shot him dead right there. The other two and Dad stayed in the barn after that and worked the fields like Mom ordered them too, but at the end of the week they were so worn down they could barely walk. Mom got them together in front of everyone and asked them what they wanted to do. They all said they wanted to leave. Mom said that anyone who wanted to leave was a heretic who deserved to die." The monotone voice he had told his story in trailed off. He wiped his eyes to clear the tears before he continued. "That's when the whole crowd attacked them. They beat them to death and then buried the bodies under the vegetable garden." The end of the story left us both shocked, Lincoln looking up at me with tear-filled eyes. "I have to leave. Dad waited too long."

There wasn't much to say to a story like that. Pulling him in, I hugged him tight. "We'll get you out with us. It'll be okay, buddy. It'll be okay."

CHAPTER NINETEEN
BRONCO

Twenty minutes later we were slipping through the cornstalks on our way to see the car. I wasn't completely ready to believe Lincoln's assertion that he had access to a functioning vehicle; it could just be youthful optimism, or a misunderstanding of the car's condition. In a car we could get to this Gogebic place in five hours, probably longer though if we drove through the night to avoid any of the entanglements that might derail us during the day. Our trek through the cornfield was longer than any of the other trips I'd yet taken out here, and Lincoln kept switching directions, making turns seemingly at random, but finally we popped out of the corn and into a clearing around several trees with a small barn centered between them. An old dirt road led away from us and into the cornfield on the other side.

"Dad used to keep stuff out here for when he was on this side of the fields," Lincoln said.

"And a spare car?"

"He had this car as a project for years. Mom never cared enough to know what he was doing, and once she started getting weird he brought it out here to hide it."

At the barn door, Lincoln fished a key out of his pocket

and unlocked the padlock, pulling the doors open. It wasn't a car, it was a truck, the model not apparent in the dark, but the body of the truck filled up nearly the entire space in the barn. It barely fit inside.

"You have to get in through the back because the doors don't open in here." Lincoln got into the bed of the truck, and I followed. In it was several gasoline cans, in signature red with the old-style flexible nozzles.

"These are full?" I asked, shaking one of them. The sound of liquid sloshing responded.

"Yeah. He used to keep gas out here in case he ran low in the tractor or something. We used to have one of those big gas containers to fuel everything up. He woke me up one night after the weirdos showed up and we filled up all the gas cans in the night and brought them out here." He slid between the seats and into the passenger bucket chair, I followed suit and was in the driver's seat. "Here." He fished another key out of his pocket. This one was a car key, clearly marked with the Ford logo. I fumbled for the ignition in the dark for a moment before the key slid into it, and a moment later the roar of the engine and glare of the lights filled the tiny barn. "Runs good!" he yelled over the noise.

"Uh-oh. It's a manual."

"What?"

"A manual transmission." I pointed at the gear shifter.

"Okay," Lincoln answered, clearly not understanding what that meant.

"It's just…going to be a bit more difficult than normal, is all. Hold on, I'm going to try and back up." I pressed my foot onto the clutch and gripped the shifter. We jerked our way backwards while I struggled to manage the car. Usually driving a car is similar to riding a bicycle, in that once you know how to do it, you're pretty much set for life; however, sit down in a manual car when you grew up on automatics, and had only driven a manual once during your Driver's Ed course 15 years ago, and you'll feel like the training wheels have been put back on. Once clear of the shed, I put it into first and did a couple of laps around the clearing. There wasn't much space for practicing my shifting, but everything felt as good as possible. We had a functioning vehicle.

"You sure they can't hear this from back at the houses?"

"No. Even when Dad ran the tractors out here, we couldn't hear them."

The truck turned out to be a Ford Bronco, which I could no longer see without automatically thinking of OJ Simpson's slow-motion getaway down an LA freeway. Daniel's restoration hadn't made it to the exterior yet, or really any part cosmetically. The side panels were mismatched, with multiple spots where he'd been grinding at the rust. It would've been a beautiful truck in some other future timeline, but this was probably as far as it was going to make it in this world. All that mattered to us was that it started and drove, that the tires were full, and that there was plenty of gas. We were set.

"Okay, let's get it parked back in there." Carefully we eased the truck back into its berth, then locked the doors and headed back to the houses. "Do you have any paper and pens back in your gaming room?" I asked Lincoln once we were trekking back through the corn.

"Yeah, a few."

"Would you be able to pass Sami a note tomorrow?"

"I guess so."

Back in his boycave, I sat and tried to think through an entire plan. Getting Sami out of the house undetected was the most difficult step. After that it was just running through the fields to the car shed. I put Lincoln in charge of plotting our car trip to Gogebic while avoiding anything that looked like a town or even subdivision if possible. Madison was the biggest city between us and there. It was sure to be a mess, with the University of Wisconsin housed there. College students had been at the forefront of the Gaia movement that'd ushered President Rodriguez into office, and they made up the majority of the Dirt faithful. Madison was sure to be a hotbed of fanaticism. Avoiding it completely was a life-or-death issue at this point.

He dug out a wire-bound school notebook and some fine-tipped magic markers, and I wrote a note to Sami, explaining the plan. "Give her that sometime tomorrow," I said, folding it and handing it to Lincoln. "Make sure no one sees it. Now, let's walk through tomorrow again and work out the signals."

* * *

It was past the middle of the night when I climbed back into my bed. My 'Let was fully charged and the WiFi network reached this far, so Lincoln and I could communicate if we needed to. I had gotten my belt out of the barn, and my holsters were reattached to it, ready to be worn tomorrow. I had decided I couldn't leave them in the room during the day; it was too dangerous to be without them now. Hooking the belt around my torso tightly and underneath my shirt let me carry them without them being seen through my baggy overshirt. It wasn't comfortable, but it'd be doable for a day.

Sleep wasn't great even though I was very tired. The past week had been an endless routine of overworking and undersleeping. Tonight was going to fetch even less sleep, and tomorrow I wouldn't get any at all. I only needed to last another forty hours or so, and then I'd sleep no matter what.

The stomping of my cabinmates woke me up as it normally did in the morning. Despite my exhaustion, I was jumpy. The guys nodded to me politely as we trooped out of the cabin and towards the breakfast table. Ozzie refused to acknowledge my presence at all. The battered look the four of us had assumed during the incarceration lingered with us, though he was looking better rested. I imagined I was the worst looking of the four, my gaunt face and heavy eyelids standing out among the entire population, a walking textbook example of the benefits of conformity and aggressive protecting of the status quo.

"You look like death warmed over," Susan frowned as she approached one last time with marching orders. "Get the dishes done on time today or you can start licking them clean."

"I'll do my best," I mumbled back as I bit my tongue. The cold metal of the handguns strapped to my chest gave me some relief. If things went south tonight, I might go looking for her before it was all over. Even though dragging my chores out might've been a nice parting gesture to Susan to let her know how much I cared about her opinions of me, it was in my best interest to get this done as quickly as possible. Finish early and I might snag a nap before dinner.

Moving with as much speed as I could without making it noticeable, I dove into the dishes. Maybe they'd assume my quickened pace was an effort to appease my overlords, having finally accepted my fate. Though my unruly appearance gave off the distinct opposite impression. I had seen better put-together homeless people sleeping behind a Seven-Eleven. Bethany was at her post per usual when I got there with my wheelbarrow, and she remained under the cover, our talking ban still continuing. She was the only one here who still showed some basic decency; she had been genuinely friendly before we got punished, and even though she'd lashed out at me with the others, she'd taken the chance to try and warn me before it'd all happened too. She didn't want to see me end up in the vegetable patch, and that passed for friendship in this world.

My mind having something else to focus on actually made the menial task I was assigned easier to do. The days here hadn't provided much to think about, just rehashing the same old thoughts that bogged my mind down and slowed my working pace. This time there were new thoughts to be had and something to work towards, which let my hands run free on the dishes and finish even quicker than I had on my best day.

Slipping off to my room after returning the final load of dishes, I laid down for a nap. With my 'Let charged I was able to schedule an alarm, as if I lived in a different world. Lincoln had clued me in on what actual time the meals were served, since he had been electronically keeping track of time since the world had fallen into the dawn-to-dusk routine. That gave me ninety minutes of sleeping before dinner started. Getting there in the midst of the crowd would be the best option, and hopefully let me remain unnoticed by everyone, unless some poor souls had to suffer the misfortune of eating at the same table as Kyle the Pariah.

* * *

The soft buzzing of the 'Let secured to my belt let me know it was time for dinner. The babysitters were already eating by the time I arrived. Sami was in the middle of them once again, so I couldn't tell if she'd gotten my note yet or not. The herd-like behavior was perfectly tailored to keep the most vulnerable members secluded from any threats. Dinner for me was swift, although not as fast as the girl who had been at the table before me. It didn't look like she'd chewed at all before she scampered away from my aura.

Finishing my meal, I went back to my room and texted Lincoln. *Did you deliver the note?*

He responded quickly. *Yes. All good.* It wasn't clear what the "all good" meant, that she had already responded positively or just that the message had been delivered. Whatever the case, we now had about another two hours of waiting to be safe. The sun was rapidly fading, but there were still people kicking the ball around in the field and chatter coming from the rooms down the hall. Everything would have to wait until the whole town was asleep. Setting my alarm for ten p.m., I tried to get some sleep, but it proved impossible. Instead, I kept watch out the windows the best I could, tracking as people headed off to their beds and left the fields empty.

It was finally time. Not a sound had been heard in over thirty minutes, and the deep dark of night had arrived. *All good over there?* I texted Lincoln.

Yes, everyone is in their rooms, he responded.

We hadn't decided on a hard time limit for when I would decide Sami was overdue and take matters into my own hands. We didn't know what kind of sleeping arrangement was going on in her room; she could be squeezed into a bed with a bunch of girls, unable to get out without waking them. I would give her as much time as possible to make it out on her own. A violent extraction was the last thing this situation needed.

The belt that'd been digging into my ribs all day long finally got removed, strapping it around my waist like normal, the guns riding exposed on my hips and the 'Let returned to my wrist. There was no turning back now, so might as well get them out in the open where they can be useful. Scooping up the empty backpack and dropping to my knees, I carefully crawled my way out of the cabin, avoiding the creakiest of the floorboards and not getting to my feet until I was in the grass. Moving quickly to the edge of the Rogers house, I crept around the edge until I reached Lincoln's window. On the sill was the key to the shed padlock and in the grass below it was a bag containing as much food as he'd been able to snatch from the kitchen that day.

Step number one was getting to the shed and gathering our supplies while we waited for Sami. Carefully unlocking the door and sliding inside, using the glow from my 'Let, I was greeted by our former possessions, our two bicycles and Sami's bag with our flashlights, protein powder and water bottles. Squeezing everything into the backpacks, I hooked them around the handle bars and wheeled the bikes out to the edge of the field.. Returning to his window and tapping gently, he lifted it open for me to climb in. It was a large window, so getting through was easy; he'd been doing it for months now. He was fully dressed, even wearing a stocking cap pulled down low on his head, looking like he was about to rob a bank.

Even though we were in the same room, we didn't dare speak, instead communicating via our 'Lets from across the room. The night before he'd drawn me a map of the house plan, which I'd memorized. Sami's room was upstairs in what used to be Carla's sewing room, but had been re-purposed when space was needed for beds. Lincoln's guesswork was that there were two other girls sharing the room with her, but he wasn't sure. He wasn't allowed upstairs anymore, because it was the babysitters' space and he was a boy. It was the best we had, so it'd be what I was working with if I had to march up there.

For an agonizing thirty minutes the two of us waiting silently in his room, him on the bed and me in a chair in the corner, counting the seconds until eleven p.m., the deadline for waiting. Finally, at 10:58, the faint grind of Lincoln's bedroom doorknob grabbed our attention. Slowly it spun open, and my flashlight illuminated Sami's face peeking around the door, eying the two of us standing in the middle of the room with a gun drawn on her. Immediately she was across the room and into my arms, burying her head in my chest, the wetness of her tears cutting through the fabric. Holding her as tightly as possible with a gun still in my hand, we had our moment in the middle of the room. We were one again and nothing was going to stop us.

Lincoln had wisely closed the door that Sami had left open. We were still in occupied territory. "We have to go, babe." Breaking our embrace and nodding, she stepped back. She was wearing a white night dress, like something out of *Mary Poppins*. "You need some real clothes." Planning Sami's wardrobe had escaped our strategy sessions, though it should've been obvious that she wouldn't be wearing her pink dress in the middle of the night. "Lincoln, do you have anything she can wear?"

"Yeah." He dug into his closet and produced a pair of jeans, a t-shirt and an old pair of sneakers. The shirt would fit well enough. The jeans were significantly too long, but Lincoln's skinny waist was close enough for them to stay up. And the sneakers were close enough to work.

"You go first," I said to him. "You're leading us." I pushed him towards the window while Sami yanked on the new clothes.

THUD. The sound above our heads probably wasn't as loud as it seemed, echoing through the quiet house, but to us it sounded like a cannon shot. It was followed with more thuds, the sounds of footsteps on wooden floors. Lincoln didn't wait; he was through the window and running for the cornfield in a flash. Sami, being practical, had gotten the pants and shoes on first. The t-shirt was still in her hand and the night dress still on, so only the crumpled denim of the too-long pants legs were visible. "Follow him," I said, pushing her through the window. Falling through, she picked herself up and chased after Lincoln as I was jumping through. The noise behind me in the house was getting louder.

The adrenaline of the escape was forcing my foot to work better than it had in weeks, the pain retreating as I pushed it harder. Catching up to Sami halfway to the corn, we glanced back at the houses for the proverbial last look. There were lights starting to flash on in the Rogers house. In the two weeks we'd been here, I hadn't seen any light being used after dark, even if they're natural gas lamps. This night it was different. An escaping babysitter would have the whole society in upheaval. Whatever tools had been stashed away were sure to come out. Still, no one was outside yet as we both grabbed our bikes and pressed forward into the corn. We still had several precious minutes before any kind of a search would get started, and by that time we'd be far enough ahead that they couldn't catch us by the time we got to the truck. If we were trying to escape on foot, they might've stood a chance of recovering us at some point, spreading out quick and trying to net us in somewhere, especially against people like us who weren't familiar with the surrounding terrain. It wouldn't work this time, though. We'd already be gone.

The trip last night had taken a while when Lincoln and I had just been walking casually through the night. This time it was a dead sprint, no regard for the cornstalks or keeping quiet. Minutes later we burst through the edge of the field and into the tree-dominated clearing that held the truck shed. "Give me the keys," I said, pushing my way forward to Lincoln who had slowed down once we were in the open. "Sami, grab us as much corn as you can while I get this out."

She paused for moment as she processed the orders before dropping her bike and running back to the edge of the field. Jamming the key into the lock and popping it free so Lincoln could pull the doors open, I climbed quickly through the bed of the truck and was back in the driver's seat in seconds. It started up as easily as last time. Taking a deep breath to concentrate, I gripped the shifter and worked the clutch, sending the vehicle rolling out of the shed easily. Dropping it into neutral and remembering the emergency brake, I hopped back out. Lincoln was already shoving the bikes into the small bed. Helping him, we had everything stowed quickly. There were only two seats in the truck, so Lincoln would spend the trip laying down on the floor behind us. But he was young; he'd be able to deal with it.

"Get the map ready!" I yelled at him before I slammed the tailgate closed. "Sami! Let's go!" I yelled into the darkness beyond the glow that the running vehicle gave off. She came running, holding the front edge of her night dress which she had turned into a makeshift corn basket. From the amount of sag, it looked like she'd managed to grab a bunch. Rushing over to her side, I got her into the passenger side before sliding into the driver's seat.

"Everyone ready!" It wasn't a question; it was a declaration. Slipping the truck into gear, we roared forward into the night.

CHAPTER TWENTY

STORM

"Turn left here," Lincoln said, navigating my driving from the back.

"How far away is this place?" Sami asked. Getting her up to speed on our plan was tricky to do since we were still in the middle of it, and Lincoln was calling out directions every couple of seconds. The modified route he planned for us was a maze of twists and turns as we avoided every semblance of a town or populated area. Back roads were the only path forward for us, and that meant we were constantly turning to avoid something.

"330 miles, but that's taking the most direct route." I veered us left down another road lined with cornfields and cow pastures.

"Do you think we'll make it there before dawn?"

"It'll be close. If we don't, we'll need to stop and hide out during the day. If any of the patrols catch us driving around, we'll be out of luck."

The moonlight was bright enough at this point that I was able to drive without the headlights on for the most part, only flicking them on briefly when we passed through wooded areas or something the moonlight wasn't lighting up. It was a very dangerous way to drive, though made safer since we were the only ones driving at this point. There was nothing we could do about the sound of the truck except hope we didn't pass any government checkpoints on the way. Even if the sound of the motor woke people up as we drove by, odds were we'd already be passed by the time they got up to look out the windows. Daytime would be a different story.

"Turn right here." Lincoln guided us onto an unmarked road. A lot of the roads out here didn't bother with street signs; if you lived here you knew the name, and if you didn't, you probably didn't have any business on this road anyway. "We're on this one for ten miles." Having the milage in mind let me increase the speed and chew up the road faster than I could on the short stretches with the constant turning.

We proceeded silently for the next 90 minutes, until Sami's voice finally cut through the blank space. "Do you see that too?" She pointed straight ahead of us, but above the street level and towards the horizon. There was a pale glow on the edge of the visible world ahead of us, distant and barely discernible in the darkness, but there.

"That's Madison," Lincoln answered. "We turn left in one mile and detour around it on the west side." He was very attached to his position of navigator.

"I can't believe they still have so many electric lights," Sami mumbled out loud. Our left turn had brought us up a small hill, increasing our view of the beckoning glow.

"I don't think those are electric lights, dear." In times past the glow of a town at night was a welcome sight; even just a small exit with a gas station and Dairy Queen could give off quite a welcoming glow when you were cruising through the dark sections of the highway. This time it was a warning.

"Fires." She nodded her understanding. "You would've thought by now they would've burned everything that needed burning."

"Once you start, it's hard to stop." I continued twisting our way west around the city.

"This is the hardest part," Lincoln said. "Madison on our right and the Wisconsin River on our left. Ahead, not much real open space." Crossing the river would've been better, but the only bridges were located in towns we couldn't afford to enter, so we had to skirt it aggressively on our journey north.

From the map this area looked the most dangerous, but it didn't appear that way as we drove through. Towns that existed on the map seemingly had disappeared, and even the homes tucked away in the open spaces on their farmlands were gone, only piles of ash left behind. "I think we're alone out here," I said after we sped past another driveway that led to nothing.

"I haven't seen a standing building in a while," Sami agreed.

"Looks like they're giving this whole area back to nature, burning out any remains of human activity." I flicked the headlights on to illuminate the former house sitting at the intersection ahead of us. We were turning right, away from the river. Only a few remnants of the house still stood, the chimney and a couple other parts that were resistant to fire.

"Wonder if they have people tearing the roads up yet? That looks like the only thing that remains out here," Sami said.

"If they were smart they'd just leave the roads. They'll start to crack up and fade away on their own. It's not like they can actually destroy the material, just tear it up and move it somewhere else." But then, I knew the futility of trying to approach these subjects with logic anymore.

"Left at the next intersection," Lincoln chimed in from the back.

* * *

The sun was just starting to appear over the horizon as we crossed the state line separating Wisconsin from the upper peninsula of Michigan. As we moved farther away from Madison, the scene had returned to what we were all familiar with prior to the shutdown, even if it was still blanketed in the blackness of no electricity. Unlike on the highway, the state boundary on these back roads was barely marked, no large sign welcoming you or bragging about whatever the state was famous for, though I honestly don't know if the upper peninsula had ever been famous for anything. "How far out are we?" I asked Lincoln, who was fading quickly behind us. Being up all night was starting to catch up with him.

"About sixty miles."

The airport was very close to the extreme western border of the state, but our roundabout route had brought us farther east than we would've been if we had driven straight there. That meant we still had sixty miles of Michigan to cross before we reached the Gogebic airport from the southeast side. The route had added significant millage to our journey, but we had avoided human contact successfully thus far, and the last hundred miles or so had been a breeze once we got into the rural woodlands of northern Wisconsin, which extended across the border. I had switched the headlights on a while ago and ran with them the rest of the way. I was more worried about hitting a deer than encountering people out here.

"Are we going to stop soon?" Sami asked. She'd been drifting in and out of sleep ever since we'd gotten into the forests. There wasn't much to look at in the dark, and the adrenaline that'd been powering us since we ran away from the farm had finally worn off.

"Yeah I think so. Sixty miles should be doable tonight when we head out again, and it'd be safer at night. Keep an eye out for somewhere soon where we can hide out for the day." Our path was currently winding through a very lake heavy area. Minnesota was well-known as the lake capital of the country, but this whole Great Lakes region was basically all the same terrain, lakes and forests everywhere.

"There's something." Sami pointed out the window. It was like a one-stop shop for all your deep woods needs—part gas station, part convenience store and part bait shop. The subject of fishing was most prominently displayed of its retail offerings. What caught my eye more suggestively was the car wash structure located behind the main building. Turning the Bronco, we did a full circle around the parking lot, seeing zero signs of anyone around. Even the windows remained unbroken. It just looked like any closed shop.

"I wonder if we can park in the car wash? It'd be hard to see us in there," I said as I steered us towards it. It was your standard "pull up and get your wheels in the tracks" structure. Both the entrance and exit had roll-up doors that were sealing it off from pulling through now.

Parking the truck next to the automated wash control panel, we climbed out. Well, Sami and I did. Lincoln was in the back and didn't seem interested in any exploring. "Do we have any tools?" she asked, nodding towards the truck.

"There might be a spare tire kit, though I forgot to look last night." Blowing a tire would've been a major ordeal, and without the jack and lug wrenches we could've been stuck fast. But the issue had slipped my mind last night.

"Looks like we're in luck." She kicked the latch at the bottom of the roll-up door. Normally a padlock would be inserted to keep the latches from being opened up, but whoever had last closed the door hadn't been too concerned with anyone breaking into the defunct car wash, probably since there weren't any cars cruising around anymore to begin with. Kicking the latch out of the way, the door shuddered up a few inches before we helped it along, opening it completely.

"Keep an eye on the wheels as I pull in." I hurried back to the driver seat. The sun was fully up now and the perfect glow of daylight was surrounding us. There were still no signs of other people, but being exposed here in the open had an unsettling effect on me. The Bronco easily rolled over the tire locks that normally guided your trip through the car, and we were safely inside the bunker with plenty of space to spare, a welcome change from the cramped shed we had departed from on the farm.

"I'm hungry," Lincoln said once we clamored out of the back of the truck. We'd been too focused on our travel to eat anything during the drive, so we were pushing ten hours of activity since we had eaten.

"Let's see what all we've got, then," I said. "It's gonna have to last us the rest of the day too." I motioned to Sami to start sorting out the food we had in the bag plus the corn. If we let Lincoln do it, the odds were he'd eat everything now. "I'm going to check the store before we close up." I grabbed my flashlight from the driver's door. "Actually, here." I paused before I left and unbuckled Sami's gun from my belt, giving it to her. Even though I was just going across the parking lot, it'd be safer if we were both armed.

The back door of the gas station was unlocked even though the door was closed. Inside it'd been cleared out in the same respectful manner the exterior had been treated. Despite being completely empty of items on the interior, the shelves were still standing and nothing had been broken inside or trashed. The store had been cleaned out like it was a moving project, not looting. Even the fountain drink supplies, the cups and lids, had been removed without any left behind. I was actually surprised there wasn't a "for sale" sign in the front window; the place had that kind of feeling to it. "Where are you?" Sami was calling from the doorway, her shadow filling the room.

"Over here." Even the magazine racks had been cleared out. Guess they were entertaining themselves reading about the behaviors of celebrities' past lives.

"Guess there isn't much to find in here." She joined me in the emptiness.

"I'm thinking the owners probably cleared the place out when things started to go bad. Maybe even the employees helped."

"It's a nice change from what we're used to."

"Did you leave Lincoln with the food?"

"He fell asleep right away. Tossed the bikes out and curled up in the back of the truck."

"I'm surprised he lasted this long." I moved our search to the back rooms. Perhaps there was something left behind in there.

"I don't think he's had any stress other than his video games for months now," Sami added, checking the bathrooms. Only the plumbing fixtures remained.

"Yeah, probably." The back rooms were empty. The building was all that remained here, not even a bag of chips forgotten.

"What do you mean by that?" Sami asked, blocking my path.

"What do you mean?"

"You said it in a weird tone. Is there something you aren't

telling me?" Her words were sharp, but the tone belied the truth behind them. She wanted to know about Daniel. We hadn't brought up that part of the saga during our car ride; there'd been plenty to tell her about the phone call with Lindsay, what Lincoln had been learning from the internet about the greater scope of our plight, and how we managed to get us out of there. "How come my dad had a fueled-up truck hiding in a barn that Carla didn't know about?"

"He moved it there when things started getting weird."

"And?"

Taking a deep breath, I told her the story as it had been related to me. By the end of it she was again in my arms, crying. "I'm sorry, babe. I wish you didn't have to hear it this way."

"And just when I had started trusting her. I thought she was finally being the stepmom I always wanted, but she was still just as evil as always." Her crying was slowing but her voice was still thick with emotion. "Oh my God," she added with growing horror. "She was going to do the same thing to you." She dissolved into tears again.

Back at the car wash we ate our breakfast silently, as Lincoln slept in the back seat, the three survivors of Carla's reign. "Should we keep watch during the day?" she asked, finishing off her allotted corn cob.

"Unfortunately, yes. There isn't much we can do, but getting caught by surprise would be even worse."

"I'll take the first watch," she said, grabbing ahold of the pull rope for the roll-up door and yanking it down, sealing us into the car wash. Only pressing your eyes against the clear Plexiglas windows on the two doors would let you see us inside of here. We might as well been back inside the ventilation ductwork of the bowling alley.

"You sure? I can stay up for a while," I said, offering her a chance to sleep.

"No, you've been up for too long already, and I can't sleep right now. You go to sleep and I'll get Lincoln up after a while."

"Alright." The exhaustion of everything began hitting me now. Sami taking charge here in the moment was a welcome relief. Letting someone else make a decision meant I could finally give in to resting, which I did aggressively.

* * *

"Kyle." Sami's voice was gentle, cutting through my fogged state like a guardian angel. "Kyle." The shaking from her hand dropped me out of the fog and back into the driver's seat of the Bronco I had re-purposed for sleeping.

"What!" I sat straight up in the fully reclined seat.

"It's getting late and I thought you should see this." She nodded her head to the front of the car wash enclosure.

"What time is it?" I stumbled out of the truck. My legs were still half-asleep and my back painfully stiff.

"It's about five p.m. You slept about ten hours."

"Why didn't you wake me up earlier? Did you sleep?"

"Look out there." She ignored my question completely. It shouldn't have been dark yet—five p.m. was still in the dusk time range this time of year—but it was darker than dusk outside the window. The swirling leaves and dust conveyed the message of what was happening. A storm.

"Have you been outside to look at it yet?"

"No, Lincoln woke me up a few minutes ago, then I woke you up."

"Lincoln!" I turned away from the view to find him. It wasn't hard; he'd followed us to the window and was directly behind us. "How long has this been going on?"

"About thirty minutes ago I noticed it getting darker."

"Let's go look at it." I led our little group to the rear door. Rolling it up, the chill wind caught us immediately, the smell of rain overpowering the previous scent of industrial car cleaning solution. The western sky was completely black. The storm front was approaching across our whole line of sight. "Did either of you see anything today? Any people?"

They shook their heads. The storm was the first notable thing to be seen all day. Our instincts had been honed to believe that storms were bad news, that they were a manifestation of our sins. Even if we didn't believe that, the vibe was still there, a thunderstorm moving across our path to salvation.

"Let's eat dinner quickly." We still had seven hours before our flight was due to depart, and only sixty miles to cover. The math was on our side, but nature didn't seem to be cooperating. "It's still too early to leave. We might run into somebody if we leave now."

Even though the storm was blocking out the sun, the early dusk light was still sufficient for seeing. Running out into the still lit world might bring us directly into contact with people before they too hunkered down to ride out the storm. Moving during the onslaught would be possible and probably safer. Government forces would be staying dry, or too busy repenting for their imaginary sins, to be roaming around the countryside. Everyone else would probably be focusing on staying out of the rain or keeping their stuff from blowing away. Noticing us driving through the rain wouldn't be easy with all the other commotion.

Retrieving what was left of the food, Sami started sorting it out, as I emptied out the last of the gas containers into the fuel tank. We had stopped once last night to refuel on the side of the road, and that had used most of our reserves, but there was a little left over. This time we were completely out of fuel, besides what was left in the truck's tank, and that was pretty low. All the extra miles and slow speeds of our winding path had chewed through a lot of gas. We'd be running on fumes by the time we reached the airport.

CRACK. The first bolt of lightning and following roar of thunder reverberated through the small structure. Lincoln let out a small yelp, jumping out of the car like it'd been struck itself. "We can't go out in that. What if we get hit?" he pled with us at the tailgate. Sami had the food sorted out into three portions.

"It'll be okay, buddy. We won't get hit." I patted him on the shoulder, trying to reassure both of us.

Sami handed him his food. "Eat this and then we'll get going."

"A plane can't land in this weather. It's too dangerous."

"It will have passed by the time the plane needs to land. We just have to be there." He did have a point, though. With the assumed lack of sophisticated guidance or tracking systems at this tiny airport we were going to, it'd be a safe bet that they wouldn't try landing in something like this. But we couldn't risk not being there. Even if we had to wait for another flight or clearer weather, it was the only lifeboat we had.

The rain had started in earnest by the time we finished our meals and were all packed up. The time on our 'Lets said six p.m. With the extra gas cans finally discarded, Lincoln had a decent amount of room to squat behind our seats. The bikes would continue with us, a hedge against running out of gas early. Though the prospect of trying to ride a bike in this weather was daunting, it would probably be easier to walk, but we'd deal with that if the situation arose.

The rain was frighteningly loud as it began pounding the roof as I eased our way back out of the car wash. Inside it'd been a dull roar, but now it felt like it was trying to hammer its way through to us.

"Turning right onto the road." Sami was guiding our trip now. Lincoln's fragile state couldn't be depended on; he was still scarred from the weather hysteria his mother had ingrained into him, probably as soon as the movement began gaining steam a few years ago.

New wiper blades were something Daniel had neglected to replace on the Bronco; he probably hadn't planned on driving it in the rain anytime soon, since he was still restoring it. That was bad news for us, since the rotting rubber was breaking off and littering the windshield as it battled against the torrent of water gushing in our vision.

"Can you dim that anymore?" I asked, indicating Lincoln's 'Let. It was contributing the least of all the factors going into my inability to see; however, it was the only one under our control.

"How's that?" She slipped the device under her oversized shirt and read it from in there.

"It helps a bit." It was pitch black now. The last vestiges of daylight had disappeared and we were genuinely driving through the dark. The headlights were doing their best, but against the rain they were being strangled mid-air, resulting in a faint glow that made it even harder to see through the glass in the moments of clarity when the wiper blade passed through my vision. The only bright spots occurred when the lightning crackled and provided a snapshot of the world around us. Even the rain couldn't obstruct our sight fully when that happened, though Lincoln continued to yelp at every strike, which added some distraction to the event.

During the next three hours we crept forward, battling to stay on the elusive pavement. Several times I drifted off the road and into trouble. Each time it had been terrifying, that we might finally be stranded, but the Bronco lived up to its name and slogged through the mud back to the beaten path of the road. The entire trip had been devoid of life, human or otherwise, though it was possible we were just missing them due to the storm. Even so, it felt like we were still truly traversing the wilderness now. The wiper blades fought a good battle, but their efforts were just too outclassed by the rain. Once they fully surrendered to the facts of life, I rolled down the driver's-side window and drove with my head out the window, uncomfortably and resulting in getting soaking wet, but improving my seeing ability and increasing our speed from the crawl we'd been maintaining.

"Is it stopping?" Sami said. She'd also been keeping her head out the window for most of the drive, trying to keep track of what road we were on.

"Maybe." My face was too wet and raw to tell anymore. The wind and rain was pelting through me.

"How close are we?" asked Lincoln from the back. His voice had returned now that the thunder and lightning had subsided.

"We're close, about ten miles to go," Sami answered after consulting the 'Let. She had attached it to her wrist so she could keep watch on it out the window. "How are we doing on gas?" She turned back to me.

I pulled my head back in to check the dashboard indicators. "Pretty low. The light is on."

"Let's hope it's got ten miles left."

Eventually it finally did get better, and soon when my head was outside, it was only the chill wind of the storm and not the icy wetness that greeted me. "Try the wipers again," Lincoln demanded from the back seat. Our heads being outside the cab had left him feeling alone inside it. It wasn't the weird family vacation vibe we had going last night that he'd grown accustomed too.

Flicking the lever up, the blades kicked into action again. Even though the rubber was mostly gone, the lack of new rain let them clear the windshield enough that the road was visible ahead of us, though still blurry. It wouldn't have been clear enough to drive if there'd been other cars to contend with, but holding to the center of the faded yellow center line was easy enough.

"This is good news for our airplane," Sami said to Lincoln, looking at him over her shoulder. "We still got a couple of hours for it to really clear up."

"Yeah, and good news for us too. I can actually speed up now." I eased my foot into the gas pedal and clutch, letting me upshift. We'd spent the entire ride since the car wash in first and second gears.

"There's a sign for the airport!" Spotting it on the side of the road, Sami called out. The standard white outline of an airplane glowed against the green background as we cruised past it. She looked back at Lincoln as the flash of the lightning lit everything up once again, the interior and exterior of the car bathed in the electric purple light of nature, Lincoln's pale face along with it. The thunderclap overlapped the visual lightning strike, indicating it had happened almost next to us, the sound and light overwhelming all of us. "Look out!" Sami's voice rang out, even louder than the thunder.

Snapping my eyes back to the road ahead, I saw what was happening in slow motion. The lightning had stuck a tree on the right side of the road ahead of us. The outline of the bolt was seared into my eyes. The top of the tree was exploding as I jammed the brake, the tires squealing and the engine revving down angrily as I choked it. The tree gave a shudder and split from the roots up. The left half, flaming at the top, tilted straight for the road and our path.

"Stop!!!" Filling the car, Sami's voice spoke for all of us. But the wet conditions meant we weren't stopping on a dime, and the branches filling up my view signaled we were out of runway. Yanking the wheel to the left, the truck went hydroplaning off the road, through the bushes, and over the ledge into a lake. Slamming into the water sent us forward from our seats. The view ahead had been distorted ever since the lightning had struck within my vision, the entire scene playing out like strobe-light images before my eyes instead of the smooth flow of reality. The tightening of the seatbelt was like I was riding a rollercoaster, the last thought I had before my face went into the steering wheel.

When I was a teenager, I would sometimes take a shower with the lights off. My family's home was small and the downstairs bathroom just had a cheap shower insert plugged into the wall. The tightness of the enclosure exaggerated the effect of sitting there in the dark with the water pouring over my head. It was a place to relax, to find my thoughts and be alone for a few minutes. That's where I was now. The pressure on my chest made me feel like I was in an even smaller shower, one you had to squeeze into. The sound of the water around me was calming, running and gurgling all over, though not over my head like a shower would. Maybe I was in the bath. That would explain why my feet were so wet and cold.

But why would I be sitting in a cold bath? If you only had cold water, you took a fast shower, barely getting wet as you wiped down whatever part needed the scrubbing. Sitting in a tub with cold water was practically torture. Looking for reality felt like I was back on the road and trying to look through the windshield being pelted with rain, trapped in the darkness that the headlights were failing to defeat and the wipers had given up on. Then it lifted, just like the rain had.

My lower half was already submerged. The truck was taking a nosedive to the bottom of the lake in slow motion, and I was literally in the driver's seat. Instinctively grabbing for the door handle with my first awakened breath, trying to push it open failed. The water pressure or something we had hit on the way was keeping the door sealed. Reaching for the seatbelt buckle was the next gut feeling, and it popped free easily, letting me fall forward a bit once it wasn't holding me into place.

My vision was returning. The shock of the crash landing had rattled my eyes. The lack of any light also contributed. We were stuck in a sinking car in the wilderness and the moon was clouded out of existence. "Sami?" I groaned out. My chest was aching from the seatbelt, and the blood in my mouth clotted the words. "Sami?" My own voice finished the process. Reality had returned.

Sami was dangling forward, the seatbelt holding her in place like it had done for me, the fresh blood still oozing down her face. Reaching out and grabbing her, she moaned; still alive, but not functioning yet. The front window remained shattered but still in place. The water was lapping through the open side windows already, filling the cab even quicker now.

"SAMI!" I pushed myself up. We were going out the back. The tail of the truck was still in the air and offering a way out. Wrapping my arm around her and popping her seat belt, she fell forward into my arm, still moaning. "Come on! Wake up, Sami!" I pulled her body with me into the rear of the truck. Aiming my foot for the floor and finding something soft there stopped the progress. Lincoln was sprawled out behind our seats. He hadn't been strapped into anything, so the crash had tossed him around, and now he was laying behind our seats in a heap with the bikes tangled up around him.

One last pull brought Sami fully out of the front seat and on top of Lincoln. The bikes were obstructing me. The crash had sent them flying around the small space and locked them together in a web of metal and tires. Pressing past them and grabbing the latch for the tailgate, it fought against me. The angle was horrible, sucking my leverage out of the situation against the old mechanism, but it finally gave in and the tailgate fell open. Grabbing the mangled bikes and pushing them upwards with all my strength, they hit the rear window with force and popped it open, the pistons retracting under the pressure. The bikes followed, teetering for a moment on the lip of the tailgate before tipping over and sinking into the water.

Grabbing at my leg, Sami was starting to come around as the water was once again lapping at her feet. The front seats had sank below the water line fully now; the open windows were letting the lake pour through them and accelerate our descent. "Get up, Sami! GET UP!" I grabbed her by the armpits and hoisted her up in front of me, her eyes fluttering through the caked blood.

"Wuts gon on?" Her voice was heavy from her barely coherent state.

"Sami, you've got to get out! Climb out!" I pushed her forward towards the open space above us. The incline was leveling out as the car took on more water, so it wasn't straight up anymore.

Still mumbling, Sami pushed forward, her wits returning with every second. The combined force of the two of us got her to the edge of the tailgate. "Can you swim? Can you get in the water?" I pushed her a little farther to the edge of the vehicle.

"Alright," she answered before flopping herself into the water.

Below me Lincoln was already starting to float as the water surrounded us. Pulling him up turned out to be harder than Sami. Even though she'd been nearly senseless, her body worked with me, while Lincoln was completely limp. Locking my left arm under his armpits and pushing forward, I found a grip with my right hand, letting me pull us both forward. My feet slipped at first, but it found a purchase on the side wall. Kicking and pushing with all my might, we made it, splashing into the water in one big jump.

Floating made things easier than they'd been in the car. Holding Lincoln's head above the water and kicking us towards shore was easier than trying to climb out of the back of the Bronco. The shore was illuminated by the faint light of the fire still burning from the fallen tree. "KYLE!" Sami's voice was battling against the sound of the water lapping against my ears.

"Yeah, I'm h…" Half the words were lost to the water, gurgling into my throat.

"OVER HERE!" her voice guided me. I kicked our way there. It wasn't far; the truck had only launched a short distance past the water's edge. Grabbing at my collar, she pulled me over to her against the shore. "I can't get up," she panted. Above us was a few feet of cliff, just exactly too high for us to reach above and pull ourselves out. "It's too muddy. I can't get up it."

"Okay, okay, just give me a minute." Panting back, the water was still too deep to stand up, but the cliff against my back gave me some support. "Can you swim okay?" I finally got out.

"Yeah, I can."

"Swim out a bit and see if you can see somewhere we can climb easier."

Diving out from our little spot against the muddy cliff, she paddled away from me. The moments of quiet meant I could feel my whole body. My chest still ached from where the seatbelt had yanked hard against my torso. My neck felt wrong, making holding my head above water harder and harder; and the front of my face felt smashed. Breathing through my nose was impossible.

"This way, Kyle! We can get up over here!" Sami was splashing back to us and leading us along the cliff until the land leveled out, the top only being a foot above the water. Sami was up first, digging her feet into the mud under the water and pushing up. She got ahold of something on top, pulling herself the rest of the way over. Next we were sending Lincoln. She grabbed his arms and I pushed from the waist and then the legs until he was over the ledge. Following Sami's lead, I stuck my feet in, propelling upwards. It was barely enough, slipping back down until Sami caught me, lugging me the rest of the way.

"Is he breathing?" I asked from flat on my back, letting the raindrops shower me as Sami started looking Lincoln over.

"Yeah, he's breathing," she finally answered. He didn't look terrible once I sat up to see him, just like he'd lost twenty pounds now that he was wet and paler than ever, just about all bone and skin. Blood was smeared around his nose and head, and it looked like there was a nasty gash on the side of his scalp. "I think his leg's broken," she whispered. His left pant leg was torn badly and the flesh under it was already a frightful shade of purple and black.

"How's the rest of him look?"

Pulling back his shirt, Sami examined him. Several scratches and a few small bruises showed up along the rest of the long body, but the leg and head where the only serious-looking ones. "A broken leg and concussion. He's lucky if that's it." As long as the head wound wasn't more serious than it looked, he'd be fine.

"Give me some light." Sami turned on the light feature of

the 'Let, directing it at his head. Carefully I picked at the flap of skin. The whiteness of his skull was visible through the opening. However, it didn't look broken or cracked anywhere, just the skin sliced through. "I think it's just a cut. Help me get him up." Together we scooped him up off the ground until I had him fully in my arms.

"You got him?" Sami asked. Even though he didn't weigh much, his awkward teenage limbs made balancing him hard.

"Yeah, I think so." I flopped his body around a bit to get it fully adjusted. "Can you tuck his arm in for me?"

Following Sami through the underbrush, we were back on the road. The tree blocking the road behind us was still flickering as the rain beat out what was left of the flames. Carrying Lincoln wasn't easy. The adrenaline that'd been pumping through my body since the lightning struck was wearing off, as the pain from my injuries forced its way back into focus. Even in a perfectly healthy state, carrying a limp body for miles wouldn't have been very easy. People are oddly shaped and not designed to be carried once they grow past infancy. Lincoln was also still soaking wet, which made him slippery as well.

"I've got to stop," I panted out, folding both of our bodies to the ground. We'd been walking for what felt like miles, our pace even slower than it'd been earlier when my foot was still freshly broken. The pain that had died off earlier was returning with a vengeance.

"I'll help you carry him," Sami said, coming back from her leading position.

"Okay. He's getting really heavy."

"It'll be okay, we can carry him together. Come on." Grabbing a hold of his legs, she took the bottom half of his weight so I could hold just his upper body. It was probably the least recommended way of carrying a person, but his length helped the situation, giving us each enough space to cradle our half and still keep moving in sync with each other. Side by side we pressed forward with Lincoln between us.

"How much farther?" I asked at a certain point. We had committed to taking breaks every twenty minutes or so. It was eating up our time, but we were able to maintain a decent pace in between, and I couldn't imagine we had much left to go.

"I think it's just behind those trees," Sami said, pointing ahead of us. The dark shapes of the trees showed against the hazy horizon of moonlight reflecting off the low-hanging clouds.

"Where's the entrance? There's probably a fence around everything else."

"On the other side, over that way." She pointed to the left side of the space ahead of us.

"What time is it?"

"After eleven."

"What? We've got to go!" Time was slipping away from us, left behind in our many steps over the last couple of miles.

"Do we go for the entrance or straight forward?" Sami asked as we raised to our feet in the delicate balancing act of holding a body while trying to stand.

"Let's go straight for now. Maybe we'll find a gate," I said, pressing us forward.

Upping our tempo, we moved forward quickly, off the edge of the road and into the thin tree line. Lincoln's mapped route had brought us to this point. If we had arrived in the Bronco we could've just circled around to the entrance, or maybe just rammed down the fence if we encountered it. Those options were less practical in our current state.

"That's the fence." It was only a few feet past the edge of the trees, the aluminum chainlink visible against the backdrop of the sky. The top of it was angled out and featured barbed wire to keep intruders out.

"I don't think we're getting over that," Sami said, glaring at the wire.

"We could if we weren't carrying him. Though it might hurt."

Once again the stillness of our world was filled with a dull roar. This time it wasn't nature; the thunder was far beyond us, the sound of an approaching jet engine, a familiar sound long missed. "The plane's here!" Sami yelled. It sounded like it was coming directly over our heads. The trees swayed gently as the silver body flashed over the top of us.

"Set him down!" I dropped myself down to release him. "Maybe we can get under the fence!" Grabbing a hold of the fence from the bottom, it had some give. "Try and slide under!"

Going flat to the ground, Sami slid against the edge of the fence.

"Ready?"

"Yeah."

Pushing upwards with every muscle in my body, straining myself against the metal fence, Sami wormed her way through, her body forcing the fence up the last couple of inches she needed for clearance.

"Now him." I dropped the fence and dragged Lincoln over to the edge. "Ready?"

"Yes!"

Pulling once again while Sami reached underneath, she dragged his body to the other side. His thinner frame slipped through easier than Sami had.

It was my turn now, but that meant Sami was alone to lift the fence. "I can't pull it up as much." Sami was trying to lift the bottom edge like I had done from the other side. Being on the inside of the fence meant she was pulling the fence against the posts instead of away from them like I'd done from my side. It fought against her more, giving her only a couple of inches of movement.

"Here, wait!" I unclasped my belt and pushed the gun and holster underneath. Running the belt through the bottom link in the fence and back through the buckle, the belt was now attached to the bottom edge. The other end of the belt went through the fence a foot higher, giving Sami the leverage to pull up on the bottom of the fence from the other side.

"GO!" She leaned her full might against the belt, forcing the fence up enough for my head to get started, the metal scraping against my face. Using my arms from the bottom was enough to get my head all the way through. Once it was free, the rest of my body followed easily.

"Go to the plane." I rolled back to my feet. "Get to the plane. I'll get him."

"I can't leave you here!"

"Just don't let them take off! GO!"

Realizing I was right, she tore off through the tall grass that was between us and the runway. The adrenaline had returned, giving me the strength to get Lincoln off the ground and back in my arms. Pushing forward through knee-high grass wasn't easy, but the outline of the plane sitting on the other end of the runway ahead pushed me forward. Even though the rest of the space was dark, the plane was glowing in the center of it. The glare from the engine and blinking lights on its wings beckoned me. The grass gave way to the hard pavement of the runway, letting me keep my steady pace forward.

"Kyle! Kyle!" Sami's voice returned, the dark shapes moving towards me down the runway, beams of light bouncing ahead of them.

"Here!" I tried to yell, but with only a croak making its way out.

"There he is!" The unfamiliar voice echoed in the darkness as their flashlight beams caught me, leaving me stunned like a deer.

"Put him on the stretcher," one of the voices commanded. The sudden burst of light left me practically blinded. Several hands grabbed at Lincoln, pulling his limp form onto the stretcher I could now see.

"Kyle, are you okay?" The voice felt familiar. In the whirlwind of light and dark it was difficult to place. Cupping his hand over the light, it broke the beam and created a glow. My brother-in-law Josh was standing there looking at me.

"Josh, I'm glad you're here." I grabbed him for a hug. His face was full and his clothes smelled of detergent. Freshly washed clothes; it was almost more of a shock than seeing my brother-in-law suddenly in a field in Michigan.

"Let's get you on the plane." He pulled me forward, chasing after the stretcher crew that was already halfway back to the plane.

Wrapping her arm around my back, Sami guided us the last hundred feet to the makeshift stairs sticking out of the side of the plane. "We made it, honey," I said, feeling the cool metal under my hands.

"I love you," she whispered, leaning forward with a kiss.

"I love you too, my dear," I whispered back once it finished. "After you, babe." I motioned for her to lead the way, up the stairs into the plane and across the country.

THE END

Follow this link to an exclusive bonus chapter, available only online.

Hey! You made it, its so good to see you here. I know you didn't expect me to be waiting here at the end of the book, but I've been here the entire time, I hope thats okay. I looked away when you were reading this in the bathroom.

I hope you enjoyed reading this story as much as I enjoyed writing it. Now that you have made it this far, its time for me to ask one last favor. The success of this book relies completely on reviews from readers like you. If you could spare a few minutes to leave your thoughts about this story on Amazon or Goodreads it would be greatly appreciated.

Kyle K Wolfson grew up in Woodstock GA, the oldest of nine children. In 2008 he moved to Las Vegas and started working in the entertainment industry. He spent over a decade working as a roadie, traveling around the country and world as an automation programmer for various bands. He wrote several novels during his free time and even sometimes during concerts.

Recently he has returned to Woodstock along with his wife and daughter to be closer to his family.

Follow Kyle on social media for book updates and his thoughts on the Atlanta Braves.
https://www.instagram.com/kylekwolfsonwritings
https://www.facebook.com/kylekwolfsonwritings

Or reach out to him via Email. kyle@kylekwolfson.com

www.ingramcontent.com/pod-product-compliance
Lightning Source LLC
Chambersburg PA
CBHW030139310726
48970CB00005B/1508